MACABRE

ALEX URQUHART

Macabre by Alex Urquhart

© 2020

DEDICATION

To my second set of parents, Sandy and Rick. You have always given me support over the years, so if this book keeps you up at night, just know it was partly your fault. Love you guys!

PROLOGUE

May 3rd, 1996. Canby, Oregon.

The Chevy Caprice sat on the shoulder of the highway, just out of sight. Every so often, the beams of passing headlights would illuminate the vehicle, but not enough to cast light upon the driver inside. The night was clear and still, like untouched water in the middle of a lake. Summer was just beginning to take hold of the crisp Oregon air, and the breeze that ruffled the pines of the trees was surprisingly warm.

Calvin noticed that his breath was fogging up the windshield. He raised his index finger and traced a line upon the glass, as if to reinforce the fact that the condensed moisture was obstructing his vision. Satisfied with the result, he wiped his digit absentmindedly against his slacks. Sweat was congealing his uniform to his back, and he leaned forward to peel the outermost layer off of his body. *Ugh,* he thought. *I'm basically shrink-wrapped now.*

Calvin looked out at the highway, noticing motorists slowing down as they passed him. Some were doing at least ten over, but he didn't mind.

Writing speeding tickets was one of the most banal parts of his job. The common line of thinking was that certain officers enjoyed doling out citations as a way to stoke his or her ego, but Calvin did not. He was not the least bit interested in being a minor inconvenience to people.

Some of his colleagues hated taking the night shift, but Calvin had always thrived in it. Out with the delinquents crawling about, waiting for someone to strike. He often framed it in his mind by using the same metaphor: The predators were all on the prowl at night, and none of them were aware that he, the real hunter, was lying in the weeds with them.

Calvin reached out and twisted the knob to the heater, bringing it to a more temperate level. *A little better,* he thought. There was no longer sweat pouring out of his every orifice, and his muscles were a little less tense. He drummed his fingers on the steering wheel, creating a makeshift beat like he was about to sing. But the only music was fleeting and ephemeral, and came from passing vehicles.

A black SUV hummed by, blasting a rap song and kicking up gravel as it went. Calvin mused upon the thumping hip-hop for a moment. It was a relatively new phenomenon, and one that piqued his interest in a way. Not in the quality of the music, but in the culture it produced. Rebellious and defiant heathens, breaking rules and finding their independence. Essentially, it was what rock-n-roll had done two decades before, produce a movement of youth that was fixated on sex and drugs. For this reason, he did not look at rap in the same derogatory way that someone else in his demographic might. It was just the cycle of generations. The new would rock the world with their own music and liberation, and the old would get pissed off about it.

Calvin wasn't even sure why he was carrying a cup of lukewarm coffee in his hand while taking the occasional sip. He was more than alert, and the joe tasted like bad breath in a cup. But still he slurped, perhaps just looking for something for his mouth to do while his eyes digested the movement on the highway.

A red blur rushed by, roaring as its engine took flight. It looked to be some sort of muscle car; perhaps a Pontiac Firebird or a Ford Mustang. It almost took him by surprise; his hands shook a little and a bead of coffee dribbled down the Styrofoam cup. Calvin looked down at the radar on his dashboard, and he was convinced that the reading was incorrect at first, for it said the red muscle-car was going eighty-eight miles per hour.

Calvin let out an audible groan. *Why did you have to do that right here?* Surely the driver should have caught a glimpse of the Caprice creeping toward the edge of the road. He could have made at

3

least a little bit of an effort to slow down. But that didn't happen, and thus, Calvin's hand was forced.

The Caprice didn't make nearly as loud of a roar as the muscle car had, but it was quickly up to sixty as it jetted onto the highway. Calvin flipped his lights on and gently pressed the gas pedal down until his headlights were shining on the metal Firebird logo that was on the back of the red car. This one must have been older, for the vehicle's front end was wide like an open mouth, instead of a pointed tip like the newer models. The driver of the Firebird brought the hunk of red metal to a stop about twenty feet ahead of where Calvin had stopped the Caprice.

As Calvin got out of the car, his first observation was that the windows were tinted almost solid black. This alone could have been a fine, but he was already beginning to feel guilt creep up into his gut about the impending speeding ticket. *You forced my hand, buddy. You forced my hand.*

When he was within a few feet of the Firebird, Calvin stopped abruptly. He wasn't quite sure what it was, but there was a distinct tingling crawling down his back. Something felt off. Perhaps it was just the feeling of looking into tinted windows. Knowing someone was seeing you while you couldn't see them.

He cleared his throat and kept walking. The

crunch of the gravel underneath his feet formed a nice little rhythm as he strode along, and strangely, it built his confidence as he approached the driver's side of the Firebird.

When he arrived next to the driver's side door, nothing happened. The driver sat idling in his seat, and there was no movement behind the black window. Calvin tapped his fingers against the glass. Nothing.

"Roll down your window please, sir."

The driver did not respond. There was no movement.

"Sir?"

Crickets.

Intermingled with his impatience was a growing sense of unease. Anyone who did not mean any trouble would have greeted him by now.

"Sir, will you please roll down your window for me?"

Finally, the glass crept downward with a mechanical buzz. It moved at a glacial pace, like the driver was taunting him.

"Good evening, sir."

It was then he saw it. Instead of a human's face looking back at him, Calvin was staring at the head of a raven. Black and sleek and terrible, its eyes faced forward, unseeing. It was atop a human torso. A bird mask.

"What on earth—"

Slowly, the raven turned toward him. Within five seconds, its black eyes were boring into his. Calvin was petrified in place, a mixture of blank shock and horror freezing him like a cryogenic chamber. The raven stared and cocked his head. Calvin was so absorbed with the mask that it took him a split second too long to register the barrel of the .357 magnum revolver raising in the darkness. He fumbled for the gun on his hip, but it was too late. There was a spark and a bang and a flash of unbridled agony before Calvin became nothing.

PART ONE

Portland, Oregon. April, 2004.

The key slid neatly into the lock, and with a flick of her wrist, Tracy Dinwoodie unlatched her front door with a *click*. She put the small sliver of a key back into her pocket, slung her purse farther behind her, and opened the door. The living room was surprisingly warm, but perhaps that was just what dwelled within her body. She felt weightless and giddy; young and fresh.

Tracy walked through her house, with the hum of a song she had heard at Le Pigeon bristling against her lips. She had been singing the tune the entire drive back, though she didn't have a clue what the words meant, for the song was in French. But the true meaning was superfluous, because at the moment it was passion, attraction, and a fluttering of lust in her stomach.

She could still smell his cologne on her shirt. Every few minutes on the forty-minute ride back home, she had gathered the collar of her blouse and had inhaled, digesting the wonderful aroma. Her lips could still feel the texture of his, even though they had stopped kissing an hour before. His strapping arms had embraced her, gently rubbing down her lower back. As Tracy recalled his tall, muscular stature and the way his jeans had created friction against hers, she felt a warm tingling sensation in the front of her pants. At forty-two, it was much more difficult for a man to stoke her sexual fire. But Matthew Lyons had done it in the shadow of the upscale French restaurant he had taken her to.

Tracy tossed her purse on the couch, and even as she was walking up the stairs, she began to undress. The decadent house that she had purchased with her ex-husband felt ill-suited to have a naked person walking around inside of it, but she needed to be free of the restricting bounds that wrapped her person as soon as possible. She crossed the landing, and before she was even in the bathroom, she was in her bra and panties. They were a matching vibrant red; a choice she had made in case Matthew had decided to finally forego chivalry and take her back to his bedroom. Alas, they would remain for her eyes only, at least for tonight.

Within seconds, Tracy was stark naked. She

fiddled with two separate knobs of her bath tub. One let the water cascade down from the faucet, and the other put a stopper from it going down the drain. She turned about and opened the mirror, grasping a small pink tube of Dr. Teal's Foaming Bath. With a tiny squirt, she watched as the bubbles formed and separated, and a pleasurable smell drifted into her nostrils. She didn't even wait until the water level was past her ankles before climbing into the bath and sitting down. The suds ascended up her thighs, disguising her whole body in soap, and she turned the faucet off. The warmth soothed her muscles, and her mind began to drift.

There it was again. Matthew's handsome smile. She pictured him, standing outside of Le Pigeon, moving closer to her. His brown hair was groomed perfectly to the side, with a part dividing the longer strands from the short. His teeth were perfectly straight, his lips thin and strong. Her mental image moved from his face downward. Tracy saw his brawny arms, and his black T-shirt tight against his pectoral muscles. She gazed upon what were likely washboard abs, and the crease of his forearms as his hands were placed against his hips. Lower and lower her mental projection went, until she saw his pelvis, and what lie beyond. She couldn't control it now. Her hand moved down through the water and began creeping inside her.

Waves of gratification shot through her

muscles. Her body relaxed further, until it was like she was about to sink through the floor of the tub and float off into another dimension, where a thousand Matthews were waiting to kiss every inch of her body. Sand dispersed throughout her eyes, and she stopped pushing her fingers. Fall asleep, or continue dwelling on the man who created a thousand butterflies in her stomach? Each choice was equally tantalizing. As Tracy debated it for a few moments longer, she drifted off.

When she woke, Tracy was suddenly cold. The water temperature had decreased dramatically; she must've been asleep for a long time. The suds had dissipated, and her body was totally visible through the water. She placed her hands on either side of her torso and pushed herself upright. She supposed she ought to feel satisfied. After all, she had just fallen asleep in a bubble bath after a wonderful date with Prince Charming. Who wouldn't be content? And yet, she felt weird and attentive, but she wasn't sure why.

Tracy looked at her hands and noticed that they were like prunes. Her skin was already beginning to crumple on its own; the water just enhanced the appearance. She tore her eyes away from her palms, a little disgruntled. The smell of the bath was still pungent, but for some reason, it wasn't nearly as pleasant.

As she sat in the lukewarm water, Tracy's eyes caught a strange shadow against the opposing wall. It was a bizarre shape, like a distorted Minotaur. She supposed it was from one of her bathroom accessories; likely her mouthwash disturbing the light that was plugged into the wall, or her blow dryer. But the shadow was a little disconcerting for whatever reason, so she moved to get out of the bath and remedy it.

A creak. Small and almost indistinguishable, Tracy would have missed it if her ears were distracted. And yet, she knew that there had been a distinct creak, and it hadn't come from the bathtub. With her chest tightening, Tracy realized she had left the door to the bathroom ajar. She stared at the hinges of the door, wondering if the sound had emanated from said hinges. Silence plugged her ears, and she waited, totally still.

It happened again. Another creak, and this one was more prolonged. Tracy was sure that it had come from the door this time. Her heart was suddenly pumping erratically like a frantic animal that had been startled out of a deep slumber. After five more seconds of silence, Tracy realized that she was holding her breath.

The door moved forward, and the small creak

was now almost deafening. It shut against the threshold of the bathroom with a clunk, and there he stood. Tall and motionless, like a statue. Tracy's eyes crept up his body, and it was like she was having a vivid dream. His arms were like tree trunks, and his neck was thick and veiny. But attached to the neck where a human face should have been, there was the snout and horns of a goat. In his left hand was a mammoth butcher's knife.

Tracy screamed.

Robert Macabre trudged down the stairs, following the trail of blood. His breath reverberated off of the mask on his face, heating up his lips, while the erection between his legs made it difficult to walk. The woman outside kept wailing, and amidst her frantic, gibberish cries were actual words that beckoned help.

"Someone, please! Please help me!" The scream morphed into a sob and then was followed by what sounded like a sharp intake of breath. Robert would hazard to guess that the stab wound to her lower left abdomen made it difficult to shout.

He crossed through the living room and was amused to find that she had shut the door. He smiled behind his mask, gripped the doorknob, and ripped it open. There she was, naked and still sopping wet, gripping the leaking hole below her belly button. When she saw him, she let out another deafening, pained shriek.

"Please help me! Help me! God help me!"

Robert gave a little shake of his head in annoyance. She knew better than anyone that there was no use making such a racket. They were out in the country, and help would never come.

Slowly but surely, the cries for help transformed into pleas, and they were directed at him.

"Please don't do this! Please! I will give you anything! Please! You don't have to do this!"

Robert just kept striding forward, and when the woman realized that her hollers would be to no avail, she gave another grunt of terror and turned back around, limping toward the white car in front of her. He calmly reached his free hand into his pocket, gripping his keys.

The woman stopped when the trunk in front of her popped open and began to look back. By the time she had twisted herself around, Robert had snatched her neck in a crushing grasp with the hand that was holding the keys to his car. Her fingers clasped around his, trying to pry them off. He chuckled at her impotence and shoved her backward with all of his strength. The back of her head was first to hit with a resounding *thud.* The sounds erupting from the back of her throat stopped, and her eyes misted over. She looked woozy from the blow to her skull. Calmly, Robert dropped the bloodied knife, caught both of her ankles and folded her securely into the open space. She still wasn't making noise when he shut the trunk.

As Robert picked up the knife and tucked it into his pocket, he set a mental timer. *Any moment now,* he thought. A couple of beats of silence stretched, and then it came. The rapid *thunk-thunk-thunk* of the woman's feet kicking against the back of the car. "No, God no! Let me out! Let me out!" *A wonderful tune,* thought Robert with another beaming grin. He strode around to the front of the white car, and hopped into the driver's seat.

The engine fired up with a growl, and Robert shifted into reverse. The path to Tracy Dinwoodie's house was long and narrow and divided a massive field in two. He initially debated backing up the entire way, but then threw caution to the wind, spinning the car around like he was in the Daytona 500. Once he was facing forward, the car shot for the road like a bullet.

Thunk-thunk-thunk. The beat continued from the back of the car. Robert gave a small chuckle, wondering when her energy would finally be spent. *Thunk-thunk-thunk.*

Stars were ubiquitous across the night sky. Robert stared upward as the vehicle continued upon the narrow path. There was no moonlight, but the stars were enough to illuminate everything in sight. *Beautiful,* he thought. *What a beautiful night.* He rolled the window next to him down.

The thunking continued from the back. Dinwoodie was relentless. Robert wondered if the noise would continue the entire ride home. Surely not. Hopefully, he would be able to make good time. It was a long trip, and he was already beginning to feel a little hungry, as he had not eaten in several hours.

As Robert came to a stop sign, he felt an itch under his mask. He raised his right glove and stroked the spot that was aggravating him, just under his nose. Then, once that desire was satiated, he felt another itch above his eye. *Screw it,* he thought, and ripped the mask off. The cool air expunged his face of irritants, and he instantly felt rejuvenated. Hell, he had never felt more alive.

Thunk-thunk-thunk.

Robert shook his head. He thought he could put up with it, hell, even *enjoy* it, but the noise was getting to him. With his gloved index finger, he reached over and tapped the power button to his radio. Instantly, a rock song blasted into the car like a lake crashing through a broken dam. The sound was even more jarring and unpleasant than the clunking from the trunk. He hit the *seek track* button once. The radio settled on an R&B slow jam.

Too dulcet, he thought. One more click of his finger brought him to the jackpot. George Strait crooning one of his favorite country songs.

"All my ex's live in Texas..."

Robert relaxed his shoulders and decreased the speed of the car. He supposed it was a bit unusual for someone of his ilk to regularly immerse himself in country music, but if enjoying the southern twang of Willie Nelson and Dolly Parton was wrong, he didn't want to be right.

"And sweet Eileen's in Abilene, she forgot I hung the moon."

Every few seconds, when Strait would pause after a line and Dinwoodie's kicking would sync up with the pause, Robert would hear more banging from the trunk. Each time, he would turn the volume dial a little to the right, trying to drown out the commotion.

"Somehow lost her sanity, and Dimple's who now lives in Timple's got the law lookin' for me."

Robert pulsed the gas pedal as he came to Highway 99. There was nigh a car on the highway, which was a little strange, even for this time of night. He looked left and right several times, admiring his own solitude. The loudest *thunk* of all suddenly jolted him from his stupor. Once more, he twisted the volume knob a little further.

"But all my ex's live in Texas."

Even through the deafening music, Robert

waited for another thump from the back. But this time, finally, none came. Was she already beginning to lose her strength? She had so much more to go. The worst moments of her life were still to come in the next forty-eight hours. Robert smiled once more.

"And that's why I hang my hat in Tennessee."

Everyone was standing. Black suits, dresses, and expensive blouses filled the room. For several seconds, the only sound was the shuffling of several documents as Judge Jeb Curry consolidated the papers in front of him.

"Bailiff, please bring forth the verdict."

A slim, balding officer in uniform collected an envelope from one of the jurors to his right. A twitchy, tattooed man in a white dress shirt flinched as the bailiff passed him, and the tall attorney to the man's right looked like he was about to be ill.

Judge Curry collected the envelope from the bailiff and took an inordinate amount of time removing the letter from inside. Once he did, Carson Welsh, who was watching the whole thing unfold, began to hold his breath.

"Would the defendant please direct his attention toward me?"

The twitchy man shifted his eyes forward.

"The verdict reads as follows…"

Welsh flattened his tie, smoothing out the wrinkles. It was a compulsive action that he took whenever he was nervous.

"On the first count, we the jury find the defendant, Rory J. Foster, guilty of first degree homicide as charged in the first count of the information."

Welsh did not smile, but elation ballooned in his chest. Foster shook his head in disgust and twitched two more times.

"On the second count, we the jury find the defendant, Rory J, Foster, guilty of second degree manslaughter as charged in the second count of the information."

Foster dropped his head to his chest. His attorney, Warren Grecko, began rubbing his shoulder in a consoling gesture. But Welsh knew this was all for show. Grecko was an abrasive man, and not one prone to sympathy.

"On the third count, we the jury find the defendant, Rory J Foster, guilty of first degree sexual assault as charged in the third count of the information.

Welsh knew it would be inappropriate to grin, but it was difficult to subdue the urge to do so. Even he, the best district attorney Portland had seen in the past thirty years, was not expecting to get the clean sweep of Foster. One more to go.

"On the fourth count, we the jury find the defendant guilty of fourth degree assault as charged in the fourth count of the information."

Welsh made eye contact with Grecko. The man was looking at him with narrowed eyes; his heavy brow and large forehead accentuating the expression. It wasn't one of pure anger or contempt, but something else. Welsh couldn't quite place it.

Curry continued to drone on like he was reading a particularly dull memo. "The sentencing will be April forth, at three p.m."

Grecko was boring into Welsh's eyes from across the court room. He never even glanced down as the bailiff placed handcuffs on Foster's wrists and led him away. Welsh finally smiled, directing it right at Grecko. *Another one bites the dust,* he thought.

Several minutes later, Welsh strode down the hall, a gaggle of reporters at his hip. Each one of them fired off questions at lightning speed, and he could only answer one out of every three at the maximum.

"Did you feel confident that this would be the verdict that was reached in regard to Mr. Foster?"

"Well, I felt confident that justice would be served. I take solace knowing that Ms. Fields family and all those who loved her will sleep soundly tonight knowing that her killer is in a prison cell."

"Was it difficult to build a case with the lack of physical evidence against Mr. Foster?"

It was a portly man who had framed the question, and Welsh became mildly annoyed just at the sight of him. He was short and squat and had a defiant expression on his face.

"Well, considering we had two material witnesses, no, it was not particularly difficult to overcome the lack of physical evidence left at the scene."

Welsh kept striding down the hall, but the reporters were abreast of him, bombarding him with more questions.

"Were there any other people of interest in this case?"

"When it is such a short trial, do you go into the verdict confident that you will get a conviction?"

"Why was Foster not charged with any sort of criminal trespassing?"

"Are you going to press for the death penalty in this case?"

Eventually, Welsh stopped at a double wooden door that he knew to be the entrance to his freedom. It was staff only beyond, so he was seconds away from basking in silence. He turned to face the cluster of reporters. Though often aggravating, he knew the men and women were just trying to do their jobs.

"Thanks, guys. Thank you."

He was sure that most of them would be agitated at this answer (or lack thereof), but there was only so much time in the day. They had more than enough to write their stories and what Welsh said now was more or less color. The meat of the articles on Rory Foster's conviction had already been supplied. Therefore, he strode through the double doors without another word. Welsh's head was down, and if he had not looked up at the last second, he would have run into Warren Grecko, who was impeding his path.

"Congratulations."

Welsh looked at the man apprehensively. He knew that Grecko was looking for a confrontation, and he was in no mood to supply it.

"Thank you, Warren. Have a nice spring."

Welsh made a move to get past him, but Grecko held out his arm like it was a barricade. When he spoke again, his voice was a whisper.

"You just signed an innocent man's death warrant."

Welsh tried to walk past, but Grecko buttressed the strength in his arm, apparently not finished with his chiding of the DA.

"You are quite the salesman, Welsh. Sometimes in there I felt like I was listening to a pitch, not a prosecution. It is no wonder that the jury was swayed by your bullshit. I hope you are proud."

Welsh looked down at Grecko's arm. Resisting the temptation to snap it in half, he leaned in toward the attorney's ear.

"I sure am proud that I beat you yet again, Warren. And remember... The local rags will *never* forget this one."

Though taller than Welsh, Grecko was nowhere near as muscular. Welsh's thick chest and round shoulders dwarfed the noodles that Grecko called arms. The attorney gave an involuntary shudder as Welsh hissed into his ear.

"Let's be honest. Deep down, you know that he did it. You know that he deserves this. You try and convince yourself otherwise... That the scourge of the earth that you so often defend are all just misunderstood. But truly, I know that you are secretly thankful that that *creature* is going to spend his life in a cell. That he won't be able to prey on your wife or daughter. So you can drop the bravado bullshit and get out of my personal space. Now."

Grecko still tried to feign self-assurance, but his front was broken. As Welsh pushed by him, he offered one more paltry attempt at a barb.

"You're a real prick, you know that?"

Welsh shrugged without looking back. "A prick who wins, Mr. Grecko. A prick who wins."

A waft of smoke had entered into the bar from the open door to the patio where people were sucking on their Camel Lights. It gave the place a feel from an earlier time, with the haze percolating and the smell of tobacco lingering. The space at the center of the bar was taken up mostly by pillars that held up the roof, and to prevent any complaints about lack of room, the architects had taken it upon themselves to attach tiny round tables to the center of each pillar, with rickety stools rounding each of these tables. Around the exterior of the bar, there were a dozen booths, with large wooden barriers separating each one as if to shield the booths' inhabitants from having unfriendly ears become privy to their conversations.

A skinny blond waitress with too much cover-up on her face walked through a crowd of people, carrying a black tray with a couple of frothing beers placed precariously on top of it. She approached a booth with two men sitting opposite of each other and smiled when she caught their attention.

"Coors Light," she said, and her voice was like a cloud: soft and high pitched and seemingly on the verge of floating away.

"Yes, thank you, Christine," said Welsh, reaching for it.

"And a Michelob Ultra," continued Christine, and the giant man across from Welsh reached his mighty paw forward.

"Thank you," grunted the bear of a man.

Christine forced a smile at both of them.

"Let me know if you guys need anything else."

"Will do," said Welsh with a closed-lip smile. Christine sauntered away.

The bear-like man stared as she walked.

"I think she likes me."

Welsh raised his eyebrows. "Do you think the same thing about strippers, Mo?"

Mo let out a girlish giggle that didn't match his elephantine body and took a sip of his beer. After he swallowed, he licked his upper lip and shook his head at Welsh.

"Never understood why you drink that horse piss, buddy."

Welsh rolled his eyes. "Oh, like Michelob Ultra is the gold standard."

"And least it has some flavor to it! Coors tastes like carbonated, dusty water."

"Mo, you could be drinking a Bud Light and I could be drinking a five-dollar microbrew and you would still think you got the better deal."

Mo chuckled again like a school girl and took another sip. There was a lull in the banter and they both gazed around the bar. It was mostly an older demographic; lots of middle-aged men and women past their drinking prime. However, sprinkled in with the baby-boomers was the occasional twenty-something slurping a cocktail and pretending to be sober.

"I suppose you maybe should indulge in something a little more tasteful, Carson. This is a celebration after all, isn't it?"

Welsh shrugged. "I guess that depends on your perspective, Mr. McCray."

Mo scratched his abnormally large nose, and shifted his thick legs around so that he was sitting a little taller in the booth.

"Well, why wouldn't we celebrate? A murderer off the streets? A violent psycho who killed an innocent young woman getting his butt reamed in the Oregon State Penitentiary every night? That makes me happier than a clam, Carson."

"I was just doing my job, Mo."

"Don't pretend you don't like taking the credit, bud, because I *know* you do."

Welsh shrugged again. "What is there to take credit for? Lives have been taken. Families shattered. Yes, justice was served, but I am not going to throw a party for myself because I made a depressing situation a little less depressing."

Mo made a strange, sarcastic face. "Whoa there, buddy, how is the weather up there on your giant moral high horse?"

Welsh's mouth jumped a little as he tried to avoid smiling.

Mo continued, unabashed. "Look, I am just

saying, think about the opposite Carson. Think if you didn't get a conviction. That scum would be out there, ready to prey on someone else's daughter, or sister. I am not saying you should walk around in a white robe everywhere like you're Jesus, but you can at least admit, you made the world a better place today."

"The jurors made the world a better place today."

"Yeah, thanks to you. So, whether you want to or not, I am going to raise a toast to you, my friend." Mo lifted his glass in the air and sloshed a little of his Michelob Ultra onto the table. Welsh laughed and shook his head.

"You are just a mess, Mo McCray."

Mo let out his infectious chortle again and drained at least three-quarters of the beer in his hand. Welsh tried to match his chug, but was only half successful.

"I will tell you one thing, Warren Grecko sure doesn't think I did the world a favor."

Mo screwed up his forehead in a skeptical gesture.

"Why the hell do you care what that shaved peckerhead thinks?"

"I don't. But he stopped me afterward in the hallway and almost made a scene. He has always been an asshole, but I have never seen him as, uh, *livid* as he was today."

"Oh yeah? What did he say?"

"Just that I had sent an innocent man to jail… Then he called me a salesman."

"Big talk coming from an absolute boob like him. Didn't he one time convince a jury that a sex offender who had raped a twenty-two-year-old in the bathroom of a gas station was innocent?"

"Yep. Perp's name was Leighton Jones. One look at the guy and you could tell that he did it. And somehow Grecko convinced those twelve nincompoops that Jones had been in the wrong place at the wrong time. And he has the nerve to call *me* a salesman."

"Jesus," muttered Mo as he shook his head and looked away. "And yet here he is makin' the big bucks in PDX. Some people just have a way of fallin' up, I tell ya."

"I'm telling *you*, Mo, if we weren't in a courthouse with a whole flock of reporters about ten feet away, I might have clocked the cocksucker."

"I would have clocked him in *front* of the reporters. That would make a hell of a news bulletin, wouldn't it? 'Crazed Beaverton man drops blood-sucking lawyer in front of entire Oregonian staff.'"

"Oh yeah? You have a lot of faith in your ability to land a good punch."

Mo shook his head. "No, the alcohol in my system has a lot of faith in my ability to land a good punch."

"That is only your second beer!"

"Well, I ain't a spring chicken, Carson. It doesn't take much to get me feelin' toasty anymore."

Welsh laughed hard this time. Mo had always had the ability to tickle his funny bone better than anyone else. It had been that way since they were in their twenties. Now, in their late forties, they didn't see each other nearly as much and virtually everything in their lives had changed, but they still made each other laugh.

"So how is Wendy? Still as feisty as ever?"

Welsh rolled his eyes. "You are the only one she is ever feisty with, Mo. And I don't blame her with all of your incessant short-jokes."

"Hey now, I am just saying, you probably shouldn't take her to Disneyland. They wouldn't let her on any of the rides."

"Five three really isn't that short for a woman, *Maurice*."

The tiny, effeminate giggle came out again.

"Anyway, she is good. Just closed on a house in Lake-O for two mill."

Mo's eyes bulged. "Who bought it? One of the Trail Blazers?"

"Nah, just some Nike mogul. Don't even remember his name."

"Hmm."

Mo finished the rest of his beer and set the empty glass down with a thud on the wooden table. "I will never understand how you got so damn lucky, Carson. Beautiful home, beautiful wife who makes six figures, kick-ass car, and a job that pays a pretty penny itself while you get to spend all of your days putting the bad guys away? I envy you, buddy. I really do."

Welsh smiled again, but under his feigned amusement, he felt a little bit of annoyance. Mo often made comments about Wendy's looks, and though they were never over-the-top, they made him slightly uncomfortable.

"Oh yeah, like you are living in the dumps. How much do you make? Seventy-five K?"

"Still less than you."

"And you own a two-story house—"

"Still smaller than yours."

"And you have the freedom to do what you want without someone breathing down your neck all the time."

"You call it freedom, I call it abandonment."

"Oh hush. We both know you are living the dream."

Mo gave a little mischievous smile, which all but confirmed Welsh's assertion about his best friend's contentment. Welsh took another tiny gulp of his Coors, and Mo teased him some more.

"Look at you with your precocious little sips. Hurry up, bud, I am already ready to call the waitress over for round three."

"Call her over? She should come without your call, remember? Didn't we come to a consensus that she was inescapably attracted to you?"

Mo cackled. "You're right. She will be here any second."

The two friends tittered away, and Welsh found himself wishing that they saw each other more often.

The smell of coffee was almost overpowering. Welsh took out the pot and siphoned some of it into a black mug. He snatched the spoon that he had set on the counter and put a single tablespoon of sugar into the coffee; no excess cream or fluff was required. Welsh's tie was loose, and he threw it absentmindedly over his shoulder so that the tip would not submerge into the hot black liquid in his mug.

"You know, you should really have some breakfast before you drink coffee. The acidity is not good for your stomach."

Wendy came up behind Welsh and kissed him on the cheek.

"I know. I'm just not hungry at all." Welsh had never been a big breakfast eater; it was all he could do to force a banana down his throat in the morning.

"Yeah, well, you are going to be famished at eleven a.m. But then you will be stuck in court or something and just have to suffer." Wendy ruffled his hair with a faux disapproving smile on her face. It was one of her many tics. She would show affection while simultaneously nagging him. Whether it was just to make the task she was proposing less ominous, or because she actually got pleasure from telling him to do things, Welsh couldn't be sure.

"I actually don't have much on the docket today. Just a couple of meetings and typing up a dossier on the Foster case."

Welsh watched Wendy stride over to the fridge and open it up for herself. Her long blond hair glistened under the overhead kitchen light, and her tiny body barely reached the top of the fridge. She was one of the most petite forty-year-old women Welsh had ever seen; her waist was slim and her buttocks tight. She would frequently wake up at 5:30 a.m. and engage in an hour of cardio, and in the evenings, she would partake in some light weightlifting as well. Her diet consisted mostly of yogurts and salads, with the occasional spattering of nuts or fruit. Almost every evening she would fix Welsh a dinner that was separate from her own, and there was a significant difference in their body compositions because of it. Welsh was thick and muscular, but he also had a gut to accompany his muscles. Wendy didn't seem to have an ounce of fat on her whole body.

As much as she tried to fight the effects that aging had had on her person, Wendy was not able to conceal all of the marks on her face. There were now small creases on her cheeks at each symmetrical point where her dazzling smile reached to, and the traces of crow's feet next to her eyes were accentuated when she grinned. Her bright green irises were as breathtaking as ever though. Welsh was often caught wondering how he had pulled it off. He wasn't ugly, but he was far from dashingly handsome.

"And what is on the list for you today, hun?"

Wendy shrugged. "Got a couple of open houses. One in Happy Valley. One in Tualatin. Also, I am showing a young couple property out in Wilsonville that is forty acres and I am ninety percent sure that it is over their budget, but you never know."

"Hey, I would say you are doing pretty good this week anyways. After the one in Lake Oswego, you might as well just take the rest of the week off."

Wendy pursed her lips and shook her head. "Oh yeah, sure, let's just throw a party because I made one sale."

Welsh smiled. "Well, I hope my little worker bee makes me a fortune, then." He got within inches of her face and snuggled his nose against hers for a second before giving her a small peck on the lips.

"Careful, hun. I may just go out on a spending spree on my lunch because of that comment."

"Well, you earned it," replied Welsh with a wink.

"What about you? What are you going to do with your day after your meetings and your dossier?"

Welsh pondered this and realized he was looking forward to an afternoon that was at least somewhat devoid of the usual pressure of his job.

"Not sure. Honestly, should be a pretty uneventful day."

Welsh smelled something burning. It was distracting enough that his attention span was firmly broken from the report he was typing. He looked up from his computer and watched as the door to his office creaked open. The skinny brunette with large ears floated daintily through the ajar doorway, carrying a stack of objects. At the bottom of her heavy looking pile was a box with red ribbon tied around it, and on top of the box were several manila folders and a couple of envelopes.

"Heya, Sam."

"Good morning, Carson. You are a popular

man," said Samantha Jennings, indicating the stack of objects in her hands.

"Popular, or just sought after?"

Sam gave him a befuddled expression. "I am not sure I know the difference in your meaning."

"Well, popular obviously has a positive connotation. If I am sought after, it may not necessarily always be for virtuous reasons."

Sam then let out a giggle, and her laugh, as always, was a little screechy. "Well, okay then, let's just say a lot of people want to speak with you."

"I'm sure. And only half of them have interesting things to say. What is in the box?"

"No idea. It isn't very heavy though."

"Oh, hey, Sam, what is that burning smell?"

Sam's cheeks flushed a little pink. "I may have gotten a little careless with the coffee pot."

"Meaning?"

"I left it on too long and now the coffee tastes like refried beans."

Welsh gave a little shudder. "Well, you can have all of it to yourself then."

Sam grinned and set the box and the letters on top of it on Welsh's desk. Welsh tried to avoid the glimpse of her cleavage as she bent over. He was at the point in his life where he was struggling with attraction to other women and felt a rush of exhilaration mixed with guilt every time he checked someone out who wasn't Wendy.

"Welp, if you need anything, just give me a buzz," said Sam with a flash of a smile, and she walked out of the office.

Welsh instantly began sorting through the articles that his assistant had left. The first item was a copy of a subpoena that he had had a detective serve a potential witness two days before. The second was a letter from a man named Brian Moses. Moses was a man who Welsh had convicted for burglary and trespassing two years before. Once a month, Welsh would receive angry letters from Moses, and they would always decry his performance as an attorney and demand that he step down, while simultaneously proclaiming the man's innocence. Welsh scanned the first paragraph of the letter, and after realizing that it was more of the same drivel, he tossed it in the trash.

The manila folders were profiles on men that Welsh was in the process of indicting. They would require a more tedious pore over than what Welsh was willing to give at the moment, so he set them aside. Finally, he got to the box, which had lit a little flame of curiosity in his stomach.

The red ribbon that twined around the box had been used to hold a letter in place. After a couple of seconds of fiddling with the ribbon, Welsh thought, *Screw it*, and ripped out a pair of scissors from the little holder that carried all manner of office supplies. He trimmed through the ribbon with ease and looked at the letter. It simply said, *Carson* in black sharpie ink on the outside. Welsh tore the envelope open. Inside, his fingers enclosed around a circular, sharp object. For a second, he recoiled. But then he gazed inside the envelope and saw that it was a DVD tucked next to a white letter.

What on earth, thought Welsh. He examined the DVD, as if just by looking at the blank object he could decipher its meaning without playing it. After a few more seconds of confusion, Welsh set the DVD aside on his desk and unfurled the white letter. He was surprised to find that it had been handwritten. With a strange feeling of apprehension, he began to read.

Dear Carson,

The day has finally come. After years of remaining in the shadows of my own mental solitude, I have decided to make my introduction. First, let me say, I have admired your work for some time. You are the most successful individual in your position in the last three decades, and I commend you for your efforts. Not to sound trite and ingratiating in my praise, but you truly are the best at what you do.

Perhaps I am reaching out because I am the best at what I do as well. Once you have reviewed my work, I believe you will come to the same conclusion. To be frank, I am more than keen to hear what you think. I suppose that is the highest form of commendation and respect, to truly yearn for one's honest review of one's work. I don't think I will ever actually physically hear your appraisal, for reasons that will soon be understood. But I am envisaging your reaction to this, and it deeply excites me.

At the time of this scribe, Rory Foster's fate has not yet been announced, but of course, the guilty verdict is inevitable. It always is when you are involved, isn't it, Carson? Your record is impeccable, your judgment swift. By my count, out of two hundred and forty-two cases in your nine-year career, you have failed to get at least partial convictions in eleven outings; by far the most prestigious of anyone in your position since the '70s. As for your failures, I would be willing to hazard a guess that they eat you alive. Perfection is a lofty goal to reach, even for someone as erudite and formidable as you. Yet, you still strive to attain it. I bet you can recall every detail of those eleven cases. I bet you stay up at night thinking of what you could have done differently.

Perfectionists are like that, Carson. We focus on every extraneous detail, trying to assemble each element in its rightful place. And no matter how successful we are, it seems like we never feel completely fulfilled.

And yet, today, I am completely fulfilled. For today, I am finally stepping out of the darkness. Today, you will be made aware of your greatest nemeses. For, as righteousness and decency rises in the world, evil must rise to meet it. For every yin there must be a yang, Carson. For every hero, there must be a villain.

To start out the festivities, I have bequeathed you with a gift. Think of it like the first symptom of this unholy disease. Know that it will spread. It will infect everything it comes in contact with, and destroy you from the inside out. Finally, when you have suffered every modicum of despair, knowing you will never be able to stop it, I will put you out of your misery. But, for now, I think you know that we are just getting started.

Welcome to my world, Carson. Let the games begin. We both already know how this is going to end, but for the sake of sportsmanship, I must say, let the best man win.

-Robert Macabre.

When he finished reading, Welsh felt a balloon of anxiety in his chest. His palms were sweating profusely, and his heart rate had ascended to an unhealthy pace. He wiped his hands on the top of his slacks, and the cognitive dissonance had already begun. *Perhaps it is some sort of ill-conceived joke,* thought Welsh. *A Brian Moses of the world, just trying to screw with me.* And yet, Welsh knew this was no run-of-the-mill hate mail from some angry felon he had convicted. This letter had been penned by a warped mind.

Welsh briefly thought about leaving the office without looking in the box. If Mr. Robert Macabre was to be believed, the contents were sinister. And yet, a frantic, disturbed curiosity had taken hold of him. He had to see what was inside.

Welsh wielded the sharp end of the scissors to perforate a hole in the masking tape that sealed the box, and then used his fingers to pry the tape completely off, which made a Velcro-like sound as he disturbed the adhesive.

The first thing he noticed was a gray packaging material that seemed to be the last barrier of defense to whatever was inside. He wasn't sure what it was for—perhaps to protect whatever fragile material was within. Or maybe it was used to subdue any sort of odor from emanating out.

"Jesus," muttered Welsh. He paused for a second to take a deep breath before ripping the material open in one fell swoop.

Sausages. Uncooked lines of sausages, coiling together like a massive cobra. That is what he saw. But they were red. A striking, sloppy red. And underneath the red, in certain sections, a dark brown color.

Sausages? No.

Intestines.

The literal smell of blood and guts infiltrated his nostrils, and the world spun. Welsh put his hand on his desk to try to maintain his equilibrium, but it was too late. It was all he could do to not land face-first in the box of intestines as he passed out.

4

The woman was still screaming. Her eyes were closed firmly shut. Three of her fingers were missing, and an incision on the side of her gut was visible. Tear tracks stained her cheeks, making pathways through the caked blood.

A close-up. Her face, only inches from the camera. Suddenly, she was pleading. "Please, I'll do anything. Anything! Just let me go!" And then another piercing cry.

It was easy to see that her naked body was fastened to a long wooden table. Her arms and legs were bound firmly by rope, and what looked like plastic wrap twisted around her forehead, keeping her skull solid against the wood. The table was covered in a blue tarp, collecting the remnants of her seeping blood underneath her body, and there was a five-foot-long mirror hung from the ceiling, only about six feet above where she lay.

The pleading continued. "Please, just let me go home. I want to go home." Then, the most horrible scream yet ripped through the speakers, as the man holding the camera seemed to have pierced her with sharp object in an unknown location. The wail continued for many long moments before it turned into whimpers.

Slowly, the camera twisted around. Into the frame came a horrifying face, that of a goat, with sharp horns and a pointed snout and a tuft of white fluff attached to its chin. The camera lingered on the dreadful mask for a few more seconds before the frame went black.

Detective Emily Arroyo turned around with a grim look on her face.

"Well, gents, it looks like it is here. The biggest case of our careers."

Detective Ray McCabe, a burly, dark-skinned man with a goatee, shifted uncomfortably next to Arroyo. Marty Flask, the police chief who looked like a spitting image of John Wayne, bit his lip and tapped the pen in his hand on the table frenetically while the two squirrelly men seated next to him swapped nervous glances. Finally, Welsh, who was stationed at the end of the table, was not even looking up. His head was resting on his hand, and he had found a spot on the wall to stare at while Arroyo spoke.

"How many times have you two watched this?"

asked Flask, leaning forward.

"Over ten times," replied McCabe silently. "Trying to pick up any new details that might help us."

Flask let a pause hang in the air before responding.

"And?"

Arroyo took the lead again. "And I think we have at least a general idea of what we are facing." She gestured at the TV that was on a stand next to her at the head of the table and then at the white letter that was now encased in a Ziploc bag in front of her. "Between the DVD and the letter, we can at least formulate a couple of theories."

"Go on," said Flask, swinging his hand outward.

"Well, he obviously suffers from an acute type of psychosis, and this is his means for sexual gratification. He seems to have a fetish for torture. And the mirror shows that he is definitely a sadist as well. He gets off knowing how horrified she must be while watching him mutilate her own body. And, like most psychopaths, he seems to possess high mental acuity. The setting in the video is nondescript, the lighting dim, the shots vague. He seems to have framed this video so as to not give anything away about his location, or obviously, his identity."

"And what have you gathered from the letter?"

prompted Flask.

"That he is well-educated. You can tell from the language used and the sentence structure that he is, at the very least, articulate. Much like the video though, there seems to be nothing that would clue us in to where or *who* he is."

"And the name?"

"Pretty apparent it is a pseudonym," said Arroyo. "There are exactly zero Robert Macabre's in the state of Oregon, and only two in the continental United States, both of whom live east of the Mississippi River. It wouldn't surprise me though if Robert was *part* of his actual name. I don't think he would be naïve enough to include his surname in any sort of manifesto, as it were. A first name isn't likely either. I would be willing to guess if anything Robert is our guy's middle name. Which obviously, is totally unhelpful, seeing as there are hundreds of men with that middle name in Portland alone."

Throughout this speech, Welsh kept looking at the spot on the wall. He still felt queasy. It had now been six and a half hours since he had found the intestines, and yet, it felt like he had seen them every second of every day for his whole life.

"Macabre seems like the most significant part of the pseudonym, wouldn't you say?" asked Flask. This time, it was McCabe who responded.

"Of course. Let me read the definition."

McCabe picked up a piece of paper from the table and used his finger to skim until he found what he was looking for. "Macabre. 'The quality of having a grim or ghastly atmosphere while emphasizing the details and symbols of death. Also refers to acts particularly gruesome in nature.'"

The chief nodded, almost sarcastically. "Yeah, I would say that fits. What about the mask?"

"Well, it may just be an attempt at a frightening disguise. Or, more likely, it could be some sort of occult symbol that is part of the message that Macabre is trying to send."

Flask nodded and looked over at the two squirrelly men seated next to him. One was extremely thin and had the distinct scarring of someone who had severe acne during puberty. The other was plump and had huge, thick-rimmed glasses.

"How much longer do you two think it will be before we get an ID on the vic?"

Ryan Dunny and Kevin Ho looked at each other apprehensively. Dunny's white lab coat was far too large for his thin body.

"Probably a couple of hours at least," said Ho. "We were working with Spade on the toxicology report when called to this meeting. No matches so far on DNA. The facial recognition software has been inconclusive."

"Jesus," muttered Flask. "All this technology

and we still have to wait eons for results. What about the package?"

"We found two sets of latent prints on the package, but they belonged to Welsh's secretary, Samantha Jennings, and Welsh himself."

"Okeydokey," said Flask sarcastically. "Emily, do you believe you could somehow trace a pertinent locale through USPS? Like, where the killer may have sent the package from, for instance?"

Arroyo shook her head. "We probably could, but my guess is that sort of endeavor would not yield any fruitful results. Even if he had physically gone to mail it, he would have found a way to conceal his identity. But I don't think he *did* go to the post office, because it would have been very risky and the clerk might have been able to pick up on the fact that he had used a fake return address."

The chief tapped his finger and turned his head. Welsh was still zoned out; it felt like his eyes were literally out of focus. Perhaps he was still in shock. Or maybe just mentally drained from the trauma of seeing the young woman's intestines splayed out in the box.

"What about him?"

Welsh finally snapped to attention and saw that Flask was staring at him. It almost looked like there was contempt in his eyes. The pair had always had a bit of an icy relationship, but Welsh could not think of a legitimate reason for Flask to not aside the ill will during the current situation.

"Well, our guy seems to have a bit of an obsession with Mr. Welsh, that is for damn sure," began Arroyo. "The obvious thing would be if he had some sort of history with him. A past convict who felt like he was wrongly convicted or faced too harsh of a sentence."

Welsh looked at the short red-haired woman standing with her hands on her hips next to the television. She had heavy eyebrows that seemed to give off the impression that she was permanently frowning, but otherwise, she was attractive. She had soft, small features and rounded cheeks, and a plethora of freckles decorated her face. Welsh had never actually personally dealt with Arroyo before, but he had heard that she was tenacious and detail-oriented.

"But I don't believe this is the case here. Truthfully, that would be too simple. The sort of mind we are dealing with is diseased. The man who wrote this letter and who filmed this video is afflicted by a form of psychopathy that I don't believe we can oversimplify by saying it has something to do with vengeance. A sexually motivated killer is driven by sadism, cruelty, and a sort-of malevolent need to manipulate. I don't think it has anything to do with something Mr. Welsh did in the past."

"Well, that is a relief," said Welsh, and he

realized it was the first words he had spoken in an hour. His voice was hoarse and deep from lack of use.

Flask seemed to twitch. "So what is it then? Why did this guy choose him?"

"He told us why. Because Welsh has been more successful at putting bad guys behind bars than any other DA in the last thirty years. He views him as some sort of all-righteous, anti-crime superhero. And he wants to tear him down. It isn't some personal vendetta. It has more to do with the perp proving *himself* and what *he* is capable of. And how do you become the best? By beating the best. Like others with his mental condition, he is driven from a stark case of narcissism, and to satiate his ego, he wants to show everyone that he can take down the biggest fish in the sea. At least, that is what I have gathered from his ramblings." Arroyo picked up the white letter in the plastic bag and wiggled it around as she said the word "ramblings."

"So, would you say Welsh is in immediate danger?"

Arroyo looked at Welsh intensely. He did not care for her expression.

"Immediate? No."

There was a dramatic pause, and Welsh felt his heart begin to thud more rapidly against his chest.

"Well, immediate enough that we should assign him a protective detail?"

Arroyo shrugged. "I think that is up to him."

Welsh looked around at all the people in the room. Everyone except for Flask was looking at him in fear and pity. Dunny and Ho almost seemed like they were afraid to get too close to him, as if being targeted by a homicidal maniac might be contagious. Arroyo appeared to feel guilty for having to tell him that he was in danger, and McCabe looked like he wanted to consolingly pat him on the back. Welsh hated it. It drove him nuts whenever others acted like he was helpless and impotent.

"I'll be fine." He tried to inflect as much strength in his voice as possible.

Flask rolled his eyes. "Carson, you don't have to act all alpha-male bravado this time. If you are being targeted, you are going to need help."

"I don't want a protective detail."

"Welsh, look—"

"No. No detail."

Flask raised his palms toward the sky in a gesture of annoyance and defeat. After a few seconds of silence, Arroyo spoke.

"If Mr. Welsh doesn't want us invading his privacy, that is his prerogative. I'm sure if he ever actually does feel like he is being threatened, he will revise his stance on the matter."

Welsh didn't reply. He looked again toward the same spot on the wall that had become his only friend. Almost instantaneously, he saw a flash of red and the coiled intestines. But this time, his disturbed mental flashback was accompanied by the woman's face from the video. Her mouth was open and the scream leaking from her lips was animalistic and distorted; a final primal cry from the frightened creature knowing her last minutes on earth were passing by. When Arroyo spoke again, Welsh did not hear her.

Emily Arroyo adjusted her reading glasses, trying to bring the font more into focus. She circled random words, looking for patterns. On another sheet of paper, she scribbled different anagrams that she found, as if the sheet contained a coded message. The actual letter still remained in a sealed Ziploc bag, but the copy that she had written was in front of her and looked like it had been edited by a particularly nitpicky English teacher, what with all of the scribblings in the margins and the underlines of words that she had found significant.

Over twenty-four hours had passed since she had first seen the letter. It was now 11:30 a.m. the following morning, and she felt as close to answers as she had been when Flask had first called her into his office. None of the theories that she had written down made any sense, and the actual tangible evidence that they had yielded nothing about Robert

Macabre's true identity.

Arroyo sipped on her coffee and noticed that it had gotten cold. The worst part was that it was still almost completely full. She had poured it into her mug an hour ago and had been so absorbed in decrypting the letter she had forgotten to take even a casual sip every once in a while.

Macabre. A word that is even spelled strange. Did it have more significance than she was giving it? She had thought it was just a general idea. Brutal, bizarre, and horrifying. But could it have an underlying connotation that she hadn't discovered? Perhaps it was a more overt clue than she thought. *Come on, Emily,* she thought. *Wrack your brain.* She circled the words "impeccable" and "erudite." Everything seemed carefully chosen. Like each word was an individual brick to the killer's foundation.

Arroyo's concentration was broken by the sound of her own name.

"Emily! Emily!"

She turned around in her chair and found McCabe jogging toward her desk.

"What?"

He came to a less than graceful stop and put his hands on his hips while he doubled over slightly and took a sharp inhale of breath.

"Ray, you really need to start doing more cardio—"

McCabe waved frantically, trying to quash her sentence. "We have to go. Right now."

"Go…? Where?"

"Mount Tabor park."

"Mount—"

"They found her! Well, what is left of her."

Arroyo's eyes bulged. "The woman from the video?"

"Yes."

"How do they—"

"You will know when you see it," replied McCabe ominously. Arroyo looked at him, and her stomach did a few nervous flips.

"Come on. Let's go. The buzzards are going to be swarming soon."

The sky overhead was completely dark and gray. The trees moved slowly and together with the wind, and it was like they were doing a strange tribal dance. A great horde of people gathered nearby, next to a large white van with the words, KATU NEWS, sprawled on the side of it. A few of the people were holding bulky cameras on their shoulders, while others in suits and ties wielded microphones, preparing themselves to go live. The short, red-haired woman and her tall partner strode across the grass, approaching the swath of TV crews and reporters.

"Let us through guys. Let us through." Arroyo held up her badge, and though they all saw it, none of them budged at first.

"People! Move your asses!"

The crowd began to grumble, and the sea parted. While Arroyo and McCabe walked through the opening several reporters jabbed recorders next to their faces.

"What can you tell us about what has happened here, detectives?"

"Witnesses say there was a homicide, can you confirm that for us?"

"Do you know the victim's name?"

Arroyo just kept walking at a swift pace. A mic got within inches of her right ear, and she swatted it away like it was a particularly large mosquito.

"Guys, we know as much as you do right now. *Please* get out of the way!"

The last two stragglers that were impeding the detective's path finally stepped aside, and both Arroyo and McCabe ducked under the yellow tape. Three deputies that Arroyo did not know were just on the other side of the caution tape, and each of them glanced at the new pair apprehensively before going back to their discussion. Someone came at Arroyo, waving frantically.

"Emily! Ray! Jesus, you guys are going to wish

you didn't come here."

Lieutenant Don Chaser stopped right in front of them, and his expression said it all. His gray mustache was curled downward, and his wrinkly forehead was scrunched in a terrible frown.

"That bad, LT?"

"Worse," said Chaser grimly. "Come on. She is over here."

Chaser whirled about and started striding toward a line of bushes. He was gangly, thin, and when he walked, he reminded Arroyo of Gumby. The long black sports coat he was wearing ruffled as it was hit by a gust of wind.

"So who found her?"

"A jogger. Name is Kennedy Washburn. She is already on her way back to the station. Though she won't be able to help for shit. Can barely talk at the moment and was shaking so bad when she tried to get in the squad car that she fell and twisted her ankle."

"Jesus… Who else is here?"

"A couple of techs and deputies. You are the first detectives on scene."

Chaser stopped as he came even with the line of bushes and gave them both a dark look. "Prepare yourself, guys. This one is going to stick with you for a while."

They rounded the corner. Hanging from a tall spruce tree was a naked torso. But where her legs and arms should have been, there were bloodied stumps. Even worse, there was a giant gaping hole in the woman's mid-section, and Arroyo could see the bark of the tree on the other side, as she had been completely hollowed out. The noose was so tight around her neck that Arroyo could see the darkened ligature marks from fifteen feet below. But what was most haunting was the mask covering her face. It was the same goat mask from the video, except its mouth had been pried open in a terrifying leer.

McCabe instantly turned away and started coughing. His coughs slowly morphed into belches, and Arroyo could tell from the subsequent noise of splatter that he was vomiting into the bushes. Arroyo continued to stare up at the dismembered torso, and instead of disgust, she felt uncontrollable anger. This was someone's daughter, mutilated and hanging from the tree. Someone's sister. Maybe someone's wife.

"Cut her down," she whispered.

"Well, lady and gents, I have good news and I have bad news."

Marty Flask was snarling as he spoke, and he seemed to be quivering slightly.

"The good news is, we have ID'd the vic. The bad news is, one of you is in for a world of pain."

Flask forcefully turned the laptop in front of him so that it was facing the same people who had met in the room the day before. The Internet Explorer window that he was showing them was emblazoned with the black logo of the *Oregonian.* The headline on the webpage was, *"Dismembered Woman Found In Mt. Tabor Park."*

"Now, the fact that this story is here is not the problem. Hell, it is now, what six p.m.? And they just published it an hour ago? Seems like they are running behind. No, the problem definitely isn't that they know the gory details of how Tracy Dinwoodie was found. The real problem is *this…*"

Flask cleared his throat sarcastically while turning the screen back around so he could read. "'A source with knowledge of the situation says the killer left a message for police at the scene of the crime. In said message, the killer used the pseudonym, 'Robert.'"

Flask looked around the room and pursed his lips. "So, which one of you did it?"

Silence. Everyone looked from left to right, like the guilty party would stand up and wave at them.

"I will have to admit, it is clever the way you did it. Feeding them enough incorrect information that it wouldn't look as suspicious when you dropped the bombshell. Pretty incredible that someone could be that clever while doing something so completely *stupid*."

It was McCabe who made a noise to start responding, but Flask cut him off by unleashing an avalanche of harried yells.

"What are you doing people? Are you trying to help him get away? You don't think he will read this shit?"

McCabe looked like he still felt a little ill from when he had evacuated his stomachs' contents in the bushes at Mount Tabor, so he went back to stony silence. Arroyo, however, tried to mitigate Flask's wroth.

"Boss—" she began.

"No! I don't want to hear it goddamn it! I am trying to run a tight ship here, but it doesn't work when one of you assholes leaks the biggest piece of intel of this case to one of these leach-ass reporters!"

Flask took a pause and ran his hand through his short brown hair. When he spoke again he was still yelling, but not with the same volume.

"I mean, Jesus, guys. Thank the lord that they didn't get the full story. And for the love of God, if I even read a single syllable of Tracy Dinwoodie's name on this website in the next few hours, I am going to have a coronary!"

"Chief, how do you know it was one of us?"

Flask looked over at Arroyo as though she was

a particularly obtuse troglodyte. Before he could lash out with another verbal berating, she continued.

"How do you know it was not Welsh?"

Suddenly, the chief's scrunched expression of anger fell.

"Welsh?"

"Yes."

Flask scratched his head roughly.

"I don't think Welsh would be that stupid."

"Maybe he doesn't think it is stupid, Marty. Maybe he is trying to be strategic."

"Strategic…?"

"Yes. Maybe he thinks that, by leaking this information, it will provoke him into a mistake."

Flask squinted his eyes. "That seems pretty calculating for someone who just opened a box of guts on his desk."

"I don't know boss… It just feels deliberate. Like, whoever leaked this is saying, 'Your move.'"

Flask shook his head. "Trust me, this is not like Welsh. And even if it *were* a deliberate move, I don't see what we have to gain by this. This undermines this investigation. It probably feeds into what the guy wants!"

Arroyo shrugged, but did not reply. Truthfully, she didn't understand the logic behind it either.

Flask sat down and rubbed his temples. "I don't know, maybe it was Welsh. Maybe it wasn't. The point is, the damage is now done. Now every one of these media outlets is going to be on us like white on freakin' rice."

"Then we need to nip this in the bud, don't we?"

Flask didn't reply.

Out of nowhere, Ryan Dunny spoke up. His voice was quiet and sounded a little hoarse.

"So what all have we found out about the vic?"

Arroyo looked over at Dunny and then to Flask, wondering if it was okay to move on from the tirade, or if the boss man had more to vent about. Flask gave her an expression that said, "The floor is yours," and she expounded on what they had discovered.

"She lived by herself outside of the city near Canby. Place is definitely out in the country. We have a team sweeping it now. So far, we have found Dinwoodie's DNA trailed throughout the house, starting in the bathroom. It seems as though the assailant ambushed her in the bath, because the tub was full of water when we got there. Dinwoodie seems to have survived the initial assault and gotten away, but she was clearly incapacitated and he caught up with her. Nothing from her attacker at the scene. At least so far. The sweep is still in its initial stages."

Arroyo gulped and let silence percolate for a few moments before continuing. "Dinwoodie was divorced. Her ex-husband is an engineer. And before you ask, he is now living on the East Coast. Anyway, she kept the house in the divorce. She was working as a dental assistant for Moretti and Brown Orthodontics in Happy Valley. Single… And we are in the process of contacting next of kin. I am going to meet with Spade soon."

Sitting next to her, McCabe gave an involuntary shudder. Edwin Spade, the coroner, was a brilliant mind and efficient at finding clues. But he was also very strange, and some, like McCabe, found him unnerving.

"And what about you two? Have we found anything that you would consider to be compelling?" Flask looked at the two forensic techs skeptically.

"Well, we still haven't found any prints on the video tape or the box," said Kevin Ho. "Not even a partial. And there were traces of a cleaning solution on the mask that was found on Ms. Dinwoodie. Bleach, baking soda, and some sort of solvent. Good enough to remove anything viable from the mask's surface. No hair, no DNA… Nothing."

Flask gave him a sardonic smile. "Okay, great… So what you are telling me is that we have basically nothing to work with, evidence-wise?

Ho tapped his fingers in front of him nervously. "Correct."

"Well, that is just lovely!" proclaimed Flask sardonically. "This case is off to a rip-roaring start!"

Edwin Spade stood next to the body, oscillating from one tool he was using to the other. He poked and prodded at the flesh of the woman's left breast, which had turned purple and pallid; the skin sagging morosely. He carried the attitude of someone engrossed in a particularly entertaining game of Scrabble. There was no revulsion at the cavernous hole in Tracy Dinwoodie's mid-section, nor disgust at the sight of her severed limbs.

"So, you are saying she has been dead for a couple of days?"

"Yes. The postmortem interval seems to be transitory in this case. The state of decay, or lack thereof, is enough to hypothesize that she has been dead for seventy-two hours or less."

When Spade spoke, his tongue slithered at every *s*. It sounded just like the lisp of someone who was flamboyant, and yet, somehow, he made it much more unpleasant. His bleach blond hair was so bright underneath the overhead light that it was almost enough to distract Arroyo from the mutilated cadaver next to her.

"So, what else can you tell me?"

Spade still didn't look up. His eyes were pinpointed on a spot next to the hole in

Dinwoodie's mid-section.

"The ligature marks around her neck are deep. She must have been hanging there for hours."

He said it not with aversion, but with fascination.

"Cause of death?"

Spade looked up at her with the traces of a smile tickling the corners of his lips. "You mean other than the mammoth hole beneath her sternum?"

Arroyo's stomach tightened. What sort of person found humor in such a bleak situation?

"Was she alive when it started?"

Spade went back to poking and prodding, poking and prodding. "Difficult to say. If I had to hazard a guess, I would say yes. The only thing I can say with absolute certainty is that the dismemberment of her outer extremities was done postmortem."

"And what about when she *was* alive?"

Spade looked up. His eyes were tiny, beaded things, and only magnified slightly by the giant glasses on the bridge of his nose. Arroyo noticed with some satisfaction that the smile on his face had vanished.

"I'm not sure I understand your meaning, detective."

"He tortured her. We can see as much from the video."

Spade looked back down. "Well, I cannot tell you exactly how he went about doing it. All I can tell you is what I have found on this cadaver, and then you can draw whatever conclusion that you prefer from said information."

"Okay."

"First, there are lacerations along her breasts," said Spade, pointing at a few purple notches next to the dead woman's right nipple. "The incisions are not deep enough to have caused significant blood loss, nor are they very wide. Small surface cuts, likely done with a knife."

Spade moved a little farther along toward Dinwoodie's head. "Next, she is missing her first and second premolars." He lifted Dinwoodie's upper lip and pointed his gloved finger toward the back of her mouth. "There also appears to be significant cavities in the flesh where the teeth were removed."

Arroyo looked at the man, mystified. "Wouldn't that be the case when teeth were removed?"

"I said *significant* cavities. As though something sharp was used to pierce the tender flesh where her premolars were detached from."

"Ugh."

"Yes, he seems to have a particular proclivity for this sort of thing, doesn't he?" Again, Spade was not possessed by fear, or revulsion. Rather, he seemed to be totally intrigued by what Robert Macabre had done to the woman on the table next to them.

Arroyo walked down to the end of the table and glanced for a second at Dinwoodie's crotch.

"What about... Sexually? Was she violated sexually?"

Spade looked up and narrowed his eyes.

"Of course she was. What exactly do you think you are dealing with here?"

"I'm not sure, Edwin. That is why I am here."

"Well, yes, she was very much violated. There is a significant contusion on both sides of the vaginal tissue, and the labia is bruised as well. The canal is considerably stretched; more so than intercourse would normally entail. It looks like she was not penetrated by his penis, but rather, a blunt object."

In that moment, Arroyo had to look away. She was a tough cookie and not one prone to be squeamish, but even she felt a little woozy after Spade's last sentence. When she addressed the coroner again, Arroyo did so while staring at the tiled white wall opposite of her.

"So he penetrated her simply to cause her pain? Not for his own sexual gratification?"

"I would think both."

"Both?"

"Him causing her pain is his means for sexual

gratification."

Arroyo looked back. Gone was Spade's look of wonderment and curiosity; it had been replaced by an expression much more enigmatic. For several long seconds, the two just looked at each other.

"So is there anything else of note?"

Spade gave her another small, chilling smile. "Well, nothing that you would consider to be of note, detective."

"I'm not sure what you mean."

"I mean... Nothing else that would give us any clues to his motive or identity."

"So, whatever else you find intriguing..."

"You would not find as such," said Spade quietly.

"And why is that?"

"You are not captivated by the dead. At least, not like I am."

Arroyo made piercing eye contact with the man. It was almost like he was trying to creep her out now. She wanted to say something fierce; to put him in his place. Instead, she turned her head and marched out of the dimly lit room.

Welsh held the miniscule pill in his hand, feeling its texture between his fingers. With his off-hand, he brought the glass of water up to his mouth, wetting his tongue. Then, he placed the pill gingerly underneath his uvula, and sucked it down his throat. The second splash of water was used to wash away the lingering taste. Next, he fingered the other open orange container, until he clung onto another tiny pill. This one for the constant pain in his back. Pain that had been there for nearly a decade, since the accident. It flared up in times of stress, or when he had performed some strenuous physical activity. The medicine would dull the pain, but not erase it entirely.

A flash of brown and red. The same coiled, thin sausages burning against the back of his eyelids. Welsh's heart rate ascended, and his equilibrium was suddenly awry. He used his glass-free hand to steady himself against the sink, but he couldn't quite make the dizziness stop. His breath had escaped him, and every time he tried to inhale, it felt like his lungs were totally compressed and impotent. Welsh's attempt at drawing air made a loud, guttural noise.

"Everything all right in there, hun?"

Welsh tried to respond, but couldn't find the oxygen to do so. He set down the glass on the back of the sink, and placed both hands down as foundation, facing his attention toward the ground.

"Carson?"

"I-I'm f-fine, Wendy."

"You don't sound fine."

"Just having a little bit of a panic attack, that is all."

Welsh heard the doorknob turn back and forth, and when he looked back up, Wendy was behind him with a concerned expression on her face.

"What's wrong, hunny? What is it?"

Welsh turned around, feeling like the bathroom was too diminutive of a place for the both of him. He walked past her, brushing her shoulder as he made his way into their bedroom and seated his rear end on their bed. He consciously made an effort to control his breathing, but every time he seemed to lasso enough air, his lungs would condense again.

"Carson? Are you okay?"

Wendy was now seated next to him, and she

looked very worried.

"Y-Yes. Well, no, I am not, but I will be."

"Carson, what is it? What happened?"

Welsh shook his head. "It will be on the news soon. They found a woman dead in Mount Tabor Park."

"A woman? Like murdered?"

"Yes."

"Okay…? I am not sure I am following."

Welsh squeezed his eyes shut. "You just… You don't want to know the details."

For a second, Wendy's face showed a bit of understanding, but then it went back to puzzlement.

"Wait, why do *you* know the details?"

Welsh felt the nausea in his stomach creep up his throat. But he swallowed, pressing it back down. He had already mentally rehearsed this moment several times over the past twenty-four hours. He had been debating not telling her at all, but then he realized it was too big of a secret not to share.

"Because the killer left me a message."

The color faded from Wendy's face.

"What?"

"He left me a letter."

A prolonged pause.

"You?"

"Yes."

Another lengthy moment of quiet. "What did it say?"

"It was… a taunt."

"A taunt?"

"Yeah. He seemed to be fixated on me. Or my track record, I guess."

Wendy paused again, thinking it over.

"Was he threatening you?"

"I don't think so," lied Welsh. "I think he was just trying to insinuate that he would get the better of me."

"The better of you?"

"Meaning we won't be able to catch him. And I won't be able to prosecute him."

"So it was like… A challenge?"

"I guess you could call it that."

Wendy ran her hand through her blond hair, and her mouth was agape in wonderment.

"Oh my God."

"Yeah."

"Oh my *God*."

"Yeah, I know."

"And you're sure you aren't in danger?"

"I think so. I mean, I think I am sure. He seems fairly intelligent. And like he doesn't want to get caught. Coming after me wouldn't exactly be the smartest thing to do if he is hoping to avoid getting caught."

"And what about me?"

Welsh looked over at her, and his heart sunk. Her lips were tightened in a timid expression.

"What do you mean?"

"Am I in danger?"

"Of course not," said Welsh, not missing a beat, and without warning, his heart rate seemed to steady. It was like the need to offer protection and consolation to his wife had superseded his anxiety. "Why would you be?"

"Well, if he wants to get the better of you…"

"Don't even think it, Wend."

"It's just—"

"Don't go there. Just don't go there. There is nothing to be afraid of."

"Really? Because you were terrified a second ago."

Welsh found his strength. He pushed himself up from the bed and did an about-face, crouching down in front of his wife.

"Trust me. Just trust me. We don't even know what he is capable of yet. For all we know, this is a one-off thing."

"Do you think it is?" Wendy's eyebrows were reaching her hairline.

"It very well could be."

"Yeah, but do you *think* it is?"

"I don't know. I'm not a detective."

"Hmm. Okay."

"This is all in its early stages. We don't know who he is, or where he is, or what he wants. But trust me when I say that this man has no intention of coming after either of us. It would be the opposite of what he is aiming for. Operating in the shadows. Taunting the police. And anyway, remember what I always tell you, the vast majority of criminals are soft. As soon as you threaten them with a prison cell, they lose their spine."

Wendy nodded, but it was more of a subconscious gesture than an actual acknowledgment.

"We are going to catch him. It won't be long."

Wendy brushed this aside with a look of impatience, like she either didn't believe him or just thought he was offering a meaningless platitude. "What was so horrifying about it? Like you said, I shouldn't know the details. How come?"

"Don't worry about that, hun."

"But—"

"Don't worry about it," repeated Welsh firmly. Wendy recoiled slightly, and Welsh instantly felt a small pang of guilt.

"Trust me. Everything is going to be fine. Like it always is."

Before Wendy could retort, Welsh gave her a swift kiss on the lips. She seemed to be taken aback by it, and her cheeks flushed pink. When he saw her reaction, Welsh let out a small chuckle.

"Twenty years together and you still act like I am your junior high crush."

Wendy sheepishly bowed her head and looked

down at the floor.

"*Twenty years* and you still blush sometimes when I kiss you," said Welsh.

"Yeah, well… twenty years and you still give me butterflies."

Without even thinking about it, Welsh went in for another kiss. Then another. Soon, their lips were locked and moving rhythmically together. Welsh put his hand on her hip and teased her pelvis with his fingers. She moved her mouth around to the side of his head and let her hot breath touch his ear.

"I love you," she whispered.

"I love you too."

The door swung shut, and Marty Flask looked up with a strange expression on his face.

"Hello, Carson." His greeting sounded ominous. Arroyo and McCabe were the only other people in the room, and they both gave Welsh a nod of acknowledgment.

"Have a seat." Flask was looking at him with narrowed eyes.

"Are you going to give me detention or something?"

McCabe laughed. Arroyo remained expressionless, while Flask twitched with annoyance. His ruddy complexion was even more reddish-purple than usual.

"Sit down, Carson."

Welsh put his rear end down on the cushioned chair, and wheeled closer to the table. It was then he noticed a folded newspaper sitting in front of Flask.

"It appears we have had a leak."

Welsh shifted his eyes around the room apprehensively. The two detectives and the police chief were all staring at him dramatically, like he was about to confess to killing Tracy Dinwoodie himself.

"Oh?"

"Yes, it seems we have had quite the outflow of sensitive information. Cheyenne Blue of the *Oregonian* is privy to this. Somehow, she has found out the killer who butchered Tracy Dinwoodie and left her remains in Mount Tabor Park is using the pseudonym 'Robert.'"

"That *is* quite the leak," replied Welsh sardonically.

"Blue didn't have the full name. Just 'Robert.' And get this. The media is now calling him 'Bob the Butcher.'"

"Ouch."

Welsh was keeping a defiant tone, but he felt his stomach clench a little. "Bob the Bucher" was a brutal nickname. It made the vision of intestines flash in his minds' eye, and his heartbeat increased rapidly.

"Now, everyone on my team is adamant that they didn't give up this, uh, *pertinent* bit of intel."

"Is that right?" Welsh could see where this was going and felt a spark of indignation at the suggestion.

"Yes. Most bizarre, isn't it?"

Welsh smiled sarcastically and shook his head. "Jesus, Marty. Come on. You think I would be that short-sighted? You think I would undermine the investigation into a case that I will likely be prosecuting? I'm not a rookie, Flask. And I have been in my position a hell of a lot longer than you have been in yours. So out of the two of us, you seem like the more likely candidate for a blunder like this."

Flask's nostrils flared. Welsh continued before the chief could unleash any sort of rebuttal.

"I don't know who did it, but it sure as hell wasn't me. What would I have to gain by doing that?"

"Welsh, did you hear me make an accusation?"

"In so many words, yes."

"Well then, you need to fine-tune your listening skills. I wasn't accusing you of anything. I was just trying to get to the bottom of this. If it was done with some sort of agenda, I would just like to understand the reasoning."

"And I would as well." Welsh nodded to

emphasize his point.

"My fear is that it's going to obfuscate the investigation. That we are going to get an avalanche of anonymous tips from every batty old lady with a weird neighbor named Robert. And it is not only the fact that we had a leak. It is the timing of it. When this sort of thing gets out this quickly, it really hampers the process of the inquiry."

"You don't have *any* initial suspects?"

Flask moved his mouth as though to respond, but Arroyo jumped in.

"It is too early to dub anyone a real suspect. But there are a couple of people I will be speaking with shortly that I think may provide some insight."

"Such as…?"

"Well, seeing as Dinwoodie was on a date in the hours preceding her disappearance, I figured it may be prudent to speak to the individual that took her on said date."

Welsh raised his eyebrows in surprise. "Really?"

"Really. Dinwoodie's coworker Margaret Ledbetter said that Tracy told her that she was going on a date on Friday evening, which was when she must have been abducted."

"Who is the guy?"

Arroyo shrugged. "I don't know much about him, yet. Matthew Lyons. He's a financial advisor for Merrill Lynch."

"The exact profession I was thinking of for a homicidal maniac."

"Like I said, it is too early to dub anyone a *suspect*."

"And who's the other one?"

Arroyo glanced at Flask before answering, apparently waiting to see if she would be reprimanded for sharing details. Flask kept a stoic expression, so she continued.

"Well, rather counterintuitively, I probed the idea that Mr. Macabre's real first name may actually be Robert. It seems like it would be too obvious to be true, right? But sometimes the most obvious answer is actually the correct one. So, I began looking into any violent offenders in the city named Robert."

"And the person you found?"

"Robert James Lacie. Fifty-two years old. Spent six years in the joint for a particularly violent assault of a cop. Known gang affiliations. And when I say gang, I don't mean like the Bloods or the Crips. Think more, Hells Angels type of thing."

"A motorcycle gang?" asked Welsh incredulously. "They have those here?"

"Apparently so."

"Wow."

"Yeah," continued Arroyo. "But the real kicker is this. He lives less than two miles away from Tracy Dinwoodie."

Welsh's eyes bulged in surprise. "Damn."

"I know. I mean, we probably won't get this lucky right off the bat, but he is worth an interview at least."

"Yeah, I'd say so."

Flask jumped in again before Arroyo could continue.

"We are trying to be proactive with this thing. With this sort of... Ritualistic, occult type of murder, it is more of a when instead of an if as far as the next one. What we can hope is he doesn't go through any sort of cooling-off period. I know that sounds morbid, but realistically, the shorter he waits in-between kills, the more likely he is to make a mistake."

"So pray that I get another box of guts?"

"Welsh—"

"I'm just saying, I'm never going to hope for another dead body. It's not my style."

Flask was visibly getting more agitated by the second. The man was tapping his fingers against the desk and shaking his head. For whatever reason, he and the DA had just never meshed.

McCabe was the next to speak. His deep, gravelly voice matched his body perfectly. The man stood above six feet tall and had such wide shoulders that his torso looked fake, like it had been designed by someone who was envisioning a real-life Hercules. McCabe's short goatee almost blended into his face, as it was nearly the same color as his dark skin.

"Now, as you are aware, Mr. Welsh, we don't generally communicate with anyone from your office while the investigation is ongoing. However, since these are extenuating circumstances, and the killer has named you in his letter, we feel that it is only right that you are given regular updates."

"Much appreciated."

"Now that doesn't mean that you are going to be made cognizant of every person we talk to, or every search warrant we obtain. But whenever there is a significant development, you will be notified."

Welsh gave a curt nod. "Okay."

"And remember, if you ever change your mind about the protective detail, the offer still stands," continued McCabe.

"Hopefully, it doesn't ever get to a point where I feel I actually need one."

Mo McCray bit into his club sandwich, and a dollop of mayonnaise congealed to the corner of his lip.

"Do you think you know him?" The words were a little difficult to decipher through the blockade of smashed food in his mouth.

"Yeah, Moose. We are best buddies. I was

actually planning on grabbing a beer with him tonight."

"Fuck off. You know what I mean."

"Well, Arroyo seems to think it probably isn't someone that feels like they have been railroaded by the justice system."

"And what do you think?"

Welsh looked down at the half-eaten burger in front of him and was surprised how quickly his appetite had faded. He glanced around the restaurant, watching a blond waitress dance between tables with two trays of food balancing on her palms. For 2:00 p.m. on a weekday, Fire On The Mountain was surprisingly crowded. This had been Mo's choice. Apparently, it was in his "top five" of Portland restaurants. They had coordinated their lunch hours together on Welsh's insistence. Now that the shock of the package he had received had worn off a bit, he had felt himself dying to tell Mo what was happening. Welsh had left out several crucial details (like the box of innards itself), but he had given Mo a basic summary of what had gone down in the past forty-eight hours.

"I don't know, Mo. I can't tell."

"You can't—"

"Part of me thinks he is just a loon. Just a maniac that chose me as a way to prove something to himself. But then another part thinks it is personal."

"Can you think of anyone that might have a vendetta against you?"

"Everyone who has been sent to jail on my behalf probably has a vendetta against me."

Mo brought his head forward, and his voice dropped a couple of decibels in volume. "But I mean like… a real vendetta. Where you actually felt like you may have made a mistake."

"I can honestly say no."

Mo's face broke into a grin. "Wow! You need to get in contact with the *Oregonian* about that. What a headline that would be! 'Local man has never made a mistake.'"

"What I mean is, I honestly don't feel like I have ever gotten a guilty verdict when the guy didn't have it coming. Sometimes the sentencing can be a little harsh, but I don't recall a time where there was a legitimate doubt in my mind about whether someone actually committed the crime."

Mo shrugged. "Then maybe it isn't personal. The guy is probably just a lunatic."

Welsh looked away, and his eyes caught a young couple spoon-feeding what looked like yogurt to a toddler in a high chair. The baby had a crazed smile on his face, as though nothing tasted better in the world than a spoonful of Yoplait.

"So he dismembered her? Then hung her from a tree?"

"Yeah. Seems like overkill, doesn't it?

Literally."

"Did they ever find the other body parts?"

Welsh raised his eyebrows.

"That's a strange question."

"I'm full of those."

"Well, no… they didn't."

"And there wasn't any like… *glaring* physical evidence left behind?"

"Not sure I can share that with you, Moose. But no, there wasn't."

Mo took another huge bite of his sandwich, and chomped down rhythmically, apparently undeterred by the conversation of dismembered body parts. Welsh had bequeathed him with the nickname Moose over twenty years before, after Mo had told him a story of a time when he and his father had gone looking for elk, and in his hunting ineptness, Mo had accidentally shot a twelve-hundred-pound moose with a Smith and Wesson M&P Sporting Rifle. It was only after the story had been relayed that Welsh had realized that Mo also had a striking resemblance to a moose, with the giant nose and general laid-back demeanor.

"Do you really think he will come after you?"

Welsh saw a hint of concern on his best friend's face. But unlike Wendy, Welsh didn't feel the need to sugarcoat the truth with Mo to protect his feelings.

"He said that he would. Not right away, but he

said in the letter that after I have suffered appropriately, that he will put me out of my misery."

"Holy smokes. Is that like... a verbatim quote?"

"Not verbatim, but pretty close."

"Jesus, Carson. What are you going to do?"

Welsh gave a half-smile, though it was not particularly genuine.

"Hope that Flask's goons catch him first."

"The Blazers stopped a six-game winning streak by the Lakers this evening, thanks to thirty-three points from Damon Stoudamire. The win marked a high point in an otherwise disappointing season thus far, with the team likely to miss the post-season."

Welsh's eyes were beginning to droop. The anchor of KATU News, Pablo Morey, droned on about the local sports teams, and his orange-tanned skin clashed horribly with his excessively white teeth. The television that Welsh was watching was a little outdated, and the color always seemed to be too vivid.

Welsh set the glass of wine that had been in his hand on the table next to the couch, realizing that if he didn't, he would fall asleep and his sweat pants would be doused in red. Out of his peripheral vision, Welsh saw Wendy walk into the living room with a long object protruding from her mouth.

"The Blazersh beat the Lakersh?"

Her mouth foamed up with the white mixture of toothpaste and her own saliva, as she brushed aggressively toward her back molars.

"That's what Pablo said. I didn't catch any of the game myself. I don't particularly have any interest in how the Jail Blazers are playing."

"But the Lakersh are like, weally good, right?"

"Yeah. Sometimes the underdog wins, even in the NBA."

"Hmm." Wendy walked back down the hallway, and Welsh distinctly heard her spit into the sink. Then, after a rush of water, there was the sound of gargling and then another spit. When she spoke, her words were clear.

"I'm going to go to bed okay, hun? I have a long day tomorrow."

"No problem. I should be in there pretty soon as well. I'm losing steam."

"Okay. Good night. Love you."

"Love you too."

Soft footsteps, and then Wendy was gone into the bedroom. Welsh tried to home his focus in on the TV, but it was difficult. His eyelids were so sandy and felt like they weighed a ton.

Welsh's mind gravitated toward the mysterious figure that had plagued his thoughts for the past two days. Robert Macabre was lingering on the periphery of his consciousness, just out of sight.

Somehow, Welsh felt like he knew exactly who the man was, even though he was completely unware of Macabre's true identity. It seemed like they had real history together. Why would Macabre choose him? Why did he seem hell-bent on torturing Welsh? The deeper down the rabbit hole he went, the heavier his eyes seemed to get. His head began to nod downward and then jerk back up, as he tried to finish digesting the mental meal that his mind had prepared for him. And every time he took a bite, he drifted down, down...

Welsh was looking up at the mountain. The green pastures seemed to dissipate the moment they hit the foot of the colossal structure, and morphed into hardened, cold bedrock with a thousand jagged edges. What was he looking for? His eyes scanned everything above him. The wind tore at his torso, and in that moment, Welsh realized that he was naked.

He placed both of his hands on his crotch, covering himself. But from what? He was alone, isolated, and cold in the wilderness. There was nobody to look at his privates or judge his impotence. Then why did he feel like he was being watched?

Welsh walked along the edge of the mountain, gazing out upon the sea of green. It reminded him of Ireland or perhaps some other foreign place where the vegetation grew and the rain descended.

Today, the sky was packed with a light cloud cover, but no water fell from above. The cold bit at his outer extremities. Why did he have to be naked? Surely, he had arrived with clothes.

It should have been tranquil and serene but it wasn't. The natural wonder of the mountain and the sprawling grassland should have put his mind at ease. And yet, all he felt was the same disconcerting sensation of a pair of eyes focused on him from some hidden place.

Welsh turned back toward the mountain. It must have been at least two thousand feet high. Or perhaps it was two hundred. The laws of space and time seemed to be muddled and opaque here, so it was difficult to guess how high the peak actually reached. His eyes scanned to the right, and then to the left. Nothing.

A soft bleat. If Welsh had not been concentrating, he wouldn't have heard it. But his eyes instantly began scrambling along the mountainside, looking for the source. And there he found it. Standing on a ledge some twenty feet above him was a goat. Welsh felt his stomach turn over as the goat bleated again, but this time, it was much louder and distorted.

There was something wrong with the creature. Where its pupils should have been, there were two blank canvasses of white, like it was possessed by a malevolent entity. From its mouth hung a black tongue, lolling pathetically like the goat had lost control of its mind. Suddenly, the loudest noise yet emitted from the animal, and it didn't take long for Welsh to realize that it was no longer bleating, but rather, screaming. A human scream.

The goat stood up, and as it did so, Welsh saw that it was no goat at all, but a gray humanoid body with fur on its chin and horns sprouting from its forehead. There was another scream, and Welsh began to internally beg for the creature to stop. But then he realized that this scream had come from his own chest. Loud and piercing and horrible, like a feeble plea for mercy. The goat-man's black pupils finally rolled forward, and he was looking directly at Carson Welsh. If looks could kill, Welsh would be cold and stiff and undeniably lifeless. The goat-man stepped forward, ready to launch himself off the cliff and down toward the vulnerable naked man below.

Welsh jerked his head with a grunt, and he was suddenly back sitting in his living room with a spittle of drool rolling down his chin and his heart thudding rapidly like he had just ran a mile. Pablo Morey was no longer on his television screen; he had been replaced by some bearded gentleman selling an extended hose for your hard-to-reach plants. Welsh rubbed his forehead aggressively, and exhaled deeply, trying to steady his heart. *Jesus Christ,* he thought.

His hands were sweating profusely, and thus, Welsh almost lost his grip on the glass as he reached for more wine to quell his nerves. *What a terrible nightmare.* The wine burned as it seeped down his throat and seemed to become even hotter when it settled into his stomach. The black tongue of the strange goat-creature was scalded to the back of his eyelids, and his arms were shaking wildly. He took another big swig of wine and then set the glass back down before pushing himself up from the couch. "Fuck me," he muttered aloud, as the pain in his joints seemed to compound when he stood. He ran his fingers through his hair, trying to assuage his body's anxiety with deep breaths.

Welsh picked the glass back up and trudged over to the kitchen to dump the rest of the wine down the drain. His hands were still shaking, and the red liquid splashed randomly throughout the sink. He lassoed the hose next to the faucet and sprayed until the lingering droplets of crimson were washed away. Welsh took more deep breaths, but he couldn't seem to relax his frantically beating heart.

He wished he had never watched the video. The ghastly, baleful mask was haunting, and every time he thought of the woman, whose name was Tracy, crucified and howling on the table, his stomach felt like a boat that had just hit a particularly rough patch of water. Why had Macabre chosen her? Why did he wreak such agony on her body? Wasn't the kill itself enough to satiate his iniquitous appetite? Welsh knew it was a fruitless endeavor to try to answer the why when dealing with a sociopathic, homicidal miscreant. But it was all he could think of. *Why?*

Welsh put both hands on the kitchen counter, and for a moment, he thought he would vomit into the sink. *In through the nose, out through the mouth,* he thought, consciously trying to make his diaphragm steady. *In through the nose, out through the mouth. You're fine. Everything is fine.* The nausea began to dispel, and his heart slowly thudded back to normal like a train reaching its final destination on the track.

Thunk. Welsh almost jumped out of his own skin at the noise. He didn't have time to process it before it happened two more times, but this time, in rapid succession. *Thunk thunk.*

Welsh glued his eyes to the front door. The noise seemed to be coming from just on the other side of the threshold, as if someone with no sense of timing or rhythm was knocking. He tuned his ears for a subsequent sound, but none came. The silence was suddenly penetrating.

Welsh stayed completely still. He waited, frozen, coiled, and still, preparing himself for another thunk.

Nothing. Just more silence. Welsh crept toward the door. Slowly, steadily, ready to pounce if need be. But it stayed shut. As he made his way out of the kitchen, his sweaty fingers enclosed around a knife that was in a block holder with six of its brothers and sisters. Welsh pulled the blade loose and tightened his grip around the hilt. His knuckles flushed white.

Within moments, he was in front of the door. His free hand reached for the handle, encircling the metal. Welsh twisted, glacially slow, as if doing it gradually would somehow be more furtive. *Breath, Carson. Breath.*

He pulled the door open, and the only thing that attacked him was the cold. There was nothing on his porch. No wounded goat-man, no blood-soaked stranger wielding an ax. There wasn't even something innocuous, like a cat or a raccoon. There was just nothing.

Welsh looked out among the trees. Their two-story house sat on the edge of the forest, like a watchtower over the wilderness. He heard crickets cooing in the night. But the sound was not pleasant; it just seemed to heighten the reality of the darkness. He could see nothing, but much like in the dream, he felt like something could see him. It was nearly pitch-black, and difficult to distinguish between what were trees and what could possibly be something more sinister. *A flashlight,* he thought. *I need a flashlight.*

Welsh turned around, leaving the door slightly

ajar. He moved silently and with purpose back through the living room and down the hallway, passing the stairs that led to their bedroom upstairs. At the end of the hallway was the double door to the closet. He placed his sweaty palms on the wooden handles and slid the doors apart, with the knife still in his right hand. His eyes probed different mounds of sweatshirts and coats, and at the foot of the closet, there was a .45 magnum pistol, a .22 caliber rifle, several hunting knifes, and a black flashlight. Welsh set the kitchen knife down and snatched up the pistol in his right hand and the flashlight in his left. He half-juggled the two objects precariously as he switched the flashlight on and the safety of the pistol off. Welsh whirled about and starting walking back up the hall, passing the stairs.

The flashlight beamed around the darkened hallway, looking for anything out of place. When Welsh got to the precipice of the kitchen and the living room, his stomach leapt up into his throat. The front door that he had left only a little ajar was now wide open.

Someone was inside the house.

Welsh felt a rush of adrenaline surge through his extremities, and he moved the pistol left and right, ready to fire. But he saw nothing except the normal furniture and blocky television. Out of his mouth escaped a small hiss as he took in air into his lungs.

He could still hear the crickets from outside, but just faintly. The freezing air prickled his arms. Welsh moved forward, waiting for the ambush from behind the couch, or underneath the counter. His body was so tense and the silence so deafening that any noise that came now would probably make him defecate in his pants.

Where could the intruder be? If not visible in the living room or kitchen, he must have been only a few feet behind Welsh during the man's foray to the closet. Which meant there was only one place he could now be.

Clunk.

Welsh looked up at the ceiling.

Wendy!

He made an about face and charged toward the stairs. Once he arrived at the steps, he bound upward, no longer caring about stealth. It took him less than ten seconds to arrive on the second landing. He ran down the hallway, passing their second bathroom and the guest room. Surprisingly, he found the door to the bedroom still shut. He swung the door open.

Wendy was fast asleep on the bed, with her mouth open and her cheek pressed against the pillow, mushing her face to the side. Her hand was dropped over the side of the bed, and the covers only partially concealed her body. Her rear end, in a pair of white panties, was sticking out with her left leg curled underneath her. She appeared unperturbed because only half her body was under the blanket. Her chest was rising and falling slowly.

Where are you?

Welsh felt like he was having an out-of-body-experience. He no longer paid any attention to any unpleasant sensations in his body. The adrenaline had cast everything else aside, and his body was powerful and ready for combat.

He pointed the flashlight down either side of the bed, checking every nook and cranny. He placed the beam on the open door to the closet and found a black void. No shape of a body, nor mask of a goat.

Where are you?

Another noise, and this one was loud. So loud in fact that Wendy stirred a little in the bed and turned over, but remained asleep. Welsh twisted about and darted out of the bedroom like a startled cat.

The beam of the flashlight went back and forth along the hall, but Welsh knew he would find nothing there. The demon had tricked him somehow, and was still downstairs, doing god-knows-what. Welsh resumed his stealthy gait, tiptoeing down the edge of each step. When he got to the bottom, he lingered there for a second, trying to steady his shaking arms and prepare for the impending shot.

Welsh ripped around the corner, brandishing

the pistol in front of him. There was no one in the hallway, so he moved forward. The kitchen was vacant; Welsh could still see the empty glass of wine where had put it on the counter. He paused again when he got to the end of the hallway before swinging his body quickly around the bend and flourishing the gun toward the living room.

Nothing.

Welsh lowered the gun, and as he did so, he realized he had been holding his breath.

"Where are you?" he whispered out loud.

Just then, he noticed that the front door was closed again. There was a still moment of comprehension before he charged forward, pistoning his arms and legs as he scrambled toward the door. His fingers fumbled with the handle, but finally found their grip. He tore the door open, raising the gun simultaneously.

And here he was again. On his front porch, looking into the darkness for something that he could not see. But this time he was armed. He moved the beam of the flashlight back and forth, illuminating shrubs and bushes and thick trees with splaying branches. The first five passes back and forth over the wilderness yielded nothing. But then he saw it.

A flash of white.

The beam had passed over it, but then when Welsh realized what it was, he focused the light back on the spot. He only got a quick glimpse of it before it disappeared into the woods. But a quick glimpse was all he needed to discern what it was.

The face of a rabbit on the body of a man.

"What is that smell?"

"Tar, I think. Or fresh asphalt."

"Why is it so strong? Jesus."

Arroyo brushed her nose with fervor, as if rubbing it would ward off the unbearable aroma. She put the Suburban in park against the sidewalk, opening the door simultaneously. She fingered the quarters at the top of her pocket, and slid them into the meter one by one, buying thirty minutes of time. McCabe walked around the back of the car and hopped up onto the sidewalk.

The morning sun was bleak and cold nipped at Arroyo's chin as she walked toward the monumental building in front of her. She passed a gaggle of people walking with their heads down and their briefcases held stiff, as if swinging it a fraction of an inch one way or another would be deemed unprofessional. The only looks that were given were to McCabe. Portland had long tried to rid itself of xenophobia and discrimination, but the city was almost exclusively white, which laid the foundation for, at the very least, a benign curiosity regarding minorities.

The detectives approached the building side by side, exchanging one last glance before they got to the entrance. The huge double doors were plated with gold handles. Arroyo took the left one and was surprised at the weight of it as she pulled it open.

When the pair got to the expansive desk with three computers and two serious-looking secretaries, they stopped, waiting for one of the women to look up. Eventually, the one on the left smiled disingenuously and asked how she could help them.

"We are here to speak with Matthew Lyons."

The woman, who had a name tag that said Charlotte, looked at her computer screen.

"Is he expecting you?"

"Uh, Portland, PD. I am Detective Arroyo, and this is Detective McCabe."

The woman could not hide the surprise on her face before giving another counterfeit grin.

"Ah, I see. Well… That doesn't exactly answer my question."

"No, he is not expecting us. But most people aren't. The ones that *are* usually are harder to find."

"Hmm, *okay*." Her voice was dripping with

sarcasm.

"If you could please just direct us to his office."

"I should probably give him a heads—"

"Not necessary," Arroyo said firmly. "Please just tell us the room number."

The woman scoffed and looked like she wanted to tell them off, then apparently remembered that she was speaking to the police.

"Um, sure… It is three thirteen."

"Thank you."

Arroyo turned and briskly strode toward the nearby elevator without another word.

McCabe couldn't stop himself from smiling as he walked in Arroyo's wake. "You ain't in no mood to beat around the bush, eh Em?"

"It's not my style," replied Arroyo, stone-faced. She punched the button embossed with the number three and waited. Eventually, the elevator doors slid open. Two minutes later, the detectives were departing the elevator and walking down the only hallway available to them.

"Three oh two. Three oh three." McCabe was looking at the plaque on each doorway as if the hallway of offices might pull a fast one and skip a number.

"Here it is. three thirteen."

Arroyo pounded four times on the door.

"Easy there, partner. Knock any harder and they'll make you pay for a new door."

"I'll just give them the door to your office. If you ever get an office."

McCabe chuckled as the door swung open. A tall, lean man with glasses and shoulder-length brown hair that was slicked back with gel looked at them with mild curiosity. He was handsome and well-built, with piercing eyes and tanned skin.

"Good morning. How can I help you?"

"Good morning. Are you Mr. Lyons?"

"I am," said Lyons, and he had a quiet voice. "Who are you?"

"I am detective Emily Arroyo. This is my partner, Ray McCabe."

Lyons' eyes shifted back and forth rapidly, but his expression did not give away any trepidation.

"I was wondering when you would show up. Come on in."

Lyons sat behind a mahogany desk, his eyes unfocused. The office was expansive and no expense had been spared on the furniture, including the sizeable desk. Hanging on the wall were several plaques, but the writing was too small to discern without standing directly in front of the awards, or whatever they were. The computer in front of Lyons was sleek and lavish-looking. Arroyo had no idea what kind of salary a financial adviser procured, but judging by the general opulence of the entire building, it wasn't an insignificant amount.

"So how long did you know Ms. Dinwoodie?"

"Three weeks."

Lyons was reclined in his chair, looking at the two of them with an indeterminable expression on his face. He had a pen that he was twiddling in his hand. Arroyo watched as it rolled through his knuckles seamlessly, passing back and forth without a hitch. *What a useless skill,* she thought.

"And the two of you were... serious?"

"I wouldn't say that. I really like her though."

He said it in the present tense and didn't even twitch once he heard the words that came out of his mouth. If Lyons were going through the five stages of grief, he would definitely still be in the denial phase.

"Where did you go on your dates?"

"The first one was pretty informal. Just testing the waters. We went to Cold Stone out in Gresham. The second we went to an Italian place... I forget the name. It was on Morrison. The third we had French. Le Pigeon."

"Nice place," said McCabe.

"I'd say. Not used to dropping a hundred bucks on dinner."

McCabe chuckled. "Especially on a third date. The things we do, man."

Lyons smiled with just his lips, but did not reply.

"So, do you think she was fairly smitten with you?" asked Arroyo.

Lyons raised his eyebrows. "I'm not sure I see the relevance…"

"Just more background, Mr. Lyons. You have to understand, we know nothing about this woman, other than what we have read and seen in photographs."

"Right… Well, yes, smitten is one word for it. I might even say infatuated."

"Infatuated?"

"Yes."

"Hmm. That seems to imply that it wasn't totally reciprocated."

Lyons brought his twiddling-pen-free hand up and waved it a few times. "No no no, that isn't what I was saying. Like I said, I really liked Tracy."

"It's just *infatuated* seems to have a negative connotation."

"Well, maybe to you, but not to me."

Arroyo looked down at the open notebook that was in her lap and made a note. *Narcissistic tendencies,* she wrote.

"As we understand it, she was married to Greg Dinwoodie for six years. Did she ever tell you why she kept his last name after their divorce?"

Lyons shrugged. "I mean… No. I just figured

that it was easier for her."

"Well, what it tells me is that she doesn't harbor ill-will toward her ex-husband."

"Maybe… I never really broached that subject. Didn't really interest me."

"You weren't interested in hearing about the ex-husband of the woman you were dating?"

If he was rattled by this inquiry, Lyons didn't show it. His face remained impassive. "It didn't seem very important."

Arroyo made another note. *Arrogant.*

"So, did you keep in frequent contact with Ms. Dinwoodie over the past month? I mean, other than when you were with her?"

"We never spoke on the phone if that is what you are asking."

"Why not?"

Lyons smiled and finally stopped twirling the pen in his left hand.

"This may sound silly, but it was kind of done in the spirit of romance, I think… I wanted to keep the spark fresh, you know? I didn't want our conversations to become tedious or dull. Absence makes the heart grow fonder, they say. I wanted our dates to be something I looked forward to every week. If you are talking to someone every day on the phone, what are you going to have to talk about when you actually see them?"

Arroyo stopped making notes and considered

Lyons. She couldn't decide if he was an egotist, a showman, or actually a hopeless romantic. Perhaps he was all three. Arroyo could see why Dinwoodie may have been infatuated. It was the mystery.

"So, how did these dates go?"

"Very well. They went very well. I would have thought you would have gleaned that when I said that I really liked her. Twice."

"Walk me through the third date. Le Pigeon." Arroyo ignored the touch of rudeness from Lyons.

"Well... What do you want to know?"

"Everything."

"Uh, okay. Starting...?"

"At the beginning," said Arroyo pleasantly.

Lyons took a deep breath and launched into his story. At first, Arroyo thought that he was sarcastically including every detail as a way to patronize Arroyo, but then as he continued she realized that he was really that thorough. The man seemed to have an eidetic memory. He spoke of Dinwoodie's mannerisms. He told them about the food they ordered and the color of the woman's skirt. He remarked about how he thought the waiter was gay, though that didn't bother him.

Apparently, the majority of the date had consisted of philosophical conversation; Lyons had taught her about the basic fundamentals of Marxism and socialism versus capitalism. They had also spoken of religion. Dinwoodie had been raised in a

Catholic family and had attended private school as her parents had been opposed to the secular education offered by public schools. However, she had told Lyons that a childhood of religion had pushed her away from Christianity, and she now considered herself agnostic. Lyons himself was an atheist.

After their expensive dinner filled with profound existential conversation, Lyons said they had kissed in the parking lot outside of the restaurant. They had come in separate cars, so when they were done kissing, they went their separate ways.

"Did she ask you to come home with her?"

"No." Lyons said it defiantly, as if he were daring the two detectives to question why.

"Did you ask her to come home with you?"

"No. I live in Canby. I wasn't about to ask her to make a half-hour drive back to my place."

"Have you slept with her before?"

With a distinct feeling of satisfaction, Arroyo watched as Lyons' face showed shock and even a little embarrassment. Even though he tried to hide it, there was no doubt that the man normally had a trace of conceit hidden in his idiosyncrasies, and if there was one thing Arroyo despised in the world, it was superciliousness.

"That is nobody's business but mine."

"Well, yours and Tracy's. But she's dead."

Silence filled the void. Lyons went back to fidgeting with his pen.

"So when did you hear about what had happened?"

"On the news. Two days ago."

"What was your reaction?"

"Well... I have a tendency to drift off on my couch when I am watching the news. So naturally, when I heard the newscaster say her name, I thought I was dreaming. Hell, I think I even laughed at first. I am a lucid dreamer, so I thought it was some sort of joke that my subconscious was playing on my conscious self. But then I kind of... twitched and I realized that I was awake."

Lyons shifted in his chair and pursed his lips.

"Honestly... It still feels like I am dreaming."

"How do you mean?"

Lyons set the pen down and rubbed his face fully with his hands while letting out an elongated sigh. He shook his head, looking over his shoulder and crossing his arms while leaning forward on the desk. When he looked back at the detectives, he was biting his lip. The man seemed to be pondering something. After at least ten seconds of silence, Arroyo reiterated her query.

"How do you mean, Mr. Lyons?"

"I took a psychology class as part of my coursework for my undergraduate degree," blurted Lyons suddenly. "I think it was just psych 201. Just the general stuff. Freud, Pavlov's dog. But I remember a section about trauma. The activity in the prefrontal cortex after a traumatic event manifests itself in nightmares, flashbacks, and anxiety. But honestly, I haven't felt any of that. These past forty-eight hours... I feel detached from my body. Like I'm in a fourth dimension and watching myself walk and talk and perform the general, repetitive tasks of my workday. I don't feel any emotion. I don't feel anger, or grief, or fear. I just feel... detached."

"Hey, I think I have heard of what you are describing. I believe it's called denial," interjected McCabe.

Lyons swallowed. "No. It isn't that. I don't know how to explain it."

Arroyo hesitated for a while before broaching the next topic.

"And, Mr. Lyons... The way she was found in Mount Tabor Park—"

"Don't."

It was almost a grunt. The word came from deep in Lyons' diaphragm.

"Sorry," replied Arroyo, and she meant it.

For another few seconds, quiet dominated the room. McCabe flattened his light purple tie awkwardly, and Lyons reached for his pen like a pacifier.

"So, can you account for your activity the night

of your date, Mr. Lyons? After you left Tracy?"

A beat of nothing, and then Lyons' face broke into a smile.

"There it is. There is the question I was waiting for."

"We have to ask—"

"I know. I know. And yes, I can. I went straight home, poured myself a glass of wine, drank it while watching a rerun of *The Sopranos*, and then went to bed."

"And is there anyone *else* who can account for this?"

The amused look on his face vanished.

"Well… No, not directly. I live by myself. Don't have any neighbors that I am particularly friendly with. But I am sure there is security footage from my apartment that shows me enter my apartment that night and not leave until the next morning."

"Right," replied Arroyo, scribbling on her notepad fervently.

"And I don't even know where Tracy lives."

Arroyo looked up.

"Are you insinuating that she was abducted from her house?"

Lyons looked frazzled. "Well, n-no, I don't know that for a fact, I just assumed since you know, it is isolated out there."

"I thought you didn't know where she lived."

Lyons gave a small scoff. "I don't, okay? Not specifically. I just know that she told me it was out in the countryside."

McCabe tried to calm him down. "Listen, Mr. Lyons. Contrary to what you might think, we haven't even assembled a list of suspects yet, or pinpointed any person of interest. We are just in the gathering facts stage. I'm sure that we won't even have to watch the CCTV footage. I bet *someone* saw you on your way back home."

Lyons nodded. "Probably, yeah."

"Excuse my partner's, uh, misgivings. She's as paranoid as they come." McCabe made eye contact with Arroyo, and they exchanged faux stony glances. This was a technique they had worked on, pretending to have some sort of friction between them while McCabe faked like he was warming up to the respondent.

"We know you didn't do anything, Matthew."

Lyons gave a small nod.

"We are just trying to make sense of this... brutality. It is just hard for me to fathom why anyone would do something like this. Hell, you know what the media is calling him? 'Bob the Butcher.' Can you believe that?"

Lyons suddenly looked like he felt sick.

"What do you think about that?" asked McCabe. "The nickname?"

Lyons pursed his lips.

"I think it is absolutely revolting."

McCabe rolled his window up, as rain droplets began to moisten the road around them. He took a quick glance at his cell phone before putting it in his coat pocket. Arroyo shifted the Suburban into drive and pulled away from the curb.

"So, what are you thinking about him?"

McCabe looked at her briefly, then turned his head away without answering.

"Ray?"

"He ain't the guy."

Arroyo looked at him in surprise. He had said it with such conviction. And one thing about Raymond Leroy McCabe was that when he was that assured about something, he was usually right.

"What makes you say that?"

"Just a hunch. Intuition, you could call it."

"But nothing tangible that points in that direction?"

"Nah. Do you have something tangible that points to the contrary?"

Arroyo slowly swerved around a construction zone, where a group of burly men in orange jackets looked to be repaving the road. The man holding the sign that said Slow looked incredibly bored. He was staring off into the distance and did not gaze in through the front windshield when the bulky SUV plodded past.

"I just get a funny feeling about him."

"How's that?

"He just seems strange to me. Like how he was so descriptive about the date with her? What man remembers that much detail?"

McCabe gave a one-shouldered shrug. "I don't deal in generalizations, Em."

"Please. A photographic memory? Telltale signs of narcissism? And the emotionless delivery that he gave that whole interview? Something is going on in that brain, Ray. Something abnormal."

"Just because he is a little strange doesn't mean he's a murderer."

"No, but—"

McCabe suddenly held up his hand and looked down at his lap.

"What?"

"Phone's ringing."

He picked up his cell and unlocked it and said his own name by way of answering. It was one of his quirks. Instead of saying, "Hello," like any other person, he would simply say "McCabe" as a form of greeting.

The conversation with whoever was on the other end of the line didn't last very long, and McCabe's responses didn't seem to give any clues about the nature of the dialogue. He said "uh-huh" three separate times, and once he even said "damn." As soon as his respondent had conveyed the information that he or she had intended, McCabe hung up with an "all right" instead of a goodbye.

"That's interesting," he began.

"What is it?"

"Toxicology came back on Dinwoodie. She was positive for LSD and some type of intravenous sodium-lactate *infusion*."

"*What?*"

"Yeah. Dunny said that the infusion was probably designed to induce feelings of panic and stress. And then coupled with the hallucinogen…"

Arroyo's eyes were wide. "Jesus Christ. Well, that doesn't seem like a concoction a middle-aged dental hygienist would usually go for recreationally, wouldn't you say?"

"I think it is safe to say that our guy inoculated her while she was tied to that table. Dunny said that it must have been a concentrated dose."

"Jesus Christ," repeated Arroyo.

"Why would he go and do something like that?" McCabe frowned in concentration.

Arroyo ground her teeth while she was thinking. She turned the steering wheel, banking down Seventy-Second Avenue in the direction of the station.

"Well, we have established that this is some

sort of paraphilic, sexual fantasy that he is enacting, right? Since she was violated numerous times. So what do sociopathic, sadistic predators get off on?"

McCabe grunted, and his nostrils flared. "Some real twisted shit."

"Fear. They get off on fear. So our guy injected her with the drugs to up the ante, as it were. The more afraid she was, the more aroused he would be."

McCabe scratched his cheek. He gave an exasperated shake of his head and muttered something inaudible before turning to his partner with a repulsed look on his face.

"This guy is one sick fuck, isn't he?"

9

Welsh's eyes were so heavy that it felt like a workout to keep them open. He sat on the couch with the gun on the table in front of him. The morning light peeked through the closed blinds and created a ray that shone across the handle of the pistol. The television was on, but the volume was turned way down so that Welsh could hear any extraneous, potentially nefarious noise.

He had slept a total of two hours the night before and cursed himself for even dozing off that much. The rest of the time he had sat in silence, listening for ominous noises outside. Welsh had drawn the blinds as tight as they would go, but they did not quite fit the window frame. Throughout the protracted hours of the night, he had frequently kept his eyes on the sliver of uncloaked glass on the window, waiting to see the rabbit mask peering into his living room.

Had the man actually been in his house? Welsh wasn't sure now. It seemed like he would've seen Macabre slinking behind his furniture or up his stairs if the demon had come inside. And what was the purpose of the invasion if nothing had been taken and no one had been hurt?

He wouldn't report what he thought had happened. For one, the more Welsh thought about it, the less confident he felt about what he had seen. Maybe no one had been in his house. Perhaps the mask in between the trees had been his own subconscious envisaging something petrifying after the terrible dream he had had. Also, if reported his suspicions, Flask and Arroyo would force a protective detail on him. The thought of a set of eyes constantly watching him, prying into his personal life and ridding him of any privacy was enough to make his insides squirm. And there were other ways to enforce security.

What he needed to do was buttress his outer defenses. An alarm system. That was what he needed first. And cameras. Multiple cameras that would capture every angle outside.

Welsh was semi-aware that his lack of sleep could be warping his thinking. A harebrained, gung-ho plan to thwart a maniacal sociopath on his own was probably not the most practical course, and one of the contributing factors to the idea was probably exhaustion. Perhaps once he slept, he would wake up and immediately call Flask. But for now, when he was stewing in it, it seemed like the only option.

His back was killing him. Welsh had foregone his pain pills for the third time over the past week. They made him feel aloof and indifferent. Numb, almost. And at the moment, he welcomed the pain. It was stoking the fire. Sparking and kindling the flame of fury in the recesses of his lungs.

A noise, but this one came from upstairs. It was immediately followed by several more sounds. A pattering of soft footsteps. Apparently, Wendy had woken up and was trudging out of their bedroom.

Welsh took a frantic look at the gun in front of him, and his eyes started scanning the room. He didn't want to discard the weapon from his person, but he couldn't let his wife see it. He looked at the large, white couch pillow next to him that was embroidered in pink trim with the word His. Years ago, they had had a matching set with one that said Hers, but it had been torn to shit by an old, cantankerous cat they had had named Walter. Welsh clicked the safety on the pistol on and tucked the gun underneath the pillow, hoping that Wendy would not insist on sitting right next to him. He found the remote and turned the volume up. Stuart Scott was rambling on about the Packers' ineptitude in free agency. Welsh tried to focus on what the anchor was saying, as if doing so would help him fool his wife. He put his arm nonchalantly over the pillow.

"Morning," Wendy said sleepily as she sauntered into the room. She was wearing her favorite baggy gray sweatpants and an oversized T-shirt.

When she caught sight of his appearance, her eyes narrowed. "Are you not going into work today?"

"No, I am. Just a bit of a slow start is all."

"Are you all right? You look really tired."

"Yeah... Just didn't get a lot of sleep last night."

"How come?"

Welsh shrugged. "Don't know."

"Was it your back? Did you not take your pills?" He did not miss the accusatory tone in her voice.

"No. My back doesn't hurt at all," he lied.

"Then why didn't you sl—"

"What are you, the sleep doctor? I don't know, Wendy. I just didn't."

Wendy recoiled, and Welsh instantly felt guilty for snapping.

"Sorry for asking about your wellbeing, I guess."

She entered the kitchen, taking great care to open up the cupboard harder than it needed to be, signaling her annoyance. Wendy brought her mug of choice down and opened a drawer in the kitchen, pulling out a light brown filter. She reached up and pulled the can of Yuban from the top of the fridge and peeled off the lid. A half of a second later, she made a noise of irritation.

"Why do you always do this? Why don't you leave the scoop to the coffee inside the can?"

"Just use a spoon."

"Ugh."

Wendy opened up another drawer. But instead of pulling out a piece of silverware, she pulled out the yellow plastic scoop that she had been looking for in the first place.

"Nice. You left this exactly where it doesn't go."

"Jesus," muttered Welsh. "Maybe *you* were actually the one who didn't get enough sleep."

Wendy scowled over at him as she released a dollop of coffee grinds into the filter, and though she was surely thinking of a nasty retort, she held it in. For the next couple of minutes, she worked in silence with a stony expression on her face as she set the filter inside the coffeemaker and pressed the on button, which corresponded with a flashing green light. Droplets of brown sizzled on the bottom of the glass pot.

"What were you doing clunking around last night anyway?"

"Huh?"

"Huh?" repeated Wendy sarcastically, making

a mocking face. "Last night! You were stomping around. I almost got up and came down to check on you. I figured you had fallen asleep on the couch like always and that is why you didn't come to bed, but then it was suddenly like you were taking a tap dancing class."

"I didn't mean to wake you."

"Hmm."

"I wasn't doing anything. Just lost my phone is all." Welsh put more of his weight on the pillow, as if Wendy would look over and sense the Glock underneath it.

"Well, did you find it?"

"Yeah."

"Where was it?"

"Just in between the cushions."

"Ahhh. So you decided to skip the most obvious place first and then circle back around later?"

Welsh now regretted starting off the unpleasantness with her. When she got in a mood, Wendy was relentless. And he had triggered it. Welsh contemplated different ways to placate his wife.

"Wait, why is the flashlight out?"

A bubble of nervousness floated into Welsh's stomach.

"I told you. I was looking for my phone."

Wendy looked over at him and made piercing

eye contact. There were several beats of silence as her brow furrowed.

"You're lying."

Welsh gave her a forced frown, as if flabbergasted by her suggestion.

"Don't give me that, Carson. Don't double down on the lie."

He pursed his lips and went silent.

"Why were you using the flashlight? Really."

"I was just looking for my phone, Wendy."

Wendy gave an exasperated, sarcastic smile and shook her head while muttering "Jesus" under her breath.

"Wendy—"

"*Nine* years together and you still feel like you have to lie."

"It's not that, Wend."

Without warning, Wendy's face, which had been beset by irritation, suddenly fell.

"Wait… Does this have to do with the letter?"

"What letter?"

"What letter he says."

"Yeah, no, of course not. It doesn't have anything to do with that." Welsh almost wanted to reach under the pillow and touch the gun, as if it was somehow a cure-all to any kind of discomfort.

Wendy looked at him, and it was like she had x-ray vision. Like she could somehow shoot one glance in his direction and know all of his innermost, personal thoughts.

"I don't believe you."

"Wendy—"

She stormed off without another word.

The dusty jukebox blared surprisingly loud considering how rusty and dilapidated it looked, and the old, mustached bartender had to lean in to hear the order of the rather obese man in front of him. The Honkey Tonk was shaking with country music, though most of its inhabitants looked rather irritated with the song selection. A hoard of bearded men in black leather jackets were circled around a pool table, laughing and seemingly trading insults. One of them had a skinny female in a short skirt sitting on his knee, and he seemed to be bucking her up and down like she was a small child. Everyone else was giving the men a wide berth, as if they were eliciting a particularly foul odor. Everyone except for the red-haired woman and her tall partner that were striding directly toward the group.

"Yo, Twigs, you solid, remember."

"I know which ones are my balls, boy."

"Then why do you keep hitting mine in? I don't need no handicap to whip your ass."

The group cackled with laughter. There were seven of them. The man who was called Twigs was lining up for a shot, while his opponent leaned against the wall casually. Three of the others were sitting on stools next to the game, and beyond them, two more figures lingered in shadow at a small table on the other side of the billiard. Arroyo noticed that the man who had the skinny woman on his knee had a ridiculous looking red handlebar mustache.

"Whose ass is gettin' whipped, boy? You had four balls left on the table when I finished last game," said Twigs.

"Yeah, you should have took pictures of that, Twigs, 'cause it ain't ever going to happen again."

Arroyo wondered why his nickname was Twigs. The man was burly; his legs looked like tree trunks.

"Never again until next game, bitch."

Another spattering of laughter rippled through the group, but stopped when the men saw the two newcomers hovering on the edge of their gang.

"Bar's that way," said the man across from Twigs, gesturing to his right.

"Oh, I don't drink," said Arroyo pleasantly.

The man and Twigs exchanged amused glances.

"Whatcha doin' in a bar then, ginger?"

"We came to talk to one of your compadres," said McCabe, stepping forward.

The man looked up into McCabe's face.

"And you are?"

"I'm Detective Raymond McCabe. This is my partner, Emily Arroyo."

"Detective, eh? I hope you ain't here to cause any trouble, Detective Raymond."

"I ain't here to cause any, but that don't mean I won't find some."

The man smiled, and Arroyo saw that his teeth were yellow and decayed.

"What's your name?" asked McCabe.

"What do you want with my name?"

"I don't want anything with it. Just wondering what to call you."

"All right then. It's Charlie."

The two stared at each other apprehensively.

"We are here to speak with Robert Lacie," said Arroyo firmly. All eyes shifted to her.

Charlie's smile faded. He considered her for a moment and then looked over his shoulder.

"You hear that, Rob? The ginger wants to talk to you."

A massive man rose up from the darkness on the other side of the pool table. When he was erect, Arroyo saw that he was at least six foot seven, and probably just on the fringe of three hundred pounds. He was wearing a leather vest with seemingly nothing under, and his arms, which were half muscular and half flabby, jiggled with his gait. Every inch of his body that wasn't his face was covered in tattoo's, including his neck. His head was totally bald and protruding from his chin was a dark gray goatee that reached almost down to his bulging chest.

"And what would a couple of pigs want with me, Charlie?" His voice was gravelly and quiet.

McCabe looked to be on the verge of some pugnacious response, but Arroyo continued before he could get it out.

"Just want to ask you a couple questions, Mr. Lacie."

Lacie smiled and revealed several silver fillings on the right side of his grin.

"Last person who called me Mr. Lacie was my lawyer."

"Can I call you Robert?"

"Depends. Can I call you Fire Crotch?"

The men all howled with laughter, but the skinny woman reached out and softly hit Lacie on the shoulder.

"Don't be gross, Robbie," she said, and her words were accompanied with a smacking of gum.

"Sorry, she's right. I've forgotten my manners. What do you two piggies want to talk about?"

"A woman."

Lacie grinned. "My kinda chat."

"One who was murdered."

The amused expression vanished from Lacie's face. The other members of the group all seemed to freeze and look at her like she had transformed into a human-sized spider. Arroyo was a little surprised at how she had come out and said it, but a flame of ire had ignited in her brain after Lacie's petty insults and general derisive attitude.

"Now why would you want to talk to me about a thing like that?" The man's tone was suddenly minacious and threatening. But Arroyo was not deterred.

"Mind stepping outside?"

Lacie shrugged.

"All right. Let's step outside."

Once they were out in the gravel parking lot behind the bar, the massive man pulled out a pack of Camel Lights, spanking the top against his meaty palm before withdrawing a cigarette. He pulled out a lighter that flipped open, sprouting flame. As soon as the tip was lit, he sucked on it so hard that his cheeks caved in and Arroyo could see the definition of his bones. He took care to blow all the smoke in his mouth in McCabe's direction, who didn't flinch.

Arroyo cleared her throat. "So you spent six years in the joint… That right, Mr. Lacie?"

"That's right." He took another draw on his cigarette. "Eight years in total, but my last sentence was six."

"First two were for possession, yeah? Meth and heroin?"

"Uh-huh." He nodded sarcastically, his tone mordacious.

"And the last six were because you assaulted a deputy, correct?"

"Yep."

McCabe chuckled. "Shit man. Now why would you go and do a thing like that?"

Lacie shrugged, with an acrid look on his face.

"No idea. Was high as a kite."

McCabe nodded, and though he pretended to be amused, Arroyo knew that he wasn't. "I'd say. R and I said that the original altercation didn't even involve you. That you just walked up to the deputy and started swinging."

"Well, I guess you can say I ain't got the friendliest attitude when it comes to pigs."

"Why is that, Robert?"

"Because they ain't held to the same standard that they enforcin', man. You tellin' me that a cop can shoot somebody point-blank who was reachin' for his wallet and not face any sort of punishment? If that ain't corruption, then what is?"

Arroyo stepped back and appraised the giant in front of her. "Are you armed, Robert?"

Lacie's eyebrows raised. "Huh?"

"Do you have a gun?"

"What does that—"

"Just answer the question."

Lacie smiled balefully and opened up his jacket. Strapped to the right side of the leather was what looked like a .45-caliber pistol.

"I can show you my permit, if you want."

"Not necessary. I'm just saying, half the time when people of your ilk put their hand in their jacket, they aren't reaching for their wallet."

Lacie's jaw contorted with irritation. "People of my ilk?"

"Yes. Criminals. Felons."

For a prolonged instant, Lacie stared at Arroyo like he was on the verge of backhanding her. His brow furrowed intensely, and his teeth grinded with vehemence. Then, all the muscles in his face slacked, and he let out a barrage of laughter.

"Look at that! The ginger has got some fuckin' balls on her! Bravo, little girl! You keep puttin' all of us *dogs* in our place!"

"My pleasure," said Arroyo humorlessly.

"Feisty little fire crotch, aren't ya? Man, I bet she busts your balls on the daily, *Raymond*, don't she? I mean, shit!" Lacie's laughter was forced and a little jarring.

"Let's just get down to brass tacks shall we, Mr. Lacie?"

"Sure, babe. Sure. Let's get down to *brass tacks.*"

"Did you know a woman by the name of Tracie

Dinwoodie?"

Lacie took another long draw on his cigarette and scattered the ash on the ground with a flick of his finger.

"Who?"

"Tracie Dinwoodie."

"Never heard of her."

"You might recognize her. She lived just a few miles from your house." Arroyo pulled out a photograph of Dinwoodie from underneath her coat. It was a headshot taken by a professional photographer in which Tracy was wearing a bright pink blouse and grinning from ear to ear.

"Sheesh. Hot little mama, isn't she?"

"She's dead."

Arroyo was expecting to see traces of consternation or defensiveness, but Lacie displayed none.

"Shame. She looks like she would be a good lay."

"Man, have some respect," said McCabe, shaking his head.

"I'm just joshin' with you, Raymond! Take a joke, man. But nah, I ain't ever seen her before."

"Hmm."

"So why do you want to talk about some dead girl?"

Arroyo's voice grew quiet. "Because she was murdered, Mr. Lacie."

"And you think, what, that I was the one who killed her because... we are sort of neighbors?"

"Well, no. But I do think it is interesting that a violent offender that lives within a ten-mile radius of a homicide victim has the first name of Robert, when the killer left a letter using that very name."

Finally, a look of inauspicious understanding came over Lacie's face.

"Shit. Is this that girl they found carved up by Mount Tabor Park? Hanging from a tree?"

Neither Arroyo nor McCabe responded, which was a response in the affirmative itself.

"This is the guy they are callin' Bob the Butcher, isn't it?"

"A truly repulsive name. But yes, Mr. Lacie. That is the one," replied Arroyo.

Lacie shook his head and scratched at his beard before flicking the cigarette on the ground and stomping on it with intensity.

"Shit, man, I have to say. This is a first. I have been accused of a lot of things, but never *satanic* murder."

"No one is accusing you of anything. And what makes you think satanic?"

"Didn't they find her with a goat mask? No arms and no legs and no guts? That's some messed-up shit, boss. Too messed up, even for a guy like me."

Lacie shook his head and brushed at his

shoulder, wiping the remnants of some rogue ash that hadn't been discarded on the ground.

"We just need for you to account for your activity last Friday night, Mr. Lacie."

"Last Friday night? Man, I can't even remember what I had for lu…"

A pause.

"Wait! I was here! Yeah, shit, I was here! I remember Friday because I damn near got in a bar fight with some tweaker that kept gettin' in my woman's face. Ask Eddie!"

Arroyo looked at him with a puzzled expression on her face.

"The bartender! He will remember it!"

"Maybe we can see some security footage of that night."

"What kind of place do you think this is? They ain't got no cameras in there."

"Okay. Then we will ask Eddie," said Arroyo with a sarcastic thumbs-up.

Within moments, Lacie was back to his mocking, cavalier persona.

"Phew, you piggies had me worried there for a second! That is a pretty twisted thing to accuse a man of!"

"We never accused you of anything."

"Yeah, yeah. But I can see it in your face, Fire Crotch. You were thinkin' it."

Arroyo had finally had enough, and the dam of

pent-up irritation burst.

"No, I wasn't. As soon as you opened your mouth, I knew you didn't have the brains for it."

Lacie's eyes bulged, and his amusement subsided. For a few long seconds, silence reigned as the man's face contorted and clenched. He squeezed his jaw and stepped within six inches of Arroyo's face.

"You got a pretty big mouth there, ginger."

The man turned from her and hocked a huge wad of spit onto the ground.

"Now get on outta here before I do something I regret. Take your spunky little ass and your pet nigger and *get*."

Arroyo looked over at McCabe, preparing for the man to launch himself at Lacie. But as always, he appeared calm. His face was stoic and expressionless, and he stared at the burly biker with what looked like indifference.

"Well, I'm sure we will see you again, Bob. If not in person, at least your mugshot in the paper," said Arroyo viciously.

She turned and began stomping away, feeling heated and ready to jump out of her own skin. McCabe, however, stayed in place. When Arroyo realized he wasn't by her side, she stopped and looked back.

"Thank you for your time, Mr. Lacie. Hopefully, we didn't intrude," said McCabe quietly.

Lacie leered at him, baring his teeth.

"And sorry about what happened to your nose," McCabe added.

"The hell you talking about? What's wrong with my nose?"

McCabe struck with such force that Arroyo cringed at the sickening noise. A splatter of blood decorated the tops of McCabe's shoes, and the elephant of a man in front of him crumpled into a heap in the gravel. Arroyo's jaw dropped and she was suddenly frozen in place with waves of shock pulsing through her.

"It's broken," said McCabe, wiping his bloody knuckles on his pants.

Welsh barely got any work done during the day. Every phone call he took, he felt like he was behind the forth wall, and watching a different district attorney field questions. The answers he gave were nondescript and ambiguous. He had an appointment with a defense lawyer named Tom Butterfield that was trying to negotiate a plea deal, and Butterfield asked him if he wanted to reschedule the meeting because Welsh's answers were so vague and contradicting.

"You seem out of it today, Carson," Butterfield had said.

If he only knew.

By the time Welsh was in his car driving home, his outer extremities seemed numb and torpid, and it was almost a surprise that he was having any thoughts at all. It was like his mind had experienced sensory overload and was shut off. The only feeling he did have was a stark sense of foreboding regarding his reunion with Wendy.

After they bickered, things usually went one of two ways. Either she wouldn't speak to him at all until the following day. Or, she would profusely apologize the moment she saw him. Wendy was strong-willed, but also genial and endearing. And fiercely loyal. The problem was, she was not above holding a grudge if the circumstances called for it. Welsh just hoped that tonight would not be one of those times.

Welsh's mind was so stagnant that he felt like he had almost blacked-out on the drive home, and when he finally pulled into his driveway, he was surprised to find that it was 7:30 p.m. Wendy was probably wondering where the hell he was, which was not conducive for a happy reconciliation. He stayed in the car for a few moments longer than what was necessary, preparing himself.

When he entered the house, he found her sitting on the couch with a mug of tea in between her thighs. She looked over at him as he crossed the threshold, and Welsh instantly knew that things were going to be okay by the softness in her expression.

"Hey."

"Hey."

"Long day, eh?"

"You could say that."

"Come here."

Wendy stretched her arms out toward him like a small child, beckoning an embrace. When he got to her, he placed his rear end on the cushion and she hugged him tight.

"I'm sorry."

"Don't be. You did nothing wrong. I shouldn't have snapped at you for asking me how I was doing."

"Yeah. I guess you shouldn't have." Wendy gave him a peck on the cheek. "But I overreacted. I was pretty rude."

"It's okay."

Welsh rubbed her back, and the rubs transformed into light scratches. Wendy seemed to softly coo in satisfaction, as her shoulders always itched.

"And you were right. I do need to be honest with you."

Her head turned toward him and they made impregnable eye contact.

"I didn't lose my phone last night. I thought I heard something outside."

Wendy pulled away, looking frightened. Her eyes seemed to pouch a little, and her lips tightened.

"Don't worry. I didn't see anything, obviously. I'm just... paranoid. And stressed."

Wendy nodded, but looked away.

"Last night, I dozed off in the chair. I had a

weird dream. When I woke up, I was on edge. Not thinking straight. That is all it was."

"Carson... I want you to be honest with me. Are we in danger?"

Welsh looked at his wife, trying to summon strength in his voice.

"No."

She nodded, but did not look reassured. Welsh instantly felt guilty for another bald-faced lie right off the bat, but he rationalized it internally by telling himself that he wasn't fibbing for his own well-being.

"But, if it makes you feel better, there are a couple of things we can do."

Wendy raised her eyebrows expectantly. "What do you mean?"

"An alarm system. Cameras—"

"I thought you said—"

"I don't think we *need* anything like that. That is why I said, 'If it makes you feel better.'"

"Hmm."

"So, it is up to you. If you want, we can up the security ante around here. I just want you to have some peace of mind. And I mean, it isn't like we are living paycheck to paycheck. We can afford some sort of home security system. It's viable financially and logistically, so there is no reason not to keep our options open."

"Mmm, I love when you talk like a lawyer to

me. Gets me hot."

Welsh laughed.

"Oh yeah, baby. Maybe it is time to discuss some early parole for your tits." He snapped the back of her bra strap flirtatiously.

Wendy giggled. "That was pretty bad. Not your best work, Mr. Welsh."

"Did you laugh?"

She shrugged and gave him a wink.

"Then the state rests its case."

Wendy suddenly perked up. "Hey, I have an idea. Maybe we just need to take an extended vacation until they catch this guy. To the house in Wilsonville."

Welsh scoffed. "Maybe if you let me renovate it. It's kind of uh, *dilapidated,* as it were. And we haven't been there since winter started. I wouldn't be surprised if there is a whole hoard of critters hibernating in there at the moment."

"Well, we should at least make them pay rent!"

Welsh laughed, harder than he had in some time. When his guffaws began to subside, there was a genuine feeling of contentment in his belly. He eyed Wendy with affection.

"I really am sorry, sweetheart. For this morning."

"Yeah… I know. I am too."

"I love you."

"I love you too."

Their lips met. Welsh had intended to just give her another small peck, but he was met with unexpected enthusiasm from his wife. She sucked hard on his bottom lip and slipped her tongue into his mouth. Welsh returned the zeal, moving his hands up and down her back and kissing her with passion. Without even really intending to, his hands were moving underneath her blouse, and hers were unfastening his belt. Soon, several articles of their clothing were on the floor, and Welsh scooped his wife into his arms in a fireman's carry, hoisting her off to the bedroom.

The red light on the phone on his desk blinked over and over. Welsh kept his head down, ignoring it and focusing on the document in front of him. He read the flummery, verbose language, trying to comprehend what was being communicated. Eventually, he got to a sentence that seemed so dense and prolix that it frustrated him enough into setting the document aside.

A week had passed since the night that he had seen the man in the rabbit mask. The seven days had been mostly uneventful. He had followed through and had a company named Sery Solutions install an alarm system in their house that would whine incessantly if an intruder encroached upon their property for more than thirty seconds without typing the code into the security pad next to their front door. It was definitely a habit that he had to get into, arming and disarming every time he went to and fro. Thankfully, nothing had triggered the alarm since they had set it up.

Welsh had also had a private contractor mount cameras at the two entrances to his house. They were set to record for seventy-two hours at a time and then loop over the previous footage. He had spent about a half hour every morning fast-forwarding through the recordings, but nothing had caught his eye.

Welsh glanced over at the blinking phone and wondered how long the person had been on hold. With a sigh, he answered the line.

"This is Carson."

A deep male voice spoke to him. "Ah, yes. Mr. Welsh, right?"

"That's right."

"I'm surprised I was able to get ahold of you. I have been calling a couple of times a day for the last week and nobody has been answering."

"Yeah, sorry about that. We are very busy here—"

"No, no, I understand that."

The door to Welsh's office slowly opened, and Samantha stepped inside, holding several items. She mouthed, "Sorry," to Welsh and set down the documents in front of him on the desk. He quickly sifted through them as he spoke, divvying up his attention while Samantha slipped back out of the office.

"Have you tried leaving a message?"

A long pause.

"No."

Welsh wondered if the man could hear the sound of his eyes rolling.

"It will make sense once you meet with me why I haven't been leaving messages, Mr. Welsh. My name is David Kane."

Welsh didn't say anything, as there wasn't anything to be said. He looked at the first item that Samantha brought, which seemed to be a copy of a subpoena. He scanned the second article, which had the Hallmark seal, and finally, he glanced at the manila envelope, which contained case files for a person named Lewis Lyday, who was being put on trial for manslaughter.

When Welsh didn't respond, David Kane continued.

"I have some information for you that I believe will be of interest."

"Regarding?"

"I would rather not say over the phone."

Welsh rubbed his eyes impatiently as hunger gnawed at his belly. It was almost time for lunch and dealing with nonsensical phone calls (which happened somewhat regularly at the DA's office) was not something he wanted to partake in.

"I am going to transfer you over to my secretary. She will be able to schedule an appointment."

"No wait—"

Welsh hit the button that said line one and then dialed star eight nine, which immediately transferred the call. He sighed deeply, annoyed at the general riff-raff that he had to interact with as an attorney. Almost absentmindedly, he fingered the copy of the subpoena. The language was as tedious as the file he had been reading before, so he cast it aside with a deep exhale. Welsh then picked up the letter with the Hallmark logo and tore at it.

Inside, he found an off-white plastic card. It was of simple design, nothing eccentric or tacky decorated the outside. It was simply embroidered with the words "A Gift For You" in a slightly darker shade of white.

When Welsh halved the card open, he was greeted with only two lines of writing:

1556 North West Plains Blvd.

-Robert.

Arroyo circled around the farmhouse, her gun pointing forward. Two deputies were in front of her and several other men tiptoed in her wake. The exterior of the giant building was rusted and in shambles; the shingles on the roof seemed to be loose and ready to tumble off. She moved swiftly and silently, waiting for a signal from McCabe, who was giving orders to the SWAT team in the front of the edifice. The only noise that came was a light rustling as she and the deputies moved past the long-leaved plants that were draping down against the gray structure. It was an aberrant and strange form of vegetation, and it made it feel like they were trekking through the jungle, and not some abandoned farm out in the country.

Arroyo's radio crackled, and she twitched at the noise.

"F-21."

She frowned at the device attached to her belt. F-21 was Lieutenant Don Chaser.

"F-21 go ahead." Arroyo found herself halfway whispering.

"SWAT team is waiting for my signal."

"Where the hell is Ray?" she hissed. The deputies in front of her had stopped moving.

"With the SWAT. They are setting up a perimeter."

"Why?"

"In case the guy is going to start spraying at us from above. There is a pretty big window on the second floor."

Arroyo processed the information. Before the operation, they had quickly mapped out the area and had just planned on two teams coming in, simultaneously. One from the front and one from the back. McCabe must have tweaked the plan when he saw the second-floor window with an open vantage point for shooting.

"Roger, that, Lieutenant."

"Shall I proceed?"

"Not yet, LT. Wait until we are in position."

"Roger that, F-33."

Arroyo chopped forward through the air, indicating to the deputies to keep moving. They all started slinking forward.

Eventually, the corner of the building came into view. One of the deputies looked back at Arroyo with a quizzical expression on his face. She simply gave a small nod, and the man, who was named Cory Hall, returned the gesture before swinging around the corner, brandishing his gun. After a beat, the gun lowered a fraction, and Arroyo realized the coast was clear, so she and the other police followed suit.

The back of the farmhouse was even more derelict than the front. It seemed to be stained with a sprawling black substance that smelled like tar. There were even a couple of holes in the wood, and the door that they came to looked like it could be kicked off its hinges by a toddler. The cops all took positions on both sides of the door, each gripping their guns a little tighter.

"Okay, F-21. Send them in."

"Roger that, F-33."

Arroyo nodded to Hall again, who stepped back, and seemed to brace his body. With a backward slide of his foot like a rhinoceros, Hall lifted his leg into the air and slammed his boot into the door, which blasted backward, completely free of its bounds.

"Go, go, go!"

One by one, they piled into the building. Arroyo was the fourth one in, and her vision was somewhat obstructed, both by the darkness and the large men in front of her, but she could still see her surroundings. On either side of the barn, there were rows of at least fifteen stables.

"Check them all!" she hissed at the men in front of her. The deputies began hovering on the precipices of each stable, before rounding them quickly, wielding their guns.

Suddenly, there was a deafening *bang,* followed by a heavy clunk and then the sound of footsteps.

"That'll be the SWAT," said Arroyo grimly. Right on cue, six men in black armor came charging down the middle aisle between the stables. One of them was yelling instructions that were not totally distinguishable, but sounded like, "All clear!" and "Watch your six!"

McCabe's voice suddenly rang out through the darkness. "Check every stable!"

She wasn't sure why, but Arroyo's eyes suddenly focused on Deputy Cory Hall, who was lingering on the edge of a stable to her right with a strange look on his face, almost like he was mentally working up the courage to swing around the corner. With a motion akin to a snake lashing out at its prey, Hall oscillated his gun around the bend. Instantly, Arroyo could tell that something was awry. Hall's gun lowered, but his face seemed to crumple in horror, and his off-hand moved to shield his nose. He began to look unsteady on his feet, swaying back and forth. Another deputy recognized what was happening and coiled his arms around Hall's midsection, keeping the man upright.

With her heart thudding like a drum Arroyo slithered forward. When she got to the area in question, she didn't even bother to raise her gun as she moved past Hall, who seemed to be fainting into the other officer's arms. Knowing that she was about to see something that couldn't be unseen, Arroyo breathed deeply and stepped onto the threshold of the open stable.

It took a moment to identify what she was looking at. It was almost unrealistic, like looking at a bizarre painting in some abstract museum. The bottom two-thirds were a woman's naked body, that was easy to see. She was tied to a chair with several distinct streams of dried blood running down her torso. But where a human head should have been, there was something much more misshapen and grotesque. The long snout of a horse. A mask? But it was too lifelike. Too gritty. This was no veneer, this was an actual head of a stallion. Squinting her eyes, Arroyo saw that there were at least fifty black seams at the point where the woman's neck met the dome of the creature. The head of the horse had been sewn on.

The others rounding the corner all cussed and covered their mouths, turning their heads away. But Arroyo kept her eyes fixed on the body, unable to look away from the monstrosity in front of her.

"Lady and gents, I am not going to lie. Feds might be comin' in on this one soon."

Marty Flask paced back and forth at the front of the table, scratching his bald head furiously. His arms were at his hips, and large sweat stains were visible on his armpits. Occasionally, he would fan himself off with the rolled-up piece of paper he had in his right hand. It wasn't even that hot in the room, but Flask was so beset by stress and consternation that his pores seemed to be overactive.

"It's going to be hard to keep them out. Hell, at this point do we even want to keep them out?"

McCabe, who was sitting across the table next to Arroyo, whistled through his teeth. Flask glared at him.

"Sure, okay, Ray. Let's get your opinion on the matter."

"I've just never been one to concede defeat, that's all."

For a fleeting moment, Flask's mouth expanded and contracted and his skin flushed red.

"God damn it Ray, look around! It's not even been two weeks and this guy has already taken us through the ringer!"

"Boss—"

"You want to trade places with me, shitheel? You want to try your hand at managing this?"

"Marty—"

"Don't you Marty me! I mean, Christ! A horses head sewn on her decapitated body!"

"I was at the scene, Chief."

"Then don't you tell me I'm conceding defeat!"

For several long moments, everyone around the table was dead silent. Flask had always been prone to outbursts, but these days, they were coming at an alarming frequency. It was like walking on eggshells. No one knew what would to set him off.

Unexpectedly, Flask pulled the chair that had been designated as his away from the table and placed his rear end in it. In that moment, Arroyo had never seen him look so exhausted. Ryan Dunny, who was directly next to the chief, seemed to subconsciously lean away, as if the heat of the man's fury may literally burn him.

"This shit is going to give me a stroke, I swear."

His voice was suddenly much calmer, and Arroyo felt a little less on edge. She watched as her boss tapped his fingers on the table anxiously.

"I can't say we won't hand it off, guys. I can probably give you until at least the end of the month. But if this shit keeps getting messier by the day…"

"I can promise you, Chief. We will catch this asshole."

Flask chuckled sarcastically at McCabe's proclamation.

"You don't even have a lead…"

"That's not necessarily true."

"You've interviewed two potential suspects and you punched one of them in the face."

"Chief—"

"I know what he said. And he probably knows he deserved it, otherwise it would have escalated. You should just be glad that Mr. Lacie hasn't filed a complaint."

"What's done is done," said McCabe, stone-faced.

"Nothing's done, McCabe. Nothing is *ever* done."

Flask swept the table in front of him with his hand, though there didn't seem to be anything that he was sweeping away.

"Shit, guys. I mean, have you ever solved a murder when the investigation lasted more than a week? When was the last time that the first round of questions didn't point you right to the damn perp?"

"I'm not sure I get what you are implying," said McCabe cautiously.

"I'm saying that every day that passes without any groundbreaking intel on the DB's is another day closer to this guy getting away."

"Well, R and I already gave us a lot of info on the new vic."

Flask used his right hand to gesture in a circular motion. "Okay, then why don't you enlighten the rest of the table?"

McCabe turned to his left and looked at his partner expectantly. Arroyo cleared her throat, as she had not spoken in at least twenty minutes, and then launched into the exposition.

"Name is Jacey Duhart. Thirty-seven years old. Single. Worked as a teller at Bank of America. Records clean. She *did* speak with police about an incident six years ago that may be of some interest. Apparently, she ran away and went missing for several days. She had bipolar disorder, and in ninety-eight, during a manic episode, she drove her car into Eastern Oregon, through the desert. When they finally found her after three days she was suffering from severe heat exhaustion and had almost died from dehydration. However, there have been no other incidents since. And she seems to have been really turning her life around over the last couple of years. Got her associates degree from P.C.C. Steady job. Nice apartment over by the waterfront."

"We will have to start asking around about her mental health. If she had bipolar disorder, and suffered a manic period that, uh, *severe,* I'm guessing she still had occasional episodes here and there," said McCabe.

Flask nodded, then turned to Edwin Spade, who was sitting halfway down the table.

"What about cause of death? Did he take her head after she was already dead?"

Spade almost seemed to slither forward in his seat. "I don't think so. I found bruising on her genitals, but other than that, no sign of the same type of torture like I found on the other victim. I think she must have been alive for the, uh, *decapitation.*"

"Jesus," muttered Flask. He turned to Ryan Dunny. "What about evidence? DNA, prints?"

Dunny had begun shaking his head before Flask had even finished his sentence. "Not even a partial. And the only DNA on the body was hers. I've never seen such a stark lack of physical evidence before."

"What about the farm house?"

Arroyo shuffled through some of the documents in front of her on the table. "Owner of the property is a man named George Swanson.

Doesn't even live in Oregon anymore. Has a farm outside of Henport, Iowa. We spoke on the phone. Sounds like he has been trying to sell the property for years. But no takers at his asking price."

"And has anybody reported a missing horse?"

"Not that I'm aware of."

Flask drummed his fingers on the table, and for a while, no one said anything. McCabe and the others seemed to fear speaking, as though steering the conversation in a way that Flask didn't want it to go would provoke another rage-induced tirade. Arroyo set the documents down and her eyes focused on the large droplets of water that were lingering on the window behind Flask. The view outside of the station was normally spectacular, but the weather had turned blustery, the sky dark, and the aesthetic effect was much less pleasing. It was as if nature was reflecting how she felt.

"What about Welsh?"

Arroyo's eyes shifted back and forth. "What about him?"

"Where is he?"

"At home, I'm assuming. I didn't ask him to stay. I didn't think it was necessary."

"Has he reconsidered the protective detail?"

"Not as far as I know."

Flask bit the inside of his cheek as he seemed to ponder the district attorney. "And how's his, uh, mental state?"

Arroyo shrugged. "He seemed sort of detached when we spoke. Didn't even ask any details when I told him about the new DB."

"And the letter didn't say anything else of substance, correct? It just had the address and his name?" asked Flask.

"Mm-hmm. The letter itself was a standard white gift card. Just said, 'A gift for you,' on the outside."

"And no physical evidence on the letter."

The chief turned to Dunny again. The boyish-looking forensic technician shook his head.

"No."

"And I'm assuming you already know that tracing where the letter came from will be next to impossible," added McCabe. "If we couldn't get traction on the package, there is no way we will get a hit on the letter. There are at least a thousand different places for outgoing mail that he could have dropped it into without a hitch."

Flask seemed to wince, and then his face broke into another sarcastic smile. He leaned forward while he wiped his brow, looking exasperated and cynical.

"Christ. It is like we are chasing a *entity* here. Like some sort of… evil spirit."

Arroyo looked around the room and saw that everyone had an air of enervation. The only person who didn't appear fatigued and repulsed was Spade, who had a strange look on his face. Arroyo couldn't quite identify it. It was something almost mimicking exhilaration. She glanced at the man, and when Spade noticed that she was looking at him, his cheeks shifted downward until his expression was much more stoic.

"So what are you two going to do next?"

Flask stared at Arroyo and then McCabe intensely.

"We are going to head to the vic's apartment. See what we can find. It might take a bit to catalog everything, but I am sure we will find something of interest," said Arroyo.

Flask nodded like he agreed, but then raised his palms in the air.

"Who knows? The way this investigation has gone so far, I'm not even sure we will be able to find her apartment."

Dolores Muldoon hobbled up the steps, her bulky posterior swerving back and forth as she huffed and puffed her way up the stairs. She was probably only in her late forties or early fifties, but the woman carried herself like she was ancient. Her gait was probably due to the toll that carrying around three hundred pounds took on her joints.

"Jacey was always upbeat. Chipper, you know? She sounded like she should be a Walmart greeter or something."

Arroyo nodded, though her attention was mostly on the massive backside of Muldoon. One misstep and the woman would come tumbling down at her like the boulder in *Indiana Jones*. McCabe was far enough behind the two of them that he probably couldn't stop the wrecking ball if it came cascading down the stairs and gathered enough downward momentum.

"I mean, I only saw her once a month when she came into the office to drop off rent. But she was always very kind to me."

Muldoon jangled the set of keys on her wrist as she struggled to find the one that would open up apartment 262.

"I knew as soon as you mentioned her name on the phone that something bad must have happened to her. A girl like that? When a detective calls asking about a pretty young lady like Jacey, you know it ain't going to be good news."

She paused as she inserted the key into the lock and then turned and made piercing eye contact with Arroyo.

"This has something to do with the woman in Mount Tabor Park, doesn't it?"

"I can't answer that, ma'am."

"That is an answer in itself."

Arroyo didn't reply.

"Pretty women don't go missing around here often enough to think that the two aren't related."

Arroyo still kept her poker face.

"Ah, sorry. I don't mean to pry. She was just such a nice girl, you know? And what happened to that other woman…"

Muldoon looked at Arroyo, hoping she would crack. When she didn't, the older woman shrugged and simply pushed the door to the apartment open, gesturing at Arroyo to step inside.

"I'll stay out here, obviously."

Arroyo nodded and stepped past. She waited just over the threshold for her partner to catch up, then once McCabe was right behind her, she pressed on. The place was incredibly spacious and was decorated more like a house than an apartment. Framed pictures of the blond Duhart and various family members festooned the walls, and there was enough furniture for a family of four. A big blue couch sat in front of a cumbersome-looking TV, and a round plush ottoman that matched the couch in navy sat perfectly spaced between the sofa and the television stand. A lamp with a chic golden cover hovered next to the couch, but it was apparently superfluous, as McCabe reached over toward the wall and flicked on the overhead light, illuminating the area.

"Roomy in here, isn't it?"

"I'd say," replied Arroyo quietly.

McCabe clicked his tongue several times and rocked a little on the balls of his feet. "So what first?"

"Well, let's just do a surface sweep first. See if we find anything peculiar."

"You got it."

Arroyo looked at some of the photographs on the wall. In one of them, Duhart was with an older woman who was also blond, and Arroyo felt sure it was her mother. In another picture, she was leaning over a small child with brown hair and a missing tooth in his smile. The boy looked a little uncomfortable, and his smile was forced. Arroyo knew that Duhart didn't have any children, so she assumed this was the woman's nephew or distant cousin.

The rest of the photographs on the wall were pictures of Duhart at a wedding reception, and then several of her with a blonde girl who looked to be in her late-teens. There wasn't anything out of the ordinary, and certainly nothing to indicate any sort of mental instability.

Arroyo reached out with her blue latex-gloved hand and picked up a small notebook that was on the ottoman. Inside, there were pages and pages of calendars, with every day for three months notarized and planned.

"Looks like she wasn't lacking any

organizational skills."

McCabe, who was standing in the kitchen and looking at more pictures on the refrigerator, glanced over at his partner.

"Planner?"

"More like a yearly to-do list." Arroyo set the planner back down without reading through it. Once they finished their first initial sweep and called in forensics, one of the guys would catalog the planner, so later, when she had more time to go through each piece of archived evidence, Arroyo would perform a more intensive scope of the thing.

"Lot of cooking utensils in here."

Arroyo looked over at the area connected to the living room that McCabe was standing in. "That's generally what one finds in a kitchen, Ray."

"But like, this is some heavy-duty shit. This is one of them juicers." He dangled the metal item that he had found on the counter in the air, making the cord flop around. Once he set it down, he pulled the fridge open and let out a loud whistle.

"Well, I think it is safe to say that we found ourselves a health nut."

Arroyo walked over and looked in the fridge. Inside, there were at least fifteen plastic containers with food inside. The top shelf was uniform with combinations of fruit in each of the containers. The second shelf looked to be all veggies, the third assorted meats.

"That's interesting."

"What, that she likes to portion her food?"

"That she has allocated certain food groups to specific shelves. It's the pattern, partner. You should look at the planner. She has dates set for months down the line. Everything in her life seems to be compartmentalized. Everything premeditated and planned for."

"Hmm."

Arroyo shut the fridge. "I'm going to go look through the bedroom."

"You do that."

There was only one door to go through, so Arroyo pushed it open and walked through it. Inside was one of the most pristine bedrooms she had ever seen. The king-sized bed was made perfectly, with every inch of the blue bedspread adhering to the mattress perfectly with no crinkles or lumps. There was a wooden nightstand next to the bed, with exactly two items on top of it: an alarm clock, and a small lamp.

Nothing stuck out, so before doing a more invested sweep of the bedroom, Arroyo strode to the other door on the wall to her left, and gripped the handle. She assumed it was a bathroom, as she had not encountered a toilet yet. Arroyo twisted the handle and pushed, but it caught on something. There wasn't a lock on the door, so it must've just been a faulty knob. With her off-hand, Arroyo shoved while torquing the handle. Suddenly, the door burst open and swung in and Arroyo stumbled a little with the impetus of her thrust. When she caught her balance and looked up, she gasped.

The bathroom was covered in red graffiti. Every inch of off-white paint was absolutely doused in color; even the mirror had been violated. Once air re-entered her lungs, Arroyo squinted her eyes and saw that it was writing. But only three words. The same sentence, penned in crimson hundreds of times on the walls:

He's wearing red.

Mo McCray drummed his knuckles on the bar, staring at Welsh apprehensively. The bar was virtually empty, except for a couple of stragglers. One older man was slumped against his arms at a booth, apparently sleeping. The bartender had not taken notice of this yet, for if he had, the older fellow would probably be eighty-sixed. Welsh occasionally glanced over, and couldn't quite decide if he thought the elderly man was homeless or not. The man had a half-empty beer in front of him, and a wallet was left carelessly on the table, so there was some evidence to the contrary. But the dark green jacket the man was wearing was tattered, and his slumped hands looked dirty.

"Good thing I am not a thief. That there would be easy pickins."

Mo swiveled around in his stool and saw the wallet in front of the sleeping (or potentially passed out) man. "What kind of thief steals from a transient?"

"Who says he is a transient?"

"I bet *he* stole that wallet in the first place."

Welsh shrugged and sipped on his beer. His eyes continued to flit around the room, digesting all of his surroundings. These days, he wasn't sure what detail would end up being important to him.

"Carson…"

Welsh looked back at Mo, who had genuine concern in his eyes.

"Yes?"

"Talk to me, buddy."

Welsh shrugged, pretending to be ignorant of what Mo was insinuating.

"'Bout what?"

"''Bout what,' he says." Mo shook his head irritably.

"Relax, Doctor Phil. I'm fine."

"We both know you ain't fine."

"We do?"

"Fuck off, man. Just talk to me about it."

Welsh sighed. He pressed index finger and his thumb against his eyebrows, and ran them along the crease underneath his forehead, attempting to rub away tension. For the past thirty-six hours since he had gotten the second letter, he had had a sharp headache throbbing behind his eyes.

"I really don't know what to say. Or even think,

Mo. I feel like I am having one long, strange dream. You know in dreams when everything is dull? When life is some weird, muffled sensory experience? Like you don't know you are dreaming but you know things are... fuzzy. That is what I feel like."

Mo gave him a prolonged stare. Welsh thought he was trying to be empathetic, but then, with perfect timing, he delivered one of his signature one-liners.

"Man, what the *fuck* are you talking about?"

Welsh laughed hard. Harder than he had in some time. His stomach seized with guffaws, and his chest wheezed as air escaped. With every passing second that he laughed, his perpetual headache seemed to fade. Mo even joined in with a few chuckles of his own, but he seemed to be mostly amused at how tickled Welsh was.

"See, this is why I never get serious with you, you shit-bird," said Welsh.

"I'm just sayin'! You sound like you are a little high, man."

Welsh cackled some more and clapped Mo on the back.

"This is why I keep you around. Only you could make me laugh when I am in the midst of a showdown with a homicidal maniac."

Welsh continued to chuckle, but Mo's smile faded a little. He took a big gulp of the Michelob

Ultra in front of him. Once he swallowed and set it down, he made penetrating eye contact with Welsh.

"Was it as bad as the last time?"

Welsh shook his head vigorously. "My end was far less graphic. I heard what the detectives found was pretty grisly though."

"You heard? You don't know specifics?"

Welsh shook his head. "They tried to tell me, but I wasn't interested. I know all I need to know about what is in this guys' head."

Mo nodded. For a second, they just looked at each other, but then both of their heads turned when they saw the bartender stride away from where he had been stationed. The skinny fellow snaked his way through tables, heading toward the elderly gentleman that was motionless on the table.

"Looks like somebody is about to get busted."

They both watched as the bartender gripped near the old man's shoulder and shook it roughly. The man did not budge, he simply groaned. The bartender told him that he needed to leave, but the man still stayed there, totally petrified in place. Eventually, after a couple of more attempts at disturbing his slumber, the bartender threw his hands up in the air and walked back to the bar, muttering away. Welsh couldn't hear exactly what was being said, but intermingled in the jumble was definitely the word "cops."

"Looks like this place is about to liven up."

"I'd say."

Mo turned back around to face Welsh.

"So… What are you going to do about this whole thing?"

"What am I going to do, or what have I already done?"

"Huh?"

Welsh shrugged his shoulders, hoping to look mysterious. "Well, I haven't exactly sat idly by, you know?"

"What does that mean? Did you finally ask for a detail?"

"No… I took some steps on my own."

A blank look took ahold of Mo's face.

"Meaning?"

"I had a company called Sery Solutions install an alarm system. And I had a guy I know put in cameras. Also, I spent some time down at Dick's Sporting Goods and now have enough ammo to take down an entire infantry unit should my house ever get invaded by hostiles."

Mo scoffed. "What, you think Bush is going to declare war on the Greater Portland Area?"

"Hey, you never know. He did just invade a country for no particular reason."

"I don't like this, Carson."

The half-amused look on Welsh's face was wiped away.

"What do you mean?"

"I don't like that you are taking this into your own hands."

"Mo—"

"You don't always have to do shit all on your own. You could ask for help instead of trying to go all *Home Alone* on this guy," said Mo quietly.

"I don't remember Kevin McAllister having an assault rifle."

"Carson, buddy, seriously. What has gotten into you about this?"

Welsh broke eye contact with his best friend and stared forward, focusing his attention on a bottle of Tequila that was sitting next to its brothers and sisters on a shelf behind the bar. He bit his lip and frowned, as if concentrating mightily on the logo that said Espolon. He could feel Mo's eyes bearing on him still. And though he was expecting another quip, Mo remained silent. Finally, Welsh sighed and said what was on his mind.

"If this guy is going to buy a ticket, I am going to make him take the ride."

Wendy had her head against his chest, her eyes drooping a little. Welsh turned the volume up a little, as the scene they were watching in *Mystic River* had suddenly gotten quiet. Wendy twitched and looked back at him.

"You know, I am not sure we should be watching a movie about some murdered girl," said Wendy groggily.

"You aren't watching. You are about to fall asleep."

"I'm just resting my eyes…"

Wendy rubbed her petite little hand against Welsh's belly, and he felt that it was warm. It comforted him, and he gave his wife a light smack on the bottom to return the affection.

"Watch it, mister. Gettin' a little frisky."

"Yep. You are right. I can't keep my hands to myself. Maybe you should put me in cuffs."

"Whoa, frisky *and* kinky."

Welsh chuckled, and Wendy's head bobbled a little with his laughter. She pressed her ear more firmly against his gut, letting her head rock with the shakes of his stomach.

"Do that again. That feels weird."

"Do what again?"

"Laugh."

"Then say something funny."

"Uh, okay. I'm pregnant."

Welsh's eyes bulged.

"Okay, you are right. That isn't funny," said Wendy quickly. Welsh roared with laughter, and Wendy nuzzled her head against his belly, letting the motion of his convulsing diaphragm move her head.

"This is so much fun! You should try it!"

"I don't know if your tiny little belly could handle my big ol' head!"

Wendy's mouth dropped as she pretended to be flattered. "Aw, my tiny belly? You are so sweet!"

Welsh laughed some more. Eventually, his chuckles subsided. He was surprised at how remarkably relaxed and upbeat Wendy was. The evening before, when he had told her the news about the second letter he had received and the subsequent victim, she had understandably spent all night on edge.

"So how are you doing?" asked Welsh.

Wendy's eyes shifted toward him. "What do you mean?"

"You just seem to be in a lot better mood than yesterday."

She shrugged, and her expression hardened. "To be honest, I have been trying not to think about it."

"Oh. Sorry."

"Don't be sorry for asking me how I am doing. I am doing okay. At least at the moment. Not as scared as I was."

"Why were you scared?"

"I wasn't afraid for me. I was afraid for you," replied Wendy quietly.

"I'm not in any danger."

Wendy smiled, almost a little skeptically.

"You know, actions speak louder than words."

"What is that supposed to mean?"

"People who don't feel threatened don't put up cameras around their house and buy big guns," said Wendy matter-of-factly.

"How did you—?"

"I am all-knowing, babe. It is time you realized that. You are married to an omniscient being."

Welsh laughed, though he did not feel altogether amused. He had been intending on keeping the newly-purchased artillery a secret.

"It's not a sin to admit that you are worried, Carson. Hell, if you weren't worried, *I* would be worried."

Welsh homed his eyes back on the television. A young boy was in the back seat of a man's car, and ominous music was playing. Since he had not been paying attention to the last minute of action, Welsh wasn't exactly sure what was unfolding, but it wasn't difficult to hazard a guess. The boy, who looked to be no more than eleven, had willingly gotten into the car of the man who was kidnapping him.

"Carson…"

Welsh looked back down at his wife.

"What?"

"I want you to promise to be honest with me."

"About what?"

"Before I tell you, I want you to promise that you aren't going to lie to me."

Wendy looked at him seriously, and though it was a somewhat tense moment, Welsh also felt a rush of fondness for his wife. Almost like a child, she took promises very seriously. It was endearing and cute and made him want to promise her the world.

"All right. I promise."

Wendy took in a big inhale, as though she were prepping herself for something unpleasant.

"Is this man going to try to kill you?"

At first, Welsh's face broke into a smile. It was such a ridiculous sounding question that he couldn't help himself. But then he saw Wendy's eyes, full of apprehension and anxiety, so his smile faded. He thought about her question hard. Moreover, he thought about the best way to phrase his answer without breaking the promise. Finally, like a long-held breath, it just slipped out.

"I'm not sure."

"What do you think it means?"

"I don't think we have enough information to hypothesize the answer to that question, Ray."

"Well don't hypothesize, just *guess.*"

"Were detectives. We don't guess."

"Yes, we do. That's *all* we do. We have just honed our guessing skills."

Arroyo shrugged and watched as a slight forensic technician named Dorian took a picture of the television. There was now fifteen people coming and going from the apartment, all wearing dark blue jackets and carrying either cameras or plastic bags. The two detectives had to frequently step out of the way as techs and pathologists hustled and bustled there way to-and-fro.

"He's wearing red," muttered McCabe under his breath. Arroyo stepped forward, watching Kevin Ho holding a video tape and ogling at it. McCabe caught notice of this too and snorted.

"What, never seen one of those before, Kevin?"

Ho hurriedly placed the tape in a bag and clasped the seal. "The opposite, actually. I'm sort of a film buff. I have a pretty big collection of VHS tapes in my garage."

"Your garage, or your mothers?"

Ho looked down, tightening his lips with embarrassment as McCabe tittered.

"Don't be a dick, Ray."

"I'm just giving him a hard time, Em."

Ho shuffled off, looking for something else to snatch up. McCabe continued to chuckle, and Arroyo softly punched his arm, giving him an admonishing stare. The man swiveled his head around the room, pretending to be incognizant of Arroyo's reproachful eyes. Her attention was suddenly caught by a redheaded, freckled man with glasses striding toward her. He was walking with purpose, and Arroyo could tell that the man had news.

"What is it?"

"The writing on the walls. It isn't organic," said Brandon McKinnon.

"So no DNA?"

"Nope."

"Then what is it?"

McKinnon gave a non-committal gesture. "I'm not one hundred percent sure. But it is waxy. And has a distinct aroma. My nose isn't as in-tuned as it used to be, but I am pretty sure it is ozokerite."

"Ozo—?"

"Lipstick," said McKinnon.

Arroyo and McCabe exchanged glances.

"Interesting."

McKinnon gave a small nod.

"Measure how high up it goes on the walls," said Arroyo.

"Huh?"

"Our vic was five three. I bet her wingspan was probably sixty-one inches, maximum. If it goes up much higher than that, maybe she wasn't the one who wrote it."

McCabe raised his eyebrows.

"Look, Duhart was bi-polar," explained Arroyo. "This seems like... something else."

McKinnon shook his head. Arroyo turned back to him.

"You disagree?"

"Look, I am no expert in graphology. But the handwriting seems distinctly female."

"Hmm."

McKinnon bobbed his head and pursed his lips as if to substantiate his point before turning back in the direction of the bathroom. Arroyo watched the nerdy-looking man duck under the frame of the door,and realized in that moment how tall and gangly he was.

McCabe moved a step closer to Arroyo. "So what do you think?"

Arroyo looked at him, but didn't answer right away, as she was trying to formulate her thoughts into articulate sentences. McCabe balked at the non-reply.

"Don't give me that, 'We aren't supposed to guess,' line. You can observe and deduct without bullshitting."

"Ray—"

"You are the one with a nose for this kind of stuff. I want to know your opinion."

Arroyo sighed and scratched at her right eyebrow. McCabe continued to look at her expectantly.

"Okay, fine. Honestly…"

Arroyo let the pause linger—not necessarily for dramatic effect, but because she wasn't totally sure of her answer. McCabe scratched at his goatee and then turned his palm through the air, trying to prompt a response. "Yes?"

"Sometimes the most obvious answer is the correct one. I think it could mean that our guy was following her in the weeks leading up to her abduction. It could be quite literal. 'He's wearing red.'"

McCabe mulled this over. "So he was following her… And she, whether consciously or subconsciously, picked up on something being not quite right."

"Yup. And even if it was subconscious, when she went into a manic state, her mind brought it to the forefront."

"So Macabre was literally wearing red while stalking her?"

Arroyo bobbed her head from side to side. "I mean, if so, what sort of subliminal message does that send? What does that make you think of?"

A pause, and then Arroyo and McCabe said the same word at the exact same time.

"Blood."

Welsh's back hurt like hell. He walked along the trail, holding a spot next to his kidneys. Once again, he had forgotten to take his medication, and now he was paying the price. He had to pause for a second as the pain surged through his body, making it difficult to move. *Serves you right, asshole. Forgetting to take your pill before a run.*

Though the pain was distracting, it was impossible not to marvel at his surroundings. He had traveled this particular trail many-a-time, but it never ceased to fill him with wonder. The forest was well lit; there was a lot of space between the trees that towered on either side of the gravel trail. The rocks were moist underneath Welsh's feet, and twice he had almost slipped when steering his body down the path. There were several prodigious maidenhair ferns reaching their slippery fingers out at him from both sides, and even a California Lilac or two intermingled with the other plants. It was quite the aesthetic trail out in the woods; not a bad place to go if you ever felt the need to be unequivocally immersed in nature.

The sky overhead was an indecisive gray, as if Mother Nature couldn't quite choose whether she wanted sun or a storm. It wasn't raining, but the air was still wet with mist. Near the top of the tree line, there was a blanket of fog. If one were to take a gander outside without actually leaving their house, they would probably estimate it to be unpleasantly frigid, but it wasn't. The temperature was just around fifty degrees; almost perfect for a light jog. Or a harried walk with a stiff back.

Wendy had tried to persuade him to stay inside, but he was going stir-crazy. All of his time during the night had been spent indoors, and he had been bunkered down for his days off as well. There was only so much television one man could watch, and he hadn't been exercising lately either. For whatever reason, cardiovascular activity was something that Welsh consistently couldn't find time for, but now that a million thoughts were waging war inside his head, it seemed imperative to move his body. The release of endorphins would surely clear his mind. And besides, it wasn't like Macabre was watching him twenty-four seven. He could afford to go on one short run.

Welsh crunched along the trail, twisting back

and forth at his waist, trying to loosen up the muscles in his back. Surprisingly, the longer he held each stretch, the less tension he felt. He even paused for a second to fully feel the tautening of his torso, pulling his arm around his chest. A sensation of warmth spread throughout the rankled area in his back, and there was a subitaneous, unexpected feeling of rejuvenation in his body. *And off we go,* he thought, pushing himself forward.

Welsh's lungs burned as he went along, but it was strangely satisfying. It was like he was shaking all of the gunk out of his chest; an unwinding of the knot in his diaphragm. The trail sloped downward, and his legs gathered speed, propelling his body along like it was a bullet. His legs were turning over so rapidly that he realized they were somewhat out of his control, and a euphoric, swooping sensation bubbled in his belly. He couldn't stop, but he didn't want to either.

Alas, the hill came to a prolonged plateau, and Welsh regained administration over his legs. His feet clopped along as he slowed down to a halt. Once he had stopped, the flickering flame that had been in his lungs became a raging wildfire, and it was quite the struggle to pull in air. Great gasps came from his mouth as he sucked, and he couldn't stop himself from doubling over and his hands from clamping onto his knees.

Without warning, the pain returned just above

his buttocks with a vengeance. Welsh even let out a groan, and then, when the agony intensified some more, he screamed a loud, "Fuck!" He had pushed himself to the limit and was reaping what he had sown.

"Fuck, fuck, fuck," muttered Welsh under his breath, walking in tiny circles compulsively, as if mobilizing himself in therapeutic, repetitive motions would somehow assuage his pain. But it didn't ease the aching at all. It exacerbated it. *Damn it, Carson. You have done it this time,* he thought. *You have really done it.*

Just then, he saw it. Movement. A small shift in his peripheral vision as something stirred next to him in the woods.

With his stomach jumping into his throat, Welsh's eyes locked onto the spot, and he froze. It had been black. Whatever had twitched behind the tree was black. Welsh continued to wait for the blackness to leap out and charge at him, but everything stayed still and silent. Even the cawing of the crows overhead had vanished, and the only noise was the sound of thumping in Welsh's ears. His own thunderous heartbeat.

Welsh remained motionless; his brain had not yet decided on fight or flight. Should he approach? Should he stand his ground and wait? Was there even anything there?

Rustling. Leaves rubbing against each other.

But not from the spot he was expecting. The noise had come from behind him. The creature, whatever it was, had somehow circled silently around the trail. In that moment, Welsh felt a stab of adrenaline, and his mind was suddenly made up. With a rough push against the gravel, he took off sprinting down the trail.

Faster. Faster. Go faster.

He galloped along, taking huge strides as the path sloped upward. A stitch in his chest seared, but he ignored it. His arms pistoned back and forth, gathering impetus as he ran wildly. The unmistakable pattering of frantic footsteps behind him sent a surge of adrenaline into his outer extremities, boosting his speed. Someone was only feet away from him, in furious chase.

The smacking from behind was growing louder as he plowed forward, and Welsh swiveled his head around to look at his pursuer. What he saw instantly made his bladder release, and his pants warm with urine. A man, all in black and wearing the mask of a bull, was closing in.

Welsh couldn't help but let out a horrible scream. It echoed around the forest, making birds perched in the trees take flight. He turned forward and wondered when he would feel the thick arms of Robert Macabre enveloping him, bringing him to the ground.

But nothing ever came. He continued to flee,

only realizing that the sound of rapid crunching behind him had stopped when he had traveled fifty feet farther. He chanced another glance behind him, and what was in his line of vision this time was almost as terrifying as the Minotaur.

Absolutely nothing. The man had vanished.

Welsh couldn't believe it. Where had he gone? What had happened to him? The chemicals coursing through his body produced absolutely absurd, nonsensical thoughts. Was Robert Macabre actually some sort of supernatural entity? Could he become invisible with a snap of his fingers? Or even take flight? If Welsh looked up, would he see the Minotaur flapping its giant brown tattered wings like a demon released from the pit of hell, ready to drag him beneath the earth? The sudden disappearance of his pursuer only made Welsh run faster.

He brought his eyes back around and only saw the root when it was too late. His right foot clunked against the bark, and he was airborne. Welsh tried to stretch his arms forward to break his fall, but they were above him in the air. As he came crashing down into the soil, the last thing he saw was a giant gray rock coming up to meet him.

Where was he? *What* was he?

The first thing he became aware of was the pain. It felt like someone had driven a blunt object through his forehead, splitting his head in two. His eyes were still closed, but light leaked through his lids. The smell in his nose was raw and earthy with a trace of iron. He tried to inhale through his nostrils, but there was some sort of blockage circumventing the flow of air.

He opened his eyes, and for a moment, he couldn't remember how he had come to be there. Or even where there was. It was like that ephemeral second just after a vivid dream where you are a blank canvass, totally unacquainted to anything of the outside world. And just like the period after a vibrant dream, there was the subsequent moment of everything rushing back.

He was Carson Welsh. He had gone for a morning run on a trail behind Roseland Park. And someone wearing the mask of a bull had driven him into the dirt.

Welsh used his arms to push himself up. The pressure in his head was staggering, and he wondered how long he could keep consciousness through the pain. He inhaled deeply through his mouth and tasted blood on his tongue. He reached up and used the index and middle fingers of his right hand to dab the spot where the blood seemed to be seeping from. When he touched it, it stung like hell. Was that a hole he felt? Had he bitten into his tongue?

Welsh snorted, trying to clear the blockage in his nostrils to get more air for his brain. He shoved his finger into his nose, and when he withdrew it, he felt a small landslide of dirt come down on his upper lip.

Why was he still alive? Macabre had had him at his mercy, alone in the woods. Why had he stopped pursuit? Why hadn't he dragged Welsh off once his forehead had cracked against the rock, wiping him of consciousness? It was a perfect opportunity.

Welsh sat there for a few minutes longer. Or it could have possibly been an hour. His brain felt scrambled; time no longer seemed like a linear thing. So he sat there while the seconds ticked by, breathing heavily.

Being that he had no possible inkling of how long had he had been unconscious, Welsh realized that he should probably get up and head back home. If it had been more than an hour, Wendy would be worried sick. But he sat there, gathering his bearings. Breathing in and out, trying not to focus on the pain. He supposed a normal person would frantically clamber onto his or her feet, trying to leave the forest as fast as humanly possible. But Welsh just sat there. The killer was no longer in the vicinity. Macabre was an alpha predator and not looking for an easy kill. He wanted to play with his food for a while first.

Arroyo studied the face in front of her, trying to decipher the expression. The woman's flabby cheeks drooped sadly, and her forehead was screwed up, like she was squinting toward the sun.

"Ms. Steens, I understand that you were close with Ms. Duhart. Is that correct?"

Amy Steens gave a curt nod of her head.

"Yes, that is c-correct."

"You met her here, right? You didn't know her before you started working together?"

"No. I mean, yes, that is right. I didn't know her before here."

Arroyo nodded and made a note on the yellow pad of paper that was on the mahogany desk between her and Steens. The two of them plus McCabe were sitting in a private room with the blinds drawn, warding off watchful eyes from the main area of Bank of America.

"How close were you?"

Steens' eyes flitted back and forth around the room. "What do you mean?"

"Did you spend a lot of time together outside of work?"

"Yes. Almost every Friday night we went out drinking together."

"Just you two?"

"Usually, yes. Sometimes Francis would come with us."

"Francis?"

"He's another teller here."

Arroyo nodded and penned another note. The conversation so far was moving painstakingly slow. Steens just seemed like one of those people that was completely awkward and socially inept around strangers, but had good intentions. In fact, Arroyo felt a strong sense of pity for the woman, and it wasn't just because she had lost a good friend. Something about her was a little off; a little broken. McCabe was eyeing Steens up and down with a penetrating stare like he could glean something valuable just by looking at her, and Arroyo had the urge to give him a nudge with her elbow.

After discovering the lipstick on the bathroom walls of Duhart's apartment, Arroyo and McCabe had canvassed the area, but had not found any material witness that could pinpoint Duhart's movements. Unlike Tracy Dinwoodie, they didn't yet have a firm timeline for when the victim had been abducted, so the first few interviews had felt a little like grasping at straws. Arroyo had eventually spoken with Lexi Duhart, who had admitted that she wasn't all that close with her sister, but she knew someone who was: Amy Steens, Jacey's coworker.

Arroyo continued without looking up as she made her notes. "Where would you usually go out to?"

"The bars."

Arroyo looked up, unsure if Steens had intended to be sarcastic.

"Oh, sorry! I didn't mean to sound like that! I didn't even… Sorry."

"It's fine. So which bars would you usually go to?"

Steens shifted her large posterior around in the chair, looking distraught.

"We would usually go to clubs. Jones's. Dirty."

"Dirty?"

"That is the name of it. It is a club on Third Avenue."

"Ahhh. Sorry, not much into the drinking scene myself."

"Yeah, I can tell. I mean, you don't look like a partyer."

When Arroyo raised her eyebrows, Steens apologized profusely again.

"Sorry! I don't mean that you look like you

can't have a good time!"

"Okay, okay, stop. Just stop. Relax, Ms. Steens. Just breathe."

Steens gave her a nervous smile, and then her expression morphed back into one that reflected pain and anxiety. She fanned herself off with her hand, and her eyes were twinkling with tears.

Without warning, McCabe leaned across the table and reached out his sizeable palms like he was trying to catch a football

"Give me your hand, sweetheart," he said soothingly.

Steens looked at him apprehensively and then reached her hand out tentatively. McCabe clasped it and rubbed lightly, giving the woman a tender look.

"It is going to be okay."

That was when the tears leaked down her cheeks. Her face contorted as if she was trying to suppress her sadness, and she used her free hand to smear her eyes. The eyeliner that she was wearing became blotchy and discolored.

McCabe patted her hand and gave her a consoling look. "To lose someone you care about is one of the worst things in the world. The only thing I can think of that is worse is to lose someone that you weren't expecting to lose. I'm sorry, Amy. I really am."

Steens could no longer subdue the emotion. She began shaking violently and released pained, prolonged sobs. Arroyo couldn't help but feel that she was watching something that she shouldn't be watching.

McCabe was not deterred. "Whatever responsibility you feel for what happened to Jacey, I want you to let go of that, okay? Let go of that right now. There was nothing you could have done. But you *can* help us fix it. I know you can."

Steens' sucked in a ragged breath and suddenly stopped her sobbing. She looked taken off guard by what McCabe had said.

"H-How?"

"I'm not sure, yet. I just have this feeling, Amy. I have this feeling that you will be able to help us catch this man."

Steens wiped her nose and started shaking her head.

"Right now, I don't think I will be of much help to anybody."

"Oh, I think you will," said McCabe softly. "See, my partner here is real good about getting people to remember things they didn't even think they knew. Associations. Faces. People."

Steens turned her attention to Arroyo, looking apprehensive.

"So, let's just let her do her thing, all right, Amy?"

Steens' hand slithered back out of McCabe's grasp, and she gave a small nod. Arroyo, feeling a little bit of annoyance toward McCabe for putting her on the spot, leaned forward and prepped her pen to take notes.

"Well, thanks for that lofty intro, Ray."

Steens gave the smallest of laughs.

"All right, Ms. Steens. So when was the last time you saw Jacey?"

"Last Thursday. Here."

"Thursday? Did she not work on Friday?"

"She called in sick."

Arroyo made a note. "Was she actually sick, do you think?"

Steens frowned and looked over at McCabe. He remained expressionless, so the woman focused back on Arroyo.

"Yes, I know she was. I talked to her on the phone Thursday night. She sounded like she could barely breathe. That is a strange question to ask."

"Well, I think it is strange that she called in sick the same day that she disappeared."

Steens' sagging cheeks retracted as she pursed her lips.

Arroyo shrugged. "Or, it could be simply a coincidence. Did Jacey call in sick frequently?"

"Well, she doesn't have a very good immune system."

"So, yes, then."

"She always seems to be catching a cold."

"Hmm."

Arroyo scribbled some more, and Steens' eyes narrowed.

"Do you not believe me?"

"Why wouldn't I believe you?"

"I don't know." Steens looked flustered.

"Describe Jacey for me, Ms. Steens," said Arroyo quickly, trying to move past any unnecessary awkward pauses. "What was she like? Gregarious? Reserved?"

"Uh…"

"Did she have good people skills, I mean?"

Steens gave a non-committal gesture with her head, bobbing it from side to side.

"When she wanted to, sure."

"Was she outgoing?"

"I wouldn't say that. She was nice to everyone, but didn't go out of her way to make friends."

"Did she have a boyfriend?"

"Uh, no. Not at the moment."

"But she *did*?"

"Yeah. For four years."

"Who was the guy?"

"Uh, his name was Logan."

"Last name?"

Steens raised her eyebrows, but then answered. "Gackstedder."

Arroyo made a note. "Four years is a long time. Did they ever think about getting married?"

"No. Well, she did. But he was never ready."

"Hmm. So I am assuming *he* broke up with *her*."

Steens nodded.

"When did that happen?"

"Six months ago. I think."

"And how did Jacey take it?"

Steens shook her head. "She was broken. She cried all the time. Even sometimes here. I would tell her to go out and smoke a cigarette whenever she would start to breakdown, and she would go cry some more in her car."

"And how long did that last?"

"Hell, she *still* wasn't really over him, you know? I think she just learned to hide it better."

"Right." Arroyo scribbled some more and underlined a few words. When she had finished the sentence, she caught Steens' eyes locked onto the yellow pad of paper, as if the woman was trying to decrypt the writing upside-down. When she saw that Arroyo was looking at her, Steens turned her attention to the window to her right as if she had suddenly noticed something completely engrossing outside.

"So, Ms. Steens, what happened on Friday?"

"What happened…?"

"Yeah, like, did you speak with Jacey at all on Friday?"

"No. She wasn't here."

"Well, I understand that, but I mean did you

speak on the phone?"

"No."

"You didn't hear from her at all." Arroyo said it as a statement.

Steens shook her head vigorously. "No."

"Did that strike you as unusual? Didn't you say you go out every Friday night?"

"She was sick."

"But wouldn't she have told you that? Wouldn't she have called you and told you that she was sick?"

"No. Me and Francis were always the ones that would contact her. If we didn't, she wouldn't come out."

"Did you try calling her? To see if she was feeling better?"

"No."

"Why not?"

Steens looked away, and there was a somewhat guilty expression on her face.

"Sometimes, it was just nice to get a break, you know?"

"How do you mean?"

"Jacey was just... a lot to handle. She was *intense*. She was never in the middle, you know? Half the time she was so happy-go-lucky that it almost freaked me out. Like, she was actually kinda wild. One time when we were walking home by the waterfront, she straight-up *dove* in. Didn't even tell me she was going to do it. Just gave me a funny look and cannon-balled into the water. She was completely plastered, but still…"

Arroyo fought the urge to smile. "Sounds, uh, *spontaneous*."

"Yeah, and then the other half of the time, she was such a sad sack that it was a total drag to be in the same room as her. She just sucked the energy right out of you. Made it all about her."

Without warning, Steens smacked her hand to her mouth and flushed a shade of maroon.

"God, why am I talking like this? I'm a terrible person."

"Amy…" It was the first time Arroyo had used her first name.

"Jesus. One of my best friends dies and here I am talking shit about her. What the hell is wrong with me?"

McCabe jumped back in. "Don't do that to yourself. Don't let yourself feel guilty for tellin' the truth."

Steens shook her head, but didn't reply. For what seemed like a long time, they all sat in silence: Arroyo making notes, McCabe trying to assuage the anguish of the woman across the table with a soothing expression, and Steens not making eye contact with either of them, focusing her attention on the same window that she would only look at after saying something embarrassing.

After Arroyo was done writing, she focused her concentration on the top half of her note pad. She had divvied the paper with a bold line across the center. On the bottom was all of the detailed transcriptions she was penning; on the top, there were at least twenty questions jotted in shorthand. Most of them were only two or three words long. *"Boyfriend?" "Friday night?" "Suspicious men?"* Arroyo looked over them, wondering which would be the best to pursue next. She decided on the one that was simply two letters: *"BP?"*

"So, as I understand it, Jacey was manic depressive, correct?"

"Manic…?"

"Bi-polar."

Steens' mouth went a little agape. "You know about that? Sorry, it's just, she never really shares that with anyone."

"Mm. Why do you think that is?"

Steens narrowed her eyes. "Would *you*?"

"I don't think it is anything to be embarrassed about. It is just a hormone imbalance."

"Well, not everyone is as tolerant as you."

Arroyo stared at the woman across from her.

Steens shook her head and gave an ashamed smile. "I'm sorry. Really. Everything I say sounds ruder than I mean it."

Arroyo didn't respond to Steens' apologies this time.

"So, in your opinion, did the breakup exacerbate her mental state?"

"Exca—?"

"Make her condition worse."

"Oh, uh… Yeah, you could say that."

"Why could you say that?"

Steens' eyes, which were still puffy from crying, shifted around the room uncomfortably.

"I don't know if she would want me to say…"

"Ms. Steens, this could be important."

Steens sighed deeply, and rubbed her mascara-lined cheeks as if to massage away an unpleasant feeling. She bit her lip, and remained silent, even though Arroyo was looking at her expectantly.

"Was she prone to having manic episodes?"

Steens looked back at the detective, and her facial expression was enough of an affirmative for Arroyo to keep pressing forward.

"Were they pretty frequent?"

"I wouldn't say that."

"Did she have more of them after the breakup?"

"She stopped taking her medication for a while after it ended with Logan… I don't know why. So yes," said Steens.

"And she didn't have any problems when she was on her medication?"

"Well, if she did, it was very rare."

"And what would these non-medicated

episodes normally consist of?"

Steens shifted around awkwardly. "I wasn't around for most of them, so I am not sure. All I know is, she would become super paranoid when she didn't take her meds. Sometimes, she would call me and just say really strange things. One night she was absolutely *convinced* that the government was going to come seize her cat as some sort of mass pet conspiracy."

McCabe snorted, and both of the women looked over at him skeptically.

"Sorry," he said, with a sheepish expression on his face.

Arroyo turned back to Steens. "So, do you remember any other specifics from these episodes?"

"Well, usually she would just start whispering to me over the phone. Tell me to tell her that everything was going to be okay."

"And what would you say?"

"That it would be."

"And then when she wasn't in a manic phase, she would act normal?"

"Yeah. Well, normal for her."

"And it didn't push you away? Her condition?"

Steens suddenly looked a little offended. "No… It drew me closer. She needed me."

Arroyo cleared her throat, trying to navigate the minefield of tact. "So, you say the *usual* episodes consisted of her whispering to you over the phone.

Asking you to tell her that everything was okay."

"Right."

"What were the unusual episodes, then?"

Steens seemed to give an involuntary shudder. "Weird stuff. Like, really bizarre. She would talk about Satan."

"Yeesh."

"Yeah. The devil. And aliens. And giants."

"Giants?"

"Yeah. That was one of the weirdest ones. She called me one night and kept talking about giants."

Arroyo frowned. "What exactly did she say?"

"Oh, I can't really remember. Just nonsense. Kept saying that a giant was after her."

Arroyo looked over at McCabe, who seemed bemused.

"Hmm."

"Oh, that is what it was!" said Steens, her voice raising a little as she recalled the particular incident.

"What?"

"She kept saying, 'He's following me. He's following me. The man in red. The giant.'"

Welsh placed his throbbing head against his palm
and felt his eyes begin to blur. Everything still
seemed a little hazy. He knew the important stuff:
He was in the station, meeting with the two
detectives that were charged with keeping him alive
and finding the son-of-a-bitch Macabre, and he was
listening to them fret about the case. But extraneous
detail, like how he was feeling and what time of day
it was, seemed to escape him. Dr. Mauve had
confirmed his assertion that he had a concussion. A
fairly severe concussion. And though Wendy had
been there when he was diagnosed and knew that he
had tripped on a tree root while running, she was
completely oblivious to the fact that he had been
running *from* someone. Welsh would not tell her the
horrifying truth. She did not need to know what had
really happened in that forest. Only Arroyo and
McCabe did.

"How tall was he, Carson?"

Welsh slipped out of his stupor, and for a second, he wasn't sure whether it was McCabe or Arroyo who had asked him the question, so he didn't know where to focus his attention. He decided on a spot on the wall behind them.

"Pretty tall. I'd say six four. Six five, maybe."

Arroyo wrote fervently on her yellow pad of paper. "What about body composition? Was he muscular? Thin? Overweight?"

"Mostly muscular. I mean, he was huge. Looked like he could lift a car. But he wasn't very lean."

"You realize you are going to have to meet with the sketch artist, yeah?"

Welsh simply nodded.

"So what was he wearing? Besides the mask?"

"Black. All black. Black jeans. A black shirt."

"A T-shirt?"

"No, a shirt shirt."

"Gloves?"

"Black gloves. Everything was black."

Arroyo and McCabe exchanged glances, and their expressions confused Welsh.

"Does that surprise you?"

"Well, a little."

"Why?"

Arroyo let a few seconds pass before she answered.

"Well, we think we have a lead on something. Here, take a look at the canvassing photos of the second vic's apartment."

She withdrew a stack of paper stocks from the manila envelope that was on the table and shuffled them until she found the one she was looking for. Welsh stared at her hand as it stretched across the table and wiggled the photograph in front of him.

"Am I going to regret looking at that?"

"No. And before you say it, it isn't blood."

Welsh pinched the photograph and set it down in front of him. It was of a bathroom. The off-yellow wallpaper clashed strikingly with the words that had been graffitied all over the walls.

"He's wearing red?"

Arroyo nodded. "Yeah. And that lines up with what Amy Steens said. One of Jacey Duhart's coworkers, and her best friend," she said, after Welsh had a perplexed expression on his face. "Duhart was severely bi-polar and had frequent manic episodes. Steens said that during one of them, she called and proclaimed that someone wearing red was stalking her. She called him a 'giant.'"

"A giant?"

"That's correct. So with that and the physical description you just gave us, I think it is safe to assert that the man who was following Duhart was the same man who chased you through the woods."

"Robert Macabre," said Welsh quietly.

"Aka Bob the Butcher," added McCabe.

Welsh frowned. "So, what, he wears red when he is stalking his victims?"

"I believe so," replied Arroyo. "At least sometimes."

"But... Why?"

Arroyo did not immediately reply. She stayed in silence, digesting his question while apparently trying to formulate an appropriate answer. Finally, after ten long seconds, she spoke in a hushed tone.

"I think he wants to stick in their memory. Maybe not consciously. Maybe he wants to just lurk in the background, like a subliminal message. I think he wants to haunt their dreams."

Several chills tiptoed down Welsh's spine.

"Anyway, toxicology came back on Duhart as well," continued Arroyo. "She was positive for LSD and a sodium-lactate infusion, just like Dinwoodie. It's a very potent mix for inducing feelings of terror and anxiety."

"Jesus."

Arroyo nodded. "So he doses them regularly while he keeps them alive to heighten their terror. The more afraid the vic is, the more intense the sexual thrill for him."

Welsh normally would have experienced some sort of revulsion; perhaps even nausea. But at the moment, he couldn't process normal feelings. Everything was too foreign and obscure, like watching an out of focus television in the dark.

"Listen, I don't want to scare you, Welsh, but we got nothin' here, man," said McCabe suddenly, and Welsh almost jumped. "No physical evidence left at either scene. Nothing on the relations. Dead-end on suspects. The list of KA's for the one person of interest we did have yielded nothing. And Dinwoodie's boyfriend is clean as a whistle. We ain't gonna collar anybody anytime soon."

Welsh frowned. "Why are you telling me this?"

"Because it doesn't look like there is an end in sight to this, and now we know he ain't just talkin' a big talk. He is after you, Welsh. He will come again."

"Okay...?"

"And you still ain't got a protective detail."

Welsh knew this had been coming. And he also knew that the detectives would be surprised by his answer.

"Then give me one."

Arroyo and McCabe swapped surprised glances.

"I thought—" began McCabe.

"I've changed my mind. Being chased by a homicidal maniac wearing a Minotaur will do that to you."

McCabe looked like he wasn't quite sure what to say.

"Oh. O-Okay. Good. Fine."

Welsh, surprisingly, felt a strong desire to laugh. The concussion was having a strange effect on him, indeed. The meeting they were having was dire; the situation tense. And yet, for some reason, he suddenly felt a little giddy. Was his brain that scrambled?

"I normally wouldn't do this, but since you are, you know, *you*... Do you have any preference on who it will be?" asked Arroyo.

"None at all."

"All right, then. Diaz and McCoy will do the honors. "

"Oh, not Diaz and *McCoy*!"

"I thought you said—"

"I'm joking."

Arroyo blinked.

"Sorry. Humor has never been my strong suit."

Welsh pointed his index finger at her. "I have come to understand that about you, Emily Arroyo."

Arroyo didn't quite crack a smile, but the corners of her mouth twitched. *Best I can hope for, I suppose,* thought Welsh.

"All right, so one of them will be stationed outside your office during the day. The other will be our night guy."

"You got it."

"And if you find yourself wanting to do anything alone, *don't*."

"Okay."

"And for Christ's sake, if you see anyone wearing an animal mask, a red coat, or even a goddamn banana suit within a hundred yards of you, tell those boys about it ASAP."

"I'll keep my eyes peeled."

Arroyo nodded, straight-faced.

"Because you said a banana suit…"

"Ah."

Welsh pursed his lips. "I'll see myself out."

"Carson."

Arroyo made penetrating eye contact with him. She had said his name with force; it had almost been stern. His concussion was playing with his mood, and Arroyo apparently did not have time for his flippant, concussion induced comedy routine when things were so tense. Her strict tone brought Welsh back down to earth.

"What?"

"Always stay hyper vigilant. Something tells me this guy has more tricks up his sleeve."

20

The coffee was too hot to drink, so he held it precariously in his hand, staring out of the kitchen window. Curiously, just the smell of the Folgers made him feel more energetic than he had been before. One of the professors Welsh had for his undergrad degree, Mr. Koch, would have waggled his finger and made a droll comment about Pavlov's dog and classical conditioning right about now. Welsh smiled while thinking about it, running his hand through his hair absentmindedly. Suddenly, he paused, looking to the left and then to the right in perplexity. Memory was a funny thing; Welsh had just recalled an anecdote from a college class that had taken place twenty-five years before, while at the same time forgetting what he had come into the kitchen for.

The hand on the small of his back made him jump, but it took him only a millisecond longer to realize it was Wendy.

"Bit touchy, are we?" she asked.

"Wouldn't you be?"

"I *am*."

"Mm."

"How's your head?"

"Better, I think. Still a little sore, but I don't feel all woozy anymore."

Wendy stood next to him and reached for the coffee pot. Welsh saw that all she was wearing was a long sleeve white blouse and blue underwear.

"Are you hot?"

Wendy winked. "Well, you married me, so…"

"Ha-ha. I'm just saying, usually you wear pants."

"Well *usually* I am getting ready go to work."

Welsh looked down at her, confused. "You're not?"

"I took the day off."

"Why?"

"No reason. Just wanted the day off."

Welsh shook his head with a playful smile on his face. "Man, if I had the luxury to do that, there is no telling what I would get up to."

Wendy rolled her eyes. "Oh yeah? What would you do, Carson? Hang out with Mo? Go to a strip club? Watch him get a lap dance?"

"Why do you hate him so much?"

"I don't *hate* him. He just makes me

uncomfortable, that's all."

"You've said that before, but you never really told me why."

Wendy shrugged and twitched like a fly had just flown into her personal space. "I don't know. He's always so suggestive. Every other sentence coming out of his mouth is an innuendo."

"So what? It is just his style of humor."

"Being crude is not particularly amusing, in my opinion."

Welsh didn't reply. He didn't want to listen to his wife rail against Mo, like she was prone to doing whenever Welsh brought him up. Instead, he looked out the window at the Ford Crown Victoria that was parked in front of his driveway. The man inside was sipping on a Styrofoam cup and adjusting the tuner to his radio. Wendy glanced up and saw what her husband was staring at.

"Just so you know, I am never going to get used to this," she said quietly.

"I know. But you know this is for the best."

"Still. To have someone in our personal space all the time. It just feels weird to me."

"It's not like he is going to watch us have sex."

Wendy raised her eyebrows. "Who says we will be having sex?"

"I don't know. I just hoped I could speak it into existence."

Wendy chuckled, but it was snuffed out almost

as quickly as it began once she gazed out at the officer.

"Just remember, hun. It isn't going to be forever. They will be gone as soon as they catch him," said Welsh, trying to soothe his wife.

Wendy continued to stare out at the car as if it were some extraterrestrial thing.

"With the way this has gone so far, are you sure that won't be forever?"

Welsh typed with fervor, letting his hands effortlessly tap the keys of the Toshiba laptop in front of him. Each line of the email seemed to come out faster than the previous one, and he realized that his fingers were moving so fast and without conscious thought that he could probably close his eyes and not make a grammatical error. When he was finished typing the paragraph, he began to read. The email was full of the verbose language that he so detested, and Welsh almost laughed when he realized it. If every lawyer was like him and despised speaking and writing in bombastic prose, why did they all do it?

Once he had clicked on the word *send,* Welsh stood up from his desk and strode out of his office. Samantha was on the phone, and barely even acknowledged him as he walked past. He mouthed the word "coffee" at her, and she gave a brusque nod of her head as she continued to try to focus on whatever the person on the other end of the line was saying.

When he was outside, he came right up to the Ford Crown Victoria that was parked against the sidewalk. Marco Diaz rolled down his window and looked up at Welsh through his sunglasses.

"I'm going to get a coffee," said Welsh, motioning at the Starbucks across the road. "That okay?"

"Sure thing," said Diaz. He was a gruff-looking man, with a buzz cut and a wrinkled forehead that made it look like he was perpetually frowning.

"If you don't come out in fifteen minutes, I will be sure to mosey on over there and get me a frappe," said Diaz.

"You do that," replied Welsh, tapping on the top of the vehicle. He waited until traffic was clear and then bustled across the street. Surprisingly, there were quite a few people milling about for it being 11:00 a.m. on a Tuesday. Welsh had to weave in and out of bystanders before he pulled open the heavy glass door and stepped inside.

The first thing he saw was that nearly every table was occupied, and the line was long. Welsh took his place at the back, towering over the small Asian woman that was directly in front of him. It took nearly ten minutes to get to the front of the line, as most of the patrons were rather indecisive about their order. When it was Welsh's turn, he made it short and sweet.

"Can I get a tall coffee with vanilla and cream?"

"You got it!" said the chipper barista with braided hair. "Name?"

"Carson."

"All right, thank you, Carson. That will be two twenty-five."

Welsh nodded, pulled his wallet out of his coat, swiped his card, and went over to the area that was designated for waiting for your coffee. Four other people surrounded him, each looking impassive and rather bored. It took no less than a minute for the barista behind the espresso machine to shout his name and slide a coffee out onto the counter.

"Thank you," he said quickly, and turned around, eager to get out of the crowd.

Two seconds later, someone thudded into his shoulder, and Welsh nearly dropped his coffee. The thin man with short black hair that had collided with him began to profusely apologize.

"Sorry, sorry, I'm sorry!"

"You are fine. Don't worry about it."

Welsh looked into the man's face and found something strange there. The man's beady eyes were boring into his, and the look on his face was enigmatic. Welsh was so absorbed with the man's strange expression that he almost missed the fingers slipping into his jacket. He wanted to rip them away, but then realized that the man wasn't taking anything. He was leaving something.

The man gave one last meaningful glance at Welsh and then stepped past. Welsh just stood there in mild shock, wanting to turn around and ask the mysterious figure a million questions. But intuition was telling him to keep moving. He didn't even turn his head to get another look at the stranger; Welsh just moved out of the coffee shop.

Once he was back outside, he waited for traffic to clear again before jogging his way back to the other sidewalk. He gave a quick nod to Diaz, who raised two fingers off of the steering wheel of the Crown Vic in greeting. Welsh wondered if Diaz thought he was being suspicious. But Diaz always looked like he found everyone suspicious, so Welsh pushed the thought away.

As soon as Welsh was back inside the building and out of range of Diaz' watchful eyes, he swiveled back and forth, making sure the coast was clear. Nobody was in the foyer but him, so he reached into his jacket and pulled out the letter that had been left there. He unfolded it, his heart thumping precipitously. The first thing he noticed was that the handwriting was slanted and small; much different than the letters that had been scribed

by Robert Macabre. And this one was only four
lines long.

*Meet me at the waterfront @ 2. Come alone. I
will help you find the man you are looking for.*

- David Kane.

At 1:35 p.m., Welsh stepped out of his office and caught Samantha's attention by waving his hand. She looked up from her computer and regarded him like he was an especially interesting insect that had landed in front of her desk.

"You always look at me like you have never seen me before," said Welsh.

"It's just my eyes. I have horrible vision."

"Why don't you get glasses?"

"Already wearing contacts."

"They don't help?"

Samantha shrugged. "Put it this way. With them you look a little fuzzy. Without them you look like part of that door behind you."

"Wow. Well keep them in, then. Hey, I'm going to lunch. I'll be back in an hour, give or take."

"You got it, captain." Samantha gave a mini-salute. Welsh chuckled and then walked toward the elevator.

Despite the faux air of levity, his heart rate had already begun to ascend. He knew he was doing something risky, and potentially dangerous. The smart thing to do would be to explain what had happened to the detectives, and let them deal with Kane. But if he did that, there would be no guarantee that Arroyo would be able to track the man down, and whatever Kane knew would be lost.

When he was down on the first floor, Welsh took one glance out toward the double-glass doors where various lawyers and other courthouse personnel were striding in and out of. Some of them would nod at him and say his name in a form of greeting when they walked past. Others, including the cantankerous Warren Grecko, gave him a scowl and looked like they were on the verge of socking him when they shuffled by. That was the thing about being the district attorney. You were either loved or despised, depending on who it was that you were interacting with and what side of the verdict they had fallen on.

Welsh looked over the bustling bodies toward the street. He could just see the tip of the Crown Vic parked along the sidewalk in front of the Multnomah County Courthouse, but he couldn't quite make out Diaz or which direction the deputy was looking.

Once he was sure that Diaz couldn't see him, Welsh made an about-face and walked down a long hallway. Two more men in suits passed him and waved, and he gave them a curt nod of his head. Once they had gone by, he watched them saunter down the hallway, and then Welsh quickly ducked out of the door that had the word's Emergency Exit written on it.

The alley outside was empty, but he still made sure to hustle in the opposite direction of where Diaz was parked. A few seconds later, he saw the taxi parked at the corner of Wellspring Avenue and Fifty-Second Street. Welsh signaled toward him and approached the car.

Once he had hopped in the back, the driver made eye contact with Welsh in the rearview mirror.

"You Carson Welsh?"

"Yes.

"Well, you sure took long enough."

Welsh rolled his eyes. "Just drive me to the waterfront."

"The waterfront? Any particular spot, or were you just planning on roaming all five blocks until you find what you are looking for?"

"You worry about getting me there, pal. That's all you worry about."

"Suit yourself, slick."

The taxi lurched forward before Welsh had had

a chance to fully buckle his seat belt, and he went careening and smacked his head lightly against the front passenger seat. He rubbed his face and gave the driver a look of contempt.

"Goodness gracious, me. Always forget how heavy my foot is."

The driver glanced up in the rearview mirror like he wanted Welsh to reply with something nasty, but was met with silence. For the entirety of the drive, they sat still, not saying a word to each other. The moment the cab arrived at the first block of the waterfront, it came to another sudden halt, and Welsh had to brace to avoid mushing his face against the front seat again.

Before the cabbie could tell him his fare, Welsh stuffed a ten-dollar bill into the man's shirt collar, causing a slight twitch.

"Keep the change. Buy yourself some tweezers to pull that stick out of your ass."

Welsh got out and slammed the door, trying his best not to look back, but he still caught the middle finger of the driver standing up in his peripheral vision.

As soon as he was outside, Welsh couldn't help but marvel a little at the beauty of the waterfront park. The cherry blossoms all around gave the area a foreign, majestic feel to it. There was only a light cloud-cover in the sky, blanketing the city in a bright gray haze. The Willamette River sat serenely next to the sprawling gray sidewalk, barely moving. The day was muggy and a little humid; Welsh felt a bead of sweat on his nape. His head began to swivel back and forth as he moved along, looking for the skinny man with short black hair.

Welsh suddenly noticed his breath becoming shallow, but not because of the physical exertion of walking. Anxiety was reaching its long, spindly fingers up through his chest, and Welsh felt butterflies flapping around in his stomach. But he wasn't sure why. There were people all around. If somehow, someway, the man called David Kane was pulling something over him, this would not be the place to do it.

Welsh saw a pack of female joggers coming toward him, and he had to side-step out of the way to let them past. None of them paid him any attention. They all just kept uniformly moving, their thighs jiggling through multi-colored spandex material, and their breasts jumping up and down. Welsh tried to keep his eyes to himself, but it was difficult. None of them could have been older than twenty-five, and there didn't seem to be an unattractive one in the bunch.

As he stepped back onto the pavement, Welsh realized that finding Kane was going to be a near-impossible task. The man had given him a two-mile radius as a rendezvous point, and Welsh had only gotten a fugacious glimpse of him anyway. How was this supposed to even work? He began to feel a little foolish for coming, and not immediately seeing the flaws of this undercooked plan.

Back and forth his head swiveled. He saw an osprey diving down toward the water, likely to gulp up an unsuspecting fish. He looked at a middle-aged woman that was power-walking past him in a purple jump suit. He caught a glimpse of more cherry blossoms, their pink petals rustling with the breeze.

And there he was. Like a specter materializing out of thin air, the man that was surely David Kane sat on a park bench with several needy pigeons nipping at his feet as he scattered bread onto the grass. The man seemed to be speaking to the birds; or was he cooing? The creatures hopped up and down, eager for a bite. Kane looked a little eccentric; his face was lit up with pure joy and his voice had a pitch that was usually reserved for puppies. Welsh moved closer, feeling uneasy.

Kane reached into his bag of bread again, tearing off a piece that was far too large. He spent several seconds shredding up the food with his long fingers, and even offered an apology to the nearest pigeon that seemed to be getting impatient. Welsh took another step forward. Once Kane's eyes flickered up and caught the man approaching, a self-satisfied expression came over his face.

"Finally. Carson Welsh, in the flesh."

Welsh stood there, towering over the scrawny,

gangly man. Welsh flexed his arms a little, like a wild animal showing his strength to a potential competitor.

"Who the hell are you?"

"You read my note, didn't you? My name is David Kane."

"But who *are* you?"

Kane shrugged.

"Just someone trying to help."

Welsh noticed that Kane's eyebrows were so bushy that they almost came together in a unibrow on his forehead. His cheeks were gaunt and he had traces of dark facial hair blooming on his chin.

"If you know something, why not go to the police?"

Kane smiled, and his teeth were yellow and he had the tiniest of gaps between his two front incisors. There was a trace of brown along his top gums.

"Why don't you sit down, Carson?"

"Oh, on a first name basis, are we?"

"Well, what would you like me to call you?"

Welsh didn't reply, nor did he sit.

"I didn't come here to mess with you, Carson. I came here because I have information that I want to share."

"Before you go any further, tell me why you don't want to share it with police."

Kane smiled again, then let out a sigh.

"You know, it would be much easier to explain this to you if we were at eye level."

Welsh rolled his eyes, and continued to stand. When Kane just gazed up at him like some sort of petulant child, he finally (and reluctantly) lowered his rear end onto the park bench.

After a few moments of silence, Kane clicked his tongue and then asked Welsh a surprising question.

"Do you have any tattoos?"

"Beg your pardon?

"Tattoos. Do you have any?"

Welsh blinked several times in total bewilderment.

"No."

"Yeah I didn't think you would. Not the type. *Me* on the other hand... I got plenty. My parents always told me that I would regret it if I got a tattoo. They said, 'It's tacky. You'll look like white trash.'" He turned over his forearm so that Welsh could see the band of black ink wrapping around his skin. It was embroidered with a pattern; triangles facing each other and meeting at the tip. "But you know what? I have never had a single moment where I regretted this. Isn't that funny?"

He looked up at Welsh with that same grimy smile. "The funniest part is, it doesn't even mean anything. You know what they told me in the joint? That I needed ink to look hard. So that people wouldn't screw with me. So I just picked this because I thought it looked cool."

Kane let out a wheezy laugh, and reached into his brown bag to tear off another piece of bread. Welsh just sat there, totally lost, and suddenly mesmerized by the ring that he saw on Kane's right hand. It was thick and gold with a thin scrawl of writing carved into it that Welsh couldn't quite read.

"You're judging me, I can tell. I don't mind, but I can tell. You're starting to lean away like being a convict is somehow contagious." There was a twinkle in Kane's eye as he gave Welsh a wry smile. "I can see it on your face. You want to know what I did. Everyone always wants to know what you did. Nosy bastards…"

Welsh kept totally quiet, waiting for Kane to continue.

"So in ninety-eight, I slept with a woman I met at a bar… Didn't really like her that much. But I fucked her anyway because I was a kid in my twenties that couldn't go five minutes without thinking about sex. It was going great. She seemed to be diggin' it. I was having a good time too, right up until a guy walked in the room. You should have seen the look on his face! Looked like he had seen a ghost. I guess that is probably normally what happens when you walk in on someone porking your sister."

The man scattered some more bread, and the pigeons flapped their wings with pleasure. "Guy's name was Marius Wicks. Deputy Marius Wicks." Kane's jaw started to clench as he retrieved the memory. "He just left without a word. Didn't think I'd see him again. Why would I? Not like I am going to buy a beer for the guy who caught me doing the dirty with his little sis. But you see, he wanted to see me again. And he did, two days later. Showed up on my front porch with his partner and a pair of handcuffs, telling me I was being arrested for rape."

The man shook his head vigorously, like he was trying to ward off a possessive spirit. "What gets me is, why didn't she have the spine to stop the whole thing? She could have come out and snuffed it out like *that*," said Kane as he snapped his fingers. "Someone can't be that evil right? Knowing your brother is sending an innocent man to jail and effectively ruining his life? Knowing he would have to register as a sex offender? Knowing everyone would see his face in the papers?

"I had my uncle post bail, so I was free for a few months while I waited for trial. One night, I am coming home from the bar, three sheets to the wind, knowing I ain't got long before I won't be able to drink, and someone jumps me. I didn't even have time to piss myself before I get dragged into an alley by four guys, all wailing on me. Broke two ribs. Fractured a bone in my face. Kicked out one of my back molars. Even as drunk as I was, I knew what was happening. Who it was. The funniest thing was, none of them wore masks. It's like they took pride in me knowing that I was gettin' my ass handed to me by a bunch of cops and I couldn't do nothing about it.

"So, three months after I get the shit kicked out of me by Marius Joseph Wicks and his goons, I am nice and healed for the trial. And I knew I had no chance. Don't get me wrong, I tried to fight it. But I didn't have no money. No one on my side. No one to step in and say, 'This is wrong.' The system is so rigged that it is almost a relief to let them win. So I took the plea deal. Six months in prison. And I rotted in there, thinking every day about Marius Wicks."

Finally, Kane took in a deep breath and made fierce eye contact with Welsh.

"So, when you ask me why I'm not going to the cops, maybe you should just look at a picture of me in the hospital after Wicks smashed my face in."

Welsh didn't say anything. He couldn't. What was there to say?

"Don't worry, this wasn't anybody you knew. This was in Tillamook County."

"If this happened in another county—" began Welsh.

"Then why don't I trust the cops here? Well,

the generic answer would be that all cops are the same. Each one is as crooked as the next. But that ain't the fact of it. The fact of it is, I haven't exactly had the best dealings with the men in blue here either."

"What—"

"Don't you worry yourself about all that, Carson. Point is, I came to you. Now, who knows? You might be as corrupt as the rest of them, and my trust was misguided. You could be in on it with all of those crooked jerks down at PPD. Isn't that what our criminal justice system is? A bureaucratic circle-jerk? Everyone in on it, talking to each other? Fighting against the people who can't fight back?"

Welsh rolled his eyes. "You got some warped views of reality, friend."

"I came to you because you are so damn good at what you do," continued Kane, ignoring this barb from Welsh. "And, in my personal opinion, you aren't going to mess it up."

Welsh reclined back a little and squinted his eyes as though he couldn't quite see Kane properly.

"Mess what up, exactly?"

Kane reached into his black jacket and withdrew a pack of Camels from his inside pocket. His other hand dipped into his jeans and removed a black lighter.

"Are you sure you are ready for this?" said Kane, pulling out a cigarette and placing it in between his lips. His hand cupped the tip of the cigarette, protecting the flame that sprouted from his lighter. Kane had a spirited, roguish look on his face, like he was teasing Welsh with whatever it was he had to say.

Welsh clenched his jaw. "Look, I have a finite amount of time out here. If you don't stop beating around the bush, I'm just going to leave."

Kane sucked in deeply. One of his eyes closed as he held the smoke in, bathing his lungs in toxic chemicals and satiating the clenching urge for nicotine. The impish countenance had changed; the man was suddenly looking very serious.

"I've seen him, I think."

Welsh didn't respond. He let the cooing pigeons and the other passersby do all the talking while he waited for Kane to continue.

"I'm not sure, but I think I've seen him, Carson. Bob the Butcher."

"You've seen him?"

"That's right."

"How's that?"

"I looked at his face."

"Screw you. You know what I mean."

Kane let out a wheezy chuckle. Welsh was staring at the man with a mix of fear and captivation. Logic would indicate that this was all a ruse; an elaborate game by some nut just out to stir the pot and get in on the action. But gut instinct was saying something different. Somehow, Welsh knew that Kane was telling the truth. Or, at least, what he believed to be the truth.

"What did you see?"

Kane took another long draw off of his cigarette while his eyes narrowed.

"Before I tell you, I think you need to be introduced to my dear friend Context. Because if I just told you what I saw without telling you anything else, it probably wouldn't make much sense."

"Just tell me whatever you think you need to tell me, Kane."

Kane blew a wad of smoke out of the corner of his mouth. "I thought we were on a first-name basis."

Welsh placed both hands on either side of the bench and clenched. His knuckles lost their color as he tried to ebb away the irritation out of his body. Kane laughed again and clapped Welsh on the back.

"Relax, man. Don't get your panties in a bunch. Okay, where to begin…"

Another prolonged inhale on his cigarette. He held this one in for longer than the others before releasing the smoke in a rattled sigh. Welsh focused on the strange ring again on the man's finger and saw that it looked like Latin engraved around the band. Before he could get a good glimpse of what the letters were, Kane launched into his tale.

"As with most stories told by bad men, it starts with a girl. Again, it was a woman that I met at a bar. She was in her forties, but bangin'. You know how some women just don't ever seem to lose their looks? Like even when they reach their sixties, you can still see at least a trace of what made all those men go crazy. Well, this chick had it. We just started talkin' one night. She had had two Long

Island iced tea's. Every other word was slurred, but she still made it sound sexy. I guess I ought to be thankful that she was smashed though, because I don't think she would have come home with me otherwise."

Kane gave Welsh another shifty, puckish look. "I know she regretted it. Hell, I probably would have if I was her. But the real mistake she made was giving me her phone number. I must have called about fourteen times over the next two weeks. I know how pathetic that is. But we've all done it, haven't we? It's human nature to want what you can't have. And when someone doesn't answer your phone calls, it makes you want to keep calling. Anywho, I never did hear back from Tracy after that night."

Welsh felt the tingling of goose bumps on his forearms.

"Tracy Dinwoodie." He said it as a statement, not a question.

Kane nodded, as his cheeks caved in for another suck on the cancer stick.

"She slept with you?"

The man gave him a side-eye. "Don't sound so surprised, Carson. Just because I got bad teeth and shifty eyes don't mean I can't woo a broad or two if they are drunk enough."

A true gentleman, thought Welsh, but he didn't say it out loud.

"Did you ever see her again?"

"Well, that is what I am getting at. I saw her twice. Once at the grocery store in the wine aisle. When she saw *me*, she almost tripped over herself trying to get away. Like I was just going to come up to her and start asking her why she didn't call me back. I called fourteen times! I *knew* why she didn't call me back."

He flicked the cig, knocking some of the loose ash onto the ground, and then he closed his mouth back around the tip. It was beginning to look spent; only a few centimeters of rolled-paper remained.

"But what I really came to tell you about was the second time I saw her. She was out jogging at Mount Tabor Park. I was walking my dog. This was about a month and a half ago. She had stopped to catch her breath, and she was checking her wrist watch. When she saw me coming toward her, she literally rolled her eyes and said, 'For fuck's sake.' If it weren't so funny it would have hurt my feelings."

Welsh leaned forward. "Did you try talking to her?"

"I didn't *try*. I *did* talk to her. She looked like she was about to take off jogging again, but I told her to hold on. I just let her know that I wasn't going to bug her or anything. That I'm harmless. She didn't seem to agree with that assessment. See, I figured out why she had cut me off. Not that I was bad in the sack. No, the reason she never called me again is because she looked me up the morning after we had screwed and found that I was a sex offender. That I had been convicted of rape."

Kane shook his head, and for the first time, he looked fairly irritated.

"She told me that if I ever called her again, that she would call the police and tell them I was harassing her. She said that if I saw her in public anymore, I better just keep my head down and not say anything if I didn't want to end back up in jail. Nothing quite like somebody making you feel like you are complete scum for something you didn't even do."

Surprisingly, Welsh felt a glimmer of pity for the man next to him, but he tried to suppress it. For all he knew, Kane really *was* a rapist, and had fabricated a sob story to get Welsh on his side.

"Anyway, I told her that was fine. I had no problem leaving her be. So I moseyed on by."

The man unclenched his index finger and thumb, letting the cigarette drop to the ground. He swiveled his foot back-and-forth over the butt, smearing the remaining nicotine on the sidewalk.

"And that was when I saw him. Standing in the trees. Staring at her."

Welsh's muscles seemed to tense.

"What exactly did you see, David?"

"A man in the woods. To my right. Probably

about twenty feet away. He was just standing there. Didn't move a muscle. He was staring right at her. I looked back to see if she had seen him, but she had taken off in a near-sprint, probably running from me, ironically enough. I don't think she saw him. Anyway, when I turned back to get a better look, he was gone."

Welsh prodded with more questions. "Okay? So you saw a man standing in the trees? What makes you think that that was Robert Macabre?"

Kane's eyes bulged. "Is that what he is calling himself? Robert Macabre?"

"Oh *shit*," said Welsh, realizing his mistake.

"The papers said that he used the name Robert, but they never said anything about a last name."

"Listen to me—"

"Robert Macabre. Robert *fucking* Macabre."

"Listen!" Welsh grasped onto Kane's shoulder with a vice-like grip, and the man recoiled a little in surprise. "You keep that to yourself, you hear? Don't you tell that to *anyone.* Unless you want to completely screw this up, you better seal your lips."

"Whoa, there, big guy. How about taking your hands off of me?"

Welsh shook his head, released Kane, and exhaled through puckered lips like he was in labor. "Jesus. This was a mistake. Coming here was a mistake."

"Relax, man. I'm not going to tell anybody. At

this point, I really ain't got anybody to tell."

Welsh kept shaking his head, but his range of motion in the disgruntled gesture was not as wide as it had been, as his trepidation began to slightly subside. A woman pushing a dark blue double stroller with two babies that couldn't have been more than six months old walked by, and as she did so, she gave Welsh a peculiar look. Her head was scrunched in a frown and she almost appeared concerned. Perhaps she had just caught wind of his irritable tone.

"So why exactly do you think this man you saw was our guy? I mean, I don't really see anything in your story so far that doesn't make it conjectural."

"You'll have to dumb down the dialect there, friend. I don't understand all of those big words."

"Incomplete. Wildly circumstantial. Inconclusive."

"I mean, if you see a guy in the woods stalking somebody that was found gutted and all cut up in the same place he was stalking her, wouldn't you find it strange?"

Welsh nodded slowly. "Yes, I would. But there is a difference between strange and guilty."

"You're preaching to the choir with that statement, Carson. But it was more than just strange."

"Still…"

"Who just stands out in the woods and stares at

passersby, huh?"

Welsh didn't reply at first. Though his thoughts were still mostly on Kane and his story, his eyes were latched onto the same lady pushing the stroller who kept glancing back at them. Did she recognize Kane? Without looking back at the pale, inordinately thin man next to him, Welsh asked another question.

"What did this guy look like?"

"I didn't see his face. He was too far away. But he was big. Somewhere in between a bodybuilder and an offensive lineman. Probably as tall as you. A little more built though, I think."

"What was he wearing?"

"He had on a heavy looking rain jacket. Kind of looked like the same material that someone would wear if they were power washing a house. But it wasn't orange. It was dark red. And the reason I couldn't see his face at all is because he had his hood up. It was kind of cloaking his face in shadow."

Welsh could suddenly hear his heart beating in his ears as he turned back to Kane.

"Black pants," continued Kane. "Brown boots, I think."

"And you didn't see his face at all?"

"Nope."

"And ethnically?"

"Eh?"

"Was he white?"

A shit-eating grin spread across Kane's face. "Of course. Were you expecting something different? All serial killers are white guys."

"He's not a serial killer."

"Huh?"

"He's not a serial killer. The FBI defines a serial killer as any person that has murdered three or more people. He has only killed two."

The smile disappeared from Kane's face. "You really think he has only killed two people?"

Welsh didn't answer.

"A mind like that. What he did to Tracy. You can't tell me that that kind of disease just started to spread two weeks ago."

Welsh squinted his eyes as the sun overhead peeked through the cloud cover, shining directly on them. It created little helix outlines on the edges of his vision, and he focused on the grass, waiting for the spirals to disappear. For the first time since he had hopped out of the cab, there wasn't a single person in sight. Just the two of them, sitting on the bench.

"You are going to have to go to the police."

Kane chuckled. "You know, I really had high hopes for you, Welsh."

"You could save lives. You could save the next Tracy," continued Welsh, undeterred.

"After I told you how she treated me, do you

really think appealing to my sensitive side is the best tactic?"

"David. Please. This could be the break in the case."

Kane shook his head. "I already told you I couldn't see any part of his face."

"You would be surprised what your brain might be able to retrieve from its long-term memory storage. And if you thought your story would serve no purpose, why did you go through all this trouble to arrange this meeting? Why don't you just meet with a sketch artist and see what ha—"

"No. No cops."

Welsh groaned. "I thought you said that you wanted to help."

"I'm interested in helping you. That's all I am interested in."

For a few moments, the only sound was the pigeons cooing and other, noisier birds from overhead cawing at each other. A slight breeze ruffled Welsh's hair as he stared at Kane with determination. The man just stared back with that same roguish smile, as if trying to bait Welsh into anger.

"You do understand that I am going to have to meet with the detectives and tell them what you told me."

"I do."

"And you do understand that they are going to

come looking for you."

"Yes."

Welsh raised his palms upward. "Then why not just go see them first?"

"Because they aren't going to find me."

This time, it was Welsh's turn to offer a mordant smile. "I think you may be underestimating their ability."

"Oh contraire, Carson Welsh. I think you are underestimating me. See, I have a knack for being... sly. If I don't want to be seen or found or bothered, I won't be."

Welsh scoffed. "So, what? I am just supposed to take what you have given me and go find every man in Portland who's wearing a red jacket?"

Kane shrugged and kept on grinning.

"I don't know what you are supposed to do. I never tell people how to go about their business. All I know is, this is a bad, bad man. Bad men need to be punished. And I figured what I saw may help the person that is in charge of doing so. The same way I wouldn't tell a surgeon how to close a severed artery, I'm not going to tell the district attorney how to put a bad man behind bars."

At that moment, Kane stood up, picking up his bag of bread and tucking it under his arm.

"Ta ta for now, Carson. It was nice to finally meet you. I hope things turn out differently for you than they did for Tracy."

With a wink, he turned around and sauntered off down the path, and though the urge was instantly quelled by common sense, there was a fleeting moment where Welsh was tempted to get up and follow him.

23

"So what do we got?"

Arroyo shook her head slowly, as if doing it too quick might provoke Flask's anger. The room was muggy and had a smell of sweat mixed with stale coffee. Most of them had been inside for far too long. The only newcomer was the chief, who had finally joined them to hear a summary of the developments of the past few hours. While Arroyo had been giving him the rundown, Flask seemed even more on edge than usual. She had noticed this before. The man's tension would heighten when they had a thread that could possibly unravel the case.

"Nothing, yet. We think the man Welsh spoke to was using an alias. There are three David Kane's that live in the state of Oregon. One is in Baker City, which, if you don't know, is about three hundred miles away from here. The second is a bartender in Florence, which is a four-hour drive. The third is in a hospital room in Ashland on the California border. Oh, and I have managed to scrounge up photos of two of them."

Arroyo shuffled through the documents in front of her on the table, until she brought up photographs of two men. One was old and haggard; someone had taken a picture of him at the kitchen table, and judging by the disgruntled expression on that David Kane's face, he was none too pleased to be documented by the photographer. The other was a mugshot; that David Kane was in an orange jumpsuit and had jet-black hair that was up in a ponytail, and his neck was covered with tattoos. He looked to be no more than twenty.

"Welsh says that neither of these men is the person he spoke to."

Flask grunted as a form of acknowledgment. "And he didn't want to talk to us because he thinks we are all corrupt?"

"Welsh says—"

"Oh, for Christ's sake, Emily, why don't you just let *him* say it then?"

Flask turned to Welsh, who was at the end of the table next to McCabe.

"Carson, enlighten us."

Welsh cleared his throat and straightened his red checkered tie.

"I think stating that Kane thinks all police are

corrupt is not too far from the truth. The origin of his, um, *prejudice*, apparently derives from time he spent in prison. His story is some cop in Tillamook County named Marius Wicks apparently took offense to Kane screwing his sister and arrested Kane for rape. He said he spent six months in OSP for it and was also assaulted by Wicks and some other cops a couple months before his trial."

"Emily—" began Flask.

Arroyo interjected quickly. "I already looked it up. Nobody by the name of David Kane has ever set foot inside a cell at OSP. And there was never a Deputy Marius Wicks that worked for Tillamook PD either."

"Jesus! So what, he made the whole thing up? Why the hell would he do that?"

Arroyo gave a noncommittal shrug and turned to Welsh without responding to Flask's question. Apparently, she was stumped too.

McCabe leaned forward to draw everyone's attention. "The thing is, Marty, his description of the person who was stalking Dinwoodie matches what Jacey Duhart told Amy Steens. Duhart called him a 'red giant.' Then, Kane said the man he saw in the woods looked like a body builder or an offensive lineman. And that he was wearing a dark red jacket."

At first, Flask looked like he wanted to offer a sardonic retort, but then whatever biting thing he was going to say suddenly evaporated off of his tongue, and his face crunched. After at least ten seconds of mulling it over, he gave his response.

"So maybe the story about Dinwoodie was true, but the name and the rest was fabricated?"

"That's what I am thinking," said McCabe with an energetic bob of his head. "Maybe there is a different reason Kane, or whatever the hell you want to call him, doesn't want to come to the police. Maybe, for instance, he has a warrant out for his arrest."

Around the table, most of the heads nodded. Arroyo, however, offered a rebuttal.

"So, why would a man that was worried enough about his own well-being to give Welsh an alias and a fabricated backstory get involved in this? Even if he saw something? If a warrant was out for his arrest, don't you think he would steer clear of a murder investigation?"

"Well, that is why I think he came to me, Emily," said Welsh. "If he has a warrant, he probably thought coming to speak to me would be safe enough to avoid arrest. He seemed weirdly confident about his ability to evade capture."

"But what does he get out of it, Carson? What does he get out of helping us find this guy?"

Welsh raised his palms upward in a "don't ask me" type of gesture.

"We need to find this man," said Flask

suddenly and loudly.

Arroyo scrunched her forehead and narrowed her eyes.

"That might be easier said than done, Marty. We don't have a photograph, KA's, background info... Hell, we don't even have a real name."

"Have Welsh meet with the sketch artist."

"And do what with that?"

"Give it to the *Oregonian*. Tell them it is a person of interest in the Bob the Butcher case."

"You think feeding a picture to a mass media outlet insinuating that this guy is a suspect is a good method for trying to get him to come forward?"

Flask slapped his hand against the desk in indignation. "Okay, then *what*, Emily? What do you think we should do?"

Arroyo threw her hands up. "Canvassing. Asking around. Checking local records. Bars, hotel rooms, restaurants. If David Kane is this man's alias, it probably wasn't a one-off thing. He must have used it before."

"That sounds a lot like looking for a needle in a haystack if you ask me," grumbled Flask bitterly.

Arroyo smiled somewhat sarcastically, but didn't respond. Flask was as hard-headed as they came. He was very good at criticizing his detective's potential solutions to problems, but not so good at offering a viable solution as an alternative. He was like the little voice in the back of your head that second-guessed every decision you made without giving you positive feedback when you demonstrated good judgment.

Flask inhaled through his nostrils, and they swelled like a bull just before a charge. He flattened the wrinkles in his tie while slowly turning his head toward Welsh.

"Setting that aside for a moment, let me ask you, what exactly were you thinking, Welsh?"

"Um… What?"

Flask's cheeks flushed. "Seems to me that a guy who just got chased through the woods by a murderous nut job would be averse to meeting strangers who slip him ominous notes in coffee shops."

"I just—"

"You just what? Decided that the protective detail we assigned you was starting to cramp your style?"

"Marty—"

"No, Welsh, seriously. If you want me to remove the detail, fine. But as long as you are under their watch, you can't just be rendezvousing with every whacko who wants to have a chitchat."

"Skip the lecture, Flask," said Welsh quickly. "If it wasn't for me meeting with this guy, you still wouldn't have shit."

"What makes you think we have shit now? We have a guy with a fake name tell us he caught a glimpse of someone standing out in the woods and now suddenly the case is solved?"

Welsh tightened his lips as if he were holding back a derisive retort, and Flask kept staring at him. At that moment, Arroyo could feel the palpable dislike between the chief of police and the district attorney. She quickly tried to steer the conversation away from where it was potentially heading.

"I think the most obvious angle to pursue is Kane's relationship with Dinwoodie, if he actually had one. We can start re-interviewing friends, family, and coworkers. See if anyone remembers Dinwoodie having a fling with this guy."

"That's a good idea," added McCabe, nodding ardently.

Flask was still staring at Welsh, daring him to continue the argument. But Welsh's eyes were now out of focus, and his fingers were tapping against the table as if he had abruptly become disinterested in the current conversation. Arroyo had a feeling this was just to further irritate Flask; acting disengaged like a junior high student in science class.

"I think it might be a good idea for Welsh to meet with the sketch artist, just for our purposes," said Arroyo. "Just so we know roughly who we are looking for."

"Maybe we can even show them to the people that we re-interview in association with Dinwoodie.

See if they remember him ever being with her. Or even harassing her."

Flask looked at both of them for a moment before resuming his piqued appraisal of Welsh.

"What do you think, Welsh? Do you think that is a good idea?"

Welsh's didn't reply, ignoring Flask's patronizing and mocking tone.

"I think we can all agree on one thing," said Arroyo. "A conversation with David Kane would be very interesting."

Welsh watched as Wendy shuffled the pan back and forth, sizzling the beef in its own juices. A screened cover was over the pan, making sure that the popping bubbles of grease didn't fly into Wendy's face. The smell of the cooking meat infiltrated every corner of the kitchen, and Welsh felt his stomach grumble impatiently. He sauntered slowly over behind his wife and kissed her on the neck, inhaling the intoxicating scent of her hair as he did so.

"Better not get too frisky, mister," she said. "Your taco meat will come out all burned to hell."

Welsh twisted around her petite body and gave Wendy a peck on the cheek. "When is the taco meat you serve me ever not burned to hell?"

He had to bob and weave as Wendy waved the spatula in his direction, pretending like she was about to give him a firm whack on the top of his skull.

"What, are you going to spank me with your greasy spatula?"

"You'd like that too much."

Welsh let out a deep belly laugh and placed his rear end on a stool. Wendy giggled too, but the laughter subsided as she glanced out of the kitchen window at Wilson McCoy, who was sitting in his Crown Vic outside, adjusting the police radio on his dashboard.

"Mo stopped by today, by the way. Just after I got home from work."

Welsh blinked several times.

"Mo did? He came here?"

"Yep. Smelled like booze."

"He did?"

"Yeah. And he was acting kind of weird. Sort of depressed, I guess."

"Hmm."

"I think it's happening again, Carson."

Welsh feigned a moment of ignorance. "What are you talking about?"

Wendy gave him a look of impatience. "Come on, Carson, you know exactly what I am talking about. His drinking."

"What do you mean, 'his drinking'? He isn't an alcoholic."

"Oh, really? What would you call someone who hasn't gone a day in twenty years without having a beer?"

"Someone who's lived a damn good life."

Wendy shrugged. "I'm just saying. I think his drinking is more of a problem than you make it out to be."

Welsh didn't answer. He was more than done with the conversation, so he strode out of the kitchen and into the living room, plopping his butt onto the sofa. He knew that Wendy could tell that he was a little irritated, but she said nothing to try to alleviate his annoyance. Welsh started fondling the table next to the couch, searching for the remote without actually looking. His fingers found a round object, and he pointed it at the television.

"Are you trying to turn on the TV with the case to my glasses?"

Welsh looked down, and sure enough, he was. He looked back at Wendy, who had doubled over with laughter. She was convulsing and wheezing, as if it were the funniest thing she had ever seen. Welsh realized that he had been frowning and relaxed the clenched muscles in his forehead. He tried to keep a stoic expression on his face, but the look of Wendy cackling and bent over made it impossible. He began to chuckle too.

"You are really tickled by that, aren't you?"

She wiped at the corner of her eye, removing a mirth-induced tear. "It's just funny how hard you were trying to be serious."

"Yeah, well, you try and be serious when you got a goofball like you roamin' around."

Wendy continued to chortle and then turned around to prod at the sweltering beef on the top of the stove. Finally, after a few more giggle-filled seconds, the jollity abated, and she turned the knob of the stove counter-clockwise to snuff out the heat.

"Only a little bit burned."

Welsh laughed and gave a sarcastic click of his tongue, but couldn't think of a funny enough reply to counter with. Wendy then put a heat-protecting glove on her hand and opened the stove, withdrawing a metal sheet filled with taco shells. She set the sheet on a brown wicker coaster and took off the glove, glancing back out the window. With a sinking sensation in his gut, Welsh noticed that her face, which had been filled with utter glee, had suddenly become a little sullen.

"What is it?" asked Welsh.

Wendy gave a noncommittal gesture and began assembling the first two tacos. Welsh had to put forth a great deal of effort not to roll his eyes. It was one of his biggest pet peeves when people made you beg to hear what was troubling them.

"Seriously, what's wrong?"

Wendy looked up at him, sighing. Once again, she glanced back out toward McCoy, who was looking bored.

"I just have a bad feeling."

"Huh? About what?"

"This whole thing. I just have this weird sixth sense telling me that something bad is about to happen."

Welsh reclined a little, taken aback.

"What do you mean?"

"I can't really put it into words. I just have this ominous feeling."

"Like… That something bad is going to happen to me?"

Wendy stared at him and he could tell that that was indeed what she had meant just by the look on her face. Her eyes were big and troubled and her lips were pursed as if she was trying not to become emotional. Welsh instantly sprung off of the couch and walked into the kitchen holding his arms out.

"Come here."

She slid snug into his arms, nuzzling her face against his neck. Welsh moved back and placed his hand on her chin like she was a small child, bringing her gaze up so that they could make eye contact.

"We are going to get through this."

Wendy sniffed and gave the tiniest shake of her head. "How do you know that, Carson? This seems like it has already gotten out of our control."

Welsh sighed. "That is in your head, sweetheart. It has only gotten out of control in your head. Nothing has happened."

As soon as he said it, Welsh felt a little prickle of guilt creep up in his chest. If Wendy knew about the rabbit mask, or the man in the Minotaur, heck, even David Kane, she would be in full-blown panic mode. But panic would not help anything, so he had to downplay the gravity of what they were facing, even if it meant lying to his wife.

Wendy's voice was so quiet when she next spoke it was almost indiscernible from the other noises in the kitchen. "I just can't imagine what it would be like if I lost you."

Welsh pulled back so he could make fierce eye contact with her.

"Nothing is going to happen to me. I promise."

Thunk.

His eyes opened wide. A stitch in his chest seared as he gobbled up a mouthful of air. His heart took great bounding leaps in his chest, and it was like he was flying. Or rather, falling. Sweat congealed the sheet over him onto his forearms, and he peeled it away like it was plastic wrap.

Bad dreams. Always bad dreams.

Welsh sat up, and he couldn't quite catch his breath. He looked over at Wendy, who was still fast asleep. Why wouldn't she be? Robert Macabre had not invaded her dreams, with his masks and wild, wicked spirit. This time, in the dream, he had been donning the black face of a crow. They had been in a clearing; Macabre had looked at him with his head cocked to the side. It was almost playful, like a dog getting ready to fetch. The man had taken a single step forward before Welsh had jerked back into reality.

Wendy's hand was curled over her face like a cat trying to block its eyes from the sun for restful slumber. The big white T-shirt draped over her coiled knees, and Welsh could see just a few inches of her bottom resting against the heels of her feet underneath the bedspread. It looked uncomfortable, like an advanced yoga pose. But Wendy remained scampering through the depths of her own dream, looking tranquil and detached.

Welsh slipped his feet out of the covers and swung his legs over the edge of the bed, placing his soles gingerly against the carpet. His head was still spinning from the dream; part of him felt like he was about to pass out, while the other part thought he could become a world-champion sprinter on this very night. It was a delirious reality; everything felt warped. His body was heavy, and for an ephemeral second, he wondered if he could even lift himself out of the bed.

Inhale. Exhale. Inhale. Exhale.

On the second deep breath, it was like some omniscient voice had yelled the word "stop" inside his brain. His pulse rate steadied, and he pictured a heart monitor becoming less frenetic with its spikes.

Hello, stress, my old friend.

Welsh felt a tiny desire to laugh as his thoughts echoed in the Simon and Garfunkel tune. What world was he in right now? A sadistic, psychopathic fiend who was hell-bent on psychologically torturing him could be out there abducting some unsuspecting lady at this very moment, and here he was feeling like he needed to giggle just moments after he had a bad nightmare?

He twisted his lower back around and looked back at Wendy, who was still corkscrewed in that odd pose and somehow looking more peaceful than ever. Welsh thought about the promise he had made her earlier in the evening.

Nothing is going to happen to me.

Would he be able to honor that oath? Even though Wilson McCoy was outside, armed and ready to defend them, and the alarm system and cameras Welsh had installed were manning the battlements, it still felt like the walls were closing in. Like Macabre was inching nearer and nearer by the day.

The alarm system. Welsh ruminated on it for a second. The strange humming noise it made when first activated.

Something was wrong.

The alarm system. He had forgotten to arm it before going to bed.

Thunk.

Almost completely in sync with this thought, a startling noise rattled from downstairs as he sat there on the edge of his bed. Silently and swiftly, Welsh opened the drawer to the nightstand next to his bed and gripped onto the hilt of the pistol that had been laid inside. After making sure that the safety button was off, he pushed himself off of the bed and moved toward the door to their room. He was not quite running, but also not walking either. His arms stayed immobile at his side as his legs did all of the work, carrying him out through the open door into the hallway.

Seconds later, he was creeping quickly down the stairs with both hands on the gun, gripping it like it might spontaneously vanish into another dimension, leaving him unarmed. When he got to the bottom of the stairs, he swung the gun around the corner like he had seen it done in the movies. The darkness of the hallway made it difficult to see, but Welsh felt fairly confident that nothing was there to greet him, so he tiptoed forward, reducing his pace as he got closer to the precipice of the living room and the kitchen.

Back and forth he moved the pistol, clearing both rooms of threat as he continued to move. There was nothing of note in the kitchen; just dirty pans and silverware stacked haphazardly in the sink. The living room looked even more in order; Wendy had made sure to straighten the pillows of the couch before going off to bed. The blinds on the windows were drawn. Welsh looked out through the gap where the blinds didn't quite touch, and saw nothing.

Perhaps he had imagined the noise.

Welsh lowered the gun and walked toward the space on the wall where the alarm had been installed. Sure enough, the green light that meant it was defused blinked in the darkness. He reached his free hand forward to the numbered touchpad, getting ready to remedy his error.

Just then, out of his peripheral vision, he saw black movement dart across the gap in between the blinds.

Welsh raised the gun and retreated, pointing the muzzle at the spot where he had seen the black shape. His finger tickled the trigger, preparing to fire. But he had to be closer to the window if he was hoping to get a good shot off. Welsh crept into the living room, ready to unload the clip through the glass.

A great deafening noise almost made Welsh's bowels evacuate. His torso went erect and his stomach invaded his throat. The sound of the doorbell had nearly knocked him over in surprise. It rang feverishly four times, and Welsh pointed the gun at the wooden door, closing one eye as if to aim. Without a second thought, he fired four times, splintering the wood in every direction and even knocking the door off of its top hinges. It slumped lamely downward with a *clunk*, and Welsh moved forward with the pistol still aimed at the spot, cocking his leg and then unleashing it with a thunderous kick, slamming the door clean off the threshold.

The first thing he saw was somebody charging toward him from twenty feet away. Welsh pointed the pistol at the intruder and was inches away from firing when he heard the shout.

"Welsh, stop! Stop! Fucking stop!" The man raised his hands. "It's me. It's me!" Wilson McCoy waved frantically, like he was trying to flag down a plane. Welsh rattled out a pained exhale and lowered the gun.

Gripping his chest tightly, Welsh doubled over. His heart literally hurt from beating so quickly. How ironic it would be if he succumbed to a heart attack here on his front porch after all that had happened.

"What the hell is going on, man?" McCoy's scream ripped apart the air, sounding primal and bizarre. "You almost just killed me!"

No body. No blood. What was happening? Surely, one of the bullets had made contact with Robert Macabre. He had been right there, ringing the doorbell, just seconds ago. But the only thing that was on the porch was a small brown package with a red bowtie and a white letter tucked underneath it.

Welsh stared at the thing like it was a coiled rattlesnake. He backed up and even felt an urge to put a couple of bullets into it. McCoy, who was wheezing and had a line of spittle on his chin from screaming, had not yet noticed the parcel. He slowly and apprehensively marched toward Welsh, as if the man might suddenly change his mind and shoot him.

"What the hell happened? What is going on?"

After a couple more steps, McCoy's eyes flickered down toward the package. Welsh gulped and gave a frenzied shake of his head.

"I ain't going to open that."

Arroyo shuffled through the photos like a deck of cards, her gloved hands barely grasping the corners of each one. She looked repulsed. Her upper lip was curled in a snarl and her brow was forced down in a heavy scowl. After she had looked over the last paper stock, she set the small stack down onto the table and shook her head, appearing a little nauseous.

"Three of these are various outer extremities. Two feet in separate photographs. Both with each of the toes hacked off. The other is of a hand missing the top half of all of its fingers. Much like the one that was actually in the package."

McCabe had his head down and his mouth contorted in disgust. Arroyo glanced at him and held out the photos toward her partner. When he looked up, he shook his head vehemently.

"Once is enough for me. Thanks though."

"Fair enough." Arroyo sat them down on the table and looked up at Welsh, who was sitting across from where she was standing.

"What are the other two?"

"Hmm?"

"Well, math has never been my strong suit," said Welsh. "But there are five photographs there and you only referenced three."

Arroyo gave him a grave look. "Are you sure you want to know?"

"I appreciate the concern, Emily, but at this point, I am already not getting any sleep. What are the other two?"

The detective sighed heavily and tapped her index finger on the table repeatedly like it was a nervous tic.

"One is of the vic's face. Or what had been his face. He had been scalped."

Welsh felt a little bit of bile raising up in his throat.

"And the other?"

"His genitals. Removed from his body."

Welsh swallowed, trying to suppress the contents of his stomach.

"Yeah, ol' Bobby B really had his way with this one," said McCabe, stepping forward with a look of utter repugnance on his face. "He was worse to the man than he was to either of the women."

"It is actually fairly surprising that he ventured

away from his usual MO," added Arroyo. "The vast majority of serial killers target the same gender and age demographic throughout their hot period. But if your theory is correct, Welsh, then it looks like this one may have been simply out of necessity."

Welsh twitched involuntarily. "When will you know if there is a DNA match on the hand?"

"Probably very shortly, depending on how fast the computers are running down at the lab."

"So he scalps the guy, then cuts off his toes, fingers, dick, and balls. That sounds like something a cartel would do," said Welsh.

"Or some gangster shit," added McCabe.

"But gangsters and drug cartels don't generally leave body parts on peoples' front porches."

Welsh let silence take the room for a couple of seconds before continuing.

"So if what I think is right, that means that this guy followed me to the park the other day."

Arroyo stared at him forebodingly but said nothing in response.

"He must be watching me pretty closely if he seized that opportunity."

"Yes. He must be."

Welsh thought he might be more afraid of that notion once someone else concurred with it, but he wasn't. He had already come to the conclusion days ago, and her agreement didn't make it worse than it already was.

Welsh sighed. "As far as tonight, my house is pretty isolated. He was there, and that means the vehicle he drives was somewhere in the vicinity. So wouldn't it be a matter of canvassing the area and seeing if any of my neighbors saw any suspicious vehicles?"

"That is on the docket for tomorrow morning."

"Hmm." Welsh scratched his left eyebrow and let himself drift away for a moment as he harnessed his next question.

"One thing I don't get... How did he know I had forgotten to set the alarm? And how come McCoy didn't see anything?"

Arroyo just looked at him with a blank expression on her face before shaking her head.

"Honestly... I have no idea."

Welsh looked away, feeling a little frustrated. He wasn't totally sure if his aggravation was with the situation, or Arroyo herself. They were detectives. They were supposed to cultivate theories and propagate answers. But here they were, with less than a trace of a clue as to who Robert Macabre actually was.

McCabe drew Welsh out of his stupor.

"How is your wife?"

"Shaken, obviously. She is with her sister right now. McCoy gave her a ride over there. I told her I would meet her there as soon as I could." He tried to put some inflection into his voice that would give

McCabe an idea of what he was trying to insinuate, and the man did not miss it.

"Look, Welsh, you don't have to stay here. You can go get some rest, man. We don't need your help to do our jobs."

"Are you sure about that?"

The patronizing question had escaped Welsh's lips before he could stop it. The detectives looked at each other and then back at Welsh with contempt.

"Look, Welsh, no one is more frustrated that we haven't gotten a lead on this guy than we are. But you just need to try and be pa—" began Arroyo.

"Don't finish that sentence," interrupted Welsh. "Don't tell me to be patient. This guy just left someone's hand on my front doorstep. I've about exhausted all of my patience, Emily."

Arroyo recoiled a little but Welsh was not deterred.

"You aren't going to find anything on that box. Or that hand. This guy is too good. Too smart to leave anything behind. Unless he wants us to... find it."

A revelation smacked Welsh over the head like a blunt object. *Of course*, he thought.

"What is it, Carson?"

"You said only the top halves of the fingers were cut off, right?"

"Right."

"Did you grab any pictures of the hand from

the techs before you sent it down to the lab?"

Arroyo pondered his question for half a second and then strode over to the whiteboard on the left side of the room. She removed the thumbtack that was holding one of the photographs in place and then carried the picture across the room. She paused for a second before handing it to Welsh.

"You sure you want to look at this?"

Welsh just reached out his hand as an answer to Arroyo's question. He snatched the photograph away from her and gazed down at it. The skin of the mutilated hand in the photo was pallid and green; there were traces of dried blood around the knuckles where the fingers had been cleaved off. Sure enough, on the third finger, there was a ring. A thick gold ring with Latin writing engraved around the band.

"So we know who got chopped up, we just don't know his real name?"

Flask was not his normal self. His usual anger was a little subdued, possibly because of how ludicrous the situation was, and maybe also due to the fact that he wasn't nearly as hostile when he was speaking to just one person. Arroyo was the only one in his office. She had spared McCabe the task of speaking to their irascible, prickly boss.

"No matches on DNA," replied Arroyo. "Obviously, no prints. But, circumstantially, we can hypothesize that the man who introduced himself to Welsh as David Kane was the one who was killed. Welsh says the ring that was left behind on his finger was the same one he saw the man wearing in the park. Which was obviously intentional. This guy has never tried to be secretive about who his victims are. This was a power play. He wanted us to know that he killed the man who saw him."

"All of this technology..." Flash didn't complete his sentence, but he didn't need to. It was one of his favorite refrains to criticize how far humanity had come and how incompetent it still was.

"We think Macabre had to have been in the vicinity when Welsh was speaking with Kane... Or whatever the hell his name is. That is the only plausible explanation for how he was able to identify the threat."

"So he saw Welsh sneak out of the courthouse and followed him to the park? Did Welsh see anybody there that could have matched the physical description given to us by Duhart and Kane?"

Arroyo shook her head. "No. He says he only saw a couple of female joggers and men in suits. No one that could have been him."

"Of course not," muttered Flask grumpily.

"Jesus, he followed him there? Aren't serial killers supposed to moonlight, or *daylight* as regular people? They are supposed to have normal jobs. Normal routines. Not stick out… How does this guy have the time to monitor what Welsh is doing twenty-four seven?"

"Maybe his job is conducive to being out and about."

Flask stared at her with an expectant look on his face. "Such as?"

"Maybe a courier. Maybe the guy who drives around giving people parking tickets. Maybe a taxi driver. Something like that."

"Hmm."

Arroyo shrugged. "It's a theory worth looking into at least."

Flask jerked his head in vexation, letting out an audible, exasperated sigh.

"This is one frustrating case, Em. One frustrating goddamn case."

"But there is good news, boss."

Flask perked up.

"What?"

"We found a partial on the package."

Arroyo watched as Flask's jaw dropped open a little bit.

"No way."

"Yep. And I know that they say they didn't touch the package, but we confirmed that the print doesn't belong to Welsh or McCoy."

"How…?"

"They always end up making a mistake, Marty. Somehow, in the end, they always falter."

Flask closed his mouth and looked down at his desk, scratching his temple for a moment before gazing back up at Arroyo. "I'm guessing since you haven't given me a name, that means you haven't been able to match it to anyone?"

"It's barely even a print, boss. You can hardly call it a partial. But it's there. If we can identify a suspect and bring them in, we might be able to match it."

"Well, shit. Maybe there is a light at the end of this tunnel, after all."

Arroyo felt a sense of satisfaction coming over her. At the very least, she had just bought herself some more time before Flask tried to hand the case off to the feds. After all, it would look better for him if his own department solved it and not somebody that had never set foot in Multnomah County. The day before, Flask had even suggested bringing in one of the FBI's profilers to consult with them. It was almost as if he was in the beginning stages of conceding defeat. But now, hopefully, he would give Arroyo and McCabe a little breathing room.

Flask looked over Arroyo's shoulder. "What about Welsh? Is he still here?"

"No. He went to see his wife. I don't know if they will stay there for a while or what. Not sure he wants to go back home and stay in a place without a front door."

"Yeah, probably not a good idea. Oh, by the way, I am going to remove McCoy from the night time detail. Tinsley will do it now."

Arroyo raised her eyebrows. "Why?"

"Well, Emily, I don't know if you noticed, but he did let our guy march up to Welsh's front door totally unchecked."

"If you think anyone else would have done a better job—"

"You just leave personnel decisions to me, Arroyo."

Arroyo pursed her lips. "Fair enough."

Flask tapped the pen that was in his hand on the desk several times and moistened his lips with his tongue, apparently unaware of how gross the subconscious gesture looked.

"You said that Welsh identified the hand by a ring?"

"That's correct."

"And it had some sort of Latin insignia engraved on it?"

"Yeah."

"What does it say?"

"I think it is Christian. It's a phrase used in Catholic and Presbyterian literature. Though, with the circumstances, it sounds a lot darker than what it actually is supposed to connote."

Flask knifed his upturned palm through the air as if to say, "Well? Continue!"

Arroyo paused for a moment to emphasize the dramatic irony.

"It says, 'He lives among us.'"

Welsh opened the door with a heavy *creak*. He looked inside the house apprehensively and smelled something that reminded him of a rest home. He flicked the switch to his right, illuminating the main room. The light from the two lamps cast bizarre shadows on the wooden walls. Welsh crossed the threshold, wheeling a suitcase in his right hand and carrying a duffel bag with various toiletries in his left. Wendy was right in his wake, a backpack over her shoulder and pulling a dark blue suitcase of her own.

"Hun, this is not that bad. I thought it would be way worse."

"Well… It was never the interior that needed the most upkeep. More just the loose shingles on the roof and the jungle growing on the lawn."

"You know, back when you first told me you were keeping this place, I thought you were making

274

a big mistake," remarked Wendy, looking around almost in awe. "But now, I am thinking it is the smartest decision you have ever made."

They had come to their second house in Wilsonville, the one that Welsh had inherited when his parents had passed. It had been a retirement home, and though his father had made no mention of it, he had bequeathed it to his son in his will. Intermingled with grief after his father had died was the shock that Welsh not only had six hundred thousand extra dollars in his possession but also a second home. He had always thought he would simply receive an expensive mortgage he would pass on to some better-off subject that was interested in the property. But alas, his parents had been sitting on a fully paid for two-bedroom house and a small fortune. How they acquired the wealth was a mystery, but it wasn't like Welsh was complaining.

"These blinds sure have been collecting dust," remarked Wendy, shaking the shades that were concealing the window to the main room and then pulling them apart. "But other than that, it looks good. Not sure why you were so reluctant about this. Staying in a tiny shack with my nosy sister seems like your worst nightmare."

Welsh shrugged. "It isn't necessarily the lack of company that worries me. Just the locale."

"But no one knows about this place." She

paused for a second, looking at him for reassurance.

"I'm sure somebody can find some connection, if they're willing to do a lot of digging. But I haven't told anybody about it, no. At least, nobody that would be interested."

Wendy scoffed. "Well, that's horrifying. Thanks for that."

"It's probably a better idea than staying at Rose's. You are the smart one, remember?"

"Smart? Or just smart compared to you?" Wendy said it like her normal teasing, but she didn't give him the mischievous look or affectionate punch on the arm that usually accompanied the jest. Before he could say something back, she gestured to the window.

"Oh, look. Our deputy-in-law is here."

Welsh turned and looked out through the window to see an unmarked black car with tinted windows pull up across the street. It wasn't the same Ford Crown Victoria that Diaz had been driving in the previous days, but Welsh had known that it wouldn't be. That morning, after only a few hours spent at Rose's house, Welsh had called Arroyo to relay the idea to stay out in Wilsonville for the time being. She had told him to wait for an hour while she consulted with her team and then had called him back with the plan. They weren't to tell anyone where they were going, and they would meet Lieutenant Don Chaser at a McDonalds in

Tualatin, who would swap the company-issued vehicle he had been piloting for their personal rig. Chaser would take Welsh's Toyota Camry back to their actual house, while they would drive the PPD-owned Chevy Suburban to the house out in Barlow. They would call Diaz on a cell phone provided to them by Chaser, and give him the address of the Barlow home, whereupon Diaz would leave the station in a new, unmarked Dodge Charger and meet them there. The plan had gone fairly seamlessly, and with a small feeling of relief in his stomach, Welsh saw the window of the Charger roll down and a dark-skinned hand flash a thumbs-up from across the street.

"I swear this is an out-of-body experience," said Wendy suddenly.

Welsh looked at his wife, who had her arms crossed and was staring at Diaz across the street with a look of disbelief on her face.

"It feels like a weird, vivid hallucination, doesn't it? I mean, last night you just shot out the front door of our house, because you were trying to stop the serial killer on our porch from coming in and murdering you. *Now*, we are basically members of the Witness Protection Program, moving into a house in the sticks with a cop living in his car just across the road. What the hell is our life?"

"I can't tell if you are trying to be funny or not."

"I'm just trying to zoom out a little, you know? Give a little perspective to the situation. Because I don't think you realize just how *insane* this is."

"Wendy—"

"I could tell you I'm not scared. But I am absolutely terrified, Carson."

Welsh looked at his wife in pity, but she didn't seem to be in the mood for accepting sympathy. She almost appeared a little angry.

"Can you imagine what it felt like last night? Waking up to gunshots? Hiding in the closet, trying not to piss myself? Not sure if the next person who would walk through the bedroom door would be you or the freaking Zodiac Killer?"

"Hun—"

"This is insane, Carson. This whole thing is just…. *Insane*. I can't even put it into words."

Welsh rubbed his eyebrow absentmindedly. "I know."

Wendy gave him a fierce look, her green eyes piercing through him like a knife through butter. "Do you? You seem pretty cavalier at the moment."

"What do you even mean by that?"

"You just seem like you are kind of minimizing the situation."

"Minimizing?"

"I mean, I'm pretty traumatized here. And it seems like you aren't all that concerned about it."

Without warning, a fuse lit in Welsh's brain.

"Are you seriously making this about you right now?"

"Well, you are not really making it about *anything,* so…"

Welsh felt his face flush, and he contorted his mouth. "Oh, what do you want me to do? Stand here, telling you a thousand times how crazy this is like you are doing? And I am sorry, but I almost came face-to-face with a man who wants to skin me alive and use my blood as mouth wash, so an existential crisis doesn't really interest me at this point in time."

"You are such an *asshole,*" hissed Wendy, unwrapping the backpack from around her and chucking it to the ground with a thud.

"Why is it always the woman who starts with the name calling, but the man who is somehow always the asshole?"

"Right, I am sure what's between my legs is dictating who is the asshole and who isn't."

"It sure is dictating *something.*"

Wendy's mouth dropped open.

"You absolute sexist prick."

Welsh stepped toward her, pointing a thick finger in her direction. "Again with the name calling."

"Again with the deflections."

"Well, what should I do then? Blubber on about nothing? You are doing enough of that."

"I'm just trying to make some fucking sense of this Carson!" She was screaming now. "Why did he choose you? Why is he coming after us?"

"He's coming after me."

"We are in this together! If you have forgotten, we are married Carson!"

"Yeah, well, we all make mistakes."

"Fuck you!"

She stormed into one of the two rooms down the hall and slammed the door with a thunderous crack. Welsh felt a vein bulging in his temple and listened to the sound of his teeth grinding. He was absolutely fuming. For a second he tried to suppress it, but then his wrath burst forth like a great wave. He dropped the suitcase onto the ground and unleashed a mighty kick, driving it backward and leaving an indentation where his foot had made contact. He did it again, further depressing the suitcase until it looked like a car that had been T-boned. Another kick. The hardest one yet. Again. Again.

Finally, the yell of absolute, unbridled frustration escaped his lips, and Welsh realized that it had been building for weeks. It started as a screech and then mutated into a guttural yowl like an animal in horrible pain. It didn't even seem like the noise could come from his body, but it did. And it continued for five long seconds. Once it was over, the pressure in his chest had seemed to abate by a fraction, and Welsh suddenly yearned to scream until all of the ennui and ill-feelings had been released from his body. The ultimate catharsis. But he didn't. Instead, he whirled about and marched out of the front door, taking great care to slam the door harder than Wendy had slammed hers.

Mo stumbled to the table, sloshing his beer onto his jacket. Either he didn't notice the rogue liquid splashing on his Columbia rain coat, or was too drunk to care, because he didn't even acknowledge it when it happened. The jukebox blared some Eminem song; the off-the-wall beat and high-pitched voice of the tune vibrated the whole floor. There wasn't anyone else in the bar besides Mo, Welsh, and the bartender, making it a mystery who had put on the vulgar (albeit catchy) rap. The bartender was sitting on a stool and reading a book called *Kiss The Girls,* apparently unperturbed by the blaring tones of Marshall Mathers. It was a strange scene. However, what was most strange was the fact that Welsh was entirely more drunk than Mo. It had been decades since such a feat had occurred.

"By the way, man, I wanted t'ask you somethin'," mumbled Welsh.

"Shoot," replied Mo, and his speech hadn't

been altered at all by the alcohol. Perhaps it was because he was so much more well-versed in being drunk.

"Why did you s-show up at my house yesterday when I wasn't there?"

A worried expression came over Mo's face.

"How was I supposed to know you weren't there?"

"You could have called."

"Don't have a cell phone and I wasn't at home."

"W-Wendy seems to think you have a drinking problem."

Mo's eyes bulged at the suddenness of the proclamation. "She told you that?"

"Yeah."

"Wow. That's, uh, *surprising*."

"Must have spooked her."

"I just asked for you! I didn't even say anything!"

Even though Welsh was absolutely hammered, he could tell that Mo was lying, but he did not call him out on it.

"Do you have a drinking problem, Mo?" asked Welsh.

"No! In fact, I think drinking *solves* a lot of my problems."

Welsh laughed, and Mo joined in. Welsh could feel his cheeks flushing as he chuckled; the heat of the alcohol was percolating throughout his body.

"Well, I'm glad you said tha', because I-I don't think you have a drinking problem. I think *I* just have a Wendy problem."

Mo's laughter slowly subsided, and he took a sip of the beer he had brought with him.

Welsh pursed his lips as he recalled what had happened earlier in the evening. "That was one of the worst fights we have *ever* had. She was so mad. Screamin' her head off. And for what? Because she said I was acting *cavalier*."

Mo narrowed his eyes. "Isn't that a basketball team?"

"I don't know what she w-wants me to do, you know?"

Mo's face was absent of any sign that he was agreeing with Welsh. In fact, he seemed to be looking at his best friend with a little skepticism.

"I do know one thing though, Mo. She gets absolutely *vicious* when she's pissed."

"Hmm."

"Tore me a new one."

"Mm."

"Don't you have anything to say?"

"No.

"You don't understand where I am coming from?"

"No."

"You should have heard the way—"

"Oh, boo-hoo," said Mo suddenly. "You're upset that your bombshell of a wife who loves you to death sometimes gets mad like the rest of the human race?"

Welsh flinched a little as though Mo had smacked him on the forehead.

"Moose—"

Mo shook his head, and the nostrils of his large nose flared. "You don't know how good you have it, Carson. That woman bends over backward for you. She does all the finances. She cooks. She takes care of you when you are sick. And she never held it against you that you can't have kids."

Welsh felt his cheeks get even hotter, but it wasn't due to the alcohol. The subject of his infertility was something that he had discussed with Mo only twice before, and both times it had been extremely uncomfortable.

"Now, a homicidal nutjob has made you his obsession, and you are upset that she is afraid?"

Welsh blubbered, trying to find an adequate rebuttal. "I-It's not that."

"Then what is it, Carson? What is it exactly?"

"She tries to change me. Makes me do things I don't want to do."

"And every woman you have ever come in contact with would do the same exact thing if they were married to you. That is how women are *programmed*, Carson. Like, biologically. To make sure that us hopeless morons that don't know our elbows from our assholes are kept in line. It's just, most of them don't look like Angelina Jolie."

Welsh looked away, his blurry vision taking in the bartender that was now eyeing the two of them with curiosity. "You weren't there—"

Mo shrugged. "No, I wasn't. But I know you, Carson. I know your temper. And I know that you are really good at making people feel like shit if they disagree with you."

"Oh, screw you."

"Case in point."

Welsh shook his head and looked away. He made eye contact with the bartender. The woman, who had a heavily wrinkled face and a long ponytail, noticed Welsh looking at her and suddenly focused so intently on her book that it was like James Patterson had found out the truth about the origin of the universe and had hidden it in his subpar fiction.

"I'm just saying, bud, you two need to stick together right now. If this guy knew what he was doing to your relationship, he would probably be happy as a clam. Now, excuse me. I gotta go take a leak."

Mo pushed himself up from the table and stumbled over in the direction of the bathroom. Welsh watched his friends' clunky feet clop along and his arms shake as he tried to maintain his equilibrium. How the man had somehow formed a string of coherent sentences when he was apparently that inebriated was baffling. Perhaps the alcohol simply affected his motor skills and not his cognitive function.

Welsh let out a sigh, feeling more agitated than ever, despite being so drunk. It was beyond frustrating to hear his best friend take sides with his wife after he had gone out of his way to meet with him just for the purposes of venting. However, what was most frustrating was that Welsh was starting to realize that Mo was right.

McCabe clicked the arrow on his monitor, letting the video fast-forward. He flexed his finger, urging the feed to speed up, but it was already zooming along as fast as it could go. He watched as the numbers in the upper right corner changed from 9:30 p.m. to 10:00 p.m., but all he saw was the same attendant pacing back and forth with his hands in his pockets.

A car pulled into the spot next to the attendant, and McCabe paused the feed and then hit rewind until the moment that the minivan had turned off the road, pausing it so he could see the plate. McCabe scribbled the number down on the notepad in front of him and then minimized the window. In another window, he typed in the number into a black screen with green font. After he hit enter several lines of writing popped up. The fact that it was not accompanied by a mugshot pretty much gave a solid answer to the question that McCabe had in his head. Sure enough…

Charles William Martin. Forty-five years old. Record clean.

McCabe let out a sigh and brought the video feed back up, clicking on the fast-forward button again. He watched as the van eventually drove off; the attendant hanging the nozzle of the pump back in its holster.

The feed read 10: 15 p.m. Nothing. 10:45 p.m. Zilch.

McCabe saw a Ford F-150 pull into the lot. He paused the feed and went through the same routine. Scribble the number down. Minimize the window. Type in the plate.

George Thomas Spencer. Sixty-three years old. This one was partnered with a mugshot of a man with a stark underbite. The green line of writing said that Spencer had been arrested for drunk-and-disorderly six years before, as well as fourth-degree assault. A standard bar fight by the looks of it. The man's face was plump and balding. McCabe clicked the thin line that made the Records and Identification window disappear again, conceding to the video.

Fast-forward to 11:15. Nada. 11:50. Nope. 12:10. Absolutely nothing.

He rubbed his eyes wearily. Sleep had been eluding him for the past few weeks. Seemingly, every waking hour was spent here, at the station, chasing ghosts. That's what Bob the Butcher was to him. An apparition. A spirit. No evidence was ever left behind. No sign that what had killed Tracy Dinwoodie, Jacey Duhart, and David Kane was anything more than a demon.

McCabe paused at 12:32 a.m. as some sort of sedan rolled into a Shell station. It was at a weird angle, so he couldn't see the make or model of the car. But it was black.

McCabe had a bit of difficulty writing down the plate this time. The numbers were just on the edge of the frame and missing the bottom halves of their symbols. He had to squint to see it. JYP272. That is what he thought he saw. He promptly typed it into R and I, but no matching vehicle was found.

Could it be a three on the end instead of a two? McCabe pressed the delete button on his keyboard and then typed a three before hitting enter.

A face popped up next to a small paragraph of green writing. It was a gaunt face, with sunken cheeks and long black hair. McCabe read the list of charges first, and his stomach clenched uncomfortably. When he scrolled up and saw the name, his heart skipped a beat.

Wendy saw the Suburban pull into the driveway, and a minute later, watched the Dodge Charger slide up against the sidewalk across the street. Her pulse ascended, and she latched her eyes back onto the book she was reading but found it nearly impossible to comprehend the words. There was a small lump in her throat and she swallowed, trying to suppress the anxiety.

Wendy had not said more than two words to her husband since their fight, and she could not decide what she was angrier at; the vicious barbs he had thrown at her or the fact that he had left afterward and Diaz had followed him, leaving her alone and unwatched in the house for several hours. At least, unwatched by friendly eyes. She had drawn the blinds to the main living room and had tucked herself into the guest bedroom that didn't have any windows, but for some reason, the hairs on the back of her neck seemed to be petrified upward the whole night, as if she could sense the presence of someone malevolent nearby.

To make the situation worse, Carson had come back stinking of booze. Wendy had imagined all the nasty things he had said to Mo, and she couldn't bear to be in the same room with him for the rest of the night. Today, since they had both decided to take time off from work until the investigation was finished, they had spent their time awkwardly finding ways to avoid eye contact and having to speak to each other. Thirty minutes before, Carson had stridden past her in the living room and muttered the word "groceries" before leaving the house.

Wendy found herself reading the same sentence over and over in the book, waiting for the sound of the door to open. Finally, the loud creak rang out and her peripheral vision caught a large figure walking over the threshold. She would have kept looking at the book, but then she noticed that he was holding something. Something red.

Roses. Carson was standing there, holding several roses in a bouquet. She moved her mouth to say something but he quickly walked over to her and placed his index finger on her lips.

"Don't. Don't talk. Just hear me out first."

He swallowed thickly and used his free hand to wipe away a bead of sweat on his temple as he sat on the couch next to her.

"I met with Mo last night. I had envisioned venting to him for an hour about what had happened while I drank my anger away. I pictured me telling him how awful you were being and him telling me that women are all crazy. But you know what? I couldn't believe it, but he took your side."

Wendy stayed frozen. She had no idea what to say or think.

"He told me I didn't know what I had in you. That you bend over backward for me. That I shouldn't be angry with you given the current circumstances. You know what I told him?"

Wendy shrugged and gave the smallest shake of her head.

"Well, actually, I told him to fuck off. But then I realized he was right."

Carson passed the flowers over to her and took her petite hand in his massive paw.

"It's been almost twenty years since we got married, and you are still the best thing to ever happen to me. I don't know what I would do if I didn't have you."

Wendy felt her face soften, and it was like a balloon had inflated in her chest.

"I remember when I was a kid, I had all these expectations for what a wife should be," continued Welsh. "Loving. Affectionate. Selfless. Cooks, cleans, takes care of you. Then, as a teen, I realized that I was setting myself up for failure by having an unrealistic vision of a life partner. And in my twenties, I went through so many women that made me look back and laugh at my expectations. Each one was the exact opposite of what I had envisioned."

He leaned in and gave her a tender kiss on the forehead.

"But when I met you, I realized that the kid in me had been right the whole time."

Wendy felt her eyes begin to well up with tears,

and at that moment, she felt a rush of passion for her husband.

"You are *everything* to me. I know I am not good at being sentimental. And I probably don't tell you this enough. But I love you. More than you will ever know."

She couldn't help it now. The first tear left a distinguishable trail down her face.

Welsh shook his head. "I am *so* sorry. I should never have gotten angry with you. This place we are at in our lives is scary. I shouldn't have ever blamed you for being scared. I am sorry that I have ever even put you in this position."

"Carson."

"I don't know who this man is. But I won't pretend that I have been perfect in my life. Whatever I have done—"

"Are you blaming *yourself?*"

Carson stared into her eyes, and he looked like a frightened child. His cheeks were slack and his jaw was twisted as if trying to fight back the emotion.

"You can't do that," said Wendy. "You can't do that to yourself. This man is *sick. Diseased.* This has nothing to do with what you have done. This only has to do with what he is."

He looked down for a second and gave the tiniest of nods.

"I'm sorry," he mumbled. "I'm so sorry."

Wendy reached out and lifted his chin up so that their eyes were locked again. Before he could apologize again, she kissed him.

"Does that mean you forgive me?"

Wendy gave a tiny chuckle and kissed him again. Soon, their lips were in constant motion, creating hot friction in the space between their mouths. She was kissing him passionately, like she was afraid she would never get a chance to do so again. She felt his hand on the small of her back begin to creep into her shirt, and almost subconsciously, she began to undo his belt, and felt the hard lump press against her wrist. Wendy leaned in to his ear and whispered, "Let's go into the bedroom."

He gazed at her for a second, and suddenly, she felt her stomach swoop as he lifted her into the air. A euphoric giggle escaped her, and he kissed her again while carrying her through the air. For a fleeting moment, they were newlyweds again, barely able to contain the passion as they hurtled toward the bed.

"I know it is cliché to say this after make-up sex, but that was the best we've done in years."

Their chests were both raising and then falling

in sync, and they were each covered in sweat. The smell of musk permeated the room, and the sheets they were laying on were completely damp. Wendy had her head on his chest, and her hand was laying against his belly.

"I agree." He gave her another peck on the lips. "It's not often you hear my voice get that high-pitched."

Wendy giggled and scratched around his belly button affectionately. "Remember the first time we had sex? In my apartment downtown?"

"Well, I remember that you told me I broke a floral vase you had with my ass."

"Funnily enough that isn't the only thing I remember you breaking with your ass over the years. How was the sex that first time? Do you remember?"

Welsh tried to summon the recollection, but nothing came.

"No. Ever since the wreck my long-term memory is hazy at best."

"Mm." Wendy almost sounded a little disappointed.

"But I do remember the time we almost got caught screwing in the hotel by the cleaning lady."

Welsh sat there, pondering the face of the housekeeper that had almost seen them copulating. But he couldn't bring up anything in his mind's eye.

After a few moments of being lost in thought,

Wendy broke the silence. "You know what we should do?"

"What?"

"We should go out to dinner tonight. Some place really nice."

"Yeah? Are you going to buy?"

She gave him a playful smack on the chest.

"Where were you thinking exactly?" asked Welsh.

"I didn't really have anything in mind. Where is the nicest place you have ever been?"

"Probably Olive Garden."

Wendy rolled her eyes while Welsh laughed.

"Okay, okay, uh… I don't know. Maybe Imperial?"

"You've been to Imperial?"

"Uh, yeah. It was for some function. A gala, I think. It was pretty nice."

A smile lit up Wendy's face. "All right then. Let's go there."

Almost simultaneously with this sentence, the phone rang from the living room. It made Wendy jump, and then she looked at Welsh with raised eyebrows.

"You have a phone here?"

"Yeah. The landlines been there for years. Phone company turned off when my folks passed. I just turned it back on this morning. But I only gave one person the number."

Feeling a sense of apprehension, Welsh hopped out of the bed in his boxer shorts.

"Be right back, hun."

He crossed the threshold into the living room and made his way over to the whining phone. With a deep breath, he picked it up and held it to his ear.

"Hello?"

"Carson?"

"Yeah."

"It's Emily."

Welsh heard the rhythmic thump of his heart in his ears as his pulse began to ascend.

"Well, I figured. You are the only one who has this number."

"You need to come to the station. ASAP," said Arroyo, and her voice was filled with some emotion that Welsh hadn't heard yet. Was that excitement?

"And why is that, Emily?"

"Because I think we found Robert Macabre."

"You can't stay?"

"Wendy, trust me, there is nothing in the world I want more than to be with you right now. But you know I *have* to go. I will explain when I get home. I will be back as soon as I can."

"What about dinner?"

Welsh looked at his wife and felt a rush of tenderness for her. She was looking up at him with wide eyes, like a puppy dog that knew its owner was about to abscond for a more important task.

"If this drags out too long, I will make sure and tell Flask I have a dinner date at seven."

"Imperial?"

"You betchya."

"Won't we need a reservation?" Wendy asked.

"I'll pull some strings."

He shuffled back and forth, gathering his wallet and the car keys and then buttoning up his shirt. His pants were still unbuttoned, and they sagged lamely and rather comically while his dress shirt looked pristine and wrinkle-less.

"You promise me you will be back for it?"

Welsh felt another bubble of warmth in his chest and stared into those big green eyes with affection.

"I promise."

He kissed her on the cheek and left the room.

Welsh stared at the face on the projector screen and felt goose bumps prickling up his spine. There was something in those eyes. Something haunting. The man's cheeks were sunken in, and it vaguely reminded Welsh of Dracula. He had had a sharp, pointed nose, and long, greasy brown hair that cloaked his face in shadow. His thin lips were pressed so hard together that there was a stark purple color to them. His expression had sort of a veiled menace to it. He looked to be ready to burst through the photograph with unbridled rage.

"William Robert Tennyson," said Arroyo triumphantly. "This picture was taken in ninety-nine, just after he had been arrested for possession and distribution of contraband; mainly, LSD. If you remember, both Tracy Dinwoodie and Jacey Duhart were positive for LSD."

McCabe, who was standing next to her, stepped forward. "Tennyson has been out of prison since two thousand two. Has a permanent address of 434 North West Ember Lane. However, the place was foreclosed six months ago, and Tennyson never updated his address on any documents. Current whereabouts unknown."

The burly black man loosened the tie around his neck and reached for a sheet that was in front of him on the table. He held it up, showing it to everyone else around the room. The picture was of a black car parked at a gas station. There was a time stamp in the upper-righthand corner, but Welsh couldn't quite make out what it said.

McCabe cleared his throat. "I pulled video from a local Shell Station on the night that David Kane's right hand was left on Welsh's porch. The Shell is less than a two-minute drive from Welsh's house, and the only pump for about twenty miles. I had to scour through hours of footage, but at 12:32 a.m., approximately thirty-six minutes from when Welsh put four bullets in his front door, I saw this black 1994 Ford Taurus roll into the lot. I ran the plate, and it was registered to Tennyson."

Arroyo then reached toward the table and grabbed a photo she held up for everyone around the room to see. It was of the package that David Kane's hand had been left in.

"As you all know, we found a partial on this package. It was barely a print, but it was there. Thanks to Ryan," said Arroyo, nodding at Dunny, who was at the end of the table. "We were able to overlay the partial with Tennyson's prints. It matched."

Welsh felt a swooping sensation in his gut. Was this nightmare nearing an end after all?

After the dramatic pause, Arroyo continued. "Now, Tennyson doesn't just have the drug charges on his record. In 1993, he was arrested for B and E, as well as battery and assault two. He broke into a woman's house in the middle of the night and beat her. Broke her jaw and cracked two of her ribs. His DNA was found under her fingernails; she said she had scratched him in self-defense."

"We believe this was his first attempt at murder but he botched it, and when Claire Foley was screaming her head off, he had to flee," added McCabe. "He tried to claim that it was just a robbery attempt, but he beat her to a pulp and nothing was taken from the house."

He looked back over at Arroyo, and the chemistry between the two of them was palpable.

"And if you folks still aren't convinced, remember that Tracy Dinwoodie was found wearing the goat mask, and we found Jacey Duhart with the head of a horse sewn to her neck," said Arroyo. "Logic would dictate that Bob the Butcher wears a different animal mask for every kill. And I bet you'll never guess where William Robert Tennyson grew up."

A few seconds of silence, and then, suddenly, it clicked in Welsh's head.

"A farm."

Arroyo looked at him and nodded. Her face was filled with triumph.

"We will get this guy, Carson."

Welsh felt like a football player ready to charge out of the locker room before a game. He wanted to stand up and chest-bump McCabe and give Arroyo a hug. But then he remembered the most important part.

"So wait, where is he?"

McCabe looked over at Arroyo apprehensively before replying. "We are getting a list of KA's, relatives, friends. He has been missing since jumping parole. Don't worry. We will find him."

Without warning, Marty Flask stood up out of his chair, and all eyes turned to him.

"We need to find him quick. Before it gets out that we have a suspect."

Arroyo's eyes shifted back and forth sarcastically.

"Yeah, workin' on it, boss."

"The leak, remember? I swear, if I read even one syllable of William Tennyson's name in the *Oregonian*, I will probably have a stroke."

Arroyo shrugged. "If you are that concerned we could issue an all-state APB—"

"No. If the leak is police, that will blow the whole thing up. If we put in something like that it won't be more than five minutes that whoever it is puts two and two together. Just move with stealth. And most importantly, *pace.* I don't want this story in the paper until the guy is in cuffs. Or dead."

"I'm already pullin' some old contacts from my time in narco. See if I can get a tip as to where this guy might be. If he is dealin', somebody out there will know how to find him," said McCabe.

"That's a good start," said Flask, nodding. "Emily, do you know who Tennyson's cellmate was when he was at OSP? If he spent a lengthy amount of time with the same person, there might be a chance that that person knows where to find him."

"Andre Crowder. Already working on tracking him down."

"Good… Good. Welsh—"

Welsh looked up.

"Keep your head down for the next few days. Don't tell anyone where you are or what you are doing. Make sure Diaz is in your shadow at all times."

"That's the plan."

"It's safe to assume that if this guy finds out that we are onto him, that he'll make one last-ditch effort to come after you. So stay inside. Try not to be seen. If he gets on your tail he could just follow you out to Wilsonville."

"Portland is small, Marty," replied Welsh. "But not that small. I don't think the chances of running into him at the grocery store are particularly high."

"Regardless. Until we nab him, lay low. Got it?"

"Got it."

Flask rubbed his hands together like he was trying to stay warm. Or rather, like he was an arch-villain hatching a dastardly plan. There was a look of calm, purposeful determination on his face.

"Now let's go bring this cocksucker down."

The phone rang only three times before Wendy answered it. Her voice seemed to be filled with nervous energy.

"Hello?"

"I'm on my way home now. Be there in twenty minutes."

Wendy made a noise of surprise. "Well, look at you. A man of your word, after all."

Welsh chuckled. "Did I ever stray? Better get ready, sweetheart. Can't go to Imperial in sweatpants and a T-shirt."

"Did you already call?"

"Yep. They have a table set aside for us."

Wendy gave a little squeak of excitement. "I guess I will have to find a blouse that I won't be totally embarrassed to be seen in."

"Pick something black. Flask says we are supposed to be inconspicuous."

"Really?"

"Well, not exactly. He sort of told me to just keep my head down and stay home for the next few days until it is done. But a promise is a promise."

"What are you talking about Carson? Until what is done?"

Welsh took a deep breath and tried to keep the excitement out of his voice.

"They know who he is, Wendy. They are looking for him now."

Silence. At least five long seconds of nothing while Wendy processed what he had said.

"What's his name?"

"I'll tell you in person," said Welsh hurriedly. "I'll explain everything when I get there."

"Do they know where he is?"

"Babe, I can't say over the phone. I will see you in twenty minutes, okay? Start getting ready. I'll swing by and pick you up."

"Okay."

"And don't actually wear black. Wear white. Or red. You've always looked good in red."

Wendy chuckled and lowered her voice.

"Better hurry. I ain't got all night."

"I'll be there before you can say Imperial. I love you."

"I love you too."

After he hung up, Welsh pressed down on the gas pedal with fervor. The big black beast sped along interstate five, passing three cars without mercy. Welsh tightened his grip on the steering wheel as the Suburban bobbed and weaved through several lanes of traffic, and the black sedan that was piloted by his protective detail tried desperately to keep up. Welsh almost felt amused at the fact that Diaz was going to have to supervise their date night from afar. But at the moment, nothing could dampen the mood; for the first time in weeks, it seemed like he was finally on the precipice of waking up from the nightmare.

William Robert Tennyson was Macabre. Welsh knew it in his gut. Just by appraising the man's mugshot, he could sense something awry there. Welsh could see it at the edges of his eyes. A covert darkness reaching its claws out of the abyss. Tennyson had a demon. It was apparent just by the expression that had been on his face.

Welsh had thought the whole time that this was some attempt at vengeance for a perceived misdeed. But he had never seen Tennyson before in his life. He had not been the one who had prosecuted the man. So why did Tennyson have such an obsession with him? Was it just a general malcontent with the criminal justice system? A blind odium toward the cyclical, self-serving reaper that puts thousands of men and women behind bars every single day? Maybe Tennyson had chosen Welsh as a vessel for his blanket loathing. Or maybe it was personal, and the district attorney had somehow wronged someone that Tennyson was close to. But do sociopaths actually get close to other people? Whatever the answers were to the riddles, they would be unveiled soon. Flask and the gang were hot on his tail. And though Welsh didn't see eye to eye with him, he had to admit that Flask was a *helluva* closer. When the man locked in on a target, that target was going down.

Pumping on the break, Welsh felt his stomach clench as he almost rear-ended the minivan in front of him.

"Shit!"

Without thinking twice about it, he raised the middle finger of his right hand, though the driver of the van was not looking. Sure, the fault had been with Welsh for tailgating, but anger seemed to supersede logic at that point in time, so he switched to the right lane and pumped the bird out of the open window as he passed.

Welsh was normally a fairly cautious, defensive driver, but at this moment, he was in such a hurry that his common frame of mind had evanesced into the atmosphere. For some reason, he was so eager to get back to Wendy. Perhaps it was the wonderful sex that left a residual feeling. Maybe because the love they had made was so passionate, it had reinvigorated feelings between them. Or it could simply be that what Welsh had told her was true. She was the only thing in the world that mattered to him.

The exit to Wilsonville finally came, and Welsh pulled off on the ramp. He was driving the Suburban like the sports car he had used to own, lurching forward at breakneck speed and cutting corners. He pistoned his foot with slightly more pressure against the accelerator, and the car reeled forward forcefully. For a fleeting moment, he felt a hankering to go even faster, but logic finally won out. Welsh looked around nervously, but then he remembered that his protective detail that was surely not far behind would be able to circumvent any speeding citation if another officer got a little overzealous about the ticket quota his bosses had assigned.

Five minutes later, he turned on to Wellspring Way, and was only two blocks away from the house. The area had only small homes, but the ones that were there formed some perfect, synergetic neighborhood. It was like each house was evenly spaced between the other, and you could almost glean a sense of what these sorts of people were like by gazing at the exterior of the buildings. Tidy, organized, and disinterested in opulence or show. He could see why his parents had chosen this particular neighborhood.

Welsh looked in his rearview mirror, but did not see Diaz's black Charger behind him. Perhaps the man was only a little behind. Welsh took a left and saw the house come into sight.

Instead of pulling into the driveway, he maneuvered the vehicle against the sidewalk. There was no point in pulling in and then having to reverse right back out. He shifted the car in park, stuffed the keys into his pocket, and hopped out of the rig.

The first thing he noticed was how much the temperature had dipped just in the twenty minutes he had been on the road. It had to have been almost ten degrees cooler, but that also made sense because the sun was barely peeking its head out from the west now. Everything was a shade of hazy blue. Welsh strode up the pathway with a bit more pep in his step than usual.

For some reason, he was actually a little nervous. It was like it was the first time he had ever taken his wife out on a date. He should have combed his hair or brushed his teeth. Welsh began to absentmindedly brush the stray follicles on top of his head, a last-ditch effort to regain some sort of administration over his do. His heart was fluttering along anxiously, as if he were about to see his high school prom date in her dress for the first time.

They should do this more often. Date nights. Nice restaurants. Ice cream. Maybe even a movie or two.

Welsh climbed the two steps to the front porch and reached out for the door handle. Without warning, his hand froze in mid-air and he felt a stab in his chest, but he wasn't sure why at first. Then his eyes locked onto the spot. There was the tiniest sliver of space in between the jam and the wood of the door. It was open.

Time crawled to a glacial pace. He knew reasonably that he couldn't be moving in slow-motion, so why did it seem like he was fighting through quick sand? He shoved the door open and heard it slam against the wall. Then, strangely, he listened to the sound of his own warped voice yelling her name like it didn't belong to him at all.

"Wendy! Wendy!"

His shrieks were primitive and discombobulated. She wasn't in the living room. And just the sheer fact that there was silence in response to his screams told him everything. It was already over.

"Wendy!"

Welsh looked frantically back and forth, first down the hallway, and then into the open door to the bathroom where the light was still on.

Everything looked untouched, collecting dust, just the way he left it. No sign of a struggle. Nothing disturbed. He must have taken her by surprise.

There was only one spot that she could be. The bedroom. Welsh hesitated, knowing that what he was about to see would rip apart his whole world. Maybe if he just walked out, there would be a mulligan. Maybe the world would reset and he would find a different scene inside this house. But no. There was no direction but forward. And forward he charged.

Welsh swung the door open with a mighty shove, nearly taking it off its hinges. And there she was. Spread-eagled out on the bed, her white blouse covered in red. His beautiful Wendy, now somewhere where he would never be able to speak to her again, with a six-inch gash across her throat.

He sat there, feeling nothing. Deadened, like it was just a peculiar dream. They all seemed so distant; two feet might as well have been two acres. Their mouths were taking turns moving, and yet, each word was rejected like his ears were sealed passageways. Welsh pictured every syllable as a physical thing that bounced and reverberated off of his skull and back out into the atmosphere. He was vaguely aware that he was shaking. Her blood was all over his shirt and hands, now dried and caked like it was just sweat.

"Carson?"

He looked up, but his eyes did not see Arroyo. They were misted over, far away from this place. This stuffy room at the police station. All he saw was the chunk missing out of her throat.

Flask was packing back and forth, compulsively rubbing his head. "Is it catatonic shock? Did he say anything in the car?"

Arroyo looked back at McCabe, who shrugged his shoulders. She remained crouched like a catcher in front of Welsh with a stony, frightened expression on her face.

"No. He didn't," said Arroyo quietly.

Flask continued to stride back and forth. "Should we take him to the hospital? For psychiatric evaluation?"

"Probably. But I don't want him to think we are making him someone else's problem."

Welsh was looking at a spot on the floor now, and his head felt heavy. He turned his hands over, seeing more caked blood on his palms and noticing a pattern of streaks that looked like lightning slicing through the muck. So much blood.

"Carson."

A small hand on his shoulder. He looked at like it was foul and useless. He almost felt an urge to bite down; use his teeth to cleave through skin and flesh and bone, so that no one would ever touch him again.

"I'm so sorry. I'm so sorry. We are going to get this fucker, I swear. We are going to make him hurt."

It was the first time that Welsh had ever heard Arroyo curse. It was a little jarring and almost unnatural. Arroyo's eyes were narrowed and her lip quivered as though she was trying to hold back tears.

"I'm so sorry—"

"Emily."

Flask said her name with reproach. Arroyo looked back at him and then stood up, her shoulders slumped.

McCabe began to speak. "We are closing in, Welsh. I got a tip from a former CI from my time in narco. He thinks a dealer named Roland Kahlil may be able to give us Tennyson. My guy is tracking Kahlil down as we speak."

Welsh didn't even perk up a little bit. Everything was still muted and out of focus, like he had just woken up from a multi-year slumber. Welsh looked up into the light and a vivid image of her body, sallow, lifeless, and covered in red, flashed in front of his face. The gaping hole just below her chin.

"She's dead."

It took a second for Welsh to process that he was the one who had said the words, for the voice did not sound like his and the assertion was so patently palpable and obvious. Why had he said it? Did he need confirmation from the detectives to reinforce the horrible truth? Had the image of her mangled throat not been tangible enough? Or had he never foreseen a world without his wife?

None of the three people said anything in response to this. They just swapped glances and stared back down at him, collapsed and nearly comatose in the chair.

"Wendy."

Just more silence. Flask was looking at him with fear in his eyes; Arroyo looked like she felt sick.

"I'll find her." Welsh realized as he said it that it did not make any sense.

"You'll do what?"

"I'll find her."

And the dam burst. For the first time in years, Welsh cried.

"Aw, hell." Flask looked away like it was something he shouldn't be watching. Welsh doubled over, and the sobs were so powerful that it seemed like his torso could combust at any moment. His eyes became swollen and his vision was almost completely obscured by the tears, but he noticed those same pale fingers reaching out and gripping onto his shoulder. For a fleeting moment, he snatched it up as though it was Wendy's consoling hand. Welsh held on tight, like it was an anchor to the world and if he let go, he would float away into oblivion. He continued to wail away, rocking back and forth and shaking violently. But the person he was crying for would never again wipe away his tears. And his heart was suddenly stone.

"Get him to a hospital." Flask's voice was stern and almost a bark. "Now."

30

"I can't believe this has happened."

Flask didn't answer. Arroyo wasn't really expecting him to.

"I have seen some pretty gut-wrenching things in my life. But watching that in there may have been the worst. I will never forget that."

Flask looked out the window as she drove along. He seemed to be focusing on every passing streetlight and sidewalk like it was the most interesting thing in the world. Outside, there was the dark golden haze that reflected nighttime on the highway, and Arroyo's eyes squinted at the road in front of her. Her vision had never been very good, but at nighttime, she was a few steps away from being legally blind. She supposed it was her own stubbornness that contributed to the problem, but she hated the look of her glasses, and contacts made her pupils burn.

"It's one thing looking at a DB that you never knew. I mean, when you see your first, it's shocking, but after the third or fourth, you become desensitized to it. It's just like looking at any other dead animal. A little revolting, but not something you are really going to lose a lot of sleep over. But that? I'll never forget what it was like seeing that."

"You said that."

"I underestimated this man, Marty," continued Arroyo as though Flask hadn't spoken at all. "What he is willing to do. I thought he was calculating. Analytical. Careful. But this shows me he is not afraid to be in prison. Or killed. Whatever sick fantasy he is playing out, he will keep doing so with reckless abandon until we stop him."

Flask grunted.

"This isn't your normal hot period," said Arroyo. "When most sociopaths are killing more rapidly, they are simply losing control. Their sexual urges to kill supersede their need to plan it all out like they did before. And then they always end up making a mistake. DNA left behind. Prints. But this isn't that. Tennyson doesn't seem to care that he is going to be caught. He's going out with all guns blazing. Hell, I wouldn't be surprised if we find out that he left that print behind intentionally."

"He wouldn't have left just a partial if that was true," grumbled Flask.

"Yeah, well, the point remains. He knows he is

going down. And he wants to take as many people down with him as he can."

"Mm."

"You don't agree?"

Flask didn't respond. He just kept looking out the window like he was reading the name of every passing business and each individual street sign.

"Marty?

"You gleaned a lot more from this than I did."

Arroyo frowned. "Well, what do you think—"

"We knew he was targeting Welsh from the beginning. You read that letter. Frankly, I am surprised that *you're* surprised."

Arroyo's jaw opened and she began to sputter in protest. "Wait, wha—? So you are saying that you knew Tennyson was going to murder Welsh's wife?"

"You know that is not what I am saying," replied Flask, his voice filled with aggravation.

"Then what are you—"

Flask twitched with irritation. "That we knew he was batshit crazy from the moment he sent us that video. And we knew he had some vendetta or score to settle with Welsh. So the fact that there was a casualty doesn't mean that this is some sort of... unmanageable evil. It just means he made good on his word."

"I wasn't saying—"

"What happened this evening changes nothing

about the way we will pursue this investigation. We were already exhausting every avenue to find Tennyson before Wendy Welsh was killed. And we are going to catch him. I promise you that."

Arroyo let this proclamation hang in the air for a while. She adjusted her grip on the steering wheel and noticed how clammy her palms had become. She watched as the speedometer slowly creeped toward the number seventy and didn't even bother to relinquish the pressure she was putting on the gas pedal. Normally, Arroyo was fairly strict about following the rules of the road. But not tonight. Tonight, it was like every mile per hour the needle climbed was another step closer to catharsis.

"Do you think Ray will come through?"

Flask gave the smallest shrug of his shoulders. "I don't know. He seemed fairly confident. But confidence has never really been an issue with Ray."

"He's pulled out the stops from his time in narco before. In the Dockery case, it definitely served a purpose."

Flask kept his voice monotone. "But there have also been times when it has been a dead end."

"Well, you are just a fountain of optimism, aren't you?"

"They don't pay me to be an optimist. And if you'd seen the things I have seen, you wouldn't be one either."

Arroyo glanced at her boss.

"I *have* seen the things that you have seen."

"No, you haven't. Not all of them."

Arroyo flicked the lever underneath the steering wheel, and the dashboard of the Crown Vic clicked rhythmically as she turned. Her thoughts went right back to Welsh, convulsing and bawling back at the station. The man had been remarkably silent on the ride over to Legacy Emanuel Medical Center. Arroyo had looked into his eyes through the rearview mirror and found only a shell. A husk of the person that had been there just hours before. When they had arrived at the hospital, the nurses reassured them he was in good hands, but Arroyo still had a bad feeling about the whole thing.

"I feel so horrible for him, Marty."

"So do I."

"Do you think he is a danger to himself?"

Flask took a moment to consolidate and organize his thoughts, biting his lower lip in concentration. "Before tonight, I would have told you that Carson Welsh absolutely loves being Carson Welsh. I would have laughed in your face if you had suggested something like that. But now, after what we just saw… I don't know."

Arroyo felt her stomach sink. "I hope they can help him. Mental health in this country isn't treated like physical health. You blow out your knee, the doctors do surgery, make you immobile for weeks and then stick you in rehab for a month. You show signs of being suicidal? They tell you you'll feel better and then send you on your merry way."

"I didn't realize you were an expert in the medical field."

The vehicle stopped at a red light and Arroyo turned her head toward him skeptically.

"Are you not concerned?"

Flask rubbed his square jaw with vigor. "Concerned is probably not the best adjective to describe what I am feeling at this point in time, Emily."

"Well, how are you feeling, *Marty*?" When she said his name, her voice was dripping with sarcasm and cynicism.

Flask sighed deeply and pursed his lips.

"I'm exhausted."

Arroyo was going to snap back with another derisive comment, but then she stopped and mulled it over, realizing the truth of the matter.

"Yeah. Me too."

31

McCabe took the shot of Jameson in a single swig, feeling it burn his throat on the way down, and when it settled in his stomach, it seemed to bubble even hotter. He grabbed the beer that he had ordered and used it as a chaser, washing the remaining bitterness of whiskey out of his mouth. The old male bartender with long brown hair and glasses was staring at him apprehensively.

"Long day?"

"You could say that."

"Want another?"

"Maybe after I finish this beer."

"You got it, champ."

McCabe looked around Danny's Bar and Grill, scanning for a familiar face. But there was none there. It appeared he would have to wait around a little longer. He glanced down at the half-empty beer and thought to himself that he should probably slow down. If he was hammered, his decision-making skills would obviously be deadened, which wasn't exactly conducive for what he had planned.

There was a huge throng of people around the pool tables on the other side of the bar, though only a few of them seemed to be actually playing. McCabe's eyes went from face to face, and none stood out. They were mostly college-aged kids, which made sense. Not many people were particularly eager to go out and get wasted in the middle of the week, unless you were in college and consumed alcohol *every* day of the week. The young men and women were loud and irritatingly jovial. At that age, it was so easy to be happy-go-lucky. All there was to worry about was finals and writing papers. They hadn't gotten out into the unforgiving world yet. All of those kids were too young to have suffered the biting reality of living. The vast majority of them hadn't lost a parent, or a sibling. So carefree. So relaxed. None of them had any idea that just a few miles from where they were was a freshly widowed man who had just found his wife brutally murdered.

The speakers were blaring some horrid mellow alternative song. The singer of said tune had barely put anything into it; his voice was intentionally muffled and indiscernible. It was a strange technique in indie rock, to sound like you are drunk and fatigued while crooning away into the audio recorder. McCabe hated it and took another large swallow of beer as if to dull the sound of the shitty music in his ears.

"You know, drinking by yourself isn't considered a healthy outlet there, friend."

McCabe raised his eyebrows at the bartender who had interrupted his stupor, but the man didn't balk. His long hair was ragged and unkempt. The man had large glasses that magnified his eyes to insect-level, and he was wearing a tie-dye shirt that had the logo of the bar printed on the front of it.

McCabe frowned. "What business is it of yours what I do in my personal time?"

The bartender raised his hands in the air in faux surrender. "I'm just saying. I don't think many people would be comfortable knowing that one of the men who is in charge of defending the city is out here putting a load on all by his lonesome. People might think said city defender might have a problem."

"How did you know—"

"That you are a cop?" The bartender wheezed in what was apparently supposed to be a chuckle. "I can tell just by looking at you. The way you carry yourself."

McCabe took another sip of his beer and held it in his mouth for a while, savoring the taste. "As much as I'd like to believe that the bartender at my favorite watering hole is that clairvoyant, you are setting my bullshit meter off there, uh…"

"Danny." The bartender completed the sentence for him, and McCabe leaned in as though he didn't hear him correctly.

"Danny? As in—"

"Don't look so surprised, friend. Just because I look like a hippie doesn't mean I can't be a successful business owner."

"Not many owners bartend at their own bar, Danny."

"How else am I supposed to get a feel for the inner-workings of this place? I bet those boys who ran up on the beach on D-Day knew a hell of a lot more about war than the politicians who made them do it."

"What a metaphor."

Danny laughed. "I'm full of witty asides, friend."

"You keep calling me that, but—"

"We aren't friends? Well, that just ruins my whole day, Raymond."

McCabe froze, staring into the man's eyes. There was a twinkle there; some sort of mischievous and enigmatic sparkle.

"Well, shit, Danny, maybe you are clairvoyant after all. Maybe you are just a stone's throw away from psychic. How did you know my name?"

The same wheezy giggle, and Danny seemed to be having the most marvelous time ribbing the man in front of him.

"You are impressed by me knowing a name? Well, *shit*."

Without warning, Danny leaned in close to McCabe and whispered, "Then you are going to be really impressed that I know that you are here to meet your CI. That he was supposed to give you an address that he got from Roland Kahlil. That this whole thing might be connected to that girl they found up in Mount Tabor Park."

McCabe could smell something foul on the man's breath. He recoiled, partly from the stench and also because he was suddenly very afraid.

"Thing is, your buddy is in so deep with Kahlil that he can't be seen meeting with a cop at said cop's favorite watering hole. That is the bad news. The good news is, we have mutual friends, Ray."

Danny leaned back with that same mischievous expression on his face. He tucked a strand of his long hair behind his ear, and the wrinkles on his face became more pronounced as he grinned.

"So how about this? You go take a leak. And when you get back, I may have something for you here."

McCabe stared at Danny nervously. Why hadn't his guy let him know about the change of plan? Could this all be some elaborate ruse?

As much as he wanted to ask a million questions right then and there, McCabe slowly pushed himself up from the stool he was seated on, causing it to scrape against the floor loudly. Keeping his eyes on Danny, he grabbed a coaster and placed it on top of his beer, as if the bartender might drop something nefarious inside. The man just let out another chuckle, grabbed a rag, and began wiping down a spot in front of him, no longer focused on the detective. McCabe turned about, his heart beating steadily, and trudged over toward the restroom.

As he opened the door, he saw that the floor was wet inside, and McCabe tried not to think about whether it was water or urine. He simply tiptoed over it to the tallest urinal, unzipped his pants, and began to relieve himself.

The door opened, and a tall stranger moseyed on by, and for some reason, chose the urinal directly next to McCabe instead of the one farther over.

"Not familiar with bathroom etiquette, eh?"

The man didn't say anything. He didn't even acknowledge that McCabe was talking to him. McCabe rolled his eyes, and as soon as he was finished, he tucked himself back into his slacks and zipped up quickly, wanting to get out of range of the man who was broaching his personal space. He went to the sink and started to wash his hands.

This did seem like the sort of thing that used to happen in narco. A change of plan at the last minute in the name of secrecy. But why hadn't his CI told him? Was he really that paranoid? Did he think Kahlil was onto him? Or, maybe, Danny was actually working for the kingpin dealer, and had somehow gotten word of this meeting. Maybe he was on the phone right now, telling someone scary and important that McCabe was here.

McCabe dried his hands on a paper towel that he discarded and pushed his way out of the bathroom. The first thing he noticed was that Danny had not kept his post at the bar. In fact, he didn't seem to be anywhere at all. McCabe's eyes rotated back and forth, but he did not see the long brown hair, nor the crinkled face. He did notice that a dark man at a booth nearby had his eyes locked onto him. The man was bald and had a menacing expression on his face. Another agent of Kahlil, perhaps?

McCabe walked toward the bar cautiously, keeping his head on a swivel. He tried not to look over at the thin, bald-headed black man that had been staring. In all likelihood, he was just being unreasonable. Some people just couldn't keep their eyes to themselves. The odds of the bald man and Danny both being in league with Kahlil and teaming up to roll over on him right here in the bar were infinitesimal. McCabe began to relax, letting his shoulders slack. His over-working, paranoid mind had just been running amuck again.

When McCabe got to the bar, he leaned over it,

looking back and forth as though Danny might be tucked into a corner hiding. He saw the kitchen door and wondered if the bartender had disappeared behind it. McCabe decided to stay put for just a few seconds longer before departing. If by chance this *was* some conspiracy, he shouldn't linger. But also, he was never a man to waist a beer. He looked down at his half-drunk Pabst Blue Ribbon and was on the verge of chugging it when he realized something strange. The coaster was no longer sitting on top of it. It was off to the side, lingering like something in a painting that had moved upon second glance.

McCabe reached out and lifted the coaster off the bar. When he saw what was underneath it, his neck swiftly turned back toward the bald man. But the stranger was no longer looking at him, so McCabe gathered the scrawl of paper that had been left under the coaster, and tucked it into his pocket.

"All right, gentlemen. The time has come." Arroyo clicked the laser pointer and directed it at the graphic that was brought up on the projector. It was a three-dimensional topographical map, outlaying various trees, hills, and even a large body of water.

"The coordinates given to us by Ray's informant direct us to *this* cabin on a hill next to Vancouver Lake, just across the bridge in Washington." She let the red dot linger on a brown spot on the map. It was vaguely discernable that it was a cabin, but it just as easily could have been part of the hill it was sitting on. "Intel puts Tennyson at this spot. This is where dealers have been instructed to drive when buying product. So it is safe to assume that this cabin is a drug house, used primarily to cook LSD and meth."

The SWAT team and various officers in front of her exchanged glances with one another, and one of the men in the front row seemed to grunt involuntarily.

"Now, the tricky thing is, the cabin is on a fairly steep hill. Meaning, that if Tennyson knows we are coming, he'll have a pretty good vantage point from up above if he starts firing."

"Is that likely?" The same deputy who had grunted posed the question apprehensively.

"If he doesn't know we are coming, I would say no."

"How would he know we are coming?"

Arroyo shrugged. "If he sees us."

A long pause as everyone gathered their thoughts. Lieutenant Don Chaser was the next to speak.

"Why don't we just come at him from the other side?"

"It's inaccessible. There was a landslide several months ago and nobody in Clark County has ever gotten around to fixing it. Essentially, it is little more than a cliff."

Chaser scoffed, his white mustache bristling as he exhaled through his nose. "Okay, so how are we going to get up there without him seeing us?"

"We will post up in this field that is a hundred yards away from the hill and proceed on foot through the trees. The forest is thick, so it shouldn't be too difficult to stay hidden for most of the trek."

"Why don't we just make this a night op?" One

of the SWAT with a thick forehead that made him look like a crab under a rock had spoken up.

"Because we can't afford to wait. For all we know, he could somehow get word of us coming, and hightail it into Canada."

"I don't like it," said Chaser suddenly. Everyone in the room locked eyes upon him.

Arroyo's eyes flicked back and forth. "You don't like what?"

"Charging up this mountain on foot, waiting for this nutjob to spot us and start spraying."

"Well, if you have an alternative, please share it."

Chaser started to reply, but then sucked the words back in and bit his lip. When it was apparent that he would not continue, Arroyo proceeded with relaying the plan.

"Once we get to the cabin, no M-80s, no smoke. No flashers either. This is a drug lab, so if we throw something combustible inside, the whole thing could go up."

"That wouldn't be the worst thing," muttered the same SWAT with the heavy forehead. Arroyo looked at him with resentment and impatience.

"Let's get one thing straight, gentlemen. We want him alive. End of story. If you shoot him, it better be because he is unloading a clip with the gun pointing in your direction. This isn't a hit. We are bringing him in to answer for his crimes. And he can't answer if he's dead."

Silence. Some of the SWAT were looking at her in defiance, but most of the deputies were nodding in agreement. McCabe was giving her an enigmatic side-eye; Arroyo wasn't quite sure what he was thinking.

"All right, well. If there are no other rebuttals, let's go catch ourselves a serial killer."

The line of men slithered through the trees with the muzzles of their MP5s knifing through the bushes, ready to fire. There wasn't a clear path to walk, so many of them had to clamber over fallen branches or rogue blackberry plants. They were all doing their best to keep quiet, but it was shocking how much noise they made. Every crack of a stick or crunch of a leaf made Arroyo's heart leap into her throat. McCabe was only a few feet in front of her, and his towering body made it difficult to see. Visibility was already an issue anyway, and she had no idea where they were going. Rigsby, the SWAT commander, was leading the way with buoyancy and poise, so she simply kept him in her sights. Or, at least, the man that she thought was Rigsby. The SWAT all looked similar, with their dark blue uniforms and their matching helmets. Each police officer stood out like a sore thumb and seemed startlingly vulnerable without headgear. Up and up they climbed, and her thighs burned angrily. The hill was getting steeper; her breath more ragged by the second. She had never worn a bullet-proof vest for this long before, and it was getting uncomfortable.

Arroyo gripped her pistol so tightly that her hands were slightly shaking. She hadn't been an expert marksman with her gun in training, so she was hoping and praying that she wouldn't have to fire it.

Crack.

Everyone tensed in unison at the noise, and Arroyo instinctively ducked her head. When she peeked upward, she saw Rigsby holding his fist into the air, signaling to everyone that they should freeze. Arroyo looked frantically back and forth for the source of the noise, but there was nothing. Not even a rabbit scampering across the woods, or a deer bolting away. Perhaps one of them had inadvertently stepped on a particularly large fallen branch. But the noise had sounded so malicious, like a predator coiling against the soil, ready to leap on its prey.

Rigsby rotated his head left and right and then froze at a forty-five-degree angle as if waiting for a subsequent sound. All that came was the cawing of several geese overhead, making their way north. It was eerie to listen to, and for some reason it made her think of those scenes in movies when a flock of birds fly away frantically to signal something ominous approaching.

Eventually, Rigsby looked back and then chopped through the air with his index and middle fingers, indicating to keep moving. They all continued their creep up the hill; slowly, apprehensively, knowing that they were at a positional disadvantage.

Arroyo heard the hiss of a radio, and everyone stopped again.

"Charlie Three to Echo One."

Rigsby dropped his supporting hand off of his gun and snatched the radio attached to his hip, bringing it to his face.

"Go ahead."

The radio crackled some more. "I've got eyes on the cabin. Lights off. Don't think anyone is home."

The other team of SWAT, which was approximately forty yards to their left, seemed to scale the hill faster than they were.

"You sure?"

"No movement. Nothing. Nobody inside as far as I can tell, Echo One."

"How far out are you?"

"Less than a hundred yards. But we got a clear view over here."

"Hold position," whispered Rigsby into the grated speaker in his hand.

"Roger that."

Rigsby again indicated to his troops to keep moving, but did so with more vigor, as if telling them that they could risk moving a little faster. Arroyo took long steps, catching stride with McCabe.

"Slow down there, champ." Hissed McCabe. "You gonna pull a hammy."

Arroyo gave him an admonishing look, and he grinned. They trekked side by side for a while, and she noticed that the trees were getting farther apart and the lighting in the forest a little better. Even the hill seemed to even out. Then, after a few more steps, they came to a muddy clearing. Each of the SWAT began piling into the clearing one by one, as if eager to have a few steps where they weren't wading through trees and brush and blackberry bushes. Ahead, the clearing morphed into the steepest hill yet; it wasn't too far from a ninety-degree angle. Atop the hill, nearly a football field away, there it was. A dark cabin, sitting in solitude. It was fairly dilapidated and reminded Arroyo of something from an earlier time. There was no trees or vegetation in a semi-circle around the front, and even on the near vertical hill, only a stray weed here and there sprouted from the ground.

Once more, Rigsby held his fist into the air and

everyone froze. He unclipped a pair of binoculars that were hanging from his belt and moved them up to his face, scanning the cabin. Arroyo watched him avidly; the only noise she heard now was the sound of her heartbeat in her ears, thudding away like a giant knocking on a metal door.

Rigsby lowered the binoculars and seemed to shrug. In unison, all of their shoulders slacked. Arroyo looked over at McCabe and was a little surprised by the expression on his face. He seemed to be almost enjoying himself a little, wearing a half-grin and narrowing his eyes roguishly. He noticed her staring, and McCabe gave her a wink.

Pop.

Arroyo was looking right at her partner when the bullet tore through his skull and pushed a cloud of red up into the sky.

McCabe's body crumpled, lifeless, and for a transient second, Arroyo's brain seemed to stall. But then the first volley of rapid noises came, and it was only after two more bodies slammed into the mud that she realized what was happening.

Pop-pop-pop-pop-pop.

"Shots fired! Shots fired!"

"Get down! Get down! Everybody down!"

The mud splattered into the air in a straight line toward her, and she dove to the left, losing her gun in mid-air, but landing unscathed. Frantic yelling echoed all around. Don Chaser's voice screamed something incoherent, and then he let out a sound like someone had punched him in the gut. Face-down in the slop, Arroyo twisted her neck around and saw Chaser lying ten feet away, squirming and holding his throat. Several streams of red were trickling through his fingers.

A louder round of pops came as someone to her right returned fire toward the cabin. She looked over and saw the SWAT crouched down with the tip of his MP5 flashing rapidly. But then, red mist spurted out of his back and he went down, unmoving.

Move, Emily. Move!

She rolled away from the fallen soldier to her left. More gunshots rang out from nearby, but they didn't seem to be coming from the cabin, nor from anyone around her.

"Go, go, go!" screamed a voice next to her, and she tucked her arms tighter to her sides and continued to roll. Arroyo felt something heavy press into her back upon another roll, so she stopped for a fraction of a second. Her gun.

"Move, da—"

A huge splatter of mud not more than two feet away showered onto her, and the man who had been talking to her was now screaming in pain. She tried to look toward the source of the shrieking but another round of pops came and it was snuffed out. One more roll of her body and then her eyes found the gun on the ground and she snatched it up.

Someone shouted something behind her, and though the sound of gunfire was too deafening to discern exactly what was said, she felt fairly certain that the word "trees" had been somewhere in the sentence. Arroyo sprung onto her feet, whirled about, and took great bounding leaps back toward the cover of brush and away from the clearing of death. She managed to tuck herself behind a giant Douglas fir, sliding down toward the base of the tree.

More shouting, and the longest volley of fire yet ripped up the brush nearby. Arroyo sat there, quivering with a loud ringing in her ears and listening to the sound of men dying. She couldn't breathe. Everything was spinning. It was chaos.

There was a body nearby, sprawled against the bushes. The head was almost completely missing, but the corpse was on its side, its chest facing her, and Arroyo could read the writing that said *CMD Rigsby* stitched into the dark blue material.

Screw this, she thought.

With a distorted snarl, Arroyo gripped the pistol tight with both hands, and ripped back around the tree, facing the cabin again. She saw a quick sequence of flashing light from the window, and aimed right at it, pulling the trigger four times in a row. The blinking light stopped for a moment and then came on again right after she had fired the rounds, accompanied by the same crackling. The mud raised in front of her, and at the last second, she ducked back behind the tree and hit the ground, listening to the thud of bullets hitting bark.

The cracking stopped abruptly, and Arroyo knew that Tennyson had to be reloading. *Now's your chance!* Again, she rounded the beleaguered tree, and this time unloaded the rest of the clip at the cabin. She saw dirt ascend all around it and knew that each of the bullets had missed. The flashing began once more, but the muzzle of the gun in the cabin was not aimed at her. It was pointing somewhere to the left, raining hell upon the SWAT that were flanking from that direction. Instead of ducking back into the trees, she crouched and reached for another magazine that was attached to her hip. With a smack and a cock, the pistol was ready to go once more.

Bang. Bang. Bang.

When the flashing from the cabin ceased, Arroyo almost dared to believe that she had hit him with one of her three shots. But then, several more pops came, and without warning, she was knocked onto the ground.

The pain took unusually long to reach her, but when it did, every color that she saw amalgamated into one, and the screech that escaped her lips sounded inhuman. It was like an animal with the world's sharpest teeth was biting into her side.

Arroyo looked down and saw that her pants were darkening with blood.

Her pelvis had to have been shattered; the bullet lodged somewhere near her buttocks. Arroyo saw the entry wound at her hip, and it was a gaping hole. A potentially fatal wound.

More shots, and wood splintered. She was lying in the dirt, waiting for one last pop to ring out and then the color black to envelop her forever. Her eyes were already beginning to darken. *Fight it,* she thought. *Fight it.* Just then, she heard a succession of loud clapping to her right. One last gasp of return fire from one of the SWAT.

A colossal boom. The loudest sound she had ever heard in her life, and the forest floor reverberated with the force of the shock wave. Wildly, Arroyo thought that they were having the world's worst timed earthquake, but the shaking stopped too soon for that. She raised her head feebly and saw the orange cloud mushrooming into the sky, topped with black. It was sprouting from the spot where the wood had been just moments before. The cabin had exploded with Robert Macabre still inside.

That was the last thing she saw before the darkness finally took hold.

The water drummed against his skull, washing the grease out of his hair. It felt like eons since the last time he had been in the shower. His skin sizzled and turned red; the knob was almost turned all the way to the left, beckoning the heat. It pained him, but he did not yield. Pain was the only thing that sharpened his dulled senses. The only thing that reminded him that he was still living. His heart still beating.

Welsh rubbed the bar of soap against the wash cloth, and then folded it in two, scrubbing back and forth until the suds had multiplied. He slapped the cloth against his inner thigh, rubbing downward past his penis. It felt dead and powerless; he couldn't imagine having sexual feelings for any woman ever again. The only one he wanted was in a body bag at the morgue, ready to be lowered into the ground and decay.

He stepped toward the front of the shower, out

of the stream of water that was drumming against the shower mat. Welsh continued to spread the soap on every inch of his skin; his goal was to be covered in white before stepping back under the downpour. He saw the dirt underneath his fingernails and realized that it was black. Her dried blood, still caked in the nooks and crannies of his body. The image was permanently burned on the back of his eyelids. Holding her broken body, protecting it from further harm, and rocking back and forth like a mother coaxing its baby to sleep. Wendy had never had the chance to be a mother. And it was his fault. His infertility. His uselessness. His inability to protect her from the monster that had ripped her throat apart.

Welsh spread the wash cloth apart until it was taut and brought it to his face. Even through the thick material he could tell that his jaw was rough like sandpaper. He hadn't shaved since he had been admitted and subsequently released from the psychiatric ward, so the facial hair had reached the point where it bristled and itched every time he rubbed his fingers against his chin. Welsh looked down at the straight-razor that was on the edge of the tub. It beckoned him casually, and he picked it up between his index finger and thumb.

The soap would serve as shaving cream like it always did. He burnished it all over his face, flattening the hairs down to his chin. Welsh began with small strokes, ridding his face of the thickest clumps of follicles first. The beard was bushiest just below his bottom lip and seemed to thin out as it crawled downward. Slowly, his strokes became longer, and after each one he rinsed the blade. He caressed his chin. Then his upper lip. His sideburns. And, of course, finally, his throat.

Welsh paused, holding the razor just above his Adam's Apple. He increased the tension of his grip by a fraction and knew that a bead of blood had appeared there. One flick of his wrist, and he would see her again. One subtle slash, and they would reunite in a place far better than here. How poetically tragic it would be. Romeo and Juliet, dying in the same place, with matching wounds on their necks.

His hand trembled and then shook. He envisioned her face, smiling and reassuring. There was nothing in the world he would like more than to see that smile just one more time. Welsh torqued the blade, ready to pull and feel his body open.

Robert Macabre had won. Without having to even lay a finger on him. He could not go on living in this thresher; a piece of meat, ravaged and continuously pounded upon by life's iron fist.

But Macabre cannot win.

Welsh dropped the razor with a clatter, and he instantly began to cry. Huge, agonized sobs, his whole body convulsing. The devil was in his chest, digging his feet in, and the sobs were the exorcism; his diaphragm attempting to heave the demon forth. His knees were weak, and they began to wobble. Welsh placed his hand onto the side of the tub and lowered himself to the mat. He hugged his knees tight against his chest and stared at the razor in front of him for a second longer before his head collapsed in between his legs. His body was now shaking so violently that even sitting seemed like a precarious proposition.

The water kept cleansing his body, pounding down upon his nape with relentless fervor. And Welsh just kept shaking; the force of his crying making his insides quiver. It felt like he would be there for eternity, wailing away, quaking and broken. The water from the showerhead just continued to come down, a proverbial storm that had consumed his world. And in that moment, it felt like the rain would never stop.

PART TWO

34

June, 2019

Dr. Leonard Freidenberg tapped his pencil against the clipboard, watching the man sitting on the couch in front of him with a passive interest. The man's sagging gut was showing the slightest bit of midriff. His muscular arms were laying on his belly and rising and falling with his expanding and contracting diaphragm. The man looked totally disinterested in their current conversation. In fact, he looked disinterested in *everything*. His demeanor was that of someone with a flaccid indifference to the world around him.

"Are you still having the dreams?"

The man gave Freidenberg a side-eye, as if it were a prodigious undertaking to answer the question.

"Sometimes."

Freidenberg waited for the man to elaborate, but he didn't.

"Are they always the same?"

Was he rolling his eyes? A small fire of indignation burned below Freidenberg's sternum.

"They are always similar. Always the screaming. Always the blood."

"And you feel… What? Guilt?"

The patient's eyes misted over, and there was an elongated hiatus of dialogue. Freidenberg wondered if the man would even reply.

"No."

"What do you feel then?"

"Nothing. Nothing anymore."

Freidenberg narrowed his eyes.

"Nothing? Nothing at all? No pain? No… regret?"

"It wasn't my fault."

"I wasn't saying—"

"My energy is all but spent on this particular topic, doc."

Freidenberg wanted to scribble something down on his notepad to give his hands something to do, but he couldn't find any useful words to write. "Do you still have suicidal ideations?"

The man's nostrils flared, and Freidenberg felt a sensation of satisfaction effervescing within him. To get the patient to show some emotion, however deleterious, was an accomplishment. Anger was better than apathy.

"No, doc, I fucking don't."

"Okay, okay. Just relax. I didn't mean to make you uncomfortable." Freidenberg felt a bizarre yearning to smile.

"I have answered that question before, Leonard. And it's patronizing that you keep asking."

"You almost—"

"Yeah! I know, doc! I know what I almost did! But I didn't, did I?"

The patient's raised voice appeared to reverberate off the walls of the office. The peculiar acoustics of the room seemed to amplify shouting. And, unsurprisingly, this room was no stranger to shouting.

"I'm just worried about you, Carson."

Welsh rolled his eyes again. "No, you aren't."

"Excuse me?"

Welsh didn't bother clarifying. He just sat back and his eyes flitted around the room, like he was hell-bent on finding something more interesting to look at than the balding psychiatrist in front of him. After coming to the conclusion that their conversation was going decidedly nowhere, Freidenberg sneered and shook his head.

Welsh caught the man's facial expression and scowled. "What? Does my suffering amuse you?"

"Amused is not exactly the word to describe

how I am feeling right now, Carson," replied Freidenberg.

"Then get that stupid smirk off your face."

Finally, Freidenberg felt a rush of anger. He tried to disguise it with a scoff, but when he spoke, his voice shook slightly with the aggravation.

"Can I ask you something?"

"Be my guest."

"What are you hoping to get out of these sessions, Carson?"

Before Welsh could verbalize the malicious retort that was surely coming, Freidenberg continued.

"You have been under the care of nearly every mental health specialist in Multnomah County at one point in time over the past fifteen years. Psychiatrists, psychologists. Counselors. You even saw a *Buddhist*, for Christ's sake. So let me ask you something… Why do you think I am going to have the answers for you, Carson? You have been seeing me for three months, and if anything, you have regressed. So why do you continue to attend these appointments if you are getting nothing out of it?"

Welsh looked shocked that Freidenberg was calling him out. His mouth briefly increased in diameter and then shrunk as he struggled to vocalize his thoughts.

"I don't, uh… wow."

"This is me being forthcoming with you.

Which is a hell of a lot more than you have ever done for me."

"I can leave." Welsh made a move to stand up. His arms braced to push himself off of the sofa.

"You certainly could. But before you do, could you at least answer my question?"

Welsh stopped. He looked at Freidenberg with contempt.

"Please. I am genuinely curious. What are you *doing* here, Carson?"

Welsh continued to glare at the doctor, but then, after a couple of seconds, his arms went slack. He reclined back onto the sofa and grinded his teeth; one last expression of his frustration. Then, his eyes narrowed and the fingers of his left hand tapped his knee compulsively. He looked back-and-forth like someone might be just over his shoulder ready to help him with the answer. Finally, after a few seconds where he seemed to be having a full-scale internal debate, Welsh sighed and closed his eyes.

"I have been a widow for fifteen years."

Freidenberg waited for a couple of beats before replying. "I am well awa—"

"My closest friend is on dialysis at the hospital. They say he has six weeks to live. Max. This is a man I have known for three decades."

"I'm sorry to hear—"

Welsh plowed on, undeterred. "Retirement

doesn't suit me. I don't have any hobbies. No friendships that I have maintained. No family members to check in on me. I mean, how much more depressing could a man's life be?"

"Carson…"

"And yet, I am not depressed. I don't have suicidal 'ideations'," Welsh said, using his fingers to make air quotes. "Getting out of bed in the morning is surprisingly easy. I feel fine most of the time. Or something resembling fine. And the question no one can seem to answer for me is… Why? Why am I not miserable? Why do I not feel like jumping in front of every semi-truck that speeds down the highway? Why don't I feel *anything*?"

The hand that was holding Freidenberg's pen froze in the air. For some reason, his pulse had started to ascend. The vexation he had felt at his impassive and aloof patient had abated. It was suddenly replaced by a sense of stimulating curiosity.

"Have you posed this question to anyone else that you have seen, Carson?"

"In so many words."

"That isn't an adequate answer. Did you directly ask them what you just asked me?"

"Well… No."

Freidenberg tapped his pen against the clipboard and furrowed his brow as he thought.

"Well, I don't think there is a simple answer. I think, first of all, you are framing it wrong. You are doing that natural human thing where you have this set of expectations of how you are supposed to feel. What you are *supposed* to do. What you are *supposed* to think. But in all reality, there is no correct or incorrect way of feeling or doing anything. Every life is a trial run. Because every life is indisputably unique. So, to get down on yourself for not feeling how society has dictated that you should feel in a particular situation is, to put it simply, a total waste of time."

"But what if I *want* to feel different?"

"Then change the way you think," said Freidenberg simply.

Welsh shook his head. "I don't *choose* my thoughts."

"No. That is true. But you choose which ones to listen to."

Welsh chewed on the inside of his cheek as he cogitated on what Freidenberg had said. The man nodded like he agreed, but his nods slowly turned to shakes. It reminded Freidenberg of something that a patient at a psychiatric care facility would do.

"That is all very good, doc. A great bit of philosophy. I'm not trying to be sarcastic either. If I were someone who was just down on his luck, I would probably eat that up. But by chance, do you have something a little more tangible for me?

Something that isn't so… vague?"

Freidenberg sighed. Again, he couldn't help but let a tiny smile spread out on his face, but this time, Welsh did not comment on it.

"Okay then, Carson… Tell me this. If you could give me one word to describe your state of mind, what would that word be?"

Welsh didn't miss a beat. It almost seemed like he had been waiting for that exact question the entire appointment.

"Numb. I feel numb."

Freidenberg reclined back, narrowing his eyes. He percussed his fingers on his notepad, then reached over and gripped the manila envelope that was sitting on the table next to him. He moistened the tip of his index finger with his tongue and began to rustle through the printed documents. Freidenberg let silence take hold of the small room, ruminating on the potential solution that he had just thought of. It was a bit unorthodox; in fact, he couldn't remember ever suggesting such a thing before. But Carson Welsh was an unorthodox patient.

"How long have you been on fluoxetine?"

Welsh scratched his temple. "Since 2005, I think."

"It was Dr. Newman who prescribed it, correct?"

"I think so."

"Two hundred milligrams?"

"Yes."

"And you have been taking it every day for fourteen years? Along with your other pills?"

"That's right."

Freidenberg scribbled another note on the pad in his lap. "I have to say, two hundred milligrams is a... high dosage, to say the least. Now, being that I went to med school and am a proprietor and purveyor of Western Medicine, I want you to know that it would be against my mandate to denounce psychotropic drugs. Being that depression and anxiety are a chemical imbalance in the brain, I have always said and will always say that the most efficient way to cure said imbalance is through the use of SSRIs."

Welsh's eyes shifted back and forth around the room; he looked unsure of Freidenberg's intentions.

"And yet... many of my patients over the years have reported to me symptoms that align with the ones you just described. Numbness. Aloofness. Apathy. The inability to emote on a level that they could before they started taking the medication."

"What are you saying? Stop taking them?"

"No. That is absolutely not what I am saying," replied Freidenberg firmly. "However, you might consider tapering down to a lower dosage. Like I said, two hundred milligrams is quite a bit."

"What should I taper down to?"

Freidenberg shrugged. "Shoot for one hundred. Then, if that is too dramatic of a decrease, go back up to one fifty."

"How slowly should I taper down?"

"I would probably start with one fifty for a couple of days. Then if you feel okay, go down to one hundred. The good thing about fluoxetine and drugs of that ilk is that they are totally nonaddictive. All that would happen even if you quit cold turkey would be you would go back to feeling how you felt before. I'm not saying *do* that. But you could, and it wouldn't kill you. There aren't withdrawal symptoms for SSRIs."

Welsh nodded, and there was a curious expression on his face. "So it isn't your recommendation, but I could theoretically dump my pills down the toilet if I wanted to and not die?"

Freidenberg smiled cynically. "It is not my recommendation. That is all I am going to say."

The twinkling stars overhead were more engrossing than they had been in years. Or, perhaps, Welsh was looking at them for the first time in years. He had never been particularly entranced with astrology, but he couldn't help but feel a little awestruck as he gazed up into the night sky and scanned for the Big

Dipper. Was that it? A lopsided square attached to a fishing line? Or was that another cluster of stars that he had just decided was the Big Dipper because he couldn't make heads or tails of the thousands of white dots blanketing the dark blue canvas overhead? To Welsh, each astrological pattern of stars had always just looked like a game of tic-tac-toe gone awry. He could never figure out why the scientists were all so determined to find shapes and patterns in the suns of solar systems millions of light-years away. It wasn't like God had left behind some subliminal message traced out beyond the celestial wonders of the galaxy. Hell, if there was some sort of omniscient, all-powerful being behind life's grand design, surely the celestial wonders themselves were the message.

The gleaming light of the half-crescent moon reflected off of the water below, and the sound of the river sloshing against the shore was undeniably calming. Welsh strode alongside the rippling water, seeing his own opaque reflection bubbling along. The reflection was a foreign thing to him; his body took up more space now than it had in his entire sixty plus years of being. It took quite a bit of exertion to pull himself along; his breath was ragged and a stitch in his chest seared every time he inhaled. But he didn't want to stop now. It had been years since the last time he had partaken in some sort of physical activity, and though the movement pained him, it was also relieving.

Welsh looked up at the moon, and the backdrop of the stars. The pit of his stomach felt heavy, and the weight only seemed to increase as he digested his surroundings. For some reason, natural wonders like rivers and stars seemed to heighten the sadness. For he could see every magnificent thing, and she could not. He was still here, and she was not. A solitary tear crawled down his cheek, and her beautiful face flickered through his mind. His chest twisted and clenched in sorrow, but somehow, it felt good. It felt... real. Catharsis through grief.

Welsh reached into his jeans pocket and pulled out the rattling yellow canister. Just an hour before, he had combined the remainder of his back pills with the fluoxetine, and as he held it aloft over the water, it felt so good to look into the little container and not know which little white pill was which. He was cleansing himself of the chemicals that had deadened his body to natural sensation for so many years. And whatever pain this brought, he would welcome it with open arms. Pain superseded indifference.

With a deep breath, he cocked back his arm like a quarterback winding up to hit an open receiver. And with a powerful follow-through, he watched as the little yellow canister traveled through the air and briefly eclipsed the stars in the sky before plunking into the water with a small splash.

Mo McCray let out a disgusting, phlegm-possessed cough. His eyes were sunken in with a yellowish-purple tinge tracing his sockets, and his cheeks were pallid. The man was thinner than he had been in years. A diminutive plastic tube was connected to a vein on his inner arm, and blood traveled toward the heavy-looking gray machine next to his bed. A separate tube sprouted back out of the machine and was linked onto his arm.

"I'll tell ya, dying is hard work my friend," he said with a wheezy chuckle. Welsh wanted to laugh to appease his friend, but couldn't bring himself to do it. He just keep eyeing the machine, fascinated and a little repulsed by its mechanisms.

Mo coughed into his hand again and smirked at Welsh. "Dialysis isn't contagious, you know that, right?"

"Doesn't make it any less disgusting."

"Yeah, right. Sorry, I hate to inconvenience you with the slow and agonizing decay of my body."

"It's okay, buddy. Nobody is perfect."

Mo let out a booming chuckle, and slowly it morphed into another hacking cough. He doubled over, clutching his chest with the hand that wasn't restricted by the bounds of the machine.

"Jesus, Mo. Your lungs too?"

Mo shook his head and waggled his finger. "It's everything! Nothing works! It is like each vital organ is seeing the others calling it quits and putting in their two weeks too! I can't breathe right, I've lost my appetite, I can't sleep, I can't pee… Hell, I haven't even taken a dump in three days!"

Welsh sighed. "I was wondering about that, actually. When I woke up this morning I thought, 'I wonder if Mo has had a bowel movement lately.'"

That same booming guffaw, echoing around the room. Welsh's mouth twitched, but the desire to laugh was snuffed out almost immediately by the heavy feeling in his chest. He spoke with lightheartedness and jocularity, but he couldn't imagine feeling okay any time soon. Perhaps quitting the Prozac so abruptly was a mistake.

"I almost forgot. I have something for you." Mo raised his left index finger feebly and pointed at the table next to his bed. On it, there was a box of tissues, two bright green earplugs and a sealed envelope propped up against the package of Kleenex. Mo reached out his fingers and latched onto the envelope, bringing it through the air toward Welsh. His arm shook mightily as he offered the parcel, and Welsh snatched the envelope immediately to alleviate the strain on Mo's arm.

"I remember when you could bench press three hundred pounds. Now you can't even lift a goddamn letter."

Mo let out another noise that was somewhere in between a chuckle and a cough and then waved his hand as if he wasn't finished explaining.

"I have firm instructions for you with this. And I want you to follow them, okay?"

"Of course, my master."

"Carson, seriously."

Welsh could tell by Mo's expression that he meant what he was saying. "What? What is it?"

Mo wheezed. "Don't open it yet. Don't open it until I am gone."

A long pause hung in the air.

"A little dramatic, don't you think?"

"You'll understand when you open it."

"Is it a gift?"

Mo's eyes twinkled. "You could say that."

Welsh looked down at the letter and frowned. "I'm not sure I should take this."

"You don't have a choice."

"You see," continued Welsh, ignoring Mo's

rebuttal. "If you are giving me a gift and don't want to do it while I am right here in front of you, the only logical explanation is that it is something you shouldn't be giving me."

"Jesus. It isn't a list of the goddamn nuclear codes!"

"I wasn't insinuating that it was something bad. What I think is that it is probably too generous of a gift."

Mo didn't say anything.

"That non-answer is an answer."

"Just take it, damn it! There is no one else I have to give it to!"

"Mo—"

"Consider it a dying wish from your closest friend. To take this letter. And to not open it until I am being lowered into the ground."

Welsh passed the letter from hand to hand and sighed. "Fine."

"Good. Great. Now while I am having you do stuff, go grab the nurse and get her to get me an extra blanket. It's colder than a witches titty in a snow storm in here."

"Yes, your highness."

Mo gave a small chuckle-cough again and then looked over at the dialysis machine and glared at it.

"You know, I am half-tempted to rip this contraption out of my body right now and call it a life. What is the point of living an extra six weeks if

I have to be in constant discomfort?"

Welsh rolled his eyes.

"I am serious! This bed-ridden life isn't for me. I honestly think I would rather croak than spend every waking minute in pain."

"But there is still a chance you could pull through."

"Yeah, and there is a chance that Ted Bundy was innocent, but I don't think it is likely, do you?"

Welsh shook his head and scoffed. "You are a real piece of work, you know that, Mo?"

"Soon to be a real dead piece of work."

Mo didn't laugh after he said this. His facial expression was akin to that of some lighthearted, self-deprecating individual that was having a grand old time mocking himself, but it was forced. As Welsh stared into his friend's eyes, he saw something there that was unexpected: Fear. Mo was putting on a facade of aloofness, but Welsh could see that underneath it all, the man was afraid. In that moment, Welsh felt his chest tighten and his stomach sink, for he realized that he too was consumed with trepidation. He was afraid of life without his best friend.

"You okay, buddy?" Mo asked.

Surprisingly, Welsh found that he was on the verge of an emotional release. His diaphragm was constricted and eyes felt hot and wet. He tried to suppress the signs of his sudden forlorn sentiment, but he couldn't.

"I'm just going to miss you."

After he said it, Welsh realized how much like a child he sounded. Like he was a young boy again, terribly frightened of loss and abandonment. Mo reached out and took Welsh's hand. Even in his sorry state, his grip was surprisingly strong. He did not speak, but his face said enough. Welsh crouched down until he was on one knee, and bowed his head against Mo's bed, letting the tears fall down his face. As Welsh continued to cry, Mo tightened his clutch. It was almost like Death was sucking Mo into the vortex, and Welsh's hand was the only thing that tethered him to reality. For a fleeting moment, Welsh could almost feel the anxiety radiating off of the bed. But eventually, the aura transformed into something more serene, like Mo had calmed through the physical connection with his best friend. It was a moment of catharsis for both of them, and slowly but surely, Mo relinquished his grip.

"I'm going to miss you too, buddy. I'm going to miss you too."

36

Easton Lowry felt a strong urge to tug on his earpiece. It chirped directly into his skull, as if the lieutenant was literally force-feeding his brain instructions. He took a sip of the soda water in front of him and squeezed the lime to delineate its bitterness. Lowry tapped his fingers on the table, watching for the giant Hispanic man to return. It was difficult to pretend that the loud voice blaring into his earbud wasn't there, but somehow, he managed it.

"*Here he comes.*" Simultaneously, Lowry noticed Jose Milano striding across the dance floor, his massive frame bumping through grinding couples and shoving them aside like they were flies. Lowry took another drink of the soda water and suddenly wished that his boss had allowed him to order something with alcohol.

Milano approached the table and eyed Lowry

with some indiscernible emotion in his face. Lowry continued to suck on the straw, feigning nonchalance and ambivalence to the massive man's presence.

"Follow me."

Lowry stood up, leaving his glass behind. He followed Milano as the man weaved through the club's traffic, passing all types of inebriated individuals humping each other on the dance floor. This go-round, the bystanders seemed to part like the Red Sea, and Milano and Lowry traveled with ease until they reached the other side of Odyssey's Nightclub. Milano approached a door that was flanked by two other Mexican men, who weren't quite as buff as he was, but just as intimidating.

"In there." Milano gestured toward the door as he spoke, and Lowry made a move to step inside. However, a heavy hand clapped onto his shoulder before he could broach the threshold.

"Wait just a minute. You think we are going to let you in there strapped like a fuckin' gangster?"

Milano reached around the front of Lowry's jeans, tugging at the handle of the gun that was tucked into its holster. Once he had removed it, he scanned the weapon with narrowed eyes.

"Redhawk revolver. Some nice heat you packin' here, gringo."

"Only the best," replied Lowry, faking confidence.

"Question I have is, why you packin' anything in this fine establishment?"

"Just covering my bases."

"Hmm." Milano looked him up and down, and it seemed like he wanted to laugh. "You a cop?"

Lowry felt his pulse ascending rapidly.

"What kind of cop carries a revolver?"

"Maybe you's tryin' to throw me off the scent."

"Look. If you won't let me in to see Mr. Bruno, I'll take my business somewhere else. That's fine. But I ain't got a lot of time here. So either let me in or tell me to fuck off, 'cause I ain't going to spend my night hanging out with you... *Amigo*."

Milano's face broke into a wide smile, and Lowry saw several silver fillings on the right side of his grin. The look was filled with spite, and for a second, Lowry wondered if the gargantuan bouncer was going to slug him. But then, Milano looked at the man to the left of the door and nodded. The man pushed the door open, and Milano gestured toward it.

"After you, my little gringo."

Lowry gave a brusque nod and strutted forward, trying not to seem like someone walking into the lion's den. He noticed a large bulge on the hip of the man standing to the left of the door and felt certain that the man was carrying a gun larger and more powerful than the revolver that Milano had taken.

Once inside the room, Lowry eyed six men that were sitting around the table. They seemed to be playing a game of poker, as each had a handful of cards and were guarding them surreptitiously. Two of the men were black, with several tattoos blanketing their skin and white tank tops drooping off of their shoulders. The pair looked to be no more than thirty. A weaselly Caucasian man with short red hair and a large nose was sitting in between the two tattooed men. On the opposite side of the table, two more burly Hispanic men were reclined in a haze of smoke, with cigarettes sagging lazily out of their mouths. Finally, a man with a cigar and giant black shades sat in the middle of the others. He had exceedingly tan, wrinkled skin. It reminded Lowry of Keith Richards, or Steven Tyler. His hair was gray and short and spiked up in the front. Every set of eyes turned toward the newcomer. The man with the tan skin and black shades cleared his throat.

"What can I do for you, friend?"

He had a bit of a Brooklyn accent. Or maybe it was Bostonian. Somewhere in the North Eastern part of the country.

"Are you Frank Bruno?"

The man smiled, and Lowry was unsurprised to see that his teeth were almost shockingly white.

"Depends on whose askin'."

Lowry smiled back. "Someone who is

interested in business."

"Business, eh? What kind of business?"

"The kind that you're not supposed to talk about at parties."

Bruno laughed, and it was almost a skeptical thing. "Well, friend, as you can see, I am in the middle of Texas Hold 'Em right now, and I am about to play a great hand, so unless the price your talkin' about is a down payment on a new Camaro, then I don't think I am interested." His goons all laughed.

"It won't pay for a new Camaro. It'll pay for a new Maserati."

The room went silent. One of the Hispanic men was smirking, while the redheaded man furrowed his brow.

"All right, you have my attention." Bruno set the cards down and consolidated them into a miniature deck. "Sorry, gents. We're gonna have to put this game on hold for a minute."

One by one, each of the men stood up and began filing out of the room, recognizing their dismissal. They all gave Lowry different looks as they passed; the red-haired man glared viciously. Once they had departed, Bruno beckoned Lowry closer.

"Come. Have a seat."

Lowry pulled out a chair and sat down slowly directly across from the man. He looked over his shoulder and saw that Milano had followed him into the room and was standing approximately ten feet away. His eyes were full of suspicion and malice. Lowry turned back toward Bruno and gestured at the hulking figure in the corner.

"Maybe we could have some more privacy."

Bruno looked over at Milano like he hadn't noticed him until that moment. "This is as private as it gets around me, friend."

Lowry shrugged, and put his hands on the table, as if he were subconsciously trying to show Bruno that he wasn't a threat. It was then that he noticed several glasses filled with brown liquid around the exterior of the table.

Bruno took notice of Lowry's attention to the glasses. "You drink bourbon?"

"Depends on what kind of day I had."

Bruno let out a gravelly chuckle. "I didn't really mean in general, friend."

"I'm going to pass."

"Suit yourself."

The man began using his hand to clear off the table of random bits of debris: cigarette ash, rogue droplets of alcohol, and what looked like peanuts.

"So... Business..."

"Business." Lowry looked at Bruno with intensity, trying to sell his part.

"You have to understand, uh..."

"Easton."

"Easton?"

"That's right."

"Funny name. Anyway, you have to understand Easton, I am an entrepreneur. I have dealings in several different... *ventures*. Some of which others consider to be, uh, *illicit* activity. So when you say business, I am not exactly sure about which product that you inquire."

Lowry smiled. "Let's just say that I've noticed that there is a lot of traffic around town lately."

"Mm." Something sparkled in Bruno's eyes. He took a sip out of the glass of bourbon in front of him and flashed his disconcertingly white smile. "Well, then, I need two pieces of information from you, Easton. One, what sort of price tag are we talkin' here? Two, what is your preference?"

"Five hundred G's."

"Five...?"

"Five hundred. Correct."

"Jesus Christ. You think I'm movin' super models here?"

"I think the market defines how much a certain product is worth."

Bruno clicked his tongue. "Well, you definitely have my attention now, Easton. So, as far as my second question—"

Lowry smiled. "Blonde. Or even dirty blonde. Petite. Nothin' extra."

"Mm. Age?"

"Young."

"How young?"

"Nineteen. Twenty. I would go for a little older if I had to, but I like 'em young."

"I may have something along those lines."

Easton nodded. "Why don't you show me then?"

Bruno's eyes seemed to narrow. "You sure aren't one to beat around the bush, are you?"

"I want to know if it is worth my time."

"What? You think I am going to take you to the girls right now? Drop everything and give you a private tour?"

"I just mean pictures."

Bruno's eyes widened. "Pictures? Why do you want to see pictures? Are you going to beat off right here?"

"Nothing nasty. I just want to see faces. Like I said, to see if it is worth my time."

Bruno didn't say anything. He didn't smile or show any emotion. He simply began to fiddle in the inside pocket of his black suit, and eventually he pulled out a phone. He unlocked the phone with his facial ID and then spent a few long moments fiddling with the touch screen. When he got to what he was looking for, he held the phone back like he could see it better at a distance. Then he flipped the screen in Lowry's direction.

The voice whispered in Lowry's ear.

"Remember, touch your temple if it's Wilson."

Lowry looked at Bruno's phone. When he saw the face in the picture and did not recognize it, he made an expression of indifference.

"Eh…"

Bruno laughed. "That picky, eh?"

"Five hundred K gives a man a right to be picky."

"All right, all right. I got something better. Hold on." Again, Bruno swiped his screen several times and then turned it back toward Lowry when he found the photo he was after. A young, slim blonde with heavy makeup and dead eyes stared back at Lowry from the picture. And Lowry knew instantly that it was Madison Wilson. His heart leapt into his throat and his breathing became irregular, but he tried to remain calm. With one fluid motion, he raised his arm and scratched his temple.

"I like that one."

"I bet you do."

Stay calm. Stay calm.

"Confirm the timeline," whispered the voice in Lowry's ear.

"How long have you been sitting on her?"

Bruno's eyebrows raised, and Lowry instantly knew that he had messed up. What kind of regular customer asks for that information? *Shit. Shit shit shit.*

"'Bout a month."

"And nobody has jumped on it?" Lowry looked behind him at Milano, appraising the massive biceps attached to the man's shoulders. Suddenly, he realized that his earpiece was pointing right in Bruno's direction, and he snapped his head forward.

"What is that in your ear, friend?"

Time froze. Lowry's stomach felt like it was cramping. His heart thudded audibly in his ears. As he looked across the table, he noticed that here was a darkness in Bruno's expression that hadn't been there before. Lowry reached into his ear and pulled out the contraption for the man to see.

"Just my Bluetooth device. For my phone."

Bruno's voice grew more menacing. "You don't strike me as that kind of businessman, Easton."

"I don't know what you are talking about."

"You don't?"

Lowry swallowed. "Look, Mr. Bruno. I am just interested in the product you sell. The girls. That is it."

"Yeah. I bet you are."

Bruno drummed his fingers against the table and made a bizarre sucking noise through his teeth. "I really bet you are. Thing is, friend... I don't move girls to cops."

Before Lowry could react, Bruno reached under the table and flipped it over, knocking the man across from him out of his seat and onto the floor.

"Run, Jose! Run! The cops are comin'! Get out!"

Lowry saw Bruno charge toward a door on the other side of the room. Before he could move, something heavy slammed against Lowry's head, rattling his skull. The world spun, and he saw the outline of the massive Mexican man clomping past him. Feeling woozy, he pushed himself off of the ground and paused for a millisecond to remove the Beretta Nano Sniper pistol that he had hidden in his sock. Then he charged after the fleeing Milano and his boss.

Once he made his way through the door, Lowry found himself in a long hallway. Milano was twenty feed ahead, pumping his arms to gather speed. But Lowry was much faster. He streaked along, closing the distance foot by foot. Finally, when he was within arm's reach, he stopped on a dime, and pointed the Beretta. With a loud *crack,* Lowry blasted a bullet through Milano's kneecap. The puff of red sprayed against the wall and the hallway was suddenly filled with the sounds of screaming. The man crumpled to the ground, writhing in pain. Lowry approached, debating whether or not to take the time to put Milano in cuffs. The SWAT would be coming in right behind them, and Milano was immobile. He could wait.

Lowry sprinted past the crippled man, but

before he knew it, his feet were no longer slapping against the ground. Milano had reached out and ripped at his ankle, causing a thunderous crash as Lowry hit the hard floor. He rolled over, his back in agonizing pain. Milano reached for his neck. Instinctively, Lowry pumped two more bullets into Milano's belly, and the screaming resumed.

Lowry stood up and hobbled forward, his whole body aching. He could still see Bruno ahead, but he knew it was too late. The man slipped through another door and in the barren hallway the sound of a lock clicking echoed throughout the halls.

Son of a bitch. Jesus Christ!

Bruno sprinted along with a stich in his chest, feeling like it was about to tear. His thighs burned like crazy; his calves felt like they may rupture at any second. He charged down the alley, his arms pistoning through the air with his hands knifed like they were scythes. Bruno's breathing was ragged and uneven, and he felt like he was about to have a heart attack. But he couldn't stop. He wouldn't stop.

The little prick had ruined everything. Bruno should have been able to smell it on him from the moment the boy walked into the room. He walked like a cop. He talked like a cop. How could Bruno have been so stupid?

Almost there. Almost there. Bruno could see the outline of his Camaro parked two blocks away. But it was already over. The police knew. They knew about the girls. The drugs. Maybe they even knew about the bodies. He couldn't stay here. He had to leave the country. Maybe fly one of the private planes he had used to transport blow and smuggle himself down to South America. Somewhere where it was hot and humid as hell and no one would wonder where he was. But first he just had to get to his car.

The cops had to know what he drove. Surely they had been tracking him for months. He would have to switch vehicles immediately. Maybe even swap plates on the car he was trading for. The first stop Bruno would make would be to visit Pete. Pete would have a beater that he could loan him. But first, Bruno just had to get to his car.

Just to his car.

Something slammed against the top of his head, and Bruno suddenly found himself on the ground, in god-awful pain. His brain felt like it was going to split in two, and he let out a pitiful whimper.

Someone was standing over him, casting his body in shadow. And the muzzle of a gun was pointing at his face. But it wasn't Eastside. Or Eastboy. Or whatever the hell he was called. It was a woman. And she looked like she would take great pleasure in pulling the trigger.

"You move a goddamn inch and I swear I'll paint this sidewalk with your brains, asshole," Emily Arroyo said through gritted teeth.

"He looks miserable."

"Good."

Detective Lowry tapped his foot and massaged the top of his head absentmindedly.

"How's the noggin?"

"Never better, LT."

Arroyo gave him a small smile, and pointed the corner of the manila folder she was carrying at her subordinates' chin. "The cringe on your face tells a different story."

"Well, did you see that hombre that tagged me? Looked like The Mountain."

"The Mountain?"

"From *Game of Thrones*."

"Never seen it."

Lowry's pulled his eyes away from the two-way mirror and gave Arroyo a look of incredulity. "You've never seen it?"

380

"Fantasy doesn't appeal to me."

"Consider myself shocked."

Arroyo kept her face impassive. "I'm sensing sarcasm."

Lowry chuckled and turned back toward the mirror. Frank Bruno was slumped forward on his folded arms, looking completely exhausted. Next to him, an older thin man with creased cheeks and slicked back hair that had lost most of its color was whispering into his ear. Either Bruno was indifferent to what his attorney was saying, or he had fallen asleep, because he wasn't moving or reacting at all.

"Speaking of said hombre, what is the word on his condition?"

"ICU," replied Lowry. "Stable. Seems I missed the vital organs."

"That's a shame."

"Ha. Since when did you become so cold, boss?"

"These men are the lowest of the low," growled Arroyo. "The scum of the earth."

"Tell me how you *really* feel."

Arroyo couldn't help but bare her teeth a little. "Did you look at any pictures of the girls he has been running? They are kids. Tortured kids. Moved and abused like they are nothing but commoditized meat. Like they didn't have families of their own or people who cared about them."

Lowry said nothing, but his lips tightened.

"Only fitting that he has a blood-sucking leach like Warren Grecko defending him."

After she said it, Arroyo looked at the thin, lanky attorney with his gelled-hair and long arms sitting next to Bruno and felt anger boiling inside her. At his best, Grecko was a sleazy obstructionist. At his worst, he was a borderline criminal.

Lowry scratched his head. "Grecko has been on a roll lately, hasn't he?"

"Every dog has its day."

"And that isn't any cause for concern?"

Arroyo scoffed. "What could we possibly have to be concerned about? We have pictures. Documents. Witnesses. A paper trail."

"But we don't have the girls."

"So you are insinuating that Grecko is going to use the girls as leverage? He would get disbarred."

Lowry stuck out his bottom lip and raised his palms in the air for a moment. "I'm just saying. Maybe we shouldn't underestimate him."

Arroyo watched as Bruno finally lifted his head. His black coat was draped around his shoulders with his arms outside of the sleeves like it was a blanket, and Grecko was patting the man's back awkwardly. Briefly, Arroyo thought of someone being consoled by a poisonous snake.

"No, detective. He shouldn't underestimate *us*." Arroyo gripped Lowry's shoulder and bucked her head at the two-way mirror. "Come on, Easton. It's time we say hello."

Arroyo opened the door with the hand that wasn't carrying the manila folder, and the two men inside peered up with stony expressions. With Lowry in her wake, Arroyo pulled out a chair and set the folder down before placing her butt in the chair and scooting it forward, the entire time making eye contact with Bruno.

"Helluva night you have had, eh, Frank?"

Bruno looked at her with hatred in his eyes, and then shifted his focus onto Lowry, who sat down across from him. The man looked like he wanted to slam Lowry's forehead onto the table. There were a couple seconds of nothing, and then Bruno flashed his teeth at Lowry in a mocking smile.

"Well, look who it is. Got that five hundred G's?"

Lowry chuckled. "I'm afraid I don't. Not at this time."

"Shame. That's a shame. How is your head, Eastboy?"

"Easton. And fine. Your dog's bark is worse than his bite."

"Heard you shot him."

"Did you hear that he deserved it?"

Bruno's face contorted into a snarl. His fingers began tapping compulsively on the table in front of him and his jaw twisted. "Is he going to die?"

"Not tonight, Frank."

Bruno used his tongue to moisten his lips, which were cracked and dry and looked like they might fall off at any second. "You must not be a very good shot."

"Trust me, Frank," Lowry said. "If I wanted to kill him, he would be dead."

Bruno grinned again, displaying his shiny pearls. But it was a totally mirthless thing.

"Mr. Bruno," Arroyo said with force, and the smile was wiped away. "As of right now, we are moving to charge you with thirty-two counts of human trafficking, fifteen counts of possession, and twenty-two counts of distribution. Those are the big ones. But if you are wondering, you are also going to be charged with racketeering and obstruction of justice. I'm sure eventually we will find enough to throw in a couple counts of murder in the first-degree, but at that point, those charges would sort of be moot, don't you think?"

"Did you come in here just to taunt my client, Ms. Arroyo?" Grecko said, and a vein was visible in his neck.

"Oh, was that a taunt? I didn't mean it as such, Warren. If I meant to taunt your client, I would ask him how it feels to know that the only suit he is going to be wearing for the rest of his life is orange."

Grecko scoffed. "Since when did you become

so ruthless, Emily?"

"Ruthless? Am I being ruthless? I thought I was just stating facts."

"No, sorry," replied Grecko. "I guess what I really meant is when did you become such a bitch?"

Lowry's mouth dropped open, and even Bruno looked over at Grecko in surprise. However, Arroyo gave the man a sarcastic lips-only smile.

"After twenty years on the job, your outlook begins to change, Warren."

"Hmm. Well, if you came in here to trade barbs, I am afraid we are not interested. I'm half-inclined to tell you to shove it right now. I can't imagine a scenario where this discussion will benefit my client."

"Then why are you here, Grecko?"

"Because Mr. Bruno asked me to be."

"But why are you here in *this* room? If you think this is a frivolous meeting, why don't you just advise your client to not answer any of my questions and then leave? I have to say, I don't think anyone here would miss you."

Grecko raised his eyebrows. "You have a lot of nerve, Emily."

"Really? Because if I am not mistaken, you were the one who just called me a bitch."

"I can call you some other things too, if you would like."

"Be my guest. You've always been the model

of professionalism."

Grecko didn't reply this time. But his eyes were filled with loathing.

"To go back to my earlier question, I think I know why you are in this room, Warren. You want me to show you what we've got," said Arroyo, opening the manila folder. "And I will happily oblige. Because, my God, this will be the shortest trial in history. The jury could be made up of twelve Italian mobsters and they would still convict you, Mr. Bruno."

Arroyo grabbed onto the first sheet in the folder and slid it across the table. "These are transcripts of text messages you exchanged with William Moon, regarding a woman named Tina Stiles, who has been missing since March thirty-first. In said messages, you offer Stiles' 'services' in exchange for a substantive lump sum from Moon. I believe the figure you two agreed upon is twenty thousand. You were never very explicit about what services you were offering, but since Stiles has been heavily suspected of being in the human trafficking circuit, it is fairly easy to infer what goods are being exchanged. Also, you will be most displeased to learn that William Moon is actually Detective Billy Heater, a ten-year veteran of PPD. You are really not good at spotting blue, are you, Frank?"

As Bruno snarled, Arroyo flipped to the next item in the folder she was looking for. Once she gripped the photograph, she pushed it forward. The photo was a grainy image showing Bruno with a young blond woman hanging on his arm. They seemed to be on a sidewalk outside of what looked like Odyssey's Nightclub.

Arroyo nodded her head at the image. "This is a screenshot of CC footage, showing you with a woman that looks remarkably like Jocelyn Rae, who has been missing since January third. Also heavily suspected of being in the trafficking circuit. Strange that this screenshot was pulled on March fourteenth, two and a half months after she went missing, wouldn't you say, Frank?"

"You can't definitively tell who that woman is from that image," interjected Grecko. "It could be anyone."

"I guess you are right. But in *this* one," continued Arroyo, picking at another photo and holding it up in the air. "In *this* one Rae is looking directly at the camera. And I don't think anyone could deny that it is her. At least not anyone that would be on a jury."

Arroyo flicked through a couple of documents and then found another snapshot that she set next to the one of the woman gazing into the closed-circuit camera. The new picture was a headshot of Rae, likely taken at a professional studio. The two images were almost certainly the same person. Grecko's face fell as he looked on at the pictures.

Satisfied, Arroyo set the photograph aside and then riffled until she came to a cluster of more paper stocks. She spread a few of them out on the table so that the images were almost directly under Bruno's nose.

"As you can see, these are pictures of contraband seized from the New Horizon, a fishing boat docked in Seattle. The raid yielded four arrests, including a man named Diego Martin, who claimed that he was moving the contraband under your instruction."

Bruno's snarl only seemed to intensify with each passing word. Arroyo felt like she could almost hear the sound of the man's teeth grinding.

"Now *this*... This is an image of your pal, Jose Milano, restraining a woman who looks remarkably like Jamie Johnson," continued Arroyo, as she picked up a new photograph and set it down on the table. "I'm sure this will be a surprise to you, but Johnson is also suspected—"

Without warning, Bruno slammed both of his cuffed hands onto the table, and everyone, including Grecko, jumped.

"Enough!"

There were a few moments of tense silence as Arroyo held eye contact with the man. His leathery skin was taut around his mouth, as his jaw twisted and his eyes bulged in fury. Bruno looked like he would take great pleasure in reaching across the table and throttling the redheaded woman in front of him.

"What the *hell* do you want?"

Grecko put his hand on Bruno's shoulder. "*Frank!*" he hissed, using the man's name as a warning.

"You know what we want, Mr. Bruno. We want the girls."

"Don't, Frank. Don't tell them *anything*."

"Where are they, Frank?"

Suddenly, when he heard the question, it seemed like every muscle in Bruno's body went slack. The contorted, manic expression disappeared, and after a few beats of nothing, a haunting smile crept across his face.

"I don't know what you are talking about."

"Screw you. Where are they, Frank?" Arroyo's voice was filled with contempt.

"Beats me."

"Tell me where they are."

"I don't know what you are talking about," he repeated.

"Listen, Bruno. You don't hold any cards here. We have enough to put you in OSP for the rest of your miserable life. If you want *any* chance of walking the streets as a free man while you are still breathing, you better tell us where to find them."

"I don't believe you."

Arroyo felt her chest jump in surprise. "What?"

Bruno gave her a grim smile. "I don't believe you. Even if I did know where they were, don't think I am naïve enough to believe you when you say there is a deal on the table. There ain't no deal."

"Frank!" Grecko's voice was high-pitched and strained. "Stop!"

"There sure as hell won't be if you don't talk," Arroyo said softly.

"Show me. Show me in writing what the deal is. Or my lips stay sealed."

"That is not really the way it wo—"

"Then screw you. I'm not telling you where they are."

Arroyo looked over at Grecko and saw that the man was sweating profusely. His face was suffused with anxiety. If a stranger was to walk into the room at that very second, they may think Grecko was the one that had just been arrested on a multitude of felonies.

"Jesus, Frank," muttered Grecko, shaking his head. "Don't speak. Don't say another word."

"You work with us, then we work with you. That is how we do things, Frank," continued Arroyo, pretending that Grecko hadn't even spoke.

Bruno looked like he was about to strike back with another biting retort, but then he apparently began to cogitate on what Arroyo had just said. He reclined back farther into his chair and started to chew on the inside of his cheek. His fingernails clacked a few times against the table, and then he sighed.

"Clock's ticking, Frank."

"All right. All right. You want something? I'll give you something."

"*Frank!*"

"Shut the fuck up, Warren. Let me talk." Bruno gave Grecko a piercing stare and the lawyer seemed to recoil. Then Bruno slowly turned his attention back to Arroyo.

"I have something for you all right. Call it a down payment of information. You want me to work with you? I will work with you. I will give you something. But it doesn't have anything to do with the girls."

Arroyo scoffed. "Then why would I be interested?"

"Trust me, Lieutenant. You will be *very* interested."

Bruno leaned forward and then looked back and forth as though he were a small child about to share a secret.

"It has to do with... past events. Something that happened a long time ago."

Arroyo didn't reply, but for some reason, she felt a chill creeping down her spine.

"I know a guy. He, uh, has done work for me in the past," Bruno said. "Officially, he calls himself a private investigator. But I like to think of him as more of a *problem-solver*. A fixer. Anyway, he has certain information. I think you'll want to talk to him, Lieutenant."

As the man's words began to percolate, a sense of dread was accumulating in Arroyo's stomach. She had no idea what was causing it, but the foreboding increased by the second. She leaned back and swallowed thickly.

"And why is that?"

Bruno shrugged, with a mysterious expression passing over his face.

"Let's just say that he might know the biggest secret that this city has ever kept."

Anton Baze sucked powerfully on his cigarette, letting the fumes infiltrate his lungs. He held the smoke in for five long seconds, before whistling it out like a tea kettle with steam. Baze flicked the end of the cig, and watched as the ash hit the pavement.

Baze's head almost grazed the sign that said Carl's Tavern. The light from the sign did not touch the spot where he was standing, and he remained cloaked in shadow. Two men stepped out of the door to the bar in mid-laugh. One of the men looked proud of himself, and Baze was certain that he was the one who had told the joke. Baze slipped his lips around the cigarette, inhaled for half a beat, and then blew the smoke in the direction of the pair that was walking past. Both heads turned, and the men jumped.

The comedian was the one who spoke first. "Jesus! What are you doing creeping behind the door, buddy?"

Baze stepped forward, and as soon as the light from the sign caught his face, the man took a step back. Baze wondered if it was his physical stature that was imposing, or the long snake-shaped scar that crawled down his cheek. More than likely, it was both.

The comedian's friend continued to walk and pulled his buddy by the wrist as he did so. "Come on," he said softly. The comedian stared at Baze for another second, transfixed by his imposing visage. Then, while muttering something indistinguishable, the comedian turned, and the pair increased their pace along the sidewalk. Baze let out the smallest chuckle; his strangely deep voice seemed to echo in the silence. But neither the comedian nor his sidekick turned back.

No cars traveled along the street next to the tavern. This was a rundown part of town, and Carl's made most dive bars look like exquisite, chic establishments. It appeared more like a log cabin than a bar; smoke even billowed from the ramshackle chimney as the woodfire pizza oven cooked another pie. But it wasn't one of those places that beckoned people in. Carl's was the place to go if you were riffraff, and you knew it.

Baze let out the longest exhale of smoke yet, and as he did so, a gravelly cough pounded his diaphragm. It sounded wet and disgusting; a telltale sign that his lungs were not a shining example of health. At this point, he would almost be surprised if he didn't die of lung cancer. He smoked almost a pack a day. Marlboro Reds. As strong as they came. He didn't pussyfoot around with his cigarettes. None of that American Spirit hippy shit. Strong. Fierce. Marlboro Reds.

Baze could still taste a tinge of whiskey on his tongue. He had tried to chase the well-whiskey with a Fat Tire, but the cheap beer had not washed all of the flavor out of his mouth. Perhaps it was also lingering in his mustache. Baze wiped at the fur on his upper lip with the cuff of his sleeve and then sniffed said sleeve. Sure enough, the pungent scent of Wild Turkey wafted into his nostrils. It only made him thirstier. He was four shots in and yet, he felt like he had just gotten started.

Was he a functioning alcoholic? Or could the life he had lived the last three years be considered functional? He hadn't worked a case in almost a month. His credit cards were all maxed out. He lived on his own. No family. No love interest. The dwindling funds in his bank account all went to cigarettes, booze, and food. And yet, Baze had never been happier. There was no stress in his life. No attachment or responsibility. Responsibility was a hassle. Sure, eventually this lifestyle would catch up to him, but for now, as he sucked on the filter of the All-American Marlboro Red, contentment filled his belly.

The sound of raised voices nearby reached Baze's ears. Several newcomers were approaching on the sidewalk.

"Just get her to the car, bro."

"C'mon, I will grab her legs."

"You are just trying to get a view of her cooch!"

"Eat shit, Ronnie."

Baze stayed in the shadow. Five young men, likely in their mid-twenties, were pulling a stumbling female along the sidewalk. Her eyes were lolling back into her head and drool was running down her chin. The girl, who couldn't have been older than twenty-two, was wearing a black tank top and a maxi skirt. Her messy black hair shrouded her face, but she still looked fairly pretty. If the girl wasn't unconscious yet, she had to be close.

The men all seemed like they could be part of a fraternity; they sported tight polo shirts of various pastel colors, and a couple of them had shades on, even though it was dark out. The one that seemed to be leading the charge was tall and stocky, with bulging pectoral muscles and tree trunks for legs. The man had a slight underbite, but with a well-defined jawline and a straight nose, like a crossbreed between Brad Pitt and a Shih Tzu. He appeared to be the one bearing most of the weight of the young woman with his hands around her waist from the back, but he was urging his companions to shoulder more of the load. Two other men were on either side and had a hold of each arm, with another pair of bro's in back looking amused. Just from one prolonged glance, Baze could tell that this wasn't five concerned gentlemen watching over their female friend who had consumed one too many vodka tonics. This was something else.

"We need to get this on video," said one of the two giggling in back.

"Let's wait until we get back to the house."

"We can send her a copy when we're done. She will probably be proud. Probably going to set a record. What's the Guinness World Record for number of cocks in the same mouth?"

All five of them erupted into laughter. The two in the back doubled over, and the man with the underbite briefly let go of the girl and clapped twice while wheezing with guffaws. "Yeah, it's not like she is going to *remember* any of this," he said.

Baze stepped out from underneath the sign, directly into their path. The pack of men froze dead in its tracks. Baze took a long drag on his cigarette, held it in for several seconds and then exhaled the smoke out of the side of his mouth.

"Evenin', fellas."

The men all looked dumbfounded. One by one, apprehension and fear began to crawl onto each face, and Baze knew they were all collectively wondering how much he had heard.

"The fuck do you want?" Underbite stepped forward, his eyes narrowing.

"Oh, nuthin'," Baze said. "Just wonderin' where you fine gentlemen were taking this young lady."

"What's it to you, Scarface?"

A smattering of chuckles spread out among the remaining four. Baze even smiled and pointed his cigarette at Underbite.

"Scarface. I like that. I *really* like that."

"I'm happy for you. Now get out of our way."

Baze chuckled. "'Fraid I can't do that, friend. You see, I'm havin' a smoke break. And this seems to be the perfect spot."

Underbite scowled and continued to move closer and closer until there was only two feet separating them.

"You want a problem, buddy?"

Baze let a pregnant pause sit on the air while he stared directly into the man's eyes. At first, his expression was stern and menacing, but then he smiled from ear to ear. With a flourish of his hand, Baze unabashedly belted out the words to the song, "Drink And Fight," by The Dropkick Murphys at the top of his lungs. His singing was loud and obnoxious, and he inflected a thick Irish accent into the lyrics.

"Well, I stumbled at two a.m. all drunk and fulla smoke. My wife said I have had enough that's it I'm sick get out."

Underbite flinched and took a step back, clearly flabbergasted by the singing. Baze did not yield, and took another step toward the man, increasing the volume of his spontaneous solo.

"So I stumbled down to Kelly's Pub, across the edge of town. And I told the boys me story and we had another round."

Underbite twitched again, and the creases in his forehead only became more defined as his frown intensified. "Are you on drugs or somethin', man?"

Baze stopped his song and pointed at the man. "You mean like the kind that you slipped in that young lady's drink? Nah, man. I'm stone-cold sober. Well... relatively speaking." Baze laughed, his baritone voice booming.

Underbite snarled. "I'm about to knock you out, asshole."

"No, you're not. And you're doing it wrong by the way."

"Doing what wrong?"

"The cigarette. You aren't supposed to swallow it."

"What cig—"

Baze took the cigarette out of his mouth and flicked the ash onto the ground. He slithered his tongue out like he had joined the band KISS, and then flipped the rollup over in his fingers. His eyes bulging, Baze slowly placed the lit end against his tongue, and grinded it back and forth, hearing the sizzle of burning flesh ring in his ears. Underbite's jaw dropped open, leaving his mouth totally agape. Baze quickly removed the cigarette from his tongue and flicked it into Underbite's open mouth.

Underbite gagged and clawed at his Adam's apple, and Baze struck like lightning. He hammered the man across the jaw with his clenched fist. For the tiniest space of time, Underbite stayed frozen in place. Then, with his mouth going slack, he crumpled to the ground. The two men holding the girl's arms let go with cries of anguish, and she fell. They charged forward, the first one swinging wildly. Baze parried the blow with his right arm and placed his left hand on the back of the man's neck. Using all of his strength, Baze brought the man's head downward while simultaneously thrusting his knee. There was a loud crunch as Baze's knee made contact, and the man grunted and then went motionless onto the pavement. His body landed right on top of Underbite and created a small barricade between Baze and victim number three. But it wasn't nearly enough, and with two rapid-fire punches to the man's gut followed by a hard uppercut to his chin, Baze's work was nearly done.

The final two, who had been giggling in the back during the initial conversation, stepped forward. One of them held a boxing stance, dancing from toe to toe. Baze waited, and after a couple of beats, the man threw a jab. Baze caught it in his palm. Summoning all of his strength, Baze crushed the fist in his grip, and the sound of knuckles cracking rang out. The man howled in utter agony.

Something caught Baze's jaw, but he felt no pain. The other one who was still standing had thrown a punch that was almost insulting. Baze quickly brought his knee in between the first man's thighs to subdue him for a moment, and while the man let out a noise like a popped balloon, Baze turned his attention toward the one who had hit him.

"Who taught you how to punch like that? Here, hit me again."

The man looked dumbfounded, but when Baze lowered his arms, he unleashed another blow in the same spot, just under Baze's right ear.

"Kid, you are doing it wrong. You're just using your forearm to punch. You got to really throw your shoulder into it. See, watch."

Baze blasted the man on the chin and watched as his body folded like a cheap suit. Four of the five were on the ground, and the other was still keeled over, holding onto his groin like something had fallen off.

"Sorry if you aren't able to have kids after that." Baze grabbed a fistful of the man's hair and pulled his head back viciously so he could look directly into his victim's eyes. "But judging by your behavior tonight, maybe that would be a good thing."

With one final vicious punch, all five of the men were down, sprawled out next to each other like they had all taken a collective nap at daycare. Rubbing his now-aching knuckles, Baze looked over toward the girl, who was on all fours, having lost the physical support of the would-be rapists.

"C'mon, sweetheart," said Baze, striding over to the girl and hoisting her up by the arm. "I think you better call it a night."

The television was blaring, but it was barely enough to keep Baze from falling asleep. He rubbed his right eye, trying to ward the sandy feeling away. The glass of bourbon in his left hand teetered precariously toward the ground, and several droplets of liquid oozed over the edge of the glass and onto the carpet.

"Whoops," said Baze, straightening the glass. He chuckled and then focused his attention back on the television. He was watching the Weather Channel. They were doing a special on the Coast Guard, and some boatsman was stuck in the sideways sheets of rain and wind, trying to explain proper procedure during rough seas while the cameraman struggled to keep the camera level. Baze was tickled pink by the Weather Channel. Not only was he deeply fascinated by Mother Nature and her fierce mechanisms, but it was also amusing to watch these poor souls stuck in the mess trying to do their jobs while they were ravaged by the wind and the rain.

Baze reached over, grabbed the remote on the table next to him, and turned the volume down. He didn't want to wake the neighbors. It was almost two a.m., and the last thing he needed was one of the stick-in-the-mud residents who lived next to him to make a noise complaint to his landlord. It would be especially embarrassing to receive a warning because of the Weather Channel. As soon as he quieted the TV, he began to nod off. It was like his body had been waiting for just a bit more silence before resting. Baze's head came down, and something wet splashed against his hand. His eyes bulged open, and he saw that half the glass of bourbon had sloshed onto the carpet.

"Shit!" Baze set the glass on the table next to his easy chair and hopped up. He immediately strode toward the kitchen, looking for the roll of paper towels. But all he found was the little brown cylinder of cardboard that signaled the roll of Brawny was spent. Baze cursed again, and headed toward the room that was supposed to be a second bedroom, but actually served as his office. He thought he remembered keeping a stray rag or two in there.

Baze entered the disheveled area, striding past the bulletin board that was covered in various newspaper articles and yarn on the left side of the room. His eyes flickered over the headline of one of the articles that read, *"Twelve Police Killed In Mass Shootout,"* and onto the table that was pushed against the opposing wall. He riffled through several items, including a box of ammo, a gun-magazine, a wad of cash, a pair of handcuffs, and a can of WD-40. Finally, next to the canister of lubricant, there was a white rag that was embroidered with the outline of flowers. Baze snatched it up and hurried back into his living room.

It was then that Baze noticed that he had left the blinds open to his living room. Standing in his boxers and a white tank top, he looked out of the window and felt vulnerable. Baze briskly walked over to the blinds and twisted them shut, his heart thumping. If there was one thing he would never sacrifice, it was his privacy.

With the rag still in his hand, Baze stepped back over next to his easy chair and got on all fours, dabbing the bourbon that had spilled onto the carpet. Most of it quickly lifted from the ground, but a couple of straggler drops remained behind. Baze furiously scrubbed the remaining liquid, but all he seemed to be doing was rubbing it deeper into the carpet.

"*Shit!*" Baze stood up, chucked the rag angrily onto the ground, and almost in contempt of what he had spilled, he picked the glass of bourbon off of the table and downed the rest in a single swig. Wiping his soaked mustache with his forearm, Baze set the glass down forcefully and plopped back into the chair.

His knuckles were still aching, and despite what he had said to his penultimate beating victim, the spot just below his ear where he had been socked twice was also a little sore. The girl, whose name was Kailey, was safe and sound back at Gamma Phi Beta, her sorority at Portland State University. She had been only able to string a few coherent sentences together, but Baze was able to glean that she was a PSU student, and thus, he drove her back to sorority row in downtown Portland. She pointed out which house was the one she was staying at, and Baze had walked her to the front door. He had gotten her to sit down on the front porch, rang the doorbell, and then left before anyone had answered. Kailey's sorority sisters would have questions. Questions that he didn't have the answers to. And being that Baze was six foot four and broad shouldered with an unsightly scar on his cheek, he might've appeared as the villain to whoever opened the door.

Baze absentmindedly rubbed his mustache and felt himself drift off again. His thoughts went to the five men, beaten and unconscious on the sidewalk. Hopefully, the walloping would be enough to deter them from preying on any other unsuspecting girls that they met in the future. But Baze knew deep down that it wouldn't. Evil wasn't malleable. It didn't change. It was rigid and resilient. Unforgiving. All the ass-whooping would do would be to change who the eventual victim was. Baze knew better than anyone that evil would survive. It would fall through the cracks and live on. It may go dormant for a while. But it would still be there. Biding its time.

That was the last thought he had before Baze fell asleep.

With a start, Baze was thrown unceremoniously out of dreamland and found himself still reclined in his chair, stinking of bourbon. A steady knocking on his front door had woken him up. He remained sitting still for several seconds, thinking it had to be a mistake. Who could possibly want to see him? But then the knocking resumed, and with a grunt, Baze pushed himself out of the chair.

His head thumped in pain as he stumbled across the living room. It was the same spot, just on the fringe of his hairline, a few inches above his eyebrows. That was where the pain was almost always centralized in the morning. Baze wasn't sure if that particular spot was where the toxins from the whiskey settled overnight, but it constantly seemed to throb after he had drunk more than two glasses of Wild Turkey.

Before opening his door, Baze peeked out of

his blinds. A redheaded woman with a stern expression was standing on the porch of his apartment. He didn't recognize her. But he didn't recognize most people, so this wasn't necessarily cause for concern. Baze flipped the deadbolt and pulled the door open.

The redhead appraised him with narrowed eyes. She looked down at his boxers and then up at the scar on his cheek.

"Anton Baze?" She sounded like she hoped she was wrong. That Anton Baze surely had to be someone more put-together.

Baze looked over his shoulder into his apartment and then back at the woman.

"Since no one else is here, I guess that must be me."

"I'm Lieutenant Emily Arroyo."

Baze kept an impassive expression, but his pulse began to ascend. He thought of the five men lying motionless on the pavement. After what they had been doing, had they really had the gall to call the police?

"How can I help you?"

Arroyo's eyes shifted back and forth. "You may hear about it on the news soon, but yesterday evening, we arrested the head of an organized crime syndicate for basically every felony we have a name for. Trafficking, possession, distribution, you name it. The man's name is Frank Bruno."

Baze stayed still, but his mind was moving at warp speed. This wasn't good. This wasn't good at all.

"As you can imagine, Bruno was fairly tight-lipped about his endeavors. His attorney saw to that. But the one piece of information we did extract was the name of a man who had done work for him in the past. He didn't mention exactly what it was that you *did*, Mr. Baze, but I can't imagine that it would be something that you would be all that eager to talk about."

Baze smiled, though he felt his stomach doing backflips. "Well, you are right about that, Red."

"Please, call me Lieutenant Arroyo."

"You got it, Lieutenant Red."

Arroyo's jaw twisted in annoyance. She looked like she wanted to tell Baze to go fuck himself.

"Surprisingly, I am not here to talk about your history with Bruno, Mr. Baze. I am here because he said you have information."

Baze raised his eyebrows. "Information?"

"Information. He wouldn't tell us exactly what it was, but he insinuated that it was something of some significance. I believe the phrase he used was, 'The biggest secret that this city has ever kept.'"

Arroyo let her words hang in the air dramatically. As everything clicked, Baze suddenly felt a yearning to laugh. *Oh, Frankie,* he thought. *You've outdone yourself this time.*

"I don't know any secrets, Lieutenant Red. I just know facts."

Arroyo narrowed her eyes. "Well, what facts do you know?"

"The fact that you should never show up unannounced on a man's front porch asking for information when he is still in his boxers."

"You can go put on—"

"I'm not interested in sharing anything with you, Red."

Baze made a move to shut the door, but Arroyo stepped forward and placed her hand on the frame.

"Wait! Think about what you are doing, Baze. The most powerful criminal kingpin in the city is in police custody, and the only person he has managed to point his finger at is you. Do you really want us to do this the hard way? To look into whatever it was you were doing at Bruno's request? I don't think that would work out well for you."

Baze smiled again, and let Arroyo stand there for a second, looking agitated and a bit frantic.

"Anyone ever tell you, you look like that chick from *The Killing*?"

"What are you—"

Before Arroyo could finish her sentence, Baze slammed the door in her face.

"What a prick."

Arroyo was back in her car, seething. She grinded her teeth, and smacked the passenger seat viciously, as if it had personally done her a great dishonor. She looked back up at the duplex and saw the man's shadow in his living room cast against the blinds. Even just the outline of Baze made her want to throw something. These days, her temper was on a shorter fuse than it ever had been before. Small things set her off. Confrontations that wouldn't have even made her blink now put a damper on her whole day. Someone like Anton Baze, who might have caused mild agitation way back when, now made her absolutely furious. Who was he to slam the door in her face?

It had started in the months following the shootout all those years ago. She had noticed that she had less patience for trivial things. Then it had morphed into a constant irritability, especially when dealing with criminals. Eventually, agitation had evolved into fury. And fury had transformed into hatred. She loathed the scum that prowled the streets. Men like Frank Bruno who preyed on the weak and unsuspecting. Those downright animals who raped and stole and murdered.

Perhaps it had been watching her partner's head explode. Ever since that bullet had zipped through Ray McCabe's skull and tore the life right out of him, things had changed. *She* had changed. Where before she had been calculating, reserved and eloquent, she was now emotional, passionate, and angry. So angry. The grief had ripped her apart for the first year. She had frequently woken up in the night sobbing, after having her subconscious replay McCabe's murder again and again in her dreams. But then, the sadness had changed into something else—hatred. And the hatred had grown within her like a disease.

As she stared at Baze's outline, the curtains suddenly opened, and there he stood. It took them only a second or two to make eye contact, and as soon as their eyes met, he smiled. It was derisive and chiding, like a young child sticking their tongue out. Baze raised his thick fingers into the air and fluttered them at her, waving sardonically. Arroyo didn't even think twice before she flipped him off.

Whatever information he possessed wasn't worth the trouble. They didn't need to make a deal with Frank Bruno. He could rot in hell. Holding her one-fingered salute in the air for several seconds, Arroyo shifted the car into reverse and pulled out of the driveway.

Welsh threw his gym bag onto the floor of his

duplex, still panting heavily. He had just finished an hour of cardio at Planet Fitness; something he had not done in a very long time. The majority of the sixty minutes he had spent walking on the treadmill, but he had also tried his hand at the elliptical, which may have been a mistake. His arms were already sore, and his heart was racing at a speed that he didn't feel like he could ever recover from. Sweat congealed the tank top he was wearing to his back. It felt like he might have to go to the emergency room and have doctors cut off the shirt with as much as it was sticking to him.

He headed toward the shower, passing the table where he had lain the letter that Mo had given him. Whatever was inside was a mystery, but Welsh had a guess that Mo had bequeathed him with something that was far more than what Welsh deserved. Maybe his house, or the keys to his car. Welsh had often made flippant, lighthearted comments about his desire to drive Mo's Audi Q7. But those asides were supposed to be in jest. Hopefully Mo hadn't taken them to heart.

The interior of the duplex he was renting was filthy. Ever since he had been widowed, the cleanliness of his homelife had gone down the tube. Welsh supposed it was only natural that such a thing had occurred, especially since Wendy had been a ferocious and persnickety cleaner. However, it wasn't just the fact of being a normal, lazy male that Welsh attributed the lack of sanitation to. He had capitulated to indifference since his wife's death. Sweeping floors and dusting counters seemed so gratuitous now. What was the point in keeping a pristine home if your life had lost most of its meaning anyway?

He had only been back to the house he had lived in with Wendy twice in the past fifteen years. And he had never returned to his second home in Wilsonville. Welsh couldn't bear the thought of stepping inside that diseased place, where her blood still stained the sheets of the bed that he had never bothered to remove. Both of his properties housed too many memories to return to; the one just outside the city held recollections that were too fond, the one in Wilsonville too tortured. So Welsh had rented a duplex downtown. It helped to be in the center of everything. Hipsters bustling back and forth, talking about vinyl records and avocado toast, and broke musicians on the street corners with an upside-down fedora collecting money. There was rarely quiet in Welsh's adopted neighborhood, and he liked it that way. For even though Bob the Butcher had been killed fifteen years before, it still felt like he was lingering in the shadows every time that there was complete silence.

Welsh stripped himself of his shorts and sweaty briefs and finally managed to peel the tank top off of his torso. He went into the bathroom, with its cracked walls and its rusty showerhead, and cranked on the knob so that hot water discharged from the cluster of holes above. It splattered onto the cheap mat that Welsh had bought from Home Depot, creating a pillar of steam that rose from the tub. Welsh was just about to step in when he heard it.

Thunk-thunk-thunk.

He turned toward the living room, feeling strangely uneasy about what he had just heard. Could someone have made a mistake? Who could possibly be calling on him? But then it happened again.

Thunk-thunk-thunk.

Someone was knocking on his front door.

Arroyo set her cup of coffee down on her desk, using the mouse to navigate her computer screen. The cursor found its way to the line of text in the report that needed to be modified, and she began to type. It was strangely therapeutic to watch her hands click and clack on the keyboard without any effort at all. Muscle-memory was the most peculiar thing. How could it be possible that our bodies were so malleable to whatever task we authorized them to engage in? How was it that Arroyo could close her eyes, and the tips of her fingers could slide back-

and-forth to transcribe the thoughts that were percolating in her brain? It was so bizarre. But welcomingly bizarre. She would zone out for a minute and a fully fleshed-out paragraph would be there. And it would actually make sense. Remarkable.

This was another one of the behavioral changes she had unintentionally adapted since the mass-killing of her colleagues outside of the cabin a decade and a half before. Wonderment of normalcy; or, at least, what most considered to be normal, but what Arroyo found not normal at all. It was extraordinary. The processes and mechanisms of human function. It was a forced-appreciation. Coming so close to death. Taking a bullet to the hip while watching her partner have his brain removed from his skull. Lieutenant Don Chaser clawing at his throat in his final moments on earth. The rest of the dead, their blood and guts scattered about. It had shoved gratitude into her being, and an admiration of life and all its micro and macro mechanisms.

It was strange how such a harrowing, traumatic event had simultaneously affected change in two dramatically different ways. The event had festered antipathy and hatred, but also produced a keen sense of awareness of the miracles of living. And Arroyo had recently been able to differentiate the two and define how she felt. She didn't hate the world. She admired it. She just despised a lot of the people who were living in it.

As she continued to plow away through her report, the door to her office opened. Detective Lowry peaked his head in through the entryway and gave her an awkward smile.

"Somebody on the phone for you, boss. Mindy said she just tried to transfer the guy directly to you, but it went to your voicemail box."

Arroyo looked at her phone in surprise. She must have been so absorbed in her report that she missed the blinking light.

"Sorry. This has been drawing my full attention. Tell Mindy to patch him through again. Who is it by the way?"

Lowry shrugged. "Not sure." He left the room.

A few seconds later, the blinking red light on her Avaya landline indicated that Mindy had re-transferred whoever was on the line. Arroyo pecked at the light and then hit the button that said, "External line one."

"Hello?"

"Hey, Red."

A pause. Arroyo felt her stomach turn over, and then her blood instantly began to boil.

"What the hell do *you* want?"

"Nice to talk to you again, too."

"Fuck off. Why are you calling me?"

Another pause. Was Baze laughing? It was pretty muffled, but Arroyo felt certain that he was chuckling. *What an asshole!*

"Well, Red, I've decided you were right. I don't particularly want you looking into my dealings with Frankie. And after some deliberation with the voices in my head, I have changed my mind."

Arroyo let out a derisive laugh. "Well, that's lovely! But I am afraid it is too late, Anton. You blew your chance. I won't be making any deals with someone of your ilk. So have a nice day, Mr. Baze."

Before Arroyo could hang up, Baze blurted his next sentence loud into the phone.

"And what if I say that I know a secret? Something that is going to change everything?"

Arroyo had taken the phone away from her ear and was preparing to press it down against the base of the landline. Slowly but surely, as she processed what he had said, she moved the receiver back toward the side of her head.

"Then I'd say you are full of shit."

Baze chuckled again. This time, it was less infuriating. Perhaps it was because Arroyo was waiting for what the man was going to say.

"Hmm. All right, Red. Well, what if I say that I have proof? A bit circumstantial, sure, but still proof."

Arroyo sighed. "Proof of what, Baze?"

"Proof that *he* is still alive. Proof that he's been here the whole time, just waiting for his moment to step back out of the shadows."

For some reason, Arroyo felt the back of her neck prickle.

"What the hell are you talking about?"

"Well, Red… What if I told you that you never caught the real Robert Macabre?"

Welsh stood naked in front of the closed door, shaking. It was partly the cold, but mostly what his eyes saw that made him quiver. The letter had been shoved under his front door and had been waiting for him ominously as he had waddled out into the living room in his towel. As he had bent over, his towel had fallen off of his waist and onto the floor. At the same time, he had seen the stylized font on the front of the letter that said *Carson*. And he was too shocked to put the towel back on.

When Welsh had torn open the letter, time had frozen. This had to be some parallel universe that he had stumbled into through a wormhole in his shower, or an alternate dimension that he had transcended to by way of a glitch in the space-time continuum. Because both of those explanations made far more sense than what was actually happening. Fifteen years had passed, but he still recognized the handwriting immediately.

Hello Carson,

I have missed you, my old friend. I have missed you terribly.

I can only envisage the look on your face when you begin to read this. The agony. The utter anguish in your eyes. It must be like stepping out of reality and into one of your nightmares. I know I still haunt your dreams, Carson. I know you better than you think. And I know how nauseated you feel right now. How repulsed. How absolutely horror-stricken you must be.

But, if you are being honest with yourself, I believe you have been aware of my fate the entire time. This story was never going to have a happy ending for you. And if you thought otherwise, you have been fooling yourself.

You should have known that this tale was only halfway told. What kind of saga ends on a cliffhanger? Surely you must have been cognizant of the fact that this was simply the intermission. My adjournment has finally elapsed, and it is time to light this fire once more. It is time to watch it burn.

Can you imagine what they will think when I open the curtains for act two?

But for every villain there must be a hero. For every evil, there must be good. It wouldn't be a fair fight without you. We are the Yin and the Yang, Carson. The light and the dark.

Once again I say, may the best man win. For your sake, I hope this time you are more prepared. For when you dance with the devil, you better know your steps.

Good luck, old friend. We will see each other soon.

- Robert.

41

Baze watched as the Chevy Tahoe climbed into the driveway. As the front end came dangerously close to his apartment, he felt his pulse increase dramatically. This was going to be the first time another person had laid eyes upon his research. His obsession. And that person was a lieutenant and a twenty-year veteran of PPD. Someone whose livelihood it was to look at information and pick it apart until a rational theory could be gleaned. Someone who knew which details were important, and which weren't. And someone who he had gotten off on the wrong foot with.

Baze had thrown on a black dress shirt and slacks and even put on aftershave. His idea was that if he looked somewhat presentable, it was more likely that he would be taken seriously. Then again, it is not like Arroyo would just forget him standing in his boxers, smelling like whiskey. But at least he would show that he could clean up.

He watched as the woman hopped out of the large

vehicle and began plodding up his driveway. She wore a scowl on her face. Baze loosened his collar and scratched at his neck. Perhaps this wasn't actually a good idea. But it was too late now. She was standing on his front porch and knocking on the door. Baze pulled it open.

"Hello, Red."

Arroyo's eyes narrowed as she looked Baze up and down. "What, are you trying to be Tony Soprano?"

"Something along those lines. I almost put on a white tie to pull it all together. But then I realized if I went full-gangster, it might not look good to someone who only knows me through a mobster."

"None of this looks good anyway, Baze. You. This situation. Bruno. It is all leaving a pretty funky taste in my mouth."

Baze smiled. "Wait until you see what I've got." He gestured toward the area behind him, and Arroyo hesitantly stepped into the living room. Her eyes scanned the walls and the furniture as if she expected to find something disreputable and perverse as decoration.

"So, Red, you were one of the detectives back in oh four, were you not? You must be one of the longest-tenured cops in Portland."

"Eighteen years," said Arroyo stiffly.

"Bet you have some stories."

Arroyo grunted.

Baze nodded. "Not one to share. I get it. Still... That long in that profession can be tough on your family."

"Don't really have one of those."

"You don't have—"

Arroyo groaned and stopped in her tracks. "Look, Baze. I did not come here for idle chitchat. Honestly, I don't even know what I am doing here. So can you get down to brass tacks, and waste only five minutes of my time instead of twenty? Show me what you got."

Baze stared at her. The lieutenant had taken him off guard. He hadn't been expecting to become pen pals or anything, but it was fairly jarring for someone to be completely averse to small talk. Part of him had expected her to be friendly as a sort of peace offering for their terse interaction that morning. Alas, she truly seemed to not give a damn about being cordial. She just wanted answers.

"Wow, you aren't exactly warm and fuzzy, are you?"

Arroyo raised her eyebrows. For a moment, Baze wondered if she would make an about-face and walk back through the front door.

"In there," he said quickly, pointing toward his office. Arroyo froze, apparently waiting for Baze to go in first.

"It isn't booby-trapped. You can go on in."

She gave him a fierce scowl and walked into the room. Baze followed suit. He watched as she looked over the table that had various materials on it, including the can of WD-40 and the gun. Arroyo had a look on her face like she smelled something funny as her eyes crossed over the different items.

"What is all of this crap for?"

"What do you mean 'crap'? These are my most valued possessions," quipped Baze, picking up the WD-40.

Arroyo didn't laugh.

"Anyway, most of the pertinent info will be on that board there."

Arroyo's head turned toward the bulletin board, with all of the various photographs and files hung on it, and the red yarn connecting certain documents to others. Her mouth slowly went agape as she looked over everything.

"Jesus," she said softly.

"Yeah. And I didn't even get paid for any of that."

Her eyes widened as she took it all in. "Are all of these case files?"

"No. Not everything. There are also newspaper articles. Photographs that I got online. Stuff like that."

"This gives new meaning to the word, 'obsession.'"

"You say obsession, I say fiercely enthusiastic interest."

Arroyo twitched. "What sparked all this?"

Baze shrugged his shoulders. "How does anything like this start? I read the paper. I looked things up online. I researched."

"And you came to the working theory that Robert Macabre is still out there?"

Baze didn't miss the skepticism in her voice. But he expected that kind of reaction.

"First, let me present the facts before you pass your mental verdict, Red."

Arroyo rolled her eyes. "Well, be my guest. Present away. And I will present how you are wrong."

Baze smiled, but didn't reply. He walked over to the bulletin board and picked up a stack of black folders that were amassed on the smaller table underneath the bulletin board. As he shuffled through the folders, looking for the one he wanted, he started to extrapolate.

"Well, there are things that are obvious, and things that aren't. I think a natural place to start would be the obvious. First, the physical stature."

Baze took a deep breath. "Carson Welsh is the only person alive that we know of that has seen Robert Macabre. Through multiple encounters, he always described the man as husky. Tall. Muscular. And then there is the Dinwoodie video, which, from what I have been told, lines up with Welsh's depiction of Macabre."

Baze pointed at the center of the bulletin board. There was a five-by-eight picture of William Robert Tennyson pinned there.

"Will Tennyson was only five foot nine. And one hundred and sixty pounds. Not exactly Arnold Schwarzenegger, was he?"

Arroyo rolled her eyes. "Well, I have *seen* the video you refer to, unlike you. And it's dark. Grainy. It is almost impossible to tell Macabre's build."

"And Welsh's description?"

"Welsh firmly believes that Tennyson is the guy."

"That's not what I was asking."

When Arroyo didn't reply to this, Baze shrugged and kept rifling through folders. As he did so, he continued to speak.

"Second obvious item... Why was there absolutely no physical evidence recovered linking Tennyson to any of the victims? No DNA. No weapons. No trophies. Sure as hell, no bodies. Nothing. When they searched his storage unit, didn't they find it strange that he had nothing that would point to him being the killer?"

The skeptical expression did not leave Arroyo's face, but it took her a while to respond. She seemed to cogitate on her answer, trying to frame the perfect refutation of Baze's argument.

"You think he would be dumb enough to keep anything in his storage unit? He was a clever man, Baze. Just because there isn't necessarily physical evidence doesn't mean a mountain of circumstantial evidence isn't proof."

Baze scoffed. "Wow, that was poetic, Red. But if we give credence to what you are saying, it would break the mold of every serial killer in history. Bundy, BTK, the Golden State Killer, John Wayne Gacy... When arrests were made, physical evidence tying the suspect to their victims was found every single time. So, you are saying that Robert Macabre was not only the most prolific killer in the last thirty years but also a forensic wizard?"

Arroyo's jaw twisted. She was getting more and more agitated by the second. Baze wondered if it was because he was making sense, and speaking to the sliver of doubt that she had in her own mind. Alas, she expressed no sign of being swayed.

"You'll need to find something a lot more concrete than that, Baze. All you are succeeding in doing is pissing me off."

He let out a booming laugh. "That doesn't seem all that hard to do, Red."

For whatever reason, Baze found that he was enjoying himself immensely. Ribbing the lieutenant was a natural exercise, as she seemed so vulnerable to teasing. Baze glanced down at her left hand and was not surprised to find that there wasn't a wedding ring. He could see why men would be averse to her, with her grumpy stoicism and general unpleasantness, but he found himself drawn to the woman. She was one of those no-nonsense, never-beat-around-the-bush type of people. And he liked that. While continuing to chuckle, Baze finally located the folder he was looking for and opened it up.

"Some interviews from those who knew Tennyson. There are a couple of interesting quotes in here. This from Wallace Brimmer. A KA of Tennyson's. He's in prison, serving ten years for multiple drug-related charges. The *Portland Tribune* did a piece a few years ago about the meth epidemic, where they talked to several dealers in the joint. There is an interesting little bit here about Brimmer's relationship with Tennyson."

Baze made a show out of clearing his throat and then read the quote from the article. "'I still find it hard to comprehend. Willie was kind of a squirrelly dude, but I would have never pegged him as a killer,' said Brimmer. 'He was always just about the dough. Making as much money as possible. Selling to as many dealers as he could. He was always cooking. Middle of the night and he would be cooking. It seemed weird that he even set time aside to kill those girls.'"

Baze looked up at Arroyo to gauge her reaction. She was shaking her head so aggressively that it seemed plausible that it would start spinning like that little girl from *The Exorcist*.

"How many times in homicide cases does that happen with witness statements, Baze? It's always, 'I can't believe he did it. He was so nice. I can't believe he's a killer.' It's never, 'Yeah, I definitely saw that one coming.'"

"Sure, I'll give you that. But when added to everything else…"

"What is everything else, Baze? What does that mean?" Arroyo's voice was shrill and full of annoyance.

For a moment, Baze stared at her with a half-smile on his face. Then, he pointed at a news article that was hung on the upper-right side of the board. A woman's face was smiling down at them. She was pretty, with high rounded cheeks and a straight smile and big brown eyes. Her hair was light blond; her skin naturally tan.

"Know who that is?"

Arroyo sighed and pressed her thumbs against her temples like he was giving her a headache. She didn't say anything for a few long moments, almost as if she were debating continuing the conversation at all. Baze twirled his fingers in the air, indicating that he was waiting for an answer. After glaring at him fiercely, Arroyo responded.

"Rachel Burns. And I know what you are going to say, but there is almost no evidence—"

"Burns is similar in age, looks and body type to the other victims, and she was killed only three months before Tracy Dinwoodie. *Three months.*"

Arroyo nodded slowly and mockingly, like she was trying to reason with a toddler. "And there is a man on death row because of it."

"It doesn't bother you that Jimmy Gleason had an alibi?"

"It doesn't bother *you* that he was found covered in her blood?"

"Do you always answer a question with a question?"

Arroyo's nostrils flared. "Gleason's alibi came from a father that desperately wanted to see his son avoid the electric chair. And, if you weren't paying attention, there were several discrepancies in his testimony."

Baze cocked his head to the side, and when he spoke, his voice was a little softer. "Discrepancies, or failure to photographically recall a night because nothing significant happened? Have you ever heard the theory that those who are innocent are actually harder to defend than those who are guilty? When someone *didn't* commit a murder, they most likely were doing something far less exciting, and thus, aren't likely to remember every detail of what they were doing. When they are interviewed, the cops always take their shaky story as an indicator of guilt, when really, it's just indicative of the fact that they weren't doing anything worth remembering."

Arroyo rolled her eyes and rubbed her hand against her freckled forehead. "This is irrelevant."

"Is it though, Red?" asked Baze. "Because Jimmy Gleason had an alibi for Burns' estimated time of death, and was only covered in her DNA when he found her two hours later. You think he murdered his girlfriend, waited two hours while dripping with her blood, and then called the police to report his own crime?"

"The jury seemed to think he did."

Baze continued like she hadn't spoken. "And it doesn't bother you that the kid was clean as a whistle before the murder? Never even got a speeding ticket. Had good grades. What sort of valedictorian randomly decides to off his own girlfriend?"

"Baze—"

"And you are neglecting the fact that Rachel Burns was killed *less than a mile away* from Jacey Duhart. A young woman that was murdered just *months* before a series of murders of other young women and only a couple football fields away from where one of the vics was found. That doesn't fire off any warning signals in your brain, Red? Come on."

A patronizing smile spread across Arroyo's face.

"You are dead wrong. Dead wrong."

"Robert Macabre killed Rachel Burns. And Will Tennyson was in prison on the night that it happened."

Arroyo just kept shaking her head. Before she could come up with another biting retort, Baze moved away from the bulletin board and picked up one of his black folders. He flicked through it at a rapid pace until he found the piece of paper he was looking for. With every passing moment, Baze could feel his heart rate increasing. He was now bounding with energy, like a cooped-up dog that had finally been let out of the house. Not only was he teeming with excitement, but it was also a cathartic exercise to finally share his work with someone after all of these years.

"These are witness statements from a bar fight in Tualatin on the night of April fifteenth, two thousand and four. Multiple people, including a John Tyson and a Michael Rau, said that the fight was instigated by one William Robert Tennyson over a game of pool gone bad. Strange that this happened on the same night that Tracy Dinwoodie was likely abducted."

Arroyo hesitated. It was a small pause, but it was

enough to make Baze feel a fleeting sense of triumph. "We don't know for sure what night Tracy Dinwoodie was abducted," she said quietly.

"Edwin Spade would probably disagree with that conclusion." Baze reached back for the same black folder that he had just been carrying and pulled out a wad of stapled files from the back of the folder. "This from the autopsy... 'The progression of contusions around the ankles and wrists indicate that the victim was bound by rope for approximately forty-eight hours before her death.' Well, since forensics says that she died on April seventeenth, isn't the logical conclusion then that she was abducted on April fifteenth? The same night that Willie Tennyson was seen at a bar nearly twenty miles away from Dinwoodie's house?"

"Conjecture, Baze. This is all just conjecture," said Arroyo. But her tone wasn't as forceful as it had been just moments before.

"I think you need to reread the definition of conjecture."

Arroyo stayed quiet for a few long seconds. She appeared to be debating the best way to attack his argument next. Surprisingly, her next query seemed like more of an actual question than a rebuttal.

"If you are right, and we caught the wrong guy, why haven't there been more killings?"

For several moments, Baze let a foreboding silence blanket the space between them. He stared at Arroyo, trying to show the ominous nature of the answer he was about to give. Maybe he imagined it, but it seemed like the woman moved a fraction of an inch backward.

"Maybe there have been, Red. Maybe there have

been ones that we just don't know about."

Arroyo shook her head in exasperation. She turned away from him, apparently too vexed with his disposition to even look in his direction. Baze took a step toward her, and she moved around quickly, shooting Baze a fierce glare as if to warn him not to come any closer. There was a brief awkward silence, and then Baze continued.

"Do you know The Nowhere Girls case on the coast?" asked Baze. "Solved a couple of years ago by a PI?"

Arroyo looked back toward him, and surprise flickered across her face. "I'm familiar with it, yeah."

"In the eighties and nineties there were five confirmed victims. Then there was a huge gap. Up until two thousand sixteen, no one even knew that it was still happening. But the killers were there the whole time, working in the shadows. They got their body count up to fifteen before they were caught three decades later."

"That was an anomaly though, Baze. How many killers do you know of that managed to operate like that, with the world oblivious to their existence?"

Baze didn't miss a beat. "The Halloween Ripper. Caught a year after. He killed twelve people—one every year for a decade. And the police were none the wiser. All in little old Oregon."

Finally, Arroyo didn't have a comeback in the chamber. Her mouth opened and then shut, and she let out a sigh.

"I know you think that that's a straw man's argument," said Baze. "But all I am trying to show you is that it is possible. That murderers don't always get caught."

Arroyo looked down at the floor and crossed her arms. For some reason, this felt like a victory. Baze knew that he hadn't exactly shown her the light, but the fact that he was making any headway into her gruff barrier of counterpoints was a small win.

It was time to show her the good stuff. Now that Baze had Arroyo's attention, she needed to see the real information that he had. With pep in his step, Baze walked back toward the bulletin board and the smaller table underneath it. He picked up a plastic bag with a small case inside it and unsealed the bag. Slowly, he pried apart the case and stuck his finger in the hole that was at the center of the DVD, and twiddled the disc around in the air until Arroyo saw what it was.

"For your viewing pleasure."

Baze walked to the far corner of the room, where there was an old-looking television on a rolling TV stand tucked away. He pulled out the stand and maneuvered it so it was directly in front of Arroyo. Underneath the bulky TV, there was a shelf with a DVD player resting on it. Several black chords jutted out from the TV and the DVD player and intertwined together until they plugged into a long white rectangular box that had several outlets along it. Baze pressed a button on the DVD player and a receiver stuck its tongue out. Baze fed it the DVD and then pressed the receiver back into the player.

"I like to think of this as my trump card."

Baze then pushed a button on the TV, and the screen flickered on. It was a security recording. Everything was either black or a dark green color, indicating that the footage was being shot at night in a place where the lighting was almost nonexistent. The camera from which the recording had been pulled was at an overhead angle, pointing downward at a man wearing a long-sleeved white shirt. The man had a rag in his hand and was wiping around the brim of a glass. The bar he stood in front of was occupied by only two people: a heavy-looking brunette woman in a flowered blouse and a bald man with glasses and a dark T-shirt. There were several empty stools in between the two people; this particular bar did not look like a thriving establishment.

"Look at the timestamp," said Baze, pointing at the bottom right corner of the TV. In small white font, the screen read, "06-04-2004. 6:02 p.m." When Arroyo's eyes read the writing, they seemed to bulge.

The bald man was staring straight forward, oblivious to whatever was around him. The large brunette was gazing at her half-empty beer glass and looking forlorn. The bartender just continued to wipe at the glass, almost compulsively, like he couldn't get it quite clean enough. Eventually, a new figure sauntered into the frame with his head down, and slid onto the stool smoothly. The bartender approached the newcomer. They seemed to exchange words, and then the bartender walked out of the frame to fetch whatever the man had ordered. Eventually, the newcomer looked up right into the camera. Even though the film was somewhat grainy, it was fairly easy to tell that it was William Robert Tennyson.

Baze walked forward and paused the video. Arroyo was frozen, staring at the frame on the TV.

"So, Red, can you explain *this*? Can you explain to

me how Will Tennyson is at the Bit House Saloon at two minutes after six p.m. on June fourth of two thousand and four? Because, unless I am mistaken, Wendy Welsh was killed in Wilsonville on this very night, sometime between six and six thirty. And, being that Wilsonville is seventeen miles from Bit House Saloon, you are looking at about a thirty-minute commute at this time of day with traffic. And yet, if you want to watch the rest of this footage, Tennyson doesn't leave this bar until six fifty-eight. So, the earliest he could have arrived at Carson Welsh's house is approximately seven thirty. And by that time, the cops were already swarming the place, because Welsh had arrived there to find his dead wife just before seven, when he placed the phone call to nine-one-one."

Arroyo seemed to have gone pale. Her eyes were wide and her jaw was crooked—Baze could hear the slight clicking of her teeth grinding together. She was still completely engrossed with the still image of Will Tennyson gazing up into the camera with a shifty look on his face. The only part of her body that was moving were her fingers. One hand was latched onto the other, and it was massaging her appendages like some sort of soothing motion to quell the discomfort within her. She hadn't broken off her piercing stare at the TV since the moment Tennyson had walked into the frame.

Baze let a couple more seconds of silence linger.

"Red?"

"God damn," Arroyo whispered.

"This doesn't make any sense."

Baze watched her. He saw the fear in her eyes. The shock.

"The man who killed my partner," continued Arroyo. "The one who shot me… He *has* to be Macabre. He just has to be." She rubbed her hip, as if it pained her when she recollected what had happened all those years ago.

Baze let silence percolate the air for a couple of long seconds before answering. He knew he had her now, so there was no point in being as frank with his arguments as he had been before. Still, he had to explain the truth to her as best he could. He spoke slowly.

"The idea of a cornered druggie who knew he was going down getting in a shoot-out with SWAT can be mutually exclusive with a deranged serial killer. They don't have to be connected. Lots of different people can kill other people."

"But… the gas station video. He was there that night. He was right by Welsh's house. And his prints were on that package."

Baze smiled wryly, wiggling his index finger in the air. He then scratched at his mustache for a second, watching Arroyo rock back and forth a little, the stress of the revelation literally shaking her.

"Have you not figured it out yet? Robert Macabre *framed* Will Tennyson."

Arroyo's eyes bulged. "But… How?"

"Well, look… Each of the first two vics were full of that substance that Macabre had inoculated them with, right? The fear serum? It contained mostly meth and LSD. And Tennyson was arrested for possession of meth and LSD back in ninety-nine. I don't think there is any doubt that Tennyson cooked the batch of drugs that went into that concoction of chemicals."

Arroyo scratched her head, and then she frowned as she thought. "So Tennyson was Macabre's *dealer*?"

"Exactly. It is where he got the stuff. I'm guessing that Macabre arranged to meet him nearby Welsh's house, so that he would be caught on camera in the neighborhood on the night that David Kane's hand was left on Welsh's front porch. I don't know if he planned for the gas station necessarily, but there all sorts of traffic-cams and CC-TV setups in that neighborhood. My guess is that he was banking on the fact that Tennyson's car would be caught on one of them."

"And the prints?"

"How much would you be willing to bet that the box that Kane's hand was left in was the same box that Tennyson used to deliver Macabre the drugs?"

Arroyo slowly nodded. "So… Macabre used the same box to deliver the hand because he knew that it would have Tennyson's print on it?"

Baze pointed at her in the affirmative.

"Jesus," whispered Arroyo.

"I know."

"But if he has been out there this whole time, and he has been killing, why has he changed his whole MO? He went out of the way to taunt us in oh four with the letters and the crime scenes. Hell, he was literally stalking Welsh. But now he's been working in the shadows this whole time?"

Baze shrugged. "Well, it wouldn't be a very good setup if the next week after Tennyson blew up in that cabin you found another body, would it?"

"Jesus," she hissed again. "Jesus Christ. How have we missed this?"

Baze let a pause hang in the air. He didn't want to make her feel guilty, but he also wanted to tell the honest truth. It was always a tricky dance, trying to be authentic while maintaining a sense of tact.

"Stubbornness. Every cop or PI is guilty of it at some point in time. When they latch onto something that has seemingly incontrovertible evidence, they ignore that little voice in their head that tells them that there is more to the story."

Arroyo gave a small nod, then pointed at the paused video on the TV screen. "How did you get this?"

Baze gave a little chuckle, and his baritone voice had an unintentional diabolical tone attached to it.

"Don't ask questions you don't want to know the answers to, Red. I'm not a cop, remember. I am not bound by the same set of rules you are."

Arroyo didn't reply to this. She was back to massaging her left hand as if it was causing her great discomfort.

"So, if Tennyson wasn't the guy... Then who was?"

Baze grinned. "I'm glad you asked, Red. I'm glad you asked."

He walked back over to the table that was underneath the bulletin board, and sifted through the stack of folders until he arrived at a particularly thick one.

"Everything I have on potential suspects," said Baze. "Now, first off, I will admit, I don't have any concrete evidence on a particular individual. And, if you asked me today to point my finger at one person and say, 'He's the guy,' I couldn't do it with any sense of actual conviction. There are some who are more likely than others, sure, but I will let you arrive at your own conclusions..."

Baze stopped, looked at Arroyo for a second, and scratched at his mustache again with his free hand.

"Matthew Lyons. Probably one of the first people that you interviewed. I have never spoken with Lyons, but as you probably know, it is not uncommon in cases like this for the killer to have a connection to the first victim. Also, who is the first person you look at in a majority of homicides? The love interest."

Baze pulled out a black-and-white photograph that showed the back end of a white sedan parked on the side of the road. There was the outline of a person sitting in the driver's seat. The angle of the camera made it look like the person had been pulled over for some sort of traffic violation. Next to the stopped vehicle, there was another car that seemed to speed past the stopped party. The car was sleek and black.

"This is a screenshot of dashcam footage taken at a routine traffic stop on the night that Tracy Dinwoodie was abducted. This was taken just after Dinwoodie had gone on her date. The black car that is passing is registered to one Matthew Lyons. Now, what's interesting about this is that Lyons told you guys that he went straight home after their date. But he lived in Canby, about a half hour south of Portland. The only logical way to get there would be to take I-5 South. And this footage was taken in Lake Oswego. So he definitely *didn't* go straight home, unless he took the most roundabout way that I have ever seen."

Baze exhaled deeply. "What is even more interesting is that this traffic stop happened just a few miles from Tracy Dinwoodie's house."

Arroyo's mouth dropped open a few inches.

"Now, I am not one to cherry-pick evidence, so I will say that Lyons does not fit the physical build of Macabre. He is lean. Muscular, but thin. Not a large man like Macabre has been described as. But I wouldn't say that rules him out necessarily. I can't think of any *honorable* reason why he would lie to the police about where he was going."

Baze set the screenshot down and perused through the other files before pulling out another photograph. This one was of a brown-skinned man with short black hair and a sharp nose. The man's neck was thick and a blocked-lettered tattoo was visible on his neck.

"Know who this is?"

Arroyo shrugged. "No idea."

"Roland Kahlil. Drug dealer that was recently released on parole. You probably have heard the name, because, as my contact tells me, one of the boys in his gang was the one that tipped you guys off about Will Tennyson's whereabouts."

Arroyo's mouth expanded a little in apparent wonder.

"What's most interesting about the theory of Roland Kahlil as Robert Macabre is Kahlil's recent prison sentence. He was in jail from June of two thousand four until March of this year. That seem like an interesting timeline to you?"

"June of two thousand four is when the killings stopped," said Arroyo softly.

"Mm. Now what I found odd is that when Kahlil was arrested, he was found with a large quantity of meth and LSD."

Arroyo slowly nodded. "So Tennyson was Kahlil's supplier?"

"One of them, I think. Kahlil moved a lot of product, so I don't think he had just one supplier."

"So he ratted out his own supplier?"

"Going back to the theory of framing ol' Willy, perhaps Kahlil saw a good scape goat in Tennyson. Maybe that was why he had one of his people give the cops Tennyson's whereabouts."

Arroyo bobbed her head from side to side, like she was tossing the idea back and forth in her brain. "Hmm… I have a hard time seeing that man as Robert Macabre. He just looks like a thug. Like a normal dealer."

"Well, what if I told you that Kahlil had a relationship with Rachel Burns?"

Arroyo leaned forward like she hadn't heard him correctly. "What?"

"Way before she dated the Gleason boy. This was back in two thousand two. Apparently, Burns had a serious relationship with Kahlil. The defense in Gleason's trail used this as anecdotal evidence that Burns was involved with the wrong people."

Arroyo let out a breath of air that was almost a sarcastic laugh. "Well, that is a strange effing coincidence…"

"I'd say."

"But if Macabre killed Burns… why didn't he take credit for it like he did for the other victims?"

Baze gave a slow shrug. "Maybe Burns was personal. Maybe, if Kahlil is the guy, he offed her because of some sort of personal vendetta, and didn't want to have anyone make the connection to him *because* it was personal. Maybe it was his first kill. A trial run that also settled the score with an ex-girlfriend."

Arroyo didn't say anything to this, so Baze continued.

"Kahlil also fits the profile. He is one burly dude. And tall. I wouldn't want to cross paths with that guy. So he fits the description physically, he has a connection with one of the potential victims, and he was the one who leaked Tennyson's whereabouts to the police. If we are just looking logically at the facts, straight observation, and deduction, this one might be our strongest case."

Arroyo didn't miss what was implied. "And not logically? Just gut feeling? You don't think he is the guy do you?"

Baze waited a while before replying to this. He rubbed the snake of a scar on his left cheek and stared at her.

"No. I guess I don't."

"Hmm."

"But my gut has been wrong before."

Arroyo nodded. "Join the club."

"Now, if we are doing the opposite... No logical evidence but weird gut feeling. Let me introduce you to Marvin Robert Wallace."

Baze pulled out a picture that was another mugshot. However, this time, the face in the picture was plump and saggy. It was a man with a large bald spot on the top of his head, and strings of gray-black hair springing out from around the spot and twirling down to his shoulders. The man had glasses and black bags drooping under his eyes, indicating lack of sleep. His cheeks were flabby and wrinkled; his eyes beady and full of guilt.

"Wallace was arrested in two thousand for luring a minor and sexual battery. He was originally sentenced to a year in prison, but only served four months after good behavior. He is obviously a registered sex offender, but has kept his record clean since the incident."

Baze tapped his foot against the ground as he gathered his thoughts. "Wallace's specialty is software development. He designs websites for local mom-and-pop shops around Portland that are looking to market to a bigger audience. Usually, he gets hired by old farts who don't even know how to turn a computer on. But website design isn't only his job, it is also his hobby. He is the system administrator on a site called TheMostDangerousAnimal.com. It is a site that talks exclusively about serial killers."

"Lovely," quipped Arroyo.

"Wallace is the only one that writes the posts on the site," said Baze. "He aggregates all sorts of information about serial killers. Their personal lives, how they got started, a detailed account of how they each committed their crimes. It seems to be less about understanding the psychology of a killer than displaying... admiration, I guess. Especially the most brutal ones. I will give you one guess on who has the biggest section devoted to him."

"Macabre."

"Yup, Bob the Butcher has quite the dedication page on Wallace's website. Listen to this excerpt..." Baze set the photograph of Wallace down and reached back into the folder, pulling out a new document. He cleared his throat and read.

"William Robert Tennyson, aka, Bob the Butcher, was particularly cunning in his exploitation of women and his dexterous taunting of the ex-district attorney, Carson Welsh. He surpasses even the Zodiac killer as the cleverest serial murderer in the last century, with his stunningly perspicacious and sapient mockery of the police all the while brutalizing at least sixteen people in a two-month period."

Baze looked up at Arroyo with a meaningful expression on his face and then handed her the paper with the excerpt on it. She took it, but responded with a shrug.

"I don't know. Just seems like some twisted fanboy to me."

"That's what I thought at first too. But then I did some more in-depth reading on this site. He knows details about this case. Details that he shouldn't know. At one point, he mentions the fact that police identified David Kane by the ring left on his hand. A detail that wasn't ever released to the public."

Arroyo jabbed her finger in his direction. "And yet a detail that *you* seem to be cognizant of."

"But I have connections. I know people. Why would a creep that sexually assaulted a fourteen-year-old girl have an in at the police department?"

"The point is, the detail is out there," Arroyo

said.

"But that is not the only thing. He claims that Carson Welsh was once chased through the woods by Macabre while Macabre was wearing a Minotaur. A story I had never come across until I read it on this site. But it's true, isn't it?"

Arroyo didn't reply to this. She was slightly frowning while reading the printout of Marvin Wallace's website.

"This guy just gives me the creeps," explained Baze. "Like I said, I don't have any hard evidence. Just a gut feeling. And my gut is telling me that something is not right with this guy. I think it needs to be looked into."

Arroyo finished reading the printout for herself and then handed it back to Baze. She looked up at the man and her facial expression was that of apprehension, like she was afraid to tell him what she was thinking.

"If I am being honest, Baze, I don't know if any of this is will get looked into."

There was a long, dramatic pause. Baze felt a flare of irritation in his chest. His throat was actually a little sore from talking so much, and yet, after all of that explanation, he hadn't moved the needle? Her response was also a little confusing. When cycling through potential suspects, the lieutenant had played along like she would utilize the information. It felt like a sudden backtrack.

Baze sighed and then shook his head.

"Damn, Red. I thought I had you convinced."

"I'm not saying you don't, Baze. But I don't have the clout to propagate a new investigation without something substantial. Without another body, or DNA evidence…"

"That video recording—"

"I know. But I am telling you right now, that may not be sufficient to shake up the bureaucracy of the police department enough to affect a real second-look at this. Like it or not, there is still a lot of evidence that points at William Tennyson. And people don't like looking at the past. Especially when the past is so ugly. I don't know if you were here back then, but Robert Macabre sent this town into a frenzy. It was chaos. If we are going to metaphorically dig up dead bodies, we better have a damn good reason for doing so. And that video is good enough for me. But it may not be for everyone."

Baze let a humorless smile spread out across his face.

"So what are you saying? You need another body?"

Arroyo gave a half shrug and pursed her lips, like she was nonverbally admitting to an unpleasant truth.

"It's only a matter of time," said Baze quietly.

Miguel Canales reclined back in his chair, falling asleep. The multitude of televisions in front of him showed all the various boring angles of the shipyard; the most interesting screen to look at was the one that showed the dock stretching out into the water, and only because occasionally a small wave would slop onto the wood. One night Miguel had actually tried to count the number of times that this had happened to keep his mind semi-occupied. Sure enough, it had led to him drifting off. Good thing there weren't cameras in the control room.

Miguel sipped on the semi-scalding cup of coffee in front of him, but it didn't seem to do any real good. The night shift was eating him alive. When you spend so many years training your internal clock around the day time, it was immensely difficult to become nocturnal. But they paid him seventeen dollars an hour to sit around and watch nothing, with the occasional tour around the facility. And when you only had a high school diploma, seventeen dollars an hour was about as good as you could do. Especially with a checkered past. So Miguel would continue to battle the yawns and yearning to collapse onto his desk.

Miguel stared at the screen that showed the dock. The water was strangely calm tonight. Almost unnervingly calm. Like even Mother Nature was trying to get him to fall asleep on the job. *More coffee. I need more coffee.* Miguel took a prodigious swig of the blistering drink in his mug and instantly regretted it. His throat seared, and he coughed. Miguel's chest heaved, and he brought his hand to the top of his diaphragm, as if holding it from the outside could quell the seizing.

The coughs came in rapid-fire increments. He tried to swallow, but his chest resisted. After hacking away for what seemed like an eternity, Miguel finally regained control over his throat. He took two deep breaths and wiped at his watering eyes, attempting to clear his blurred sight. Just as he was doing so, Miguel noticed movement in his peripheral vision. It had come from one of the five screens in front of him.

Miguel froze. Perhaps a bird had fluttered into the frame. It was rare, but it wouldn't be the first time it had happened. He concentrated his vision on the screen and saw nothing.

False alarm.

Miguel turned his attention back toward his coffee, wondering if he should give it another go. But more movement snapped his attention to the screen in front of him.

What he saw made his heart clench. A massive cloaked figure wearing all black slid quickly behind a storage container.

Someone was inside the facility.

Miguel leapt up from his chair, his pulse suddenly going at warp speed. He fumbled around on the desk, grabbing onto the bulky flashlight.

Moments later, he was outside, the chill biting at his neck and wrists. The beam from the flashlight swiveled back and forth, trying to catch movement. It shined over the sizeable shipping containers, casting new shadows where there hadn't been before. On the side of one of the containers, he saw the outline of a body, and almost had a heart attack. It took him a couple of seconds to realize it was his own shadow.

Miguel crept forward, wondering if he should call the police. He was security, but of course, he didn't have a gun. He didn't even have a baton. At that moment, Miguel had never felt more vulnerable. Whoever the intruder was couldn't mean well. Best-case scenario, it was a bum looking to crash for the night. Even that didn't seem like a desirable situation. What if the bum in question was mentally unstable?

It was too quiet. Even the water wasn't making as much noise as it normally did. Miguel took quiet steps, hoping not to alert the intruder to his presence. But what would he even do with the element of surprise? As he moved forward in the darkness, Miguel began to realize that the best thing to do would be to retreat into the control room, lock the door, and call the police.

Thump.

Miguel's head swiveled to the right. The noise sounded like it had come from somewhere nearby.

Breathe. Just breathe.

Should he call out? What if the intruder was still oblivious to his presence? For some reason, with a chill creeping up the back of his neck, Miguel thought that that was unlikely. It felt like a set of eyes was firmly fixed on him.

Thump thump.

The noise made him jump almost a foot in the air, and he released an involuntary gasp. Miguel was almost certain that the sound had emitted from behind one of the three giant shipping containers in front of him. Or perhaps inside one of them.

Go back inside. Go. Back. Inside.

Just then, he noticed that the container on the left was slightly ajar. A sliver of darkness peeked out from the door to the container. Miguel knew instinctively that the door had not been opened when he had arrived for his shift earlier that evening.

The intruder was inside.

Miguel tiptoed forward, swallowing thickly. He had no idea what he was going to do or even why he was still moving. He was utterly unarmed and impotent. But a horrified, insistent curiosity was spreading through his chest. Who was it in there?

He placed the tips of his fingers on the door and took a deep breath. Surely, if someone was planning on ambushing him, it would have been over by now. Only slightly reassured, he gripped tightly and ripped the door open with the loudest creak he had ever heard in his life.

Darkness. It was pitch-black. No movement as far as he could tell.

Miguel's fingers reached forward and above his head, searching for the chain that would pump light into the container. After a couple of seconds of fondling air, his sweaty fingers latched onto the cold links of metal dangling overhead. With one last inhale, he pulled down, and light flooded the container.

In the center of the space, a woman's body was rotating in mid-air, suspended only by a coil of rope around her neck. She was naked and soaked in crimson blood from head to toe. Her face was concealed by something. A pink veneer with a flattened snout in the middle of it.

A pig mask.

Miguel didn't even have time to take another breath before he passed out.

"Does this feel like a dream to anyone else?"

No one answered Arroyo's question. She looked from face to face, expecting to see horror, shock, and repulsion. Instead, she found nothing but serious and attentive expressions. There was even perhaps thinly veiled excitement among her subordinates. After all, none of them had been around back then. None of them knew the hell that they were about to be dragged through.

"Sorry, I just... I can't believe this is real."

Easton Lowry was seated at the table to her right; Arroyo was still standing. The detective was looking up at her with something resembling sympathy in his eyes. Out of all of them, he was maybe the only one who actually knew a little about who she was on a personal level. The other two detectives at the table, Andre Giuliani and Gary Fairfield, took her orders but rarely asked her questions. She barely even recognized Owen Anders and Marcus Austin, the two forensic techs that were sitting at the opposite end of the table. Arroyo was not usually one to call meetings like this that involved so many people, but it wasn't a usual time. The world had been turned upside down.

"As you all know, twenty-seven hours ago, a security worker at the Vigor shipyard on Swan Island found the body of a woman hanging in a shipping container. Victim has been ID'd as one Maria Cable, a twenty-two-year-old caregiver at Cascade Terrace."

Arroyo pulled out a picture from a folder in front of her and set it on the table. It was of a pretty blonde with pale skin and numerous freckles on her cheeks. "Cable had been missing since Wednesday night, where she was likely abducted from her studio apartment in northeast Portland."

Arroyo pulled out five more photographs and felt a lump rising in her throat. These were of the crime scene itself. The one she had spent seven hours at the night before. And yet, it was just as lurid and grotesque to look at the mangled body in photographs as it had been to look at Cable in person.

"This was how she was found. So far, we haven't been able to pull any DNA off of the pig mask. At least none that wasn't Cable's. But I think it is safe to assume who is behind this killing. There is only one person with this kind of signature."

Arroyo then gestured toward the opposite end of the table where a rugged figure was leaning forward in his chair with a stony expression on his face.

"If any of you are wondering, this is Anton Baze. Baze is a private investigator that we have brought onto our team as a consultant. And he is going to tell us a little bit about Robert Macabre."

Baze kept his face impassive, and Arroyo wondered what the man was thinking. He was good at hiding any trace of emotion; Arroyo supposed this was a learned skill. You probably had to be somewhat furtive with your thoughts and feelings when you worked with gangsters.

Gary Fairfield, a large man without a hair on his head, cleared his throat. His bald dome gleamed underneath the light, and when he spoke, his high-pitched voice was possessed by phlegm. "Excuse me, LT... Macabre? Weren't you there when Macabre got himself blown up?"

"William Tennyson was a rabid dog. But he wasn't Robert Macabre."

"How do you know this?" demanded Fairfield. "Just because the girl was wearing a pig mask? How do we know this isn't a copycat?"

Baze suddenly leaned forward, and his imposing presence commanded the attention of the entire room. "Excuse me, uh, *sir*... How long have you been a detective?"

"Seven years. What about you slick?"

Baze ignored the remark. "In your seven years, have you *ever* seen a copycat killer? Hell, in your whole life, have you even heard about a real copycat killer?"

Fairfield's nostrils flared. "And why are you the expert?"

Baze shrugged. "I never said I was an expert. But you don't have to be an expert to be right."

"Where did you come from anyway?"

"Southwest Portland."

Fairfield bared his teeth in a sardonic smile. "Well, aren't you just a wiseass? Lieutenant, where did you find this guy?"

Arroyo's mouth moved as she went to respond, but Baze beat her to the punch.

"She was looking for a new detective. That's how she found me. She said that the bald guy on her team wasn't cutting it."

"Listen, jerk,"

"No, you listen, Off-Brand Bruce Willis. Copycat killers only exist in fiction. The fact that you even suggested it makes you sound like you have never worked a real homicide case."

Fairfield's face turned a marvelous shade of red. "And how many have you worked? Jesus Lieutenant, does Mike know about this guy?"

He was referring to Mike McGrath, the newly

promoted chief of police. Arroyo felt a quick burn of irritation at Fairfield. They hadn't even officially started their investigation, and here he was, already trying to go over her head.

"No, Gary. Mike is going to have very little involvement in this case. He has barely even finished moving into his new office."

"Nice try though, Mr. Clean," muttered Baze.

Before Fairfield could come back with another insult, Arroyo raised her voice.

"Guy's that is *enough*."

Silence fell like a blanket over the room. Fairfield seemed to be embarrassed at the reprimand; Baze, however, just looked amused.

"Gary, I know it sounds nuts," said Arroyo, seeming flustered by the interplay. "Up until three weeks ago the thought didn't even enter... the *stratosphere*. But then I met Baze. And he changed my mind. In a little bit, he will explain to you everything that he explained to me, and if you still don't have any doubts that the real Macabre was never caught, then I don't know what to tell you. Regardless, we now have the homicide of a young woman that was found in an animal mask, and her body shows distinctive signs of torture. Genital mutilation, knife wounds from head to toe, contusions, and rope burns around her chest indicating that she was bound in place for well over twenty-four hours. Even if we are now living in

461

some alternate universe where this isn't the work of Bob the Butcher, we still got a real sick fuck on our hands."

Andre Giuliani, a muscular man with thick lips and a massive forehead, shifted in his chair and pointed at the crime scene photos that were on the table.

"So, I am guessing we weren't able to pull any useful footage from the cameras in the shipyard?"

Arroyo shook her head. "No. The computer that the cameras feed to was completely destroyed. Looks like someone curb-stomped the modem."

Giuliani grunted. "How on earth did Canales not notice him entering into the facility with a dead body?"

Arroyo exchanged looks with Lowry. They had discussed this particular question earlier in the evening and had arrived at a somewhat unsettling conclusion.

"Well, Vigor doesn't have any security watching the cameras during operating hours, since they have so many people coming and going. My guess is, Macabre waited until foot traffic was light and entered the facility with Cable folded up in a duffel bag. If anyone did see him, it might not look suspicious because people haul maritime equipment in and out of there all day long. My guess is, he broke into that shipping container later in the day, and hid there with Cable's body until nighttime."

"What if someone randomly entered into the container?" asked Giuliani.

"He probably locked himself in with the key. Most of the containers are padlocked from the outside, but the doors spread enough even when they are locked to fit a key through."

"So, if he entered into the facility before it was officially closed... surely someone would have seen him," said Giuliani slowly.

"We spent all day interviewing employees at the facility. No one saw anything," said Arroyo, and she realized how tired she sounded after she said it. "Like I said, he must have waited until foot traffic was light. Or nonexistent. There was probably a very short period at the end of the day before Canales manned his post that would have been perfect for him. Where most of the workers had already gone home."

Giuliani exchanged glances with his partner, Fairfield. They both looked a little skeptical of the information that was being presented.

"Okay, so my question is, why here? Why this place?"

This time it was Lowry who had spoken. Arroyo shook her head and gestured toward Baze.

"Why don't you take this one, Anton?"

Baze percussed his fingers on the table and looked at Lowry, who only maintained eye contact with Baze for a couple of seconds before looking away.

"Back in oh two… Well, I *think* it was oh two," said Baze. "A woman named Erin Kennedy was walking home from the bar when she was dragged into the bushes and sexually assaulted. Miguel Canales was arrested and charged for the crime. But he was found not guilty. It was one of only eleven times that Carson Welsh did not get at least a partial conviction in a criminal trial that he was prosecuting."

"The *Portland Tribune* and the *Oregonian* both picked up the story, and were calling it Welsh's biggest failure," said Arroyo, piggybacking off of what Baze had said. "It was actually somewhat remarkable that Canales got off, because his DNA was found on the victim's shirt."

Lowry frowned and twisted his mouth to the side, like he was trying to work out how Canales could have been innocent.

"It was a hung jury," continued Arroyo. "Completely split. Somehow, some way, they bought Canales' story. Instead of reconvening a week later with a new jury, Welsh decided to not to re-prosecute. That was why he received so much criticism from the press. He let a likely rapist go free. But if you ask Welsh, he would probably say that it would have been a waste of time. The same problems that arose in the initial trial wouldn't just go away. Right or wrong, he figured that a conviction was not likely."

"So this is Macabre's way of taunting Welsh for his failure?" asked Lowry.

For a moment, everyone seemed to look back and forth between Baze and Arroyo.

"That's what it looks like," said Arroyo slowly. "For whatever reason, Bob the Butcher still thinks he has a score to settle with Carson Welsh."

Welsh ate his dinner slowly, forking the pasta up into his mouth like he had just learned how to consume food. The garlic on the noodles was strong; Welsh had a feeling that it would take at least a day to get the taste out of his mouth. The only sound in his kitchen was the slurping noise he made whenever he sucked a noodle through his puckered lips.

Looking to his right, Welsh observed the shotgun that was resting against the table like a wicked dinner guest. The safety mechanism wasn't even on, and a shell had been pumped into the chamber. If need be, Welsh could grip the gun in a heartbeat and blast somebody half to hell if they advanced on him. This was how it had been in the past couple of weeks since he had received the letter. Every noise made him jump two feet in the air. Every shape in his apartment looked like the face of an animal in the darkness. Welsh's heart seemed to have achieved a resting rate of one hundred beats a minute. But it wasn't anxiety. It was more like a demented anticipation for the impending confrontation.

Somehow, deep down, he had always known this story wasn't over. Something had always felt off about William Robert Tennyson. A drug dealer who opened fire on a SWAT team when he was cornered? That didn't feel like Macabre. The man was cunning. Deceitful. A cloven-footed entity that outwitted and outmatched his opponents through sheer perspicacity and shrewd will. Not some skinny little shit who peddled hallucinogens. Welsh still remembered how he felt when he heard what had happened to the police's prime suspect fifteen years before. An immediate sense of apprehension. The saga felt incomplete, even then.

Welsh had told no one about the letter. And he would not. He was ready for the apotheosis of this confrontation. The culmination of fifteen years of despair and angst was finally about to come to a head. He was now positive about what he had vaguely suspected all those years ago. One of them would end up dead. And it would most certainly be from the other's hand.

The doorbell ringing rocked Welsh out of his stupor, and with a loud clang he dropped his pasta-tainted fork onto the ground. Instantly, his hands latched onto the shotgun and he leapt onto his feet, his heart suddenly squirting along like a startled fish. He crept forward, aiming the muzzle at his front door, his finger taut around the trigger; a single twitch of the muscles in his primary appendage and the person behind the door would be blown apart.

Welsh slid up against the door. He could feel his breath bouncing off the wood and the smell of garlic slid into his nostrils as he placed his eye against the peephole. When he saw the person standing there, he felt almost as much shock as he would if it had been Robert Macabre.

It was Emily Arroyo.

There was a moment of incomprehension, and then, when he realized that he would have to answer the door, Welsh internally cursed and scrambled over to the nearby couch. Clicking the safety of the gun off, he stuffed the shotgun in between the cushions and the back pillows. Once it was mostly concealed, Welsh whirled about and went back to the door. Taking a deep breath, he swung it open.

Arroyo was looking at the ground, but when the door cleared the threshold she slowly peered up. They made eye contact, and Welsh clicked his tongue.

"I have to say, Emily, I never thought there would be a day where I would find you on my front porch."

Arroyo didn't smile. Her face looked grim.

"Something wrong?" asked Welsh.

"May I come in?"

Welsh cocked his head to the right and gave her a fake grin. "I have a feeling that I am not going to like this conversation."

"Carson, we need to talk. May I please come in?"

Welsh let the smile slowly drip off of his face. With his right hand, he gestured for Arroyo to pass over the threshold. She did so slowly, as if his living room might contain traces of dangerous radioactive material.

"Take a seat," said Welsh, tapping Arroyo on the shoulder while pointing at the kitchen table. His one and only goal was to keep her away from the couch. She obliged, pulling out a chair next to where he had been eating. He followed suit until they were at eye level, only a foot away from each other.

"I didn't mean to interrupt dinner."

"Yes, you really put a dent in my enjoyment of Chef Boyardee's exquisite cuisine."

Arroyo apparently couldn't even bring herself to fake a guffaw. She just stared at Welsh with a slight frown on her face.

"How have you been?"

Welsh chuckled. "Don't bog us down with

small talk, Emily. We haven't talked in years. Why on earth would you care how I have been?"

"I do care," said Arroyo, sounding a little offended.

"Hmm."

"But you are right. I didn't come here to chitchat."

"I figured as much."

Arroyo sighed. She let a few seconds pass before she continued.

"Carson. I have some bad news."

Welsh felt his chest tighten, but he tried to play it off. "What is it? Did something happen to my wife?"

Arroyo's mouth expanded rapidly as words seemed to escape her. Welsh quickly continued so that she wouldn't have to find something awkward to say.

"Emily, I am already broken beyond repair. I have been since that day. Whatever you are about to tell me couldn't possibly compare to what has already been done."

Arroyo sighed again; this time it was deeper and more of a guttural noise. Finally, she let the words escape her mouth.

"The body of a woman was discovered at the Vigor Shipyard yesterday evening. Young lady named Maria Cable. Twenty-three years old. She, um… She was found wearing a pig mask."

Welsh felt the goose bumps rise on his arms, but it wasn't from shock. It was something else. Something that should have been much more disturbing to him—excitement. But he had to feign astonishment and consternation. So he let out a hastily concocted stutter followed by a two-word sentence, as if he was too flabbergasted to vocalize a coherent thought.

"Copycat?"

Arroyo shook her head.

"No. No… Um, Carson, evidence has come to light that throws everything we did into question. We uh… We think we were wrong about William Tennyson."

"Oh? Evidence, you say? What kind of evidence?" Welsh tried to inflect tension into his voice.

"A local PI pulled security footage from a bar on the night that your wife was murdered. Tennyson was there. Miles away from the house in Wilsonville."

Welsh didn't have to fake anger this time. It suddenly came pouring out of him like water from a faucet.

"What? Security footage? How…? How did you *miss* this?"

Arroyo stuttered a little before responding. "The fingerprints on the package. The gas station footage. It was all pointing to him."

"So you neglected contradicting evidence?" demanded Welsh.

"We didn't neglect it. We were unaware of it."

"Oh, so not negligence, just incompetence."

"Carson, I did not come here to listen to a tirade, so drop the bullshit," said Arroyo, and her voice was filled with ire. It threw Welsh off-balance. Arroyo had always been calm, stoic, and unshakeable. It was definitely surprising that she had resorted to fury so fast. Hell, Welsh couldn't even remember if he had ever seen her angry before.

"The bar was sparsely populated. And no one came forward because no one recognized him, or even came close to figuring out the significance of his presence that night. Think about all of the times you have been to the bar in your life. If you caught a passing glance at somebody in a dimly lit place while you were potentially inebriated, do you think you would immediately recognize that person if you saw them on the news weeks later?"

Arroyo's speech still held traces of the fiery disposition that she had just displayed, and Welsh didn't think it a good idea to continue to wind her up, so he stayed silent.

"You have the right to be angry, Carson. But not at me. Not at us. Everything pointed at him. If Tennyson had survived and you were the prosecuting attorney, do you think you would have gotten a guilty verdict with the evidence at hand?"

Welsh thought about it for a second and then realized that she was right. Given what they knew, it would have been extremely irrational to suggest that Tennyson had been innocent.

"Of course, I would have."

Arroyo nodded. "Yes, I know you would have. You were probably the best DA on the West Coast during your prime. How many cases did you even lose? Eleven?"

Welsh met her eyes and felt a hint of suspicion. Why had she come armed with this fact?

Arroyo brushed a hair out of her face that had apparently come loose during her bout of anger. Then she sighed.

"Maria Cable was found at the Vigor Shipyard. Miguel Canales works security at the Vigor Shipyard. He was the one who found the body."

It took a moment for it to process, but once it did, Welsh's stomach jumped into his chest. "Wow. *Wow*," he hissed through clenched teeth.

"He's obsessed with you, Carson. He always has been. I am not sure why he chose you, or why he took a fifteen-year hiatus, but he's back now. Back to taunt you. Back to finish what he started. For whatever reason, you have always been in his crosshairs. You are the biggest fish left to fry."

Welsh kept silent. He wasn't exactly sure where she was going with this.

"Carson… He is going to try and communicate with you again. A letter, a note through the mail slot on your front door, another body part. Something will come soon. I want you to be prepared for that. Are you prepared?"

Welsh still maintained his reticence. For the briefest moment of time, they made eye contact, and it was as if she was reading his mind.

"Has it already happened, Carson?"

He looked away, and thought of the note that he had received. It made loathing course through him like an electrical current. He quickly became so absorbed in his hatred of Macabre that he completely forgot to answer Arroyo's question.

"Carson?"

Welsh twitched out of his stupor and saw Arroyo looking at him with narrowed eyes. He thought of Macabre again, and then subconsciously looked over at the couch where the shotgun was buried in between the pillows.

"No, Emily. Of course not. He hasn't sent me anything."

Baze watched the house across the street with mild interest. The fingers of his right hand absentmindedly scratched his mustache, and he wondered if he should come back in an hour or so. The driveway was empty, and he was virtually positive that the man was not home yet. The commute from the office where the man worked was forty-five minutes on a good day, so perhaps he was stuck in traffic. Baze looked through the tinted windows of his Chevy Impala and knew that the vehicle might look conspicuous to some of the nearby residents. It was one of those neighborhoods where the locals probably all had a mental tracker of the cars that traveled and parked in the vicinity. That was the case with a lot of the ritzy neighborhoods around Portland.

The house was off-white with multiple stories and vast windows on the second floor, and Baze wondered why one person would need that much space. There had to be at least seven rooms inside. What purpose did each of them serve? The house was lined with a pristine cedar deck that climbed up to the front door. Beneath the deck there was a small metal grate that shed light into whatever lay beneath. Baze imagined a woman naked and shackled in a dark basement with only a few slivers of light grazing the ground; the illumination catching the bloodied parts of her face whenever she moved next to the grate, her screams for help drowned by a gag shoved back against her uvula. Perhaps this was the ultimate form of torture. Hell on earth, with an impassable window just feet away that led to freedom. Was Baze only twenty feet from the demon's lair? He had no idea, but something about the giant building was unsettling.

Outside, gusts of wind ripped through the branches of nearby trees. For a fringe summer day, the weather wasn't particularly pleasant. It wasn't raining, but the sky sure seemed to be threatening an oncoming downpour. Baze let the warmth that crept out of the vents on the dashboard warm his fingers as he suspended his hands midair just inches in front of the heater. How was it this chilly in June? Only in the Pacific Northwest.

From far away down the street, a pair of headlights maneuvered in Baze's direction. Something big and black had just turned onto the road and was listing toward him. Baze subconsciously leaned back as the Ford Expedition drew nearer, and his breath froze in his mouth when the blinker turned on just in front of the driveway. He was home.

The Expedition parked, and after a few moments of nothing the driver's door opened and the lean man uncoiled his long legs and slid out of the SUV. It was the first time that he had ever actually seen him in person, but Matthew Lyons carried himself like Baze imagined him to: With a quiet, sleek confidence.

As he moved toward the house, Lyons tucked something into the pocket of his black slacks, and then shut the door to his vehicle, completely oblivious to the Impala that was stationed across the street. Baze watched as the man sauntered up the deck and then pulled out a set of keys. He pointed the keys at the slot on the deadbolt, but then, without warning, Lyons froze. Baze's chest constricted as the man slowly turned his head back in the street's direction. Had he suddenly just processed the alien vehicle that was positioned across the way? Could he sense that Baze was watching him? Lyons' eyes seemed to lock onto the Impala and Baze had a sudden urge to throw the car into drive and speed away. But then the moment passed, and Lyons went back to unlocking his front door. Within moments, he was inside the house and the door was shut. Baze expected the lights in the house to turn on, but for some reason, they didn't. The darkness stayed still, and Baze felt a tingle on the back of his neck as each moment passed. What on earth was Lyons doing in there in the dark?

Baze's head jerked back, his tongue lolling out slightly. It took a couple of seconds to regain his center of gravity, as his head had slumped forward and sleep stretched out its warm fingers toward him. Baze reached forward and torqued the knob that coordinated the temperature in the cab of the car, making the arrow on the lever point at blue. The cold bristled against his cheeks, and he instantly felt more awake.

This wasn't the first stake out he had partaken in, but every other time he had simply been waiting for an opportunity to strike. When Frank Bruno told you to send a message by beating the snot out of some client that had wronged him, all you had to do was bide your time and wait for all eyes in the neighborhood to shut. This task was much more open-ended, and consequently, much duller. As he sat there, trying to ward off sleep while simultaneously focusing on the still-dark house across the street, Baze pondered leaving the neighborhood and going home. That is, until he saw the small junker Toyota Avalon slide down the street and pull into Lyons' driveway.

Baze leaned back into his seat, trying to become invisible. The tinted windows would already do that job for him, but being at a lower vantage point felt safer. As the Avalon came to a halt and the wiry man with glasses and a black hoodie crawled out of the driver's seat, Baze felt a chill pass over him. The scrawny man walked up to Lyons' front door and hammered on it frantically. Even from the back, Baze could tell that the man was panicked about something. He compulsively moved his head from shoulder to shoulder as if he had a kink in his neck that he couldn't quite get out. After a few seconds, the door opened and Baze saw Lyons' face peek out of the darkness.

What followed was a heated, but mostly hushed conversation. Baze only caught a stray phrase every so often when Lyons' or the wiry man would raise their voices. He distinctly heard Lyons screech, "*My fucking house!*" and then what sounded like the man replying with, "I didn't know what to do!" What followed this interplay was a whispered discussion that was inaudible. After a minute or so of whispering, something Lyons said set the man off, and he screamed at the top of his lungs.

"*You need to get rid of your shit, man! They got him, man! They are coming for us next! What do we do?"*

Lyons' maintained his hushed tone, but the malice in his facial expression was clearly visible. The skinny man threw his arms in the air in frustration and stormed off of Lyons' front porch and back toward his Avalon.

Lyons watched from the threshold of his house as the man skidded out of the driveway and sped away. Baze expected the door to slam shut, but it didn't. It remained open as Lyons stared out at the street while the skinny man drove off in a huff. Why was he so focused on the departing junker of a car? Was Lyons trying to memorize the license plate? But then, Baze realized that it didn't look like the man was looking at the Avalon at all. In fact, it looked like he was now starting directly at the Impala across the street.

Baze caught his breath. He was imagining it. For all Lyons knew, no one was inside the car and it belonged to someone simply visiting one of his neighbors. Baze tried to relax, waiting for the front door to shut.

But it didn't. It opened farther. And Lyons' lanky figure stepped out of the darkness. His eyes were definitely latched onto the Impala now.

He began to walk toward it.

"Fuck a duck," hissed Baze, and without thinking about it, he pounded the push-button start, and the engine revved on. Now he had no choice.

Lyons would have heard the engine. Baze chanced a glance to his right, and he saw that Lyons' pace was quickening. He threw the gearshift into drive, and Lyons broke out into a run toward the vehicle. Baze's whole torso seemed to compress as he pressed the gas pedal downward, and the car darted forward with Lyons only ten feet away.

Baze's chest thumped erratically as he bolted down the road, not letting his foot relinquish any of its might on the pedal. He looked in the rearview mirror and saw something eerie. Lyons was standing frozen in the middle of the street, watching Baze's car from behind like a sentinel. He didn't even move a muscle. He just stood in the road, staring as the car maneuvered out of the neighborhood and back toward the freeway.

"So wait... What did the guy say again? Something about they got him and they are coming for him next?"

"He said, 'They are coming for *us* next.'"

"And you have no idea who this guy was?" Arroyo paced back and forth behind her desk, looking contemplative but also like she felt a rush of elation.

"Not a clue," replied Baze. "He was kind of

sketchy looking. His demeanor. He seemed like one of those guys that appear normal most of the time but then blow up and talk like a complete psycho when they are pissed."

"And Lyons couldn't calm him down?"

"It didn't look like he was even trying. He just seemed annoyed that the guy had the gall to show up at his house."

"Hmm." Arroyo tapped on her desk and bit the inside of her cheek as if she were chewing on some profound existential question.

"Something is going on here. I am telling you. Something isn't right about this guy." Baze tried to punctuate his point by leaning forward and lowering his voice, but Arroyo didn't seem to notice. She was still lost in thought.

"What are you thinking, Red?"

Arroyo looked up quickly, like she had forgotten that Baze was in her office. Then, when she processed what he had said, she let out a long breath and shook her head.

"When are you going to stop calling me that?"

"When you dye your hair blond, maybe. Then I'll call you blondie."

Arroyo shuddered. "Jesus, okay, never mind, that's way creepier. Anyway, I am just thinking about Lyons. I am trying to remember what he was like when me and Ray interviewed him."

"And what are you coming up with?"

Arroyo's lips tightened and her hands drummed absentmindedly on the back of her chair as she apparently tried to formulate her thoughts into a cohesive sentence.

"He was weirdly emotionless about the whole thing with Tracy. Sort of detached. Ray seemed to think that was a coping technique. Anyway, he also had an eidetic memory. Like he recalled weirdly specific things about his date with her."

"An eidetic memory is a telltale sign of high intellectual acuity," remarked Baze.

"Mm."

"And psychopaths are almost always intelligent."

"Mm-hmm."

"Do you think the guy could be a killer?"

Arroyo stared at him, and her eyes lost focus.

"Honestly, I don't know."

Baze felt a little bit of frustration at the non-answer, but he didn't say anything.

Arroyo turned both her palms into the air and shrugged her shoulders. "I don't know. What do you think? Do you honestly think it could be him? Give me your real opinion."

"I've never talked to the guy. But if you say he was emotionless during your interview, and we know that he lied to the police about his alibi, *and* I just saw him meet a strange man on his front porch who said something about 'someone' coming for them," Baze said, using air quotes when he said the word someone. "I think it's definitely worth pursuing, Red."

Something in Arroyo's expression changed. She was now looking at Baze with apprehension. "And how do you plan to pursue it, Mr. Stake Out?"

"Not sure you actually want the answer to that."

Arroyo looked at him with trepidation in her eyes. "I don't know what you are thinking, but I can already tell I don't like it."

"You knew what I was when you brought me on board. You knew what I do."

"No... No. We do this by the book, Baze. If you want, we can interview him again—"

"And say what? That it was me watching him outside of his house?"

"I didn't ask you to do that."

"I didn't say you did. But since we lack any actual evidence and he has no connection to the new vic, what would you even say in an interview? 'So uh, we don't really have anything that proves it, but just curious, are you a homicidal maniac?'"

Arroyo jabbed her index finger at him aggressively. "So what do *you* want to do then?"

Baze shrugged, pretending to be indifferent to the conversation. "Leave the snoopin' to the snooper, Red. Don't burden yourself with knowing specifics."

The lieutenant glared at him, and he expected her to shoot him down again. But she didn't.

"Whatever you are going to do, don't get caught."

The glass to the window on the back door shattered, but the sound of the car alarm on the street covered it up. Baze reached through the now open space and toggled the lock beneath with his gloved hand to pop the door open. He knew it wouldn't be long before the neighbor would turn off the alarm that Baze had triggered, so he moved with purpose and determination so that the noisiest part of this endeavor would be over by the time silence ensued. Sure enough, he made it just inside Lyons' house as the alarm went quiet.

The ski mask over his face made him hotter than hell. It had been a long time since he had worn it, and Baze had forgotten how uncomfortable this ensemble was. The long-sleeve black shirt and jeans combined with the mask over his face was not only boiling, it was also itchy. Hopefully, this task would be done quickly. There was only a brief period in the day where it was dark outside and Lyons wouldn't be home, so Baze had a finite amount of time to accomplish this.

Baze moved the beam of the flashlight left and right and saw a washer and dryer sitting across from a gargantuan water heater. The laundry room. He crept along and avoided stepping in a litter box at the last second. Baze shined the flashlight on the box and saw several fresh turds decorating it. Lyons had a cat? *Weird,* thought Baze. He stepped over the litter and toward the door on the other side.

With a quick pull, Baze ripped the door open and found himself staring inside a kitchen that had several dirty dishes in the sink. With his heart starting to pound faster, Baze slipped through the kitchen and under the archway that led to the next room. A big leather couch took up most of the space of the living area; it was propped up across from a huge television, and on the other side of the room, there was a staircase. Baze let the beam of light wash over everything, but did not see the item he was looking for.

If there was any sort of photo or video proof of illicit activity, it would be on the computer. That was the theory anyway. Robert Macabre had shot a video of himself torturing the first victim, Tracy Dinwoodie. That led Baze to believe that the man was a documentarian of sorts, at least when it came to his facinorous hobbies. If there were more photos or videos, they might be on his computer.

As the seconds ticked along, Baze began to scramble. It was like every passing moment where he didn't find what he was looking for upped his sense of urgency. Lyons wasn't due to be home for at least an hour, but there was a chance that the man could surprise Baze. Baze looked left and right, and tossed a blanket off of the couch, hoping that he would find a laptop underneath it. But he knew it wouldn't be there. If anything, it would be in Lyons' room, which was on the second floor.

With the hand that wasn't holding the flashlight, Baze pulled out the SIG-Sauer from the waistband of his underwear, pointing the muzzle at the staircase to his left. There was not supposed to be any inhabitants in the house, but there was always a remote possibility that someone could be there. A loaded gun never hurt in situations like this.

The staircase was steep and seemed to creak on every other step. One of the creaks echoed onto the landing above, and Baze had a wild, albeit brief thought of Lyons waiting to ambush him on the floor above. He tried to push the unhelpful vision aside as he ascended the steps. Nothing was on the landing, so Baze stepped onto it and creeped down the hallway.

Baze came to a door on his left and paused. He breathed deeply, letting the remaining tranquility he could find wash over him. He put his hand on the doorknob, squeezing ever so slightly and turning it to the right. The door made a noise as he pushed it open, and Baze paused, listening for any sounds of activity in the room.

Dead silence. Baze breathed heavily and shoved the door ajar. Almost immediately, his eyes locked onto it.

A silver Mac sitting on the bed.

Baze rushed over to the computer and set the gun and flashlight down so he could work. From his pocket, he pulled out the adapter that would plug into the Mac's primary port, as well as the little black device that his hacker friend had sold to him for a thousand dollars two years ago. The device was called The Raptor. The Raptor functioned as a storage device on steroids, as well as a cloning mechanism. It would bypass the Mac's security measures with ease and copy the hard drive in less than five minutes without breaking a sweat. Baze plugged the adapter into the USB port on the side of the mac and then plugged The Raptor into the adapter. On The Raptor's tiny screen, Baze clicked the button on the side, and a prompt came up on the black screen of the Mac.

Copy Hard Drive?

Baze clicked the button on the side again, and the device began to blink green. It started with slow, intermittent flashes, and then it became a strobe light. Within moments, The Raptor was copying information at light speed.

It took only two minutes and thirty-two seconds to clone the hard drive, but it felt like an eternity. When the green light finally stopped flashing, Baze was greeted with a new message on the screen.

Cloning finished.

Baze ripped the adapter out of the USB port, and pulled The Raptor apart from the adapter, shoving both in his pocket. With another deep breath, he picked up the gun and flashlight and whirled about, leaving the silver Mac behind.

"You need to see this, LT."

Arroyo looked up and saw Easton Lowry in the frame of the doorway to her office. He had a troubled expression on his face.

"Already?"

"Huh?"

"Another vic already?"

"Huh? No. It's something else. Something unrelated."

"What is it?"

"Just come look."

With her eyebrows raising to the precipice of her hairline, Arroyo stood up and followed Lowry out of the office. He led her through several rows of cubicles until he came to one manned by a skinny man with glasses.

"What have you got, Raj?" asked Arroyo.

Raj Patel, the forensic computer specialist, glanced up at her and it looked like he felt nauseous.

"We just received an email from an anonymous IP. Centralized in Belgium, of all places. Whoever sent it must have been using a VPN that rerouted the IP to Europe. The return address is blank. Whoever sent it was somehow able to mask the server that the email came from."

"Jesus, Raj, just tell me what was in the email."

Patel gulped. "Pictures. Pictures of a man. And... a girl." He swallowed again as if bile was rising in his throat.

"What sort of pictures?"

"Pornographic."

Arroyo let a couple of beats pass, totally flabbergasted. "Somebody used a VPN and a masked email address to send us porn?"

"Not normal porn. The girl is quite young."

Silence. Several goose bumps stood at attention on Arroyo's arms, and she waited for what felt like a long time before replying.

"How young?"

"Probably no more than thirteen."

Her mouth was suddenly very dry.

"Jesus Christ."

"I feel like I am going to be ill," said Patel.

"Open the pictures."

Patel looked at her like she was nuts.

"Lieutenant, they are very disturb—"

"Open the damn pictures, Patel. Now!"

Patel swallowed thickly again. He maneuvered his mouse to a minimized browser window and clicked on it. Then he opened the downloads folder and selected the first image with a double click. There was a half second of nothing, and then the image blew up onto the screen. A pre-teen girl, naked and in tears, was sprawled on a bed. A lean man with chiseled abdominal muscles towered over her, looking ready to mount. His hand was over her mouth and his face was beset with a sort of demonic energy.

"This is the least graphic of them," said Patel quietly.

"Does he kill her?"

Patel's eyes bulged. "What? No! It's not like that. See look. There is a picture included in the email that isn't part of the set. It is a yearbook photo."

Patel hovered his mouse back to the downloads folder and selected the last picture that had been copied. When he clicked on it, a photograph of a pretty teen with pale skin and freckles and a shy smile blew up on the screen. It was just a headshot with the name Melissa Stout written under it.

"I did a quick search on her," continued Patel. "She is a senior now at Tigard High, so these pictures are five or six years old. I also googled the name in association with any news stories, but no hits. Looks like she kept the assault under wraps."

Arroyo's mind whirred like a Turing System processing the information as fast as she could.

"Bring up the first photo again."

Patel sighed and brought up the initial picture once more. Arroyo looked at the man's face on the screen and felt fury bubbling in the pit of her stomach.

"Matthew Lyons."

Patel's mouth dropped open. "You know him?"

Arroyo didn't respond to this. She turned to Lowry and put her hand on his shoulder.

"Let's get a damn warrant."

Welsh put his phone down, breathing heavily. His eyes were strained from reading the lengthy article. It was probably not a good idea to consume too many more news stories on his phone, but he hadn't been able to wait to get home when he had seen the headline on this one. Arroyo had texted it to him with no explanation, and for a moment, when he saw the word *arrest* in large font, time had frozen. But it had turned out to be something out of left field.

Matthew Lyons, the man that Tracy Dinwoodie had been seeing just before she was killed, had been charged with statutory rape and possession of child pornography. Apparently, he had been a part of an online forum of men who gathered images and videos of teenage girls being sexually assaulted and exchanged them. It was fairly jarring to read, and initially, Welsh had thought Arroyo was insinuating the news was proof that Lyons was actually Robert Macabre. But it wasn't at all. The news article actually said that the Macabre killings and Lyons' transgressions were unrelated, and that though they hadn't completely ruled Lyons out as a suspect, the investigation was moving in a "different direction."

Welsh hadn't texted Arroyo back. He had no idea what to say. Was Welsh supposed to be happy? Fascinated? Repelled? It was hard to process, especially since Arroyo had sent him the text right when he was preoccupied with an incredibly difficult task.

His shrink, Dr. Freidenberg, had thought it a good idea to revisit his past. That it would prove to be some form of catharsis to reenter the place where the trauma had occurred. And Freidenberg hadn't meant in a metaphorical sense either. Welsh was now sitting parked across the street from his second house in Wilsonville. The very spot that Wendy's throat had been slashed and her body discarded carelessly like a candy wrapper. The point of the exercise was to confront the pain, acknowledge it, and then release it. That was the bullshit Freidenberg had spouted, at least; Welsh couldn't see how this could possibly help. And yet here he was, ready to go inside. But Welsh was not motivated by grief or cleansing himself of sorrow. Mostly, he finally wanted to see what this place had become. And, unsurprisingly, it had not become anything pleasant.

The lawn was comically overgrown, and vines crawled up the side of the house like the earth was trying to suck the building down into the abyss. Several shingles were missing off of the roof, and the once pristine concrete front porch was cracked in several places.

Welsh sighed. He thought of the article about Lyons one last time and then put the phone in his pocket. *Wow, Arroyo,* he thought. *Impeccable timing.*

After getting out of his car, Welsh slammed the door as if it had caused him a great disservice by existing. He was partly irritated at Freidenberg for suggesting this stupid task and partly irritated at himself for giving into the burning curiosity. Finally, he was now a little irritated at Arroyo for sending him that news article, but he wasn't sure why.

Taking long strides, Welsh was on the front porch in less than five seconds. He toggled the knob to the front door to make sure it was still locked, and sure enough, it was. He quickly jammed his key into the lock and flipped the deadbolt. When the door opened, the smell of mold and dirt was the first thing that found its way into his nostrils.

From his vantage point on the porch, it looked like the inside of the house was still mostly clean. A little dusty, but there weren't any weeds sprouting out of the floor or any rat droppings tucked into the corner of the living room (at least as far as he could tell).

Welsh took a deep breath, still standing on the threshold. Without warning, he became overcome with emotion. His chest was suddenly tight and his eyes burned. Nothing had prepared him for what he would feel when he had arrived here. And it didn't feel good. But it was too late now. He was here.

With one giant step, he was inside. It was bitingly chilly, even though the air outside wasn't particularly cold. Ahead, everything looked exactly as it had ten years ago. Welsh shuffled forward, and his foot caught on something. With wild spasmodic motions of his arms, he was able to maintain his balance, but barely. What the hell was that? Welsh looked down and saw a floorboard that jutted out above the others. Had it been like that in '04? He couldn't remember.

Like he was being pulled by some otherworldly magnet, Welsh found himself floating toward the bedroom. The bedroom where she had died. He had to see it. He had to see what it felt like to look at the place where his life had been turned upside down all those years ago. Welsh had thought that he had never wanted to lay eyes upon this place again. But now that he was here, he needed desperately to see what it felt like to look at the exact spot where the love of his life had been taken away from him.

Welsh came to the door. With a twist, he pulled on the doorknob and threw the door open.

Oh my God.

The mattress was still there, but absent of sheets. It had a dark brown stain coloring nearly the entire thing. However, that wasn't what had turned Welsh's stomach upside down. He had expected to see the blood stain. What he hadn't expected to see was the mask of the raven that was now sitting on the bed.

"I know it was you."

Arroyo's eyes narrowed as she stared at the mustached, scarred man that was sitting across from her. Baze gave her a mischievous, lips-only smile.

"I haven't the slightest idea what you are talking about."

"Mm. So even after our last conversation where you made it clear you were going to pursue Lyons, you are going to feign ignorance? Even though he was just arrested thanks to an anonymous tip from an untraceable email?"

Baze didn't respond. He continued to give her that smile that was partly amusing but also partly aggravating.

"Well, even if you don't want to take credit, or blame I guess for doing whatever illegal thing that you did, I know it was you. And thankfully, it worked, so *I* don't have to answer the chief on why our special consultant got arrested."

Baze raised his eyebrows. "It worked? How do you figure?"

Arroyo frowned and paused for a second before answering. She was sure that Baze was aware, but they had already conducted a search of Lyons' residence, and had found nothing that linked him to the killings. Thanks to Baze's exploits, they had been able to cross Lyons' name off the list.

"We ruled out a suspect, while also putting that perverted asshole behind bars. How do you figure that it *didn't* work?"

"Well, because we are as close to catching Robert Macabre as you were fifteen years ago," quipped Baze.

Arroyo felt a spark of irritation. Perhaps it was due to the fact that she had spent so many hours in this building fighting stagnation in the case in '04, and this arrest felt like a success. Baze wasn't used to police investigations. He didn't know what it was like to sit around for days at a time, scouring over every useless detail without making any headway on catching the man you were after. And it was because of him they had arrested Lyons! The man should have felt at least a little bit of triumph.

"In the meantime, I am not really sure why you brought me in here. I am not going to admit to anything, and you don't have anything to gain by me doing so." Baze made a move to stand up, as if the meeting between them was somehow over.

"Sit down, jackass."

Arroyo's voice was so stern that it made Baze freeze in his tracks. Slowly but surely, he lowered his posterior back into the chair across from her desk.

"I didn't bring you in here to admit to anything, or even to tell you, you did a good job. Contrary to whatever you may believe, you are not the only one who finds leads."

With that, Arroyo opened the manila envelope that was in front of her and pushed it across the desk. Baze looked down at the photographs in the folder and pursed his lips.

"Canvassing photos from the crime scene at the shipyard. Now, I am sure you know this, but forensics doesn't just take photographs of the body. They are also always instructed to take pictures of the crowd. Anybody that is standing behind the yellow tape gawking is documented and filed."

Arroyo reached for the photos and pointed at the bottom left corner of the picture that was on top of the stack. She tapped on the head of a blond man that was lurking behind the crime scene tape and sighed.

"Now, I have mulled it over in my brain several times. He retired a year ago, but since he worked on the original case back in oh four, perhaps he just has an active interest in knowing who the killer is. He definitely still has connections within the department, so maybe someone tipped him off."

Arroyo paused, took a deep breath, and shook her head. "But the more I think about it, him being at *this* crime scene doesn't fit. The first one in fifteen years, and he shows up within two hours of her body being discovered? Before it got out that this was even the work of Macabre? No, Baze... It just doesn't make sense. Not at all. I can't think of an innocent explanation for Edwin Spade being in this photograph of the crime scene. And yet, here he is."

Arroyo and Baze waited on the doorstep, looking at each other apprehensively. The echo of the doorbell still pinged around Baze's ears, and he felt very out of place. This neighborhood was too ritzy for him. The lawn next to the house too perfectly kept. His eyes swiveled back forward when he caught movement out of his peripheral vision, and a blond head moved swiftly past the long, rectangular window next to the door.

The door opened, and a spindly man with beady eyes stood there, looking like he was trying to dissimulate his misgivings about the pair that was standing on his front porch. Edwin Spade gave them a smile that was supposed to be warm, but was actually just chilling. His teeth took up too big of a portion of his face, and his beady eyes sunk too far into his cheekbones. The oversized glasses on his face had a weird effect on his pupils.

"Hello, Emily."

"Hello, Dr. Spade."

Spade chortled. "After all of these years, we still aren't on a first name basis?"

"Well, Doctor, I can't say we ever had a personal relationship, so I will continue to address you like a colleague. Hopefully, the formality doesn't bother you."

The smile wiped off of his face, and it was replaced with something stony and resentful. Spade turned to look at Baze, and his eyes latched onto the scar on the man's cheek.

"And who is this?"

"This is Anton Baze. He is a special consultant that we have brought on board to our investigative team."

Baze stuck out his hand, and when Spade slithered his cold palm into his grasp, Baze made sure to squeeze with a little more force than he usually put into his handshakes.

"Nice to meet you, doc."

"And what are you consulting Ms. Arroyo on, exactly? Something extra perplexing?" The man said it with heavy sarcasm in his voice.

Before Baze could respond, Arroyo jumped in.

"Why don't we go inside, Spade?"

"Sure thing, *Emily.*" Spade stepped aside and gestured behind him, and Arroyo and Baze slowly sauntered into the house.

Moments later, they were in the living area, sitting on a couch that gave off a pungent and almost unpleasant leathery scent. Spade was in a recliner across from them, with his legs folded and both of his hands gripping his right kneecap. He was staring at Baze for some reason, and the look on his face was unsettling.

"So, Ms. Lieutenant and Mr. Consultant, how can I help?"

Baze glanced at Arroyo, and she was staring at Spade with dislike etched across her face. Arroyo set the folder she was holding unceremoniously onto the black ottoman in between them and flipped it open. Spade's eyes traveled down to the photograph of the disfigured body hanging there, complete with a pig mask. His face seemed to lose a bit of its color.

"Well, Doctor, as I am sure you are aware, last Tuesday, a woman named Maria Cable was found hung in a shipping container at the Vigor facility not far from here. Her body was mutilated. Contusions around her wrists. We think that was from the rope, as she was likely kept bound for at least twenty-four hours. Lacerations all along her body. Probably from a serrated knife. Genital bruising and tearing, indicating that she was violated with a blunt object…"

Baze wondered if Arroyo was being intentionally clinical as a way of somehow talking in Spade's preferred form of discourse.

Arroyo leaned forward. "Now, Doctor... I know you still have contacts within my department. But you do look fairly shocked at this particular moment in time, so perhaps no one told you that Robert Macabre is killing again?"

After a moment of nothing, Spade began shaking his head appulsively.

"No, no... That's impossible. That's simply impossible. Tennyson. It was Tennyson. We all know that. *You* know that! He shot you, didn't he?"

"Drop the pretense, doc. Ain't nobody given you an Oscar."

Both Spade and Arroyo turned their heads to Baze, whose voice was filled with spite. He could already tell from the two minutes he had spent in Spade's presence that he did not care for the man.

"I'm sorry? What is it that you are implying?" asked Spade.

"I'm not implying anything. You already knew about this."

A flash of panic scurried across Spade's face. His voice was a few decibels softer when he spoke next.

"I did, did I? That's news to me."

"Hmm. What do you think, Red?"

Arroyo narrowed her eyes while looking at Spade. "I think the doctor here is going to have trouble explaining why he was in this photograph at the crime scene." She reached under the first photograph of Cable hanging naked from the shipping container and pulled out the picture where you could just make out Edwin Spade lurking in the corner of the crowd behind the yellow tape, with shifty eyes and an uncanny demeanor.

Spade looked down at the photograph, and that same panic quickly lit up his eyes again, but it passed almost instantly, and was replaced by the smile he intended to be lighthearted and jovial but just looked downright strange.

"Wow… Is that what this is? You think that because I am in this picture that I am implicated in this?"

When Arroyo didn't reply right away, Spade let out a bizarre and mirthless laugh. It reminded Baze of a crow cawing. "Well, this is something, isn't it? When I woke up this morning, I saw this day going a lot of different ways, but never did I envision myself being accused of mass murder."

"We aren't accusing you of anything, doc," replied Baze quickly. "But the fact that you were at this crime scene is, let's say, a little *strange*."

"Well, surely it is a sign of my guilt. Better have me arrested. Might be tough to find a judge that issues warrants based on that, though. Is being photographed a misdemeanor or a felony?"

Arroyo suddenly leaned forward, and when she spoke, her voice was stern. "Spade, *enough*."

This clearly took the man off guard, because he leaned back like she had just breathed a mini spout of fire.

"Listen, Doctor. I don't want to be in this room with you for any longer than I have to be. I'm not looking to grill you, or to spend an hour going in circles about Robert Macabre. All I want is a reasonable explanation for why you were at that crime scene last week."

Spade's mouth opened and then closed, and there was an elongated spell of quiet. It was like the man realized that he didn't have a quick and biting retort, so he swallowed his response altogether.

"Doctor? It's a simple question."

"Okay… And the simple answer is that Vigor Shipyard is only five blocks away from here. When I heard about the scene, I was naturally curious. So I walked down to the pier. And I didn't see a goddamn thing. Is that helpful?"

"Who told you about it?"

"The crime scene?" asked Spade incredulously. "You said it yourself, Lieutenant. I worked for nineteen years in that department. You think I don't have any sort of connections left from my entire career?"

"It just seems odd to immediately contact an ex-coroner in the hours after a brutal murder," said Arroyo.

"I was contacted *because* it happened so close

to here. It's not like I receive regular updates on all the homicides in Portland."

"So, who within the department is close enough friends with you to tell you about nearby dead bodies?"

"That is none of your business," snarled Spade.

"Why not, Spade?"

"Because you gain nothing from me telling you who my source is, while I lose something from telling you who my source is. Fact of the matter is, I heard about it because it was close to where I live. I walked down to check it out. End of story."

"But just a second ago you acted like you were absolutely flabbergasted when I mentioned Robert Macabre," countered Arroyo. "And now you are freely admitting you were at the crime scene."

"Goddamn it, Emily! I told you! I didn't see anything! I don't know anything about that! If by some infinitesimal chance Macabre is actually still out there, I had absolutely no idea that that was him. I didn't even know what it was until you showed me that picture."

Arroyo didn't reply to this. She leaned back and eyed Spade with suspicion. While she reclined, Baze moved forward. His voice was ever so quiet when the next two words came out of his mouth.

"You're lying."

The whisper came out like a hiss. It evidently took Spade and Arroyo off guard, because they both looked at him with bewildered expressions.

"Excuse me?" Spade's tone was different now. There was something a little foreboding there.

"I've talked with a lot of liars in my life. You sound like all of 'em."

For a fleeting second, Baze thought that he could see a glimpse of a monster that was lingering in the protective shell of Edwin Spade's body. Something flashed in the man's eyes. Something malicious and dark. But it passed in a nanosecond, and that familiar bizarre smile spread across Spade's face.

"I think you two better leave now," he whispered.

Baze didn't hesitate. He placed both hands on the couch and pushed himself up onto his feet. Arroyo was looking up at him with an expression of consternation and perplexity, and Baze could tell that her frustration had shifted onto him.

"C'mon, Red. You heard the man."

Baze began to slink out of the room, staring at Spade the whole time. It took all of the effort in his body not to vocalize the thought in his head.

See you soon, doc.

Macabre was watching him.

There was no other logical explanation. The man was stalking him again, teasing and taunting Welsh from the periphery. This was his preferred method of cruelty, at least when Welsh was involved. Macabre wanted his adversary to be constantly looking over his shoulder, oblivious to when the attack would finally transpire. It made Welsh's insides squirm with anticipation every time he thought about it. The last confrontation was coming.

It should have scared the hell out of him, but it didn't. Welsh was no longer afraid of being followed, even though Macabre was clearly trying to torment him. The man had somehow known that Welsh would go to Wilsonville and had placed the bird mask on the bed in a taunting gesture. The only other alternative was that Macabre had broken in years before and left the token for Welsh to find, so that he would know that the real killer had never been caught. But that didn't sound right. Macabre had gone dormant on purpose—he wouldn't have left clues to his continued existence.

What was most perplexing about the whole thing was the fact that Welsh hadn't told anyone of his planned foray to the house. Freidenberg had been the one to suggest it, and Welsh hadn't relayed the idea to anyone.

Freidenberg...

No. No. That wasn't possible. This connection with Macabre went back almost two decades, and Welsh had met his new shrink just months ago.

Then again, perhaps Welsh meeting the doctor just as Macabre resurfaced wasn't a coincidence.

Oh, come on. He is almost seventy, thought Welsh. This train of thought was categorically insane. But that was what Macabre did to him. It is what the man wanted, for Welsh to be so paranoid that he questioned each and every relationship and interaction in his life.

His mind whirring, Welsh pulled up to his apartment and pulled the keys hostilely out of the ignition. The bird mask was now sitting on the front passenger seat. He wasn't going to hand it over to the cops. He wasn't going to tell Arroyo. He wanted a chance to end this on his own terms. He wanted revenge. If Arroyo knew that Macabre was back to stalking him, she would get in the way. And Welsh didn't need that.

The steps up to the front door to his apartment were slick, and he almost biffed-it on his way up. His right hand went out to brace himself, and the key that he had withdrawn from his pocket skittered away across the concrete step and into the bushes.

"Shit!"

Welsh bent down and moved to his right, as he saw the silver of the key glinting in that direction. As he reached into the bush, the color red caught his eye and he looked up. A classic sports car was parked across the street.

Was that a Firebird?

Welsh stared at the tinted windows and was perplexed. He had never seen that car in this neighborhood before. Not that he had a photographic memory of every vehicle that came and went, but he thought a Firebird would have burned itself into his recollections. It was such a sweet ride.

He looked for a few seconds longer, and then, like a man who had been caught staring at an attractive woman's breast, he pointed his attention quickly somewhere else. *Have some dignity, Carson,* he thought.

But then the engine revved.

Welsh felt a tingling sensation creeping up his spine. It was a very strange feeling to know that someone could see you when you couldn't see them.

The engine revved again. Whoever was behind the wheel was keen to show off the powerful engine of the sports car. *Asshole,* thought Welsh, and he turned away, knowing that this was likely just some rich jerkoff overcompensating for something.

But then the passenger window rolled down, and Welsh saw the sleek head of a raven staring at him. One not unlike the mask that was now in the front seat of his car.

He didn't even think twice. Adrenaline forced him off of his front steps and toward the maniac that was in the car across the street. Welsh knew that he was unarmed and vulnerable. But the deep-seated loathing that was coursing through his veins overruled anything else. He had to get to the car. He had to get his hands around Robert Macabre's throat.

Just as he took off running, the car's tires spun so fast that smoke puffed out onto the street. And then, like a bullet, it shot forward with a screech. Welsh pumped his arms and his legs in sync, trying fruitlessly to catch the fleeing vehicle. But the effort was folly. By the time he got to the street, it was already a block away.

Welsh squinted his eyes, trying to memorize the license plate. But it was dark out, and the Firebird was already thirty feet away. At the first street it came to, the car turned to the right. Welsh thought about hopping into his own vehicle and leaving in pursuit. But it was too late. Once again, Macabre was gone.

Edwin Spade let his head drop against the pillow as he pulled the covers up over his naked body. It was a warm night; Spade usually slept in the nude as a preference, but tonight, it felt like a necessity. Sweat instantly pooled up on his lower back and in his armpits, and he realized that it was going to be difficult to fall asleep. He had a fan, but the obnoxious sound that it made offset any sort of cooling effect.

His glasses lay sitting on the nightstand next to his bed, and everything was now blurry as his eyes took in his surroundings without any assistance. Spade had been born with horrible vision, and every time his he took off his glasses, it was like looking at a different dimension, where everything was distorted and strange.

For some reason, the face of Emily Arroyo floated to the front of Spade's consciousness, with her ludicrously red hair and sickly pale complexion. When he had first known her, Spade had actually found her attractive. But that was back when his sexual appetite was insatiable; his libido yearning for any woman with a pulse. Now that he was in his fifties and his sex-drive had faded significantly, Spade's tastes only adhered to the young and supple. And Arroyo was definitely not young and supple. The bags under her eyes were heavier than they had ever been. Her face looked like it hadn't been touched by the sun in eons, and her breasts seemed to sag to the middle of her body. Combined with her acrimonious and prickly attitude, Spade now found himself repelled by her.

And then there was that strange man that had accompanied Arroyo. The bushy mustache hanging over his upper lip. The snake-shaped scar that inched up his cheek. The man called Baze was tall and thick and didn't seem like someone you would want to trifle with. There was a darkness in his eyes that Spade couldn't pinpoint. The man seemed like he almost welcomed confrontation.

Spade felt himself sinking into the mattress, and slowly, the heat that had been uncomfortable became much more pleasant. It was only in that moment that he realized how exhausted he was. His body ached for no good reason at all. Father Time had a way with everyone, but he seemed to hold quite the grudge against Edwin Spade. Spade's joints pained him whenever he moved. His stomach could no longer process certain foods. His vision had somehow gotten worse. It all added up to a distinct feeling of enervation and fatigue when his body finally hit the mattress at night. Day-to-day life was much more of a battle now.

As he lay there, pondering the heated interaction with Arroyo and Baze, a sandy feeling dusted over his eyes. The familiar sensation of falling off the edge of a cliff hit him like a semi-truck, and within moments, Spade was asleep.

Crack.

Spade convulsed in his bed spasmodically and was thrown unceremoniously out of slumber like someone had dumped a bucket of ice water onto his bed. His heart was throbbing wildly, and it took a few seconds for him to gather his bearings and realize where he was.

He was naked in bed, and a loud noise had just woke him up.

Spade reached out for his nightstand and fumbled for his glasses, and in his panicked state, he felt his fingers knock the bifocals off of the nightstand and onto the ground.

"Shit!"

Spade pulled the covers away from his body and maneuvered his legs gingerly off of the side of the bed, careful not to step on the fallen specs. Just as he was about to slide off of his mattress he heard a soft creak.

His bedroom door slowly opened. An intruder in all black stood in the doorframe. Though blurry in Spade's vision, the figure didn't have a distinguishable face. Where there should have been a nose and a mouth and eyes there was blackness.

Spade screamed.

The figure darted forward and Spade heard the *crunch* of the man stepping on his glasses. Spade tried to roll out of the man's grasp, but before he could, a hand closed around his larynx, snuffing out the scream. The black figure pummeled Spade across the jaw, and the room spun. Before he knew it, he was lying on the ground next to the bed, completely exposed and lacking any sense of direction.

"What were you doing at the shipyard?"

The voice was gravelly and warped as it shrieked and Spade madly thought of Christian Bale's Batman. Before he could even formulate a response, the fist slammed against his forehead and propelled the back of his dome into the wall. Everything was spinning.

"Answer me, motherfucker! What were you doing?"

Spade only had one thought, and he somehow managed to vocalize it.

"Who are you?"

Once more, the fist slammed against his jaw,

and Spade tasted hot iron in his mouth.

"Not so bright, are ya? *Answer the question! What were you doing at the shipyard?"*

"D-Did A-Arroyo send you?"

The figure pumped back his fist, ready to strike once more, but Spade threw his arms up pitifully.

"All right, all right! Stop! Please! Jesus! I was just looking for information!"

The man in black stopped, and he seemed to cock his head.

"You better provide a lot more than that if you want to keep your teeth."

This time, the man unleashed a forceful kick right into Spade's gut, and all the air in his diaphragm shot out like a popped balloon. Spade rolled onto his side, trying to find any sense of equilibrium left in his body. Intermingled with the pain was a new fire bubbling in his belly—Anger.

"You won't get away with this," he said through gritted teeth. "You'll never get away with this."

The man in black hit him square in the nose, and it broke upon impact. Spade let out a pitiful squeak as blood poured down his face and seeped into his mouth.

"Stop! Stop! Please!" He held up his hand to protect his face from any more blows, and the man reached out and snatched his first two fingers and bent them back so viciously that they felt like they were about to snap off.

"Please!"

Spade's pleading voice sounded inhuman, even to his own ears.

"Start talking, asshole. Start talking and you won't have any broken fingers."

"There was a leak," Spade heaved, though it was difficult to speak. "There was a leak."

The man grabbed Spade by his forearm and lifted him up before dumping him back onto the bed.

"The hell does that mean?"

"Back in oh four! When Macabre was first killing! Someone was giving the *Oregonian* information about the case."

"And?"

"It was me! I was the source! Cheyenne Blue, the reporter, she paid me for the info."

The man reached out and grabbed Spade by the throat again. This time, he didn't squeeze as hard, but it was enough to rob Spade of some of his air.

"Keep going, Doctor," rumbled the man, and his voice still sounded like a demon.

"Someone on Arroyo's forensics team told me about the scene on the night that it happened," whispered Spade, as a whisper was all he could manage over the hand gripping his throat. "They told me that Macabre was back."

"Who was it?"

"His name is James Wills."

The man suddenly relinquished his grip and Spade instantly scrambled backward on the bed like a frightened cat.

"So... What, when you heard that Macabre was back you thought you would go poking around? See if you could find anything that you could sell to the reporter? You were trying to profit on the girl's death?"

Spade froze, and though he could only see the outline of the man in black, it was like a lightbulb went on over his head.

"It's you, isn't it? The consultant?"

Before he could process what was happening, something heavy that might have been the man's fist but also could have been a brick swooped through the air toward Spade's temple. He didn't notice it making contact, but it must have, because Spade didn't wake up until hours later, sprawled out on his bed and the man in black nowhere to be found.

Welsh hobbled along with his back feeling like a thousand fiery needles had penetrated it. Whenever he exercised for too long, the injury flared up so much that it made it difficult to move. Even moderate exercise like walking put too much strain on the muscles in his lower back. He had to stop for a second.

There was a bench nearby and he plopped onto it with a *thunk*. Once he was stationary, the pain subsided enough that he could take a few calming breaths to reassert a sense of tranquility in his body. The bookstore next to the green bench that he was sitting on was tinkling with some catchy melody that reminded Welsh of Christmas music. He couldn't make out any of the words, but the tune was welcoming. The sign dangling just above him and to the right said Annie Bloom's Books. Surprisingly, he had never ventured past this particular nook before. He had taken many a jaunt in downtown Portland, but still always seemed to find new shops and restaurants that had seemingly sprung out of the ground.

The Firebird had not reappeared since its initial manifestation two nights before. And yet, Welsh still felt like a set of eyes were upon him. No matter where he went, it was like he was being watched. He couldn't tell if that was just the festering paranoia that had plagued him for the past fifteen years, or if he really was perpetually being followed.

Either way, he didn't care.

Walks around town now had multiple purposes. Not only did it serve as a form of light cardio to keep his heart beating long enough to put a bullet in Robert Macabre's forehead, it also served as a form of reconnaissance. He was gathering information. Who did he see multiple times during his forays downtown? Who was acting suspiciously, trying to camouflage surveillance by pretending to do something innocuous?

Better yet, where was that damn Firebird?

Though Welsh hadn't actively admitted it to himself, there was also a more ominous reason for being in public. If he spent his time in places where it was easy to be seen, surely someone would be watching.

I'm right here. Come and find me.

The Glock attached to his hip was heavy, and whenever the hilt brushed against his midriff, Welsh felt the cold, rough edge of the grip tape wrapped around it. His hands always seem to sweat more profusely than what was normal, so the last time he had been at the shooting range, the instructor there had suggested grip tape, so the gun wouldn't go spiraling out of his hands mid-shot. Welsh didn't think Macabre would attack him in a crowded area, but he couldn't rule somewhere *next* to a crowded area. His plan was to take a detour down a backstreet if he sensed someone following him, and hopefully his pursuer would take the bait. Then, Welsh would be ready to pull the Glock whenever he heard the first footsteps.

And yet Welsh knew that even if Macabre *was* always watching him, the man would be clever enough to avoid a trap. Welsh wasn't the type to just skip down a dank and dark alleyway for fun.

After feeling the last remnants of pain depart from his body, Welsh placed his hands on either side of his hips and pressed himself off of the bench. Perhaps maintaining a slower pace was the key to the muscles not seizing, so he took miniature steps while passing the bookshop. He glanced in and saw an old lady with a drooping turkey neck looking at a nearby shelf, apparently perplexed by a book that was not there. She seemed to be oblivious to the set of eyes that were now on her.

That was how people were. They would never notice someone looking at them unless the person was in direct proximity. Welsh had always liked to people-watch. It was fascinating to see the behavioral habits of individuals that somehow clung to the illusion that they were anonymous.

Welsh turned his eyes back toward the street and saw several interesting passersby, both walking past him and across the intersection. He saw an old man with fluffy white hair and a thick Adam's apple. There was an overweight gentleman in sweats and flip-flops with the traces of a beard tickling his jaw. Next, a skinny blond woman with sunglasses and an inordinate amount of makeup on her face. Each person had a completely inimitable gait and distinctive idiosyncrasies within the way they carried themselves. Everyone seemed to project something unique. Even the ordinary-looking man with jet-black hair.

Time froze. Welsh's heart battered away in his chest like an animal trying to break its glass enclosure.

It couldn't be.

Ignoring the stabs in his back, Welsh pushed himself up and broke into a fast-paced walk. A new wave of people came toward him, and the man vanished into the crowd. Welsh started brusquely shoving past every stranger that got into his path, and he clipped a couple of them, including a large man in a suit.

"Watch where you are going!"

Welsh ignored him and continued in pursuit of his target. At first, Welsh thought he had lost him, but then, there was the same head of black hair weaving in-between bodies some twenty feet ahead. The head turned back around, and they made eye contact.

The man broke into a run.

Disregarding the agony in his back, Welsh began to piston his arms and legs together to gather speed, and in a few seconds, he was sprinting.

Faster. Must. Go. Faster.

Welsh's ragged breath rattled out of his mouth, and he realized that he couldn't keep this speed up for long. Surely, his heart would implode or his legs would collapse upon themselves if he pushed them much longer. Up ahead, his target took a sharp right turn, and galloped away down Thirty-Fifth Avenue. Ten seconds later, Welsh rounded the same corner, and immediately came to a halt.

The man had disappeared.

Welsh looked to his left and his right, but didn't see him. He even bent over and peeked under a parked car, looking to see if the man was hiding there. But, of course, he wasn't.

Conceding defeat, Welsh doubled over with a stitch in his chest searing. He placed his hands on his knees, panting wildly. But even after he regained control over his labored breathing, his heart continued to patter away in his chest. The enormity of the revelation that Welsh had just come to propelled his pulse like fuel on a fire.

It didn't make any sense. How could it be possible? Welsh turned over each possibility in his head, but none of them seemed to fit. No matter how hard he thought, he couldn't come up with a rational explanation for what he had just seen.

Because David Kane was supposed to be dead.

53

Arroyo held the piece of paper into the air so that each detective could see it. The sketch was actually fairly haunting; the man had sunken eyes and a gaunt look about him, and even in the drawing, his expression conveyed malice. Arroyo gave it a little shake, as if to emphasize the significance of the picture.

"This is the man that Welsh saw yesterday on Capitol Highway near Annie Bloom's Bookstore. He goes by the pseudonym of David Kane. His actual name is a mystery. As I am sure many of you know from scouring over case files, Kane was presumed to be a victim of Macabre fifteen years ago. We came to this conclusion after Macabre left a severed hand on Welsh's front porch that was mistakenly identified as Kane's. Along with the hand, there were five photographs of a male victim who had been mutilated. Extremities and genitals removed. Face scalped. Tops of the fingers chopped off on the hand too, so no chance at prints. No matches on DNA of the hand either."

Arroyo looked down the table of men and made eye contact with Baze, who was smirking at her for some reason. She had been a little leery of him over the past couple of days. When he had told her about Edwin Spade, she had become instantly suspicious. How could he have found out that Spade was the leak that quickly? Arroyo was beginning to regret bringing Baze on board, due to his deviant antics. The man had apparently successfully ruled out two suspects, but at what cost? Hopefully, whatever he had done would not become their undoing.

"Whoever David Kane actually is," continued Arroyo, "He is a pathological liar. Welsh said that in their initial conversation, Kane proclaimed to have been falsely accused of rape, and that he had served time at OSP for it. This was false. No record of anyone with that name was ever in OSP. Kane also said that he had been beaten by an officer named Marius Wicks before he went to prison, which was also false. Officer Marius Wicks never existed."

Arroyo slapped the picture down on the table and looked from face to face.

"So, why would this man have any desire to concoct this web of lies? What motive could he possibly have to come forward as an eyewitness and then fake his own death by leaving a body part in a box that had Will Tennyson's prints on it? Lowry, you want to field this one?"

"Because David Kane is our man."

Arroyo gestured at Lowry with her index finger. "Pretty easy to put two and two together, isn't it?"

"But why even come forward at all? If you are the killer, why make contact with Welsh? Wouldn't you want to stay as far away from suspicion as possible?" asked Fairfield, who looked perplexed.

"You are speaking about it from the point of view of a normal criminal. Evading suspicion. That is not Robert Macabre. He has no desire to keep quiet. He just thinks he is smarter than all of us."

"Maybe he is right," muttered Giuliani.

"And how the hell did we not find a match on the hand?" demanded Fairfield. "It is not like we are talking about the stone-age of forensics back then."

"The DNA didn't match anybody in any known database," replied Arroyo. "My pet-theory is that Robert Macabre killed a transient and placed his own ring on the vic's finger to make us think it was him."

"Tell them about the ring, LT," said Lowry while he raised the pencil he was holding in the air.

"Ah, yes. The ring itself was engraved with a Latin phrase. It translates to, 'He lives among us.' Originally, it is supposed to be some sort of religious connotation, but here, I think this was one of Macabre's cryptic clues about his actual identity."

The room was silent for a little while before Baze unexpectedly broke the void with a chuckle. Arroyo looked at him with fiery resentment and made a sarcastic gesture with her hand.

"Something to say, Anton?"

"Nothing of significance, Red. I just find it mighty hard to believe that we are going to make quick work of finding a man that, before yesterday, had not been seen in fifteen years."

Arroyo closed her eyes for a second, trying to suppress the rising tide of anger within her. "Well, thank you for that, but I think your opinion on how laborious this endeavor is going to be is a little irrelevant. And I fail to see any sort of humor embedded in this particular subject, Baze."

Baze scoffed. "Yeah, well, you fail to see the humor in most things, Red."

Everyone seemed to collectively fidget in discomfort, and Arroyo felt her cheeks growing hot. Baze wasn't her subordinate, but that didn't mean he could treat her with disrespect.

"Jesus Christ," murmured Fairfield. "When is this guy going to get eighty-sixed?"

"Same day you grow hair, shitheel," growled Baze.

Fairfield started contorting his mouth as the

muscles in his face worked to express his fury, but Arroyo stopped the impending tirade by raising her voice and gesticulating aggressively in Baze's direction.

"*Finding* this man is the only thing that matters! And we will find him, no matter what! We start by circulating this image to the press. KATU news, channel six, the papers, everybody. I want everyone in Portland to have eyes on this sketch. Next, we will pull case files. We will re-interview those that knew Dinwoodie and see if Kane was actually telling the truth about his relationship with her. We will dig up old canvassing photos. Interviews with neighbors. Bystanders. If anyone, *anyone* involved in this case has ever known or spoken with the man who calls himself David Kane, we will know about it."

Fairfield drummed the middle and index fingers on his right hand against the table, and Arroyo noticed that he was chewing the inside of his cheek. "And you're sure about this guy, LT?"

Arroyo nodded, her body full of conviction. "I know one thing. If we find David Kane, we find answers."

Carrie Leon pinched the skin of her arm, looking for a lump of pale blue. The needle in her hand twitched as she brought it closer to her body, and the baby on the carpet cried louder. Leon ignored it and continued to search for the perfect vein. That damn kid was always fussing. No matter how much attention she paid to her son, the fucking boy would always cry. There would be periods of time where Cory would go quiet, but the whining and crying would always start up again, like an alarm clock that had a snooze button but would never turn off. It was to the point now where Leon would just let him sob until he got tired of doing so.

As Leon finally pinpointed the perfect spot to pierce her flesh with the tip of the needle, she saw that Cory's wet eyes were latched onto her as she moved to inject the drug into her body. Somewhere in the back of her mind, where the last traces of a polluted and diseased form of morality still lingered, a small voice told her how wrong this was. Doing heroin in front of your seven-month-old baby. Even someone as sick as she was could sense the depravity of her actions. But the yearning for the rush was too powerful. And Cory's brain was nothing but a clump of mush anyway. There was no way he would remember this when he was fully grown.

Leon tapped the needle, getting it ready for the imminent penetration by knocking away the miniature bubbles that threatened to impede the process.

Those big blue eyes were staring right at her now. They were wide; Cory seemed to be totally absorbed in what was happening. Leon looked away.

"Didn't your mother ever tell you it was rude to stare?"

She let out a husky laugh, as if it were the most droll and charming joke she had ever told. The boy started to howl again, and as the seconds went on, his crying and screaming amplified by the second.

"Stop cryin', you little shit. You're going to make my ears bleed."

But the baby wailed and wailed away. Cory's face contorted horribly, and Leon wanted to slap him. The way his mouth twisted and his eyes squeezed did not inspire pity, but rather, loathing.

This was not the life that she wanted. She had never asked for a child. She had never prepared to take care of one. All that little goblin had done was eat and shit and cry and cling to life since the day he was born. He was like a little parasite, slowly sucking the remaining life force from her. The only way she could cope with the constant barrage of noise and god-awful smells that the boy produced was through her little needle.

With a sigh, Leon pressed the back end of the needle down, ignoring the droplet of blood that oozed out of the pinprick in her arm. It took a few moments, but then the rush came. Her stomach soared, and her body felt as light as a feather.

"Ah, hell," said Leon, leaning back and closing her eyes. She sat there for what felt like a second or two, but could well have been five minutes, bathing herself in the sensation. It was the best feeling on planet Earth. Leon had no doubt about that. Heroin could make your pain go away. It could make the cold, forbidding world feel warm. It could make the baby stop crying.

Leon opened her eyes. Cory was no longer bawling. The boy was frozen, staring at a spot just over her shoulder.

"What the hell are you looki—"

Leon saw the shadow dance across the carpet. Before she could process anything else, an arm with crushing strength was wrapped around her throat.

Her eyes rolled back and she saw the shape of the giant man standing over her. He was wearing all black, including the gloves on his gargantuan hands. But he didn't have a face. At least, not a human face.

It was a rooster's head on a man's body.

The man lifted her off of the couch and the remaining air left in her mouth was vanquished. Leon clawed at the arm around her throat that was lifting her up, but the man's grip just tightened. Leon kicked fruitlessly, as if her jerking legs could somehow produce air for her lungs and get the rooster-man to release her.

Something wet tickled her palm, and Leon's eyes lolled to the side to see a droplet of heroin running down her forearm. Then the needle glinted ephemerally in the air. Her attacker was holding it just above her face.

Leon tried to let out a scream, but all that came out was a grunt. Her eyes flickered down to her son on the carpet. Cory was watching the action unfold with his head tilted to the side and his eyes full of curiosity.

Without warning, the man released her. She got a brief, sharp intake of air, but then a gloved hand chopped just underneath her chin, and breathtaking pressure was forced upon her jaw. The rooster-man squeezed her jowls, and her mouth popped open in response.

A half-second later, the heroin needle was jammed down her throat.

Leon retched, and bile foamed up through her mouth. She tasted the stomach acid and something horribly bitter swirling around her tongue. Leon felt herself fall forward off of the couch, and her diaphragm began to heave. But before she could throw up, the same gloved hand clasped over her lips. She couldn't breathe. Everything was spinning. The needle was lodged in her throat.

Leon's eyes locked upon Cory, and there he sat, completely still. Totally unmoved by the sight of his mother reeling and writhing in front of him. And suddenly, the ground began to separate from her hands and knees. She was moving upward, and Cory was still motionless on the carpet, staring at her. Further away she floated, with the boy only politely curious about what was happening. As the rooster-man carried her away, all Leon saw were those big blue eyes locked onto her, completely impassive to her impending absence.

55

"This is some sick shit, LT."

Arroyo gave the smallest of nods in Lowry's direction. The man had a penchant for stating the obvious whenever he felt uncomfortable, and it sometimes got on her nerves. If there was one thing that did not need to be pointed out, it was the repugnant nature of what they were looking at.

Arroyo stepped toward the grisly scene in front of her, and she realized that the sight reminded her of a painting—with the clash of color and the abstract, yet intentional incongruity. She wondered if on some level Macabre thought of himself as an artist. How much time did he spend perfecting his work before it was ready for viewing?

For whatever reason, this one smelled worse than the others. The stench of rotting flesh and dried blood permeated the forest. Arroyo wondered if she had been dead for more than forty-eight hours. This wasn't exactly a hot spot for foot traffic, out in the middle of the woods. They got lucky that Nicole Childs had decided to go for a jog down a generally non-frequented trail. But why had the killer chosen this spot, as opposed to the public place where he had hung Tracy Dinwoodie's torso? Maybe David Kane suspected that the police had circulated his picture to the public. Maybe he couldn't risk venturing into busier areas.

Lowry moved side by side with Arroyo, watching as the forensic techs took a multitude of photographs of the pale woman that was suspended by her neck from a tall Douglas fir. The woman's lips were blue; her eyes were rolled almost completely back up into her sockets. Her entire head was bald with noticeable abrasions all over it, and Arroyo was certain that she had been roughly shaven as part of the torture. Each side of her head was caked with blood, and where the ears were supposed to be, there were two gaping holes that looked to be where most of the blood was emanating from.

"Jesus Christ," muttered Lowry, and he ran his hand through his short black hair. "Let's cut her down already."

"Not yet, Detective," said Arroyo quietly. "We have to preserve the scene best we can."

"Why? He hasn't left shit behind so far. Why would he now?"

"Because every killer makes a mistake. I have said it from the beginning."

Lowry shook his head in disgust as he stared up at the mauled woman dangling twelve feet above the ground. "This is a nightmare."

Captain Obvious with another guest appearance, thought Arroyo.

"Mm."

"The sooner we get her down, the sooner we can work on getting an ID."

"All in good time, Lowry," murmured Arroyo. "All in good time."

"This one looks older than the rest. Probably early forties, if I had to guess. Anybody reported a missing middle-aged woman?"

"Not as far as I know."

"Cause of death? I mean, just from looking at that," said Lowry, gesturing emphatically at the body.

"My specialty isn't forensics, Easton."

"But if you had to guess."

Arroyo eyed the dead woman, with her bald head and dried blood covering her body. There were several noticeable punctures around the mid-section.

"The stab wounds to the abdomen look fairly significant. If she hadn't already passed from the blood loss due to the head wounds, she wouldn't have lasted long after those."

"Head wounds," said Lowry blankly, as if he couldn't quite wrap his mind around such a concept.

"The ears."

"Wha—? No, obviously I know you are talking about the ears, LT. I was just thinking…"

Arroyo shifted her focus from the scene to Lowry's befuddled face. "Yes?"

"What do you think he did with the ears?"

Arroyo sighed so deeply that she almost felt the remaining energy drain out of her like the last swirls of water in a bathtub.

"I have a theory. But I hope I am wrong."

Welsh didn't know why he had opened it.

As soon as he had seen the little white package with the red ribbon tied around it, he had known exactly who had sent it. And he had known that whatever was inside was bad news.

And yet, he couldn't help himself.

His fingers shaking, he had pulled off the ribbon, thinking wildly of an engagement ring. That was what it looked like, with its neatly bowed decoration and the tidy slanted writing that was on the miniature card on top of the box. Welsh had even felt the most bizarre desire to laugh when he had read the two words that were on the card. "Old friend." Like he and Macabre were exchanging sentimental gifts with each other.

Now, the two bloodied ears lay askew on the tissue paper, and Welsh was surprised by the fact that he didn't have the urge to throw up. He remembered when the intestines had been plopped on his desk, and the feeling of sheer dread before he passed out. Now, though still shocking, he didn't feel that innate terror. There wasn't any nausea. The world wasn't spinning. Was this what it had come to? Had he become so acclimated to the horrors of the world that a pair of dismembered body parts barely even shook him?

His hands still slightly shaking from the adrenaline, Welsh picked up the note that had been in the box with the ears, and reread the man's penmanship. Another set of chills crawled down his back as he looked over it for the second time.

Do you hear me coming?

"You need protection."

"I don't need shit."

"He's going to kill you, Carson."

"If he wanted to kill me, wouldn't he have done it already?"

Arroyo looked away from Welsh and let out a heavy, rattled sigh. The only other people in the living room of his apartment were the two remaining forensic techs sweeping the place for prints. They dusted various surfaces and picked up random items, and Arroyo saw Welsh give the techs an irritated side-eye, like they were crossing some line by touching his personal items.

The set of ears that belonged to Carrie Leon were now on their way to the evidence locker, and Arroyo was glad that she did not personally have to look at the tokens of Macabre's strange fantasy— the scene in the forest had been gratuitous enough in its display of brutality to last her a lifetime.

"You don't understand, Welsh. You are his crown jewel. You are the reason for everything that he does."

"Well thanks, Emily, that's heartwarming…"

"His hatred of you runs so deep. Whatever perceived transgression that you committed toward him all those years ago is motivating *all* of this."

Welsh twitched, and a shadow of anger passed over his face. "He's a psychopathic killer, Lieutenant. I think we have moved well past the stage of revenge. You think someone with a mind like that *wouldn't* be killing if it weren't for some longstanding grudge?"

"I don't deal in hypotheticals. All I know is, he wants you dead. He told you so, remember? In the very first letter. He said once you have suffered the final modicum of despair, he would put you out of your misery."

Welsh shook his head and pushed out an annoyed breath. "You memorized that?"

"Not every word, but I do recall that."

"And what makes you think this is the final, uh, *modicum* of despair? Why would this dead junkie have any bearing on my happiness?"

Arroyo let a few seconds of nothing pass, trying to gather her thoughts. She felt a mix of chagrin and something like irritation, or maybe it was slight disbelief.

"Didn't realize you had become so aloof, Welsh. I have to say, it's not a great look."

"What was the woman's name? Carrie something?"

"Carrie Leon."

Welsh's chest seemed to inflate with passion as he launched into a tirade. "Didn't you say she was full of heroin? And didn't CPS storm into her apartment and take her one-year-old child, who was found screaming and covered in its own shit, having been abandoned for over twenty-four hours? Why the *hell* would I feel sympathy for that, Emily?"

Arroyo felt the muscles in her shoulders tense up, and she had to work to subdue the rising heat of ire that was simmering underneath her skin.

"Because no one deserves to be tortured, Welsh. No one."

Welsh grunted and turned his head away. One of the techs was examining a nearby bookshelf as though it contained the secret to all human existence. Welsh pointed at him with his thumb and looked back at Arroyo.

"Why are your goons still in here? You think he stopped halfway through his foray into my apartment to read *Sometimes A Great Notion*?"

"Protocol, Welsh. Just because he hasn't left evidence behind before doesn't mean we will stop searching."

"Lovely. Well, I hope Mr. CSI over there finds

a real page-turner."

"Doesn't it make you want a detail, Carson?" asked Arroyo through gritted teeth. "Knowing that he broke in here to leave a box with body parts on your living room table?"

The look that Welsh gave Arroyo in response was a look that she had never seen before. He briefly appeared inhuman. Demented. Full of absolute hatred, all the way to his core. It passed quickly, but even just seeing his jaw twist and his eyes widen and every crease in his face taut with rage for a second was jarring.

"I had a detail once before. Remember, Emily? Now, this may just be my poor memory, but if I recall correctly, my wife still ended up dead."

A frozen, penetrating silence rocked the room. Arroyo briefly thought of an old record player screeching to a halt like in the movies. Like one of those scenes where everyone stops what they are doing to turn and stare at the two people that are in the middle of a heated argument.

"I don't need anybody watching over me, Lieutenant. I can handle my business."

Arroyo felt a sense of dawning comprehension as she watched the man across from her.

"Oh my God. You *want* him to attack you."

Welsh didn't say anything, but a half-smirk crept over his face. He shook his head like she was the most foolish person in the world, and then glanced over at the tech that was still standing by the bookshelf, looking like he was trying with all of his might to avoid peeking over at the two of them.

Arroyo stepped closer to Welsh, invading his personal space without a hint of apprehension. She lowered her voice and spoke every word with a sharp cadence.

"Listen. I don't know what world you think you live in. But this isn't the movies. You aren't about to go on some Tarantino style retaliation tour, avenging your murdered wife. This is real life. And in real life, the bad guys get caught and go to jail. If you tried *anything*, you would be the one to suffer. Big-time. No matter what this man has done to you, or anyone, you killing him would only make things worse for you. So whatever ill-conceived strategy of retribution you are pondering, you better drop that shit right now and come back to reality."

Welsh rolled his eyes, and Arroyo felt a strong urge to slap him.

"It isn't a joke, Welsh!"

"Am I laughing?"

"If you do something stupid, I will have no problem arresting you. If nothing else, at least it would wipe that stupid smirk off your face."

Welsh's upper lip curled into a slight snarl for a moment before he gave Arroyo a humorless smile. It was in that moment that Arroyo felt genuine dislike emanating from the man across from her.

Whatever goodwill and trust had been built between them was gone. They had never exactly been friends, but now, it seemed like they were a lot closer to enemies.

"I think you better leave, Emily," said Welsh quietly.

57

He was stumbling through a thick forest. The trees were so dense that even though he knew it to be daytime, the darkness was still enveloping. The branches swooped low like timeworn, wicked arms reaching down to snatch him. Welsh looked over his shoulder and felt a presence that he could not see. A set of eyes were watching him. He was sure of it.

Welsh continued to trudge on, but this time at a quicker pace. He was unaware where he was heading, but something called to him, like a faint beacon in the dark. Instead of a physical place, it was more like a gravitational feeling that pulled him forward.

Something rattled in the brush ahead.

Welsh froze. It had sounded like a serpent. But how would a rattler make its way into this terrain? Didn't they normally dwell in the desert? His eyes scanned over the forest floor, searching for the thick, slimy coils of a snake.

It happened again. The rattling noise. Welsh looked frantically back and forth, trying to locate the source of the sound. There it was. On the ground, just ahead. Something coiled up and gray.

The vibration of the rattle swirled up toward him again, and Welsh realized that the creature was just taking in long, labored breaths.

"Hello? Are you all right?"

What a silly thing to ask of a snake. But as soon as he said it, the gray mass began to unfold and Welsh realize that it was not a snake at all. It was much larger. In fact, it was downright massive.

The goat-man stood seven feet tall, staring down at him. It almost reminded Welsh of a centaur, with powerful legs and a muscular torso to match. Its mouth opened and out lolled that repulsive black tongue. The tongue curled up and came within an inch of touching Welsh's chin.

He screamed. The loudest, most powerful cry he had ever let out in his entire life. Sheer terror rumbled through his body. And it wasn't just his voice he heard reverberating around the forest. There was someone else's too. It only took a few seconds longer to realize that the goat-man was yelling right back at him. But the sound was jarring and out of place. It was a woman's scream. High-pitched and splitting the cold day in half.

This was the sound of Robert Macabre's victims.

Welsh jerked forward, and with one last echoing shout, he was sitting upright in his bed, covered in sweat.

No forest. No demonic creatures. Just him, here in his bed, having just been thrown out of one of the worst nightmares of his life.

He panted wildly, his chest convulsing in rapid, dramatic intervals. Welsh closed his eyes, as if he could ward himself of the boogeyman that was seared into his consciousness. The black tongue kept flashing through his mind in quick, staccato sequences, like reading through a flipbook.

The pistol was lying on his nightstand, facing out. For some reason, Welsh had a strong urge to reach out and grab it. Hold it close to his chest like it could soothe the fear pulsating within him. His mouth was dry and his throat sore from shouting.

Water. He needed a glass of water.

Welsh pushed himself out of bed, and his legs were rubbery and seemed like they could collapse at any moment. His underwear was plastered to him like saran wrap, and he realized how profusely he was sweating. Welsh strode forward quickly, ignoring the impulse in his body to collapse and have a panic attack while curled in a fetal position on the carpet.

When he got to the kitchen, his right hand was

shaking so badly when he went to collect a glass from the cupboard that he nearly dropped the thing. Welsh paused for a second, setting the glass on the counter and placing both hands on either side of it, taking steady, rhythmic breaths. Slowly but surely, his frenetic pulse began to beat slower, and the tension in his chest eased.

Welsh turned the faucet on and collected a substantial serving of water that he brought up to cool his lips. It poured down his throat, and the sense of relaxation continued to burgeon within him.

You're fine. You're just fine. Everything is okay.

He set down the glass of water and looked into the living area. The room seemed lighter than it should have been; a little illumination was coming through a space in the curtains that were not completely drawn over the large window. Welsh sauntered across the carpet, feeling most of the strength returning in his legs. He reached up to bring the curtains together, but something outside caught his eye. He pinpointed his focus on the street outside of his apartment.

A motionless figure garbed in all black was standing in the middle of the road. A man's body with a fox's head. The yellow eyes of the mask were staring right into his living room. Right at him.

"Oh, shit!"

Welsh scrambled about, crashing into the couch and nearly tumbling to the floor. He scrambled forward on all fours like a gorilla until he was back up on his legs and sprinting toward the bedroom. He lowered his shoulder and the door slammed against the wall with a thunderous smack. The pistol lay exactly where he had left it, and Welsh snatched it up quickly, his sweaty hands slipping on the grip. He whirled about, expecting to see the fox mask coming toward him in the darkness, but there was nothing.

For a few long seconds, all he heard was the sound of his heart clumping along in his chest like a horse that had been on the wrong end of a whip. His hands shook, waiting for the moment that the mask would appear, and he wondered if his aim was steady enough to put a bullet into the broad side of a barn, let alone a moving human being. Everything stayed still. Then, after another few beats, he realized his own stupidity.

Don't let him get away!

Welsh charged forward, tensing his finger around the trigger. He burst into the living room and almost skidded to a halt when he saw his surroundings.

The front door was open. But Robert Macabre wasn't in his line of vision. And he hadn't cleared the corners when leaving the bedroom.

Just as he came to this epiphany, an arm

wrapped around his throat and pulled his body back. Welsh had a quick thought to point the gun behind him, but simultaneously, Macabre reached out with a vice-like grip and held his wrist in place. For a moment, both of their bodies quivered with the tension as they grappled. Then, with his free hand, Welsh reached over his shoulder and clawed at the man behind him. His hand closed around the snout of the fox and he pulled forward.

The mask came off.

For one evanescent second, Macabre relinquished his grip in shock. And that was all Welsh needed. He ripped the gun forward and then wrapped it around his waist. Without even realizing he had done it, the gunshot went off with a colossal boom, and the remaining force around Welsh's neck released. He heard the sound of Macabre's giant body thudding to the ground behind him in a heap.

A loud, torn breath inflated Welsh's lungs, and he collapsed onto his hands and knees with dizziness. He swallowed air in great heaving gulps, and the room continued to spin. But there was no sound of movement behind him. Macabre was still.

Was it finally over?

Just as this thought skittered across his consciousness, a shadow moved on the floor in front of him. Then, the worst pain he had ever felt in his life seared into the back of his leg. The agony was so powerful that at first, the scream was robbed from his lips, and all that came out was a pitiful hiss. Then Welsh bellowed out a distorted, jagged cry of absolute torment. He reached back and his fingers brushed against the hilt of the knife that was now embedded into his hamstring.

All traces of remaining light in the room were briefly eclipsed by something gargantuan passing over him, and then Welsh saw the back of the hulking figure moving with surprising speed toward the door. He was just going to leave him here? He wasn't going to finish the job?

"Come back, you bastard!"

Welsh saw a glob of spit shower out of his mouth as he screamed it. Shockingly, Macabre turned back toward him. It was almost a subconscious reaction; a normal human response to turn toward the disturbance. Macabre had forgotten that the fox mask was discarded onto the floor.

It was only a short glance, but it was enough. Welsh saw folds of rubbery skin. He saw a sharp nose and thick lips, and a chin with a small button indent in the center. Curtains of light brown hair fell around the face, cloaking the man's black, soulless eyes in shadow. It lasted half a second before the man finally vanished over the threshold of Welsh's front door. But Welsh had seen it. Even through the soul-splitting agony in his right leg, he felt a sense of triumph mushrooming in his chest. For he had finally seen it.

The face of Robert Macabre.

58

The morphine made him so drowsy that it was difficult to hold his head up to listen to what Arroyo was saying. He wanted to close his eyes and recline back into the hospital bed and sleep until the last traces of pain in his leg dissipated.

"—is what it sounds like. And you definitely didn't recognize him?"

Welsh shook his head back and forth, which proved to be difficult. His head felt like someone had poured a bag of cement into his skull. At the same time, the bed seemed unstable and the room around him was slightly shimmering, like it was all a mirage in the desert. Arroyo was right in front of him, and her freckled face loomed forward. Welsh saw that there was a trace of skepticism in her eyes. Behind her, the disgruntled nurse stood with an irritated expression on her face, waiting for the conversation to be over. Clearly, the woman felt like this exchange could wait.

"No, Emily. I've never seen him before in my life."

"Hmm. Well, the sketch artists will be here soon. Maybe once you see his face in front of you again, it will jog your memory."

"I'm telling you, I don't know the guy. Even if he came into this room right now and sat down in front of me, I wouldn't be able to tell you who he is."

"So think there is no connection? He just chose you randomly?"

Welsh did not miss the faint sarcasm in her voice. But he was so exhausted that the only rebuttal he could offer was a faint chuckle and a sigh. Arroyo shook her head and looked down at the screen of the phone in her hand, apparently checking the time.

"We are analyzing ballistics on the bullet that we found in your bedroom door. It's early, but suffice it to say that if you did hit him, it was a grazing blow at a best."

The nurse that was standing behind Welsh crossed her arms and rolled her eyes, apparently having thought that the conversation was dwindling before that moment. When Arroyo showed no signs of getting up to leave, the nurse let out a huge sigh and walked out of the room, throwing her hands up in the air in exasperation. Arroyo didn't break eye contact with Welsh, oblivious to the peeved woman behind her.

"Hopefully, there will be DNA," murmured Welsh.

"So far we haven't found any on the carpet. So I think that is probably unlikely. Honestly, he probably faked the whole thing. Feigned like you hit him so that your guard would be down."

"He was already choking me out, Emily. Why would he need to try and trick me?"

Arroyo didn't say anything to this. She just stared at him, apparently unable to come up with a satisfactory answer herself.

"Can we be done for now, Lieutenant? I've had about all I can handle tonight."

"Sure. But I am going to wake you up when the sketch artist comes."

"Oh, joy."

"This can't wait, Welsh. We need to get this image circulated as quickly as possible. If he knows you saw him, there's a good chance he will be in the wind."

"No. He won't leave. Not while I am still kickin'."

"I don't know how much *kickin'* you will be doing on a bum leg."

"Well, the doc says it's just going to be managing pain. That if I have a high pain tolerance, I should be up and walking in no time."

Arroyo stood up, putting her phone in her pocket while gathering the manila envelope that she had brought with her off of Welsh's bedside table.

"One last thing, Welsh, I hope tonight has made you come to your senses as far as a detail is involved."

Welsh wanted to roll his eyes, but found that he did not have the energy to do so. Arroyo stood there for a moment, waiting to see if he would respond, and when he didn't, she simply walked away.

The new nurse that had wandered in front of him was cute. She was short, blonde, and petite, with an infectious smile that showed off startlingly straight teeth. He had woken up to her adjusting something on his bedside table, and she had grinned down at him when she had seen that his eyes were open.

"Morning!" she said brightly. Judging by the tone in her voice, she was oblivious to the fact that she was speaking to someone who had been stabbed in the leg by a homicidal lunatic. Either that, or she simply had one of those personalities where nothing could shake her out of a good mood.

Welsh grunted, pushing himself up in the bed. Light flooded through the drawn curtains that were covering the window on the east side of the room.

"Time is it?"

The woman dropped a piece of paper that she had been carrying, and when she bent to pick it up, Welsh got a glorious view of her rear end. Something tingled just below his pelvis, and he tried to push his focus onto something else.

"Ten," replied the woman.

"Sheesh. I slept that long?"

"When your body is recovering from such a substantial wound, extra sleep becomes essential," she said with a small nod. Apparently, she was not incognizant to his situation after all.

"What's your name?"

"Claire," said the nurse, and she flashed her pearly whites once more. She was breathtakingly attractive. So much so that just looking at her stirred something deep in Welsh's stomach.

"Well, Claire, I hope I wasn't drooling too much when I was sleeping."

Claire giggled. "Everything was dry as far I saw."

"I guess that means I didn't wet the bed either."

Another cute chuckle. "I will let that remain a mystery. Don't want to embarrass you too much."

"Yikes."

As she continued her tasks, adjusting the IV bag attached to his arm and looking at the dressing on his leg, Welsh couldn't help but compliment her.

"You have a lovely smile, you know that?"

Claire's cheeks tinted pink, and she beamed at him. "Well, thank you. That is very sweet."

She brought her hand up and patted him gingerly on his left kneecap, and as she did so, Welsh noticed a glint of silver on her hand. A wedding ring. For whatever reason, he felt a pang of disappointment. Perhaps it showed in his face, because Claire suddenly looked a little bashful, and she made her way out of the room.

"One last thing, Claire," said Welsh, making the woman stop in the threshold of the doorway. Her face looked apprehensive, like she was scared that he might ask her on a date.

"My friend Mo is at this hospital. Should be in room two sixty-three. That's where he was. Could you tell him I said hi?"

"Mo? What's his last name?"

"McCray. Mo McCray."

Claire's face fell. For the first time, her expression didn't show any of the bubbly, vivacious energy that had been there. Instead, something sullen twinkled in her eyes.

"I guess you haven't heard. I'm so sorry. Mr. McCray passed away three days ago."

59

"*That* is Robert Macabre?"

Baze let a long pause hang in the air. He stared at the sketch that Arroyo was holding up in the air. The cheeks looked time-worn, and even in the drawing, sun kissed. The lips were thick and shapely; the nose sharp and a little large. A curtain of straggly hair fell on either side of the face; having been parted unceremoniously on the top of the head. The man had unique features; he was a strange-enough looking individual that blending into a crowd seemed like it would be an inordinately difficult task.

"He looks like Steven Tyler," quipped Gary Fairfield. The men around the table chuckled.

"I was thinking Keith Richards," mumbled Lowry.

"Surprised you know who that is," countered Fairfield. Another ripple of laughter spread out through the room. For the first time, the small task-force of investigators had a collective air of optimism. They were closing in on their target, and the excitement was palpable.

"No DNA left behind," said Arroyo. "Bullet didn't even touch him, looks like."

"Oh well. We don't need DNA. We know his face," said Fairfield roughly. "I'm assuming you've already been handing out that sketch to the media."

"It will only be a matter of time before we get a positive ID," said Arroyo hopefully. She picked up the picture and wiggled it about in mid-air. "I don't know who this is. I don't know where he is. I don't know how it all started. But it ends with this man."

Arroyo took a deep breath and exhaled with dramatic flair. It was like she had been preparing for this moment for years; like she had rehearsed what she was going to say in the mirror when the time finally came.

"We are about to get our guy, gentleman. And this nightmare will finally be over for good."

For a few long seconds, the weight of her words blanketed the room in quiet. The detectives all exchanged anticipatory glances. Baze almost regretted having to bring everyone back down to earth.

"And what about David Kane?"

The air went out of the room like a popped balloon. Arroyo percussed her fingernails on the sketch which now laid on the table in front of her. For a long while, she seemed to have a full-scale internal debate on how to best answer the question posed.

"You are right, Baze."

"I know, Red."

Arroyo pressed on like Baze hadn't responded at all. "One seems to be tied to the other. David Kane, or whatever the hell his name is, is connected to Robert Macabre. I feel confident that if we find one, we will find the other."

"When you say connected—" began Lowry.

"I mean that we may be looking at a possible accomplice."

In response to this, Fairfield let out a long breath and shook his head slowly. It reminded Baze of an old man that was ruminating on the younger generations and internally deeming them unfit for the world they were taking over.

Arroyo shook her head cogently. "I don't mean like two separate killers. I think the signature is too unique on each of these killings to have it be done physically by two different people. I don't think Kane is involved in the actual killing, but he is somehow helping Macabre."

Baze knifed his upturned palm through the air. "Please, *elaborate.*"

"I mean... Kane is sort of an underground figure, right? He uses an alias and rarely shows his face in public. I mean, he is off the grid. Maybe he has some avenue to protect Macabre's identity in a similar way."

"But we just saw Macabre's face."

"Right. Maybe he has a way to identify potential targets?" suggested Arroyo.

"So Macabre doesn't pick his own victims? C'mon Red."

"I don't know, Baze. I'm just floating out ideas."

Lowry leaned forward. "And what would Kane get out of it if he's not the one doing the murders?"

"Probably a sexual fantasy."

"Huh?"

"Crimes like this are almost always sexual in nature," said Arroyo. "They sure as hell are for Macabre. Fetishizing death. It could be a violent erotic fantasy of Kane's that he lives out by proxy through Macabre. A form of voyeurism, you know? But instead of watching people have sex, he watches people kill people. We know that Macabre has filmed himself doing unsightly things before. Maybe Kane is the sole recipient of Macabre's home videos."

Lowry squinted his eyes. "Would he really risk that? Leaving evidence in someone else's possession?"

"I don't know. I don't think so. But hell, I can't think of anything else that seems any more likely. I mean, maybe they both partake in the killings. Or maybe Kane is actually the mastermind behind the whole thing and Macabre is just... his blunt instrument."

Baze let a few moments of quiet play out before he vocalized his thoughts.

"And what about none of the above?"

Everyone around the table seemed to collectively frown. Arroyo let her eyes slowly swivel back and forth before locking back on to Baze as if to indicate that she was missing something.

"Meaning?"

"Meaning, what if the man who calls himself David Kane is not actually in league with Macabre? And what if *that* isn't actually Macabre?" Baze gestured ardently at the sketch that was sitting on the table.

"What the hell are you talking about? The man who attacked Welsh last night *has*—"

"I am not disputing that. But what if *that* isn't actually what he looks like?"

"How could—"

Baze waved his hand randomly through the air to mitigate her question. "First, serial killers are lone wolves. The whole hallmark of a psychopath is the inability to relate to others. That's what makes them what they are. A lack of empathy."

"Then how do you explain Kane's

involvement?" asked Arroyo. "The ring? The fact that the supposedly dead and dismembered individual was seen very much alive in Welsh's direct vicinity?"

"I wouldn't explain it by saying he's an accomplice. I know in my *gut* that David Kane is not working for or with Robert Macabre."

"Fine, okay, let's say that's true. Let's say Kane's immersion in this case is totally random. What on earth would cause you to think that *this* is not an accurate depiction of our killer?" Arroyo picked up the sketch and fluttered it in the air as a sign of her vexation.

Baze shrugged. "It was a dark house. The assailant only glanced back for half a second, according to Welsh. It seems like it would be difficult to get a perfect snapshot of someone's features based on one glance."

Arroyo briefly bowed her head in sync with the inflection of her next sentence. "*Okay,* sure. That's all good, but what is your angle here? What is really motivating this line of thought, Baze? Why do you *really* think this sketch could be inaccurate?"

Baze didn't answer right away. He mulled over how to verbalize his thoughts in a way that wouldn't make him sound stupid or stubborn.

"Because of how personal this is, Red. It's thought out too carefully. It's too…. vindictive. It is someone that is absolutely seeking revenge on

Welsh for a perceived misdeed. It has to be. It just can't be someone he has never seen before. That doesn't fit with anything we know so far."

"Baze, you can't just ignore eyewitness—"

"I'm not ignoring anything. I am telling you what I think. You don't have to agree with it. But you invited me to this little party because you value my opinion, correct? Well, my opinion is that there is no way that Robert Macabre is someone that Welsh has never met or spoken with before."

Arroyo shook her head. She let out a large sigh, like a parent that was not angry at their child, but disappointed. She absentmindedly rubbed her hip like it was causing her some discomfort, and Baze realized that she was massaging the exact spot where Will Tennyson had shot her all those years ago.

"Great. And it is my opinion that you are wrong, Baze."

Baze took a sip from the Styrofoam cup, and the scalding black coffee seared his throat. He coughed, and felt a spittle of saliva running down his chin. Baze wiped at it with his forearm, trying to ignore the feeling of pain in his esophagus from the scorching liquid that he had poured into his mouth, unaware of how hot it was. Gas station coffee was not generally so blistering, but apparently, the attendant inside Shell had just made a fresh pot.

Baze watched from his car as the digital numbers above the pump crept higher and higher at an alarming rate. Gas prices normally peaked at the beginning of summer, but this year, it was shocking how astronomical they had gotten. Baze waited for the pump attendant to make his way back over to his car, but the boy with the scraggly mustache and the backward red hat was having a conversation with a man in a sleek black Infinity just in front of Baze's Impala. What could they possibly be talking about? The man in the Infinity seemed like he would regard minimum wage gas station workers with irascibility and contempt. The boy with the scraggly mustache gave his respondent a sarcastic-looking smile, and turned around, trudging away. It was at this point that Baze heard an indistinguishable shout from inside the Infinity, and though the boy ignored it and kept walking, his facial expression seemed to become stonier.

The attendant walked up to Baze's car and pulled the hose out of the tank, attaching it back to the pump. His expression was positively surly as he leaned down and made eye contact with Baze.

"Need a receipt?"

"Nah. I don't think I can return the gas."

The boy didn't laugh. He either didn't get the

joke or was still perturbed by his interaction with the man in the Infinity.

"Everything okay, friend?"

The boy seemed to jump a little. "Yeah. Guy in front of you is just a douche."

"What happened?"

The boy looked back at the Infinity, which still hadn't driven away, though its brake lights were on, as though the driver was preparing to shift out of park.

"Man, that dude is just a prick," said the boy, and he had a bit of a hillbilly accent to his speech. "First, I seen him pull up, so I go up and try to make some conversation, and I guess rich dudes like him don't like talkin' to guys like me, because he told me to hurry up. So I was like okay, guess he's not in the mood to chat. So I hurry up. Then, when I was done, he accuses me of giving him the wrong change. He paid cash and gave me a fifty for twenty bucks worth of gas. I gave him thirty back, and then he starts saying he gave me a hundred-dollar bill. I showed the guy the fifty and he still flipped. Like I just carry a fifty-dollar bill around as change. I mean, shit. You think I would have an effing job if I was ripping people off?"

The boy was talking loudly, and Baze wondered if the man in the Infinity could hear him. Apparently, the boy came to the same realization, because when he next spoke, it was in a hushed tone.

"Honestly, I ain't not pussy, but the dude was kinda scary."

"What do you mean?" Baze shot another glance at the Infinity, which was still stationary on the pavement in front of him.

"His eyes, man. I don't know."

"Hmm." Baze was secretly praying that the man would not get out of the vehicle and accost the boy again for his change. He didn't want to be seen.

"Anyway, you need a receipt?"

"Nah." Baze kept his eyes locked on the black vehicle.

"Do you know him or something?"

Baze looked up at the attendant. For someone seemingly unsophisticated and obtuse, the boy had just displayed a keen sense of intuition.

"Never seen him before in my life," lied Baze.

The boy kept his eyes on him for another couple of seconds, and Baze could tell that he was unconvinced.

"Well, have a good night."

The boy walked away with his head down. Baze sat motionless in his car, watching the figure retreat back toward the main building. Then, his eyes locked back onto the Infinity, which began to roll forward. Baze waited for a few moments and then fired up his engine as well.

A pragmatic, logical person like Arroyo would

not understand. An eyewitness had described a suspect, and Arroyo was now convinced that Robert Macabre was a spitting image of the man in the sketch. Case closed. But Baze was unorthodox. Even though logic was telling him that Macabre had to look similar to the physical description that Welsh had given, his gut told him that there was more to the story. Macabre had to be someone with a personal vendetta against Welsh. And he had always trusted his gut over his head. Therefore, when Warren Grecko pulled his black Infinity out of the Shell station and onto the highway, Baze shifted his Impala into drive, preparing to follow.

60

Warren Grecko was a prickly man.

Though Baze had only been watching him for two days, he had seen numerous instances of Grecko treating people with condescension or outright viciousness. From chiding the Starbucks barista over mispronouncing his name to yelling at an old man who was walking incredibly slowly through a crosswalk, Baze had to guess that Grecko didn't have many friends. It was difficult to maintain amicable relationships with people when your temper seemed to flare up over the drop of a hat.

But being kind was apparently not a prerequisite to being a successful defense attorney. The brief research Baze had done on the man yielded some interesting facts: Grecko had been on a hot streak lately; he had successfully gotten a "not guilty" verdict in each of the last three cases he had worked, and the five before that had concluded with plea deals weighted heavily in favor of the defendants. Due to this, some truly deplorable people were serving light sentences or simply still out on the street. The prime example, Dwayne Crowe, a sex offender who had been accused of assaulting a thirteen-year-old girl. Due to Grecko's unrelenting defense of his client, and the fact that the only witness in the case had mysteriously decided against testifying, Crowe had gone free. This provided some extra motivation for Baze as he continually pursued Grecko. Even if Grecko wasn't Macabre, he was still a terrible human being, and if Baze could find something incriminating to give to his new friends at the police department, so be it.

In the past twenty-four hours Baze had spoken with two different people who had known Welsh and Grecko, and it was no secret that their relationship was strained, to say the least. Grecko had repeatedly served as Welsh's punching bag in court, having lost every one of the twelve cases he had worked in opposition to the DA from 1999 to 2004. This had stoked an open rivalry between the two, to the point that the men would regularly trade barbs whenever they interacted.

Baze, whose obsession had been the Macabre case for years, had frequently delved into the revenge angle, seeking people who held grudges or were open about their dislike of Welsh. The problem was, there weren't many people who seemed to truly despise the man. He was regarded as the best district attorney Portland had had in decades and credited with putting scores of heinous men and women behind bars. A folk hero, in a way. The only person that Baze could find in the legal system that had a bone to pick with Welsh was Warren Grecko.

Even more interesting was the fact that the most recent victim, Carrie Leon, had been defended in court by Grecko in 2016 for drug-related offenses. It was the only case in the 2016 calendar year that Grecko had lost. Leon had been sentenced to a year at Coffee Creek Correctional Facility. A victim of the killer who had been defended by the only person with a notorious grudge against Carson Welsh? That was worth looking into, at least.

Over a span of forty-eight hours, Baze had followed Grecko all over town. He watched him from several tables away at a Chinese restaurant, and then later from across the lobby in a Starbucks. Baze even surveyed Grecko as he went to-and-fro from court, sitting idly in his Impala as the man slithered from one obligation to the next. So far, it had been a strange task. Grecko had done nothing even remotely incriminating, but Baze found himself more and more intrigued as hours went by. Something was off. Something was tickling at Baze's subconscious, but he couldn't put a finger on what. Maybe it was just the way Grecko carried himself, with cold, calculating purpose, and a complete disregard for niceties or tact toward the bystanders he interacted with. It was like Grecko was advertising his lack of empathy to the rest of the world.

As the hours passed, Baze couldn't help but marvel at his own aptitude for stalking. Grecko seemed to be completely incognizant of the figure who was constantly in his shadow, making subtle observations and taking notes. At first, Baze had aired on the side of caution, but when Grecko had failed to show even the slightest hint of awareness to the investigators' constant presence, Baze had decided to keep pushing the limit. If the attorney was going to be this oblivious, then Baze was going to watch until his curiosity was satiated.

Therefore, on a sultry Tuesday afternoon, Baze found himself racking forty-five pound weights onto a barbell, slyly watching the man out of the corner of his eye. Baze was naturally an athletic man, but not very fit. He hadn't been to a gym since the late nineties, and that occasion was almost solely to hang out with the woman he had been dating at the time who had an ardent proclivity for exercise. Due to his long intermission between workouts, even racking the weights onto the bench-press station seemed to cause a shortage of breath. He huffed and puffed as he prepared himself to bench one hundred and eighty-five pounds; a fairly standard amount of weight for someone of his size and stature. He shot a side-eye at Grecko and saw the man finishing a set of military presses near the racks of dumbbells. Grecko was surprisingly muscular, or perhaps just cut. The definition of the shoulder muscles that peeked out of his cutoff T-shirt was stark. He looked like he could at least hold his own in a fight.

After loading one forty-five-pound weight onto one side of the bar, Baze's eyes flitted back over to Grecko, who was looking in the direction of a perky little brunette in yoga pants and a tank top. The young woman was doing squats with a twenty-five-pound plate in her hand, and Grecko's eyes were feasting on her body. It wasn't an unnatural thing for a man to lay eyes upon an attractive woman at a gym, but the intensity and unabashed stare was unsettling. What Baze wouldn't give to hear what the man was thinking. Great ass? Nice legs? Or something… else?

Slowly but surely, Grecko looked away from the woman and turned in Baze's direction. Eager to avoid suspicion, Baze let his eyes travel down to the weight in his hands as he pushed it onto the bar. He felt a bead of sweat commuting down the back of his neck and felt more apprehensive about the impending bench press. If loading the plates onto the bell was so strenuous, what would an actual set look like?

Don't be a pussy, Anton. You'll press this bar like a feather.

Baze finished racking the weights, readying himself to do the routine. As he rolled his shoulders to loosen them up, he couldn't help but shoot another glance at Grecko.

His heart jumped into his throat. The man was across the gym, but for some reason, looking right at Baze. Baze bent his head down and stared at a wet spot on the floor like it was the most absorbing thing he had ever seen. He let ten long seconds pass, looking at the floor and pretending to be bobbing his head to the music that was blaring over the gym's speakers. There could be many innocuous reasons for Grecko staring at him. After all, he was a six-foot-three mustached man with a snake-shaped scar slithering along his cheek. People stared. It wasn't a new phenomenon. Baze let his discomfort pass. When he looked up again, Grecko had vanished. Perhaps he had gone to the locker room, or to the water station to fill up the bottle that he had been carrying.

With one last deep inhale, Baze sat on the bench and plopped backward. He put his hands on the gnarls of the barbell, braced his legs on either side of him, and pushed the weight into the air. As he held it with his arms straight, one hundred eighty-five pounds felt far too heavy for him. It had been decades since he had bench pressed anything, so perhaps starting at a lighter weight would behoove him.

Screw it, thought Baze. He lowered the weight down onto his chest and then pumped it back into the air with a grunt. It was a difficult rep and put more strain on his elbows than he was expecting.

One, he thought triumphantly with his arms straight again.

He lowered the weight once more and bounced it off his chest a little, and this time, the motion was much smoother. Baze didn't have to put as much effort into getting the damn thing up.

Two.

Down, and back up. He was getting in a groove now.

Three.

Easy enough. *Maybe you aren't such a pussy after all,* he thought.

Four.

Five.

Baze felt his arms going out, and quickly re-racked the weight, exhaling as he did so. He took several deep breaths, reestablishing his equilibrium. His arms felt surprisingly spry for the amount of exertion he had just put forth. Maybe a second set wasn't out of the question.

He sat up, looking over his shoulder for Grecko. Baze caught the head of black hair streaked with gray lingering by the dumbbell rack. The man was no longer looking in Baze's direction. Instead, Grecko was flexing his right shoulder and admiring the tautness and definition of the muscle in the mirror. Baze rolled his eyes and turned his head back forward.

After thirty seconds or so of recovery, he rolled onto his back and slid under the bar. His hands found the sweet spot on the bar and with a grunt, Baze pushed the weight back into the air.

One.

Pump that iron, baby.

Two.

Pain shot through his chest, but it was a good kind. Maybe getting into a workout regimen wasn't such a bad idea.

Three.

Four.

Baze felt his triceps protest the workload, and his pectoral muscles were on fire.

Five.

Six.

On the seventh rep, his arms were quivering with the tension, but he was able to push the barbell up relatively easy by arching his lower back and thrusting his legs into the ground.

Seven.

On rep number eight, a shadow danced across his chest just as he lowered the weight down. When the barbell hit his upper abdomen, a set of hands latched onto the spot in between the gnarls, and pressed down. Just like that, one hundred eighty-five pounds had been turned against him, pinning Baze to the bench and digging into his torso with crushing power.

Grecko's face snarled over him; his jaw was twisted in anger and a vein bulged near his temple.

"Think you're fuckin' sly, do ya, pal? Think I'm stupid, eh?"

Grecko continued to shove the barbell downward with surprising strength, and Baze had no chance of releasing himself from the pressure.

"I don't know who you think you are, or who you think I am. But if you keep following me, you are going to find out *exactly* what I do."

Baze couldn't even cry for help. The weight was compressing his chest so much that all that came out of his diaphragm was a pitiful moan of pain. Soon, breathing was going to be very difficult.

"Go back and tell whatever rat-faced fuck that hired you that his money ain't worth the pain that I will cause you. And if you keep skirtin' around in the shadows, I'm going to find him too. And I swear, the both of you will learn all that you need to know about me."

The pressure on the bar released, but Grecko's face lingered over Baze for another moment. He pointed his index finger right at the spot in between

Baze's eyes.

"Screw. You."

With that, Grecko vanished. Baze heard footsteps clomping away across the gym. The weight of the barbell now felt like a thousand pounds squashing his chest. He pressed as hard as he could with his arms, but all of the strength in his muscles had dissipated. Baze could not breath, and his face was flushed. He grunted, and the pain overwhelmed him, and with a feeling of panic, he saw that the barbell had only moved a couple of inches upward. Baze propelled his legs with all of his might into the ground and arched his lower back as high as it would go. Still, the weight would not budge.

"Ahh!"

He couldn't lift it. He was stuck. The barbell began to grind into his trunk once more, this time with a vengeance. Baze let out a primal moan, and could feel his whole body straining with the effort of fighting the load.

"Whoa, whoa, whoa!"

Suddenly, Baze saw a new set of dark hands clasp onto the barbell, right in between his. A half a second later, the pressure released. The large African-American man standing over him quickly pulled the weight up into the air and set it back onto the rack. Like someone who had been under water for too long, Baze sucked in a ragged, twisted breath, and then he began to cough.

"Holy shit, dude, are you all right?"

Baze hacked away, his diaphragm contracting rapidly, and he felt an urge to vomit. With a couple more torn breaths, he suppressed the bile rising in his throat.

"That was some messed-up shit!" said the man incredulously. "At first I thought he was spotting you. Are you okay, man?"

Baze, whose sternum was aching, couldn't manage to speak. It took all of his effort to regain his breath. So instead, he simply nodded.

"Are you sure, man? Do you need water?"

This time, with another gravelly cough, Baze shook his head.

"Man, who was that guy?"

Baze looked up at his rescuer, and saw the dark face screwed up in absolute horror, like he had never seen something so demented. Finally, after another couple of inhales and exhales, Baze was able to respond.

"Just some fuckin' psycho," he wheezed.

Welsh flicked through several channels, ambivalent to the programs that were airing on most of them. He rustled around on the king-sized bed that he was lying on, unable to get completely comfortable. After a minute or so more of channel surfing, he came to a weather report. The sprightly and clean-cut weather man gesticulated at seven digital boxes, all with a corresponding day of the week emblazoned along their top portion. Each one was fit with seven bright yellow suns, and the numbers underneath the suns varied from eighty-two all the way up to ninety-four. In other words, it was going to be really damn hot. At least for Oregon.

Welsh absentmindedly touched the bandage on his hamstring and felt a bristling of pain in response to the contact. It had been a week and a half since Macabre had attacked him in his home, and though the wound was less painful now, it was still somewhat debilitating. He now had a heavy limp whenever he walked, and every once in a while, speckles of crimson would appear on the bandages. The stitches had not yet burst, but every time he exerted himself, droplets of blood would appear on his leg, as if warning him to stop moving.

He and Arroyo had come to somewhat of a compromise. There would be no detail. No uniformed officer skirting around in his shadow every time he went to do anything. But she had not let him preserve the status quo. Arroyo was determined to keep Welsh safe, and thus, he was now staying in room 325 on the third floor of the Comfort Inn in Tualatin, approximately thirteen miles from his apartment in Portland. He was instructed to lay low, and if he had to go outside, he was to wear sunglasses and a hat (as if this paltry attempt at a disguise would fool anyone). But since his injury, he had mostly been immobile. Any time he actually needed to leave his hotel room and move a significant distance, he would use the crutches that the doctors had lent him. It was almost somewhat embarrassing—he had essentially been rendered a cripple from one measly injury to his non-dominant leg. But he was no longer a spring chicken. With old age came a prolonged period of healing any time damage was inflicted upon your body.

Welsh wriggled about some more. The place

was stuffy; the air-conditioning system on the far side of the room blew out cool air half-heartedly, even though he had cranked the knob to full blast. His hand twitched with something like restlessness. The longer he laid on this bed and contemplated his broken life, the more antsy he felt.

The face of Robert Macabre was now almost seared to the back of his eyelids. Every time his mind wandered, he would picture the leathery-skin and shoulder-length hair of the killer. The man had only appeared for a fraction of a second in a dark room, but Welsh could vividly envision the emotions in his expression, curiosity followed by panic. Macabre had never meant for Welsh to set eyes on him. But he had. And Welsh still had no idea who the man was. No matter how much he wracked his brains, he couldn't produce a name or any tangible association. And though he had told Arroyo and the other officers a different story, Welsh had a sneaking, albeit vague sense of familiarity. Something scratched in the depths of his mind every time he pictured the face, but for the life of him, he had no idea what it meant.

Welsh sat up, now positively perturbed by the stuffiness of the room. He was in khaki shorts and a T-shirt, but he just couldn't get comfortable. There was a tightness in his chest, like the world's smallest dumbbell was perpetually laying on his navel. It was this sensation that he had come to associate with a lack of exercise. Every time he was stationary for a protracted period, that familiar heaviness in his chest would return. This was also accompanied by a rapid frequency of negative thoughts, like his brain was upset by the unhealthiness of his body.

Screw it. Welsh pushed himself off of the bed. When he set his legs down onto the carpet, his hamstring burned in protest. But it wasn't as bad as it had been in previous days. Hell, it actually wasn't that bad at all. It hurt, sure, but it wasn't the crippling agony that had been there before. He took a step, and then another. He could do this. *No point being immobile now.*

He was going for a walk.

Welsh braced himself against the railing of the bridge, looking down upon the water. The sunglasses on his face partially obstructed his vision, but he could still mostly take in the beauty of his surroundings. The Tualatin River was murky and opaque due to its shallowness, but it had a distinctly Oregon feel to it. Across the river on the opposite bank, mammoth Douglas firs cast shadows down on the water, and the trees were so thick that it was difficult to see anything beyond. There was nigh a cloud in the sky, and the sun beat down hard on Welsh's forehead; several globules of sweat glistened just above his hairline, and he breathed hard as his body fought to stay upright. But it was a good feeling. The exertion was relieving stress, and the serene aesthetics of the park propagated a sense of tranquility within him. He had needed this.

There were only a few people trudging along the wooden bridge. Welsh saw a young mother in active-wear pushing her baby along in a stroller, and a tall man struggling to stay abreast of a large Siberian husky that was plodding along in front of him. Most of the passerby were individuals partaking in some sort of exercise, though all of them appeared to be having a much easier time than he was with physical activity. One young woman darted along at a near-full sprint, her blond ponytail flopping from side to side. But her face looked relaxed and purposeful, like it was nothing at all to push her body to fifteen miles an hour. *Oh, to be young and healthy.* Welsh used the various people exercising around him as motivation to force himself out of the mini-intermission he had taken and back into his limp-plagued slog along the bridge.

When he got to the other side of the crossing and back onto the sidewalk, an eerie feeling came over him. It was one that he had become all too familiar with. The feeling of a set of eyes on him.

Welsh scanned the area left and right, but saw no one of consequence. After an uncanny moment of looking from face to face of the remaining bystanders in front of him, he came to the stark realization that he was being paranoid. Arroyo had told no one where he was staying, not even any of her detectives. He had been transported directly from the hospital to the hotel—Arroyo herself had driven him. Hell, they had even taken him out through one of the emergency exits of the building that led into an alley, where Arroyo's car had been parked. Combined with the fact that he had a scruffy beard tracing along his jawline, and a Portland Trail Blazers cap pulled over a pair of Oakley's that rested on the bridge of his nose, it seemed very difficult to fathom that someone that knew who he was could be watching him.

However, when Welsh made it ten feet farther, that same internal alarm that was pinging warning signals to his nervous system was now louder than ever. Someone was definitely watching. He could feel it in his gut. Then he saw him.

Standing underneath a tree, some twenty feet off to the left, was David Kane.

Welsh didn't even think twice about it. The adrenaline pumping through him warded off the pain in his leg, and he moved as fast as he could in Kane's direction. Surprisingly, the man did not move. His eyes were wide and his spindly body was tense, but he held his ground. He didn't even flinch when Welsh shoved him aggressively against the bark of the tree and held him in place by the scruff of his T-shirt.

Welsh's voice sounded warped and animal-like as he spoke. "Who the *hell* do you think you are? What do you *want*?"

"Carson," said the man softly.

Welsh slammed Kane's body against the tree, causing the man to let out a grunt.

"You working with him? Huh? You two best pals?"

"Carson," repeated Kane, and it sounded like he was pleading.

"Why are you fucking with me, huh? *Why are you fucking with me*?" Welsh's voice had become a screech.

This time, Kane didn't say anything. He simply closed his eyes and let out a deep breath as Welsh continued to pound him against the tree. Anger like Welsh had never felt in his entire life coursed through him like an electrical current. The question that came spitting out of his mouth made little sense, but it was the only thought he could formulate.

"What *are* you?" he shrieked.

When Kane didn't answer, Welsh caught the man by his jaw and squeezed as hard as he could.

"What do you want, huh? What do you want

from me?"

Kane's wide eyes swiveled back and forth, and a squeal seemed to seep out of his chest.

"S-srop hmph."

"*What?*"

Kane pointed at Welsh's hand, which was still squeezing the man's jaw. Welsh released his grip, but latched back on to Kane's T-shirt and pressed even harder against the bark.

"Stop him," Kane croaked. "You have to stop him."

Welsh felt like someone had bludgeoned him over the head with a gavel. Complete and utter perplexity and bewilderment hit him, and without even thinking about it, he loosened his grip on Kane.

"What?"

"You are the only one who can end this. You have to stop him." Kane's voice was a whisper; his dark eyes were filled with a fiery hatred, but it wasn't directed at Welsh.

"What are you talking about? Who is he?"

"December thirteenth, nineteen ninety-five. That's when it all started."

Waves of shock palpitated through Welsh's entire body. He looked at Kane like the man was some otherworldly force, some omniscient being that could somehow stare into his soul.

"How do you...?"

Without warning, Kane propelled his knee into Welsh's groin. Welsh doubled over and felt Kane's fist slam into his gut. He collapsed onto the grass, his head bouncing off of the ground and coming two inches back into the air like a basketball that had gone flat. There was no oxygen left in his lungs, and he frantically tried to suck in air while holding his pained midsection. Disorientation plagued his senses, and it took him several long moments to realize that he was face down in the grass, his sunglasses askew on his nose and his hat lying a couple of feet away.

Six ragged breaths later, Welsh had finally regained control over his lungs. He rolled onto his back with a loud groan. Nausea percolated in his stomach from the blow to the groin. Welsh swallowed and took two more giant inhales of air to calm the seas within his stomach. Finally, his metaphorical ship began to steady, and now that his mind was no longer possessed by pain, he turned his head toward where Kane had been standing. The need for more answers was almost physiological, like a gnawing hunger that was now eating at his gut. But there would be none. David Kane was long gone.

As Baze drove his Impala down Interstate-5 two days after his incident at the gym, his chest was still sore. There was a spot just above his sternum that caused an immense amount of pain whenever he pressed against it. It had been the spot that had taken the brunt of the weight of the barbell as it had cut against him. It was just a bruise, but still one that went deeper than most.

Baze kept his eyes open for troopers lurking on the side of the freeway or merging from one of the off-ramps, for his seatbelt wasn't on. Wearing it caused incredible discomfort, due to the soreness in his torso, so he was pacing himself as he cruised down the road at fifty-five miles per hour, at least twenty miles slower than he normally ventured when commuting I-5.

Revenge was on his mind. Anton Baze was a lot of things, but a victim wasn't one of them. He didn't allow himself to be bullied. Many boys and men had tried to inflict pain upon him over the years, and they had quickly learned that Baze was wired differently than most. He had won almost all of the fistfights he had partaken in, and the rare ones he had lost, he had still inflicted a significant amount of damage on his opponent. A boy in high school named Zep Carlson, who had been a senior when he was a freshman, had beat the pulp out of Baze back when he was five foot six and the runt of the litter in his class. But Baze had broken Zep's nose and blacked his left eye, and afterward, the boy had always avoided him in the hallways like he was a rabid wolf. And that was how Baze liked it.

Grecko would not get the best of him. Someday soon, the score would be settled. For the past forty-eight hours, Baze had spent a good portion of his time internally stewing about the ways he would inflict pain upon the coward who had jumped him. Next time, it would be a fair fight. And Grecko would regret attacking Baze when his guard was down.

But now was not the time for that. Grecko would be watching for him. Baze could no longer follow the man around town, hoping to see something unsightly or suspicious. At least for a while, he would have to focus on something else. Someone else.

Therefore, he had scheduled an appointment

with Marvin Wallace, the man who created the website TheMostDangerousAnimal.com, an obsessive fanboy site having to do with all things serial killers and Robert Macabre. Baze had made sure that Wallace was not privy to his ulterior motives; the man thought that Baze just wanted to pick his brain about Macabre. He had no idea that Baze was analyzing him as a possible suspect.

The incoherent ramblings about Macabre on the site were not exactly damning. It could just be that Wallace was a normal, pathetic serial killer fanboy. There were plenty of those around. Hell, many killers had a cult Internet following. Manson, Bundy, Richard Ramirez, the Zodiac. It was as if scores of faceless people behind computer screens thought of it like fiction. They were fascinated by the gore, the horror, and the demented psyches of all the psychopaths, without ever considering that those men had ripped families apart and stolen daughters and sons from loving parents. The Internet-mob of bloodthirsty heathens were too fascinated by death to realize the tragedy of it all.

Maybe Marvin Wallace was just a common, desensitized Internet troll that reveled in stories of torture and morbidity behind his computer screen, but was actually a giant sissy in real life.

Or maybe not.

Wallace had put forth details of the original string of killings in 2004 that were not public knowledge. He had somehow known that Carson Welsh had been chased by a man wearing a Minotaur through a forest while Welsh was on a jog. He had also published candid photos of Tracy Dinwoodie on his website that Baze could not find anywhere online or elsewhere. The photos were innocuous enough. Most had been Dinwoodie attending work functions or training for the half-marathon that she had run in late 2003. Perhaps Wallace had a knack for aggregating difficult-to-find photographs from somewhere on the Internet. Or maybe he had accrued said photos because the man had had a vested interest in Dinwoodie's personal life leading up to her death.

Baze would never know until he asked. And he had been wanting to ask Marvin Wallace questions for some time.

After taking the exit off of the freeway into Gresham, Baze ventured past several suburban neighborhoods before taking a side-street and ending up in a rural-looking area, with overgrown vegetation and dilapidated houses on both sides of the road. Eventually, he came to house 462, and the navigation system built into the car told him he had arrived at his destination.

Moments later, Baze was knocking on the front door of what was not much more than a cabin. It took two long minutes before the door was finally answered, and when it was, it opened up slowly like the house itself was apprehensive about Baze's presence.

Marvin Wallace looked even worse in person than he did in photographs. The man had a drooping gut that jiggled when he walked, and massive tree trunk sized legs. His pockmarked skin was ravaged and red, like he had fought a decade-long battle with acne and lost. A pair of thick-framed glasses ballooned his pupils, and on his forehead, a constellation of sweat beads lingered. Wallace had long, stringy brown hair that went down past his shoulders and swirled strangely around his ears. He had on khaki shorts that didn't quite reach his knees, and a black T-shirt that simply said Natural Selection across the chest.

"You must be Mr. Baze." His voice was high-pitched and over-enunciated.

"You must be Mr. Wallace."

"Call me Marve," said Wallace, shaking Baze's hand, and his grip was strong. Baze could feel calluses along the man's palm, and the skin he touched was like sinewy sandpaper. "Come on in."

Baze slid through the door behind Wallace. There was only one room inside; an expansive area that doubled as a living room and a kitchen. In the living room, there was a brown loveseat that was stained with something dark on one of the cushions, and a black ottoman that seemed to serve as a footrest. Next to the loveseat, there was a rickety-looking desk that held a giant computer monitor and two gargantuan servers on either side, both with mounds of wire curling out of the back. The thing that was most striking about the room was the complete lack of decoration on the wall. There were no photographs, artwork, or any sign that the houses' inhabitant cared about creating a welcoming atmosphere. Also, there was a very strange and somewhat repugnant smell radiating from nearby. If Baze had to guess, the stench was likely emanating from somewhere behind the only other door in the room. It was a peculiar scent; it reminded him of mold, but with a tinge of sweetness intermingled with the mildew.

Wallace indicated the loveseat for Baze to sit in and then pulled the computer chair away from the desk for himself. When he sat down, the chair creaked in protest, and Baze wondered how much more weight the thing could take before it would implode.

"Sit, sit," mumbled Wallace, again gesturing at the loveseat. Baze gave the seat an apprehensive glance before carefully placing his rear end on the cushion that wasn't stained.

Wallace had his eyes locked on Baze's face. He was staring with a penetrating curiosity, and the intensity of his gaze made Baze want to look away.

"You are an interesting-looking fellow, I have to say," said Wallace, and his lips twitched with the traces of a smile. "How did you get the battle-wound?"

Baze raised his eyebrows. He couldn't remember the last time someone had the gall to ask him about his scar. He wasn't sure if he respected the man for having the nuts to say what he was thinking, or feel offended.

"I lost a fight with a goose."

Wallace let out a chuckle, and his laugh was even higher-pitched than his speaking voice. "I don't know if I believe you."

"You would be wise not to."

Wallace twitched his head. "Well, color me intrigued."

Baze opened his mouth to respond, but Wallace continued before he could.

"I know, I know, appropriate social convention dictates that I develop a good-natured rapport with my respondent before we exchange secrets. But I have never really been one for appropriate social convention."

"Shocking," quipped Baze. Wallace let out another weird, high-pitched giggle.

"So, how can I be of service to you, Mr. Anton Baze? You're interested in cracking the Bob the Butcher case on your own, eh? Looking to usurp the credit from the police?"

"Actually, the police have brought me on board to their investigative team as a consult."

Wallace raised his eyebrows. "Have they now? Interesting. Interesting. Do you have a penchant for catching serial killers, Anton? Or does this one in particular somehow fall into your area of expertise?"

"The latter, I think. I would consider my preoccupation with Robert Macabre an active hobby, but those who know me might lean toward calling it an obsession."

Something twinkled in Wallace's eyes. "Well, we have that in common, Anton. We most certainly have that in common."

"Perhaps your knowledge on this subject surpasses my own."

"I have no doubt that it does. If anyone has studied Robert Macabre more than yours truly, it would be a surprise to me."

The nonchalant way Wallace said this was surprising. It was as if he had no notion of how arrogant he had come across.

"Hmm. Well, I hope so."

"So what is it that you wanted to ask me?"

Baze took out his iPhone, unlocked it, and opened the recording app. "Do you mind?"

Wallace shook his head. "Be my guest. You could make this into a podcast episode for all I care."

Baze set the recorder down on the ottoman and pressed the red record button. "So first things first…" He let out a dramatic sigh. "Who do you think it is?"

Wallace let out a deep belly-laugh, as if Baze had just uttered the most amusing sentence he had ever heard.

"Wow! You go right for the throat! I like it! No buttering me up or bloviating on about all of your grandiose theories! Getting right to the juicy stuff. You are a ballsy one, Mr. Baze. Quite ballsy indeed. But to answer your question, I don't know what his name is, nor do I particularly care."

Baze narrowed his eyes and let the incredulous silence speak for him.

Wallace's grin stretched across his whole face. "Surprised? You thought I would care to know Macabre's birth name, or what he kept as a day job? You think I want to discover the facade that he constructed in his day-to-day life? No, Mr. Baze… That is superfluous information to me. For what you consider to be his identity is simply a disguise. Knowing that his actual name is William Robert Tennyson, or Robert E. Lee, or Robert effing DeNiro has all the same effect on me. None. For Macabre is who he *truly* is.

"You see… what I am interested in is his psyche. His inclination for affecting terror and predilection for the subjugation and control of his victims. His tools, his… modus operandi, as it were. What really *drives* him. Is he a domineering, sadistic killer that seeks power? Or one motivated by hatred? All serial killers fall into one of those two categories. They are sexually motivated by domination and control or sexually motivated by unbridled, uncontrollable loathing. I would tend to guess that Macabre is the latter. But what really fascinates me is *why*."

Baze gave a slow nod, but it was more of a sardonic, mocking thing. "Uh-huh. Well, that was a very wordy explanation. I have to say, you sound almost in admiration of him."

"Not admiration. Fascination."

"Mm-hmm. Some of the excerpts from your site seem more like adulation."

Wallace waved his meaty paw in a dismissive gesture. "Semantics, semantics. I would be lying if I said that my, uh, *preoccupation,* is an altogether healthy exercise. I mean, I run a website dedicated to serial killers for Christ's sake!" He let out that strange giggle again.

Baze froze, staring at Wallace with unease rising in his chest.

"Some of the passages are disturbing."

Wallace seemed to be immensely enjoying himself. He tittered away with raucous laughter, wheezing a little as his big belly shook.

"Well, please—what do I call you? You said you were a private investigator. Do I call you private? Please, *private,* elaborate on that statement if you would."

"Take this, for example," continued Baze, trying not to be deterred by the man's strange behavior. He cleared his throat, pulling out the small notebook from under his coat that he had brought with him. After flipping to the appropriate page, he began to read.

"'Macabre seems to have perfected the art of stalking. The man has a fixation with involving himself in his victim's lives well before they are taken. It is part of his sexual fantasy, the thrill of the hunt. Notably, Macabre would wear a red jacket while on his predatory reconnaissance missions. Conventional wisdom would obviously suggest that a stalker blend in and appear inconspicuous. But this sort of tactic is what made Macabre so cunning. He would subtly burn himself into the subconscious of his targets, slowly stoking a sense of unexplained dread. They would be able to sense that something was awry, but not know what. This, ultimately, is another important component of Macabre's sexual fantasies: fear.'"

Baze set the notepad onto the ottoman, and took a deep breath, after having read the long paragraph he had penned.

"You had to dig deep through old case files to find that detail, Marve. The red jacket. That came from the second victim, correct?"

"Public record. I had a right to those files, as

does everyone else. And you clearly pored over the same documents, since you already know said detail and which victim it came from."

"Mm. Touché. I have to say though, I never have referred to these young, beautiful women as *targets*." Baze could not keep the contempt and disgust out of his voice.

"The purpose of my website is to get into the killer's heads," replied Wallace slowly. "I disassociate myself from the women, and have to detach from the real horror that has been inflicted upon them. Otherwise, I would never be able to produce compelling content." Baze was pleased to see that the giggly predisposition Wallace had had before had vanished.

"I see." Baze swallowed thickly. He wriggled his nose, trying to ward off the odd smell that was still finding its way into his nostrils. He flipped through his notepad, eventually arriving at the quote he was seeking. This time, he launched straight into the material without an introduction.

"'It is a well-known fact that serial killers over the last fifty years have a penchant for returning to the scene of the crime. In between hot periods, these men find their way back to the area where they last struck, and most of the time, they masturbate. It serves as a subsequent sexual release and tides them over in between kills. However, Macabre is too calculating to participate in this, for he knows that it greatly increases the chances of him getting caught. Furthermore, it is common knowledge that Mr. Macabre is a noted documentarian of his work, which removes the need to revisit the places where the murders were committed."

Baze peered up at Wallace, and there was a mysterious look in the man's eyes.

"How could you possibly know that? That he doesn't return to the scene? Have you staked out every one of the crime scenes over the last fifteen years?"

"It is observation and deduction, *friend*. He has no need to do so."

"And contrary to what you stated here," pressed Baze. "It is *not* common knowledge that Macabre is a documentarian. In fact, I would like to know more specifically what it is that you are referring to."

The man's eyes continued to twinkle. "The video—"

"Of Tracy Dinwoodie? Interesting that you know about that. Because the details of that video were never made public."

Wallace paused, and he bit his lip. For the first time, something other than the zany, self-satisfied energy possessed his person. Something darker.

"You are aware of it."

"And I am a consultant on the case. I work with the police department."

This was a bit of a fabrication. Baze had known of the video long before Arroyo had brought him onto her team. But for argument's sake, he kept this shred of knowledge under wraps.

"What is this?" asked Wallace suddenly. His voice was tinged with the beginnings of something that resembled vexation. He was catching on.

"One other thing I want to ask you about, Marve. You state on your site that Robert Macabre once pursued Carson Welsh through a forest trail while wearing a Minotaur."

Wallace's lips were pursed, and his cheeks were beginning to flush.

"It's true. That really happened. Scary, huh? Imagine being chased by a psycho in a bull mask. Especially somewhere secluded." Baze lowered his voice by a decibel, and it was now somewhere close to being a whisper. "How do you know these things, Marvin? How are you privy to the particulars? I looked it up online, and after scouring Google for an hour, I found that your site is the only one that references the story with the Minotaur. What I want to know is… why?"

Wallace looked genuinely frightening now. His jaw was twisted, his pudgy cheeks red and slightly quivering. But the eyes. The eyes were what looked most disturbing.

"So this is why you made this appointment?" he asked softly. "You think it's *me*?"

"No, Marvin, I don't think that." *Not yet,* thought Baze. "But when things don't add up, I want to know why."

"Look at me," hissed Wallace, and there was no mistaking the fury in his voice now. "Do I look like a killer to you?"

"Psychopaths come in all shapes and sizes, Marvin. But that's not what I am insinuating." *Again, not yet.*

Wallace shook his head spasmodically, as if warding off a fly that was buzzing around his head. "Why did they send you? If the police thought I was a suspect, why wouldn't they send a detective?"

"They don't think you are a suspect. Hell, most of them don't even know you exist."

"Then why are you here?"

"Like I said. Things aren't adding up here," replied Baze, gesturing toward his notepad.

"I am not going to divulge my sources to you, *private*," spat Wallace. "I see no reason why I should have to."

"You don't."

"I won't."

The interview had gone off the rails. Perhaps Baze had approached it the wrong way. He looked back at his notes, trying to get the discussion back on track.

"My next question—"

"I am not answering any more of your

questions," interrupted Wallace. "In fact, I would like you to leave now."

Baze sighed. He closed his notepad and slowly tucked it back into his jacket. With a grunt, he pushed himself off of the loveseat. Before turning for the door, he looked down at Wallace and his eyes narrowed.

"Well, it would be a lie if I said it was nice talking to you, Marve. I really hope I don't have to see you again."

He turned toward the door, and the same repulsive scent hit him again, as if moving the particles of the air disturbed the odor.

"One last thing, Marve. What the hell is that horrible smell?"

Something flickered in Wallace's eyes. It was mostly indiscernible, but Baze thought he caught a hint of *something*. The look was quickly gone, and Wallace suddenly plastered that familiar mocking smile onto his face.

"What smell?"

63

Welsh sat at the small table in his hotel room with his head in his hands. He rubbed his fingers around his skull, trying to massage away that headache that was now pulsing just above his eyes. His leg was on fire, and his back was now aching as well. Since he had disposed of his pain pills, his back had only troubled him in times of stress. Once he had pushed through the initial withdrawal symptoms, the rankled nerves just below his shoulder blades had slowly healed. It was almost ironic; the pills, which he assumed was the only thing making his pain manageable, were actually tethering him to the discomfort. But now, after Kane had once again made a cryptic appearance, Welsh's back was worse than it had been in years, and he was left to ponder the night that caused his injury twenty-four years before.

December 13th, 1995. It had taken months after

the incident to fully recall what had happened, but now, Welsh remembered it vividly. He had just wrapped up the successful prosecution of a man named Ian Freeze, who had brutally assaulted his wife. The evidence had been circumstantial at first—the defense had claimed that the wife's bruises were made by a third man whom she was having an affair with. However, Welsh had been able to get something close to a confession out of Freeze when interrogating the man on the witness stand. Though Freeze had not actually copped to the crime, he had broken down into tears and repeatedly uttered, "I'm so sorry," over and over after a brutal and unrelenting series of questions from Welsh. The guilty verdict had been delivered on December 12th, and Welsh had spent the following day cooped up in his office, getting caught up on mounds of paperwork that had accumulated during the trial. He had finished typing up a report at 7:30 p.m. on the 13th, and had set off on the commute back to his house, eager to get home to Wendy.

The traffic light had turned yellow just as he was about to reach the intersection on Brooklyn Avenue. Welsh remembered pressing fervently on the gas pedal and darting forward just in time to catch the light. He could still see the Toyota Avalon suddenly barreling toward him in the darkness and recalled the horrible feeling of powerlessness as he tried to slam onto the brake, all the while knowing it was too late. The most striking thing about the moment of impact was the sound. Two tons of metal compacting was the loudest thing Welsh had ever heard. And that was the last thing he remembered before he had been propelled into darkness.

The next thing he knew, he was lying with his head on the passenger seat, his senses momentarily broken. There was the sound of a woman screaming, and the smell of gasoline, and the world was upside down. His whole body hurt so bad that he thought death was imminent. Welsh had vomited and then lost consciousness once more. Hours later, he had woken up in the hospital, unable to recollect why he was there or what had happened. The morphine had mostly subdued the pain, but any time he moved, it was like someone had gripped his heart and squeezed. The nurse had told him that he had been in a car accident and had a severe concussion and a spinal fracture, as well as a ruptured disc in his back. At first he had thought it had been a mistake; he had no memory of any car accident. But then Wendy had shown up a short time later, frantic and sobbing. She had been the one who had told him he was lucky to be alive. Luckier than the other person involved, at least.

Lydia Cross, the pilot of the Avalon, had died at the scene. The coroner's report had found more than three times the legal limit of alcohol in her system. It was a wonder she had made it as far as she did, being that she was likely blacked out. Cross had been traveling at least sixty miles an hour when she slammed into Welsh, flipping his car onto its side. Cross had broken her neck due to the whiplash, and if that wasn't enough to kill her, the Avalon's engine had caught fire and burned her body to a crisp. It was a wonder the gas tank hadn't exploded during the fire. If it had, Welsh probably would have met his maker too.

He had tried not to feel guilt in the months after the accident, but the task was difficult. Cross had sent him to weeks of rehab and had caused permanent damage to his back. He had had surgery to repair the ruptured disc and had been stuck with a stack of medical bills. And yet, Welsh couldn't stop thinking about how he had killed someone. Sure, the fault lied with Cross for daring to get behind the wheel, but Welsh couldn't help but wonder what would have happened if he had pressed the brake when the light had turned yellow instead of the gas pedal.

Now, as he vigorously rubbed his forehead while slowly rocking back-and-forth in his chair, his mind was fixed on Cross. How could the accident have any connection to Robert Macabre? What could a fatal car wreck two and a half decades before have to do with a demented serial killer? No matter how hard he wracked his brains, Welsh could not possibly see how the two things could be linked.

And yet, Kane had somehow known. He had somehow tracked Welsh to the hotel specifically to bring him this information. But why? What was Kane's angle? How did he fit into all of this? And if Welsh's accident and Macabre were somehow connected, how had Kane found out?

Welsh let out a loud noise of frustration that was partly produced by the pain in his body, but also by his inability to make sense of what had just happened. He compulsively began to rub his thighs, the synapses in his brain firing off at rapid intervals, desperate to concoct a solid explanation. Lydia Cross. A young, troubled woman trying to make a better life for herself, all the while struggling with her addiction to alcohol. Cross had had a steady job, and a long-term boyfriend. But she had not been able to overcome her sickness. And it had cost her dearly.

Welsh focused on the dead woman, desperately trying to dredge up details that he had long forgotten. What had been the boyfriend's name? Alex? Allen? It had started with an *A*. Could this all have been set in motion by a vengeful, psychopathic boyfriend who had lost his significant other? When Welsh had tossed the idea back and forth in his head a couple of times, he almost rolled his eyes. Robert Macabre was a sadist; a creature that had been molded for years. The notion that a lover had turned to serial murder as a coping mechanism for the pain was almost laughable.

Who else that was associated to Cross could be connected to the killings? Welsh wracked his brain while continuing to massage his headache-riddled dome. Suddenly, a huge spasm of pain spread through his lower back.

"Jesus!"

It was as if thinking of the incident was causing a physical reaction in his body. Like the dormant pain that had gone quiet had roared back to life because of his thoughts of the accident. Welsh took in several deep breaths, trying to quell the perturbed nerves in his back, and through a sort of slow meditation, he was able to make the feeling abate. He had to calm his mind. Control his thoughts. His back would get worse if he continued to stress. And a tranquil mind was able to produce a solution to a problem better than a frazzled one. The solution had to be lying somewhere in the depths of his memory. Welsh closed his eyes, determined to find the answer. *Breathe in, breathe out. Breathe in—*

A boy. There had been a boy. Lydia Cross had had a son that CPS had taken away due to her drinking. It had happened just days before the accident. It was thought that this was some of the motivation behind her bender; one of the reasons that she had been hammered in the first place. What had been the boy's name? He had been fourteen or fifteen at the time. He remembered seeing the boy's photograph in the paper two years after the accident. It had been a mugshot. The boy, whatever his name was, had been arrested for assault. Someone in his office had told him that it was Lydia Cross's child. He remembered the kid having long brown hair that fell over his shoulders, and wide, dark eyes. As Welsh scraped the plumbs of his memory bank, the mental image he produced of the old mugshot looked more and more like a young version of the man who had plunged a knife into his left leg two weeks before.

Was this it? Was this the answer to all of the cryptic messages? The key to all the riddles? Was Robert Macabre this boy? The son of the woman that Welsh had killed in the car accident?

Just as he had this thought, a noise shook Welsh out of his rumination. His head snapped to the right, pinpointing the source of the sound. Welsh watched in shock as the doorknob to his hotel room began to twist. Could it be Arroyo? But why wouldn't she knock?

The door opened inch by inch. It was as if everything was in slow motion, and Welsh was frozen in time. A loud creak rang out as the hinges of the door protested the movement, and all of the air in Welsh's lungs was gone. It couldn't be.

And yet, when the door was finally ajar, there

he was. Appearing like a demon that had been summoned by Welsh's dark thoughts, Macabre stood in plain sight, unmasked and unhinged. The man's long hair cloaked his wide eyes in shadow, and the folds of wrinkly skin around his plump lips stretched into a leer. Everything clicked at the exact same time that Welsh realized that his fate was sealed. This was the son of the woman who Welsh had killed in the accident.

Robert Cross.

64

Baze stared at the bulletin board, lost in thought. He had cleared away most of the newspaper articles and clutter. All that remained were the images of the four men that he had accrued in the last twenty-four hours. He stared at each one, carefully examining the different nuances in their facial expressions, as if a scowl here or a fake grin there could signify malevolence. But as hard as he tried, the images would not speak to him. His collection of suspects just continued to sneer, mocking him silently.

First, there was Warren Grecko. The photograph of Grecko was the man shaking hands with the mayor, and scowling at the camera like he absolutely detested being at the charity event. Baze absentmindedly rubbed the sore spot on his chest as he peered at Grecko. Something was not right there. Something lingered behind the man's eyes. A cold hatred; a sort of unrelenting fury that threatened to envelop anyone who stood in his path. Out of all the suspects, Grecko was the most logical. A volatile, angry man that had an open grudge toward Carson Welsh. It definitely made sense. Baze came closer to the photograph and nearly ripped the picture down. He had not yet forgotten the ambush in the gym. It made his chest tighten, and his face feel hot.

Almost as if to not let his anger get the best of him, Baze tore his eyes away from Grecko and looked at the next picture. The photograph he had acquired of Edwin Spade was a staff picture from the police department. The picture was old; Spade's blond hair did not have the traces of gray that it had now, and when he had nearly beaten him to a pulp, Baze had noticed a set of crow's feet that were absent in the picture. Other than that, Spade looked as unpleasant as ever, with his cold eyes and lips-only smile. After initially ruling Spade out, Baze had circled back around to the idea. The man had seemingly provided a logical explanation for why he had been at the crime scene where Maria Cable had been found, but the more Baze cogitated on Spade's reasoning, the more skeptical he felt. Spade had been remarkably quick to the scene—and who in the police department would tip him off anyway? Whose first thought when a body is discovered is to immediately contact a *former* coroner? Spade had been involved in the case since the beginning. If a person had enough clout and acumen to steer a homicide investigation a certain way, it was plausible that that person had been within the ranks of the police the whole time.

Next, Marvin Wallace's ugly mug stared at him from a low-res photo that Baze had plastered next to Spade. Baze had pulled this particular photograph from Wallace's website, in the "biography" section. The photo looked like something you would see on the back of a hardcover crime-fiction book. Wallace was standing up with his arms crossed, trying to look tough. But a strange smile seemed to tug at the corners of his lips, like he wanted to laugh. Baze felt his skin crawl as he looked into Wallace's eyes. It was almost as if he could still smell the rancid stench that had been present in Wallace's cabin during the conversation the previous day.

Finally, there was the sketch of David Kane hanging there, with a thumbtack holding it in place. Kane's face looked gaunt; his cheeks were hollow, and the shadows drawn under his eyes were quite dark. As he stared at the picture with a sense of foreboding, Baze could not deny that Kane was somehow deeply involved in this case. The most likely explanation was that he provided some assistance to the killer, perhaps in exchange for videos of Macabre's torture porn. But Kane didn't match Welsh's physical depiction of the killer, and Macabre was not stupid enough to intentionally show his face to his primary target. So, accomplice was the only theory that made sense. If Kane *was* solely responsible for the killings, it would be very difficult to find him. David Kane seemed to have mastered the art of living off the grid.

Last and definitely least (at least in Baze's mind), was the possibility that Macabre was none of the above. The sketch that had been drawn based on Welsh's visual of the attack in his apartment propagated this theory. Arroyo and her team now firmly believed that Robert Macabre had leathery skin, and thick lips, as well as shoulder-length brown hair. But, for whatever reason, Baze did not agree with this line of thinking. Welsh had said that he had never seen the man before. If that were the case, it couldn't be Macabre. Baze was certain of one thing: Macabre's grudge against Welsh was deeply personal, to the point that Macabre constantly obsessed over his perceived adversary. It couldn't be a randomly chosen fixation, where Macabre had read about Welsh and decided that he was deserving of psychological torture. If Baze was certain of one thing, it was that Welsh had unwittingly spoken to Robert Macabre at some point in his life. Perhaps Welsh had not gotten a good look at the attacker, or the person that had broken into the man's apartment was someone else entirely. Whatever the explanation, Baze's gut told him that the man in the sketch was not the one he sought.

He stared at each of the photographs again, one by one. If he had to rank them from most to least likely, it would go Grecko, Wallace, Kane, and Spade. Logic pointed to Grecko, but if Baze was being honest with himself, gut instinct pointed to Wallace.

Baze sighed and scratched at his mustache. He pondered his next move, knowing that the break in the case would not come easy. Macabre was an absolute magician about covering his tracks. Every murder attributed to him so far had yielded nothing.

What about murders that hadn't been attributed to him? Baze was one of the only people who believed that Rachel Burns, the woman who had been murdered several months before Welsh had received the first letter, was a victim of Robert Macabre. It was like a trial run. A demo for more grandiose things to come. Could that mean that neither Dinwoodie *nor* Burns was Macabre's first victim? After all, the hand that had been left on Welsh's porch did not belong to David Kane. The photographs that had accompanied the hand were of someone else entirely. Someone they had yet to identify. If Macabre had been able to pull that off, who was to say that he hadn't committed unspeakable acts before? Sure, there wasn't any forensic evidence or leads from the known victims. But what about the unknown ones?

Baze drummed his fingers against the table underneath him for a second, and then he headed over toward his computer at a brisk pace, firing up the monitor. It was time to search for answers in unorthodox places. It was time to look into the past.

Though he hadn't expected the job to be easy, Baze also hadn't planned on looking for a needle in a haystack. The sheer volume of violent crime was staggering, and Baze had to wonder what the statistics would look like in more metropolitan, urban states that didn't have such a vast expanse of rural country. Since the sixties, Oregon had just over five thousand homicides reported to the FBI. And 2018 had been the deadliest year on record, with 172 murders.

A decent-sized chunk of the homicides in the past ten years could be attributed to two different serial killers that had lived remarkably close to each other on the Oregon Coast. The first had been active from 1984 all the way until 2016, targeting mostly teenage girls. The man had killed his first five victims haphazardly, making no effort to conceal his exploits. However, after the police had nearly caught him, the man had made a concerted effort to disguise his killings as accidents or suicides. A drowning here. A young, pretty girl with her wrists cut there. The man had displayed a streak of ingenuity and had operated unchecked for three decades. But he couldn't be Robert Macabre, because he was dead.

The other purveyor of serial murder was a man who had been dubbed The Wolfmask, or the Halloween Ripper. The predator had killed a young man every Halloween night from 2007 until 2016 in various cities all over the state, and also murdered a middle-aged couple on the night he was caught, October 31st of 2017. But his MO was different than Macabre. The bodies of most of his victims had never been found, and the man targeted a completely different demographic. Also, as far as Baze knew, the Halloween Ripper was still shackled up at a psychiatric ward in Salem.

Another big portion of homicides in Oregon since 1960 stemmed from domestic disputes. Deranged, drunk husbands strangling their wives to death, or hysterical, violent women shooting their cheating significant others. Then there was gang violence; most of which happened in the rough areas of Portland. It wasn't as bad as other major cities, but to act like Portland was devoid of drive-by shootings or park stabbings was silly. It had its problems, just like every other metropolis.

Baze's eyes began to burn as he continued to stare at his computer screen. He had been reading stories of murder for nearly two hours, and it wasn't exactly an uplifting exercise. The depravity of humanity knew no bounds, especially when it came to violence. Baze had even read one article about a man on death row who had hacked two of his friends to death with a samurai sword on a camping trip. It had not been pre-meditated; the man had carried the sword with him as sort of a grown-man's play-toy, and after a couple of hours of doing hallucinogens at the campsite, he had decided that the next most logical thing to do was to bisect his two buddies. Spontaneity and all.

Another case of ghoulish first-degree murder was a couple who had carried out a short-lived white supremacy campaign, murdering four people in their spree, including a traveler who had offered to give them a ride after a jazz festival. The couple had forced their driver to take them sixty miles down Highway-20, before shooting him point-blank and leaving him in the woods. The driver had been black. During the spree, the other victims were the husband's step-parents and the driver of a vehicle that the two had car-jacked. It was an inexplicable series of events; the only minority in the group of people that had been killed was the young man who had offered them a ride. It seemed like a strange way to carry out their supremacist manifest, targeting three Caucasians. But perhaps those ideas were just a guise under which to enact their violent tendencies.

Perhaps the most brutal tale had been the case of a middle-aged man who had abducted a thirteen-year-old girl and kept her in his basement for twenty-seven days in 1999. The man, Earl Voight, had repeatedly raped the girl, eventually impregnating her. After an ill-conceived escape attempt by young Lizzie Sanders, Voight had stabbed the girl 114 times. He had been caught three days after the murder and had spent fourteen years in prison before finishing his last day on earth in an electric chair.

After the Sanders story, Baze rubbed his eyeballs in frustration. This whole venture was going exactly nowhere. It had seemed like a good idea at first, but now, he was starting to wonder if he had just wasted two hours forcing himself to study humanities most dastardly deeds. It was very unlikely that there was some connection that everyone had missed for fifteen years.

Baze decided that he would peruse only a few more articles before calling it quits. There was almost certainly nothing to find, and he was getting tired. He clicked and scrolled with malaise, slowly becoming desensitized to the stories of graphic, non-fiction horror on his computer screen. A shop manager being shot to death in an armed robbery. Meh. A homeless person who had had their throat slashed with a broken beer bottle by a rival transient. Whatever. An old man who had gotten his head blown off during a home invasion gone wrong. Oh well. The man had been ninety-four anyway.

Everything he read seemed useless to the task at hand. That is, until he read the story about the fallen police officer.

In May of 1996, a young deputy had made a routine traffic stop in Canby, Oregon, some twenty miles outside of Portland. The officer had been blasted through his left eyeball by a round that had come from a low-caliber gun. The archived news article had said that the murder had been committed by a tweaker named Eddie Hayes, as Hayes had been arrested with an eight ball of cocaine and a Beretta pistol stashed in the waistband of his underwear just two miles away from where the officer had been gunned down. But as soon as Baze read the name of the officer, the world came to a stop.

Dozens of chills prickled down his spine, and an army of goose bumps raised along his arms in unison. He brought in a huge intake of air, and Baze had to place his hands on either side of him to keep him from getting dizzy.

Everything finally clicked in the span of a second; the time it took to read the name. This was it. This was the missing puzzle piece. It was almost shocking how reading one name in an archived news article could form such a crystal-clear picture of something so convoluted and strange. The theory was wild—but it had come so fast after seeing the name that Baze knew it was true. This was everything. All packed into three syllables.

He took a deep breath, and more chills spread out over Baze's body. His heart thumped along at a rapid pace, and he was full of resolve as he read the name of the slain officer in his mind one more time.

Deputy Calvin David Kane.

The lights to the building went off with a loud clunk, casting everything inside into darkness. No one remained in the building, but the ADT alarm system that would bring a uniformed officer to the source of the disturbance was now defunct, thanks to the vandalized power box. A shadow passed along the side of the building, and the man in the ski mask found his way to the back door. The figure quickly removed both of his gloves and withdrew the two hairpins from the back pocket of his jeans. After three long minutes of toggling with the lock, there was a click and a creek, and the masked man put his gloves back on and pushed the door open, looking over his shoulder one last time to make sure no one was watching.

Once inside, Baze moved with purpose toward the staircase that he knew to be on the other side of the hallway. His heart was thundering along in his chest, and he felt a swooping sensation in his stomach. Baze rounded about the staircase and almost stumbled as he began trekking up the stairs. The way he saw it, he had a short window before anyone realized that something was awry. Five minutes was generally the amount of time it took a passerby to notice that things were amiss. Like how the building that was normally illuminated was now cast in darkness.

After six seemingly endless flights of stairs, Baze was on the third floor. He felt several beads of sweat streaming down his exposed neck and percolating at the top of his long-sleeved black shirt. His hands were shaking now; a bi-product of the adrenaline galloping through his nervous system. He subconsciously read the plaques on each of the doors that he passed, even though he knew where he was headed.

There was a soft clunk in the hallway ahead, and Baze's heart skipped a beat. He froze in his tracks. Was this wild escapade about to be all for naught? Was someone lingering in the darkness, waiting to pounce? The silence seemed ominous and heavy. He tiptoed forward, and his whole body was tense, like a cat that was stalking its prey.

After a few more moments of nothing, Baze decided he had imagined the noise. No one was here right now, waiting to thwart him. He had carefully vetted this plan; it wasn't like there was some unforeseen detail that would prove to be his downfall. Baze quickened his pace, remembering the five-minute rule. He passed three more doors with plaques before arriving at the one he had come for. He read the inscription, and though he knew what the name would be, his heart seemed to do a backflip. This was it.

For the second time in minutes, Baze withdrew his hairpins and went to work. This time, he was much more technical and proficient in his work, and the lock clicked open in a matter of seconds. Baze scurried into the office, his eyes passing over the sofa and the mahogany desk before arriving at the three rows of cabinets. He instantly lunged for the cabinets, pulling the first two open simultaneously and the third one after that. Thankfully, the organizer of said drawers saw the virtue in alphabetizing his files, making Baze's task a thousand times easier. He quickly rifled through the folders, and within seconds, arrived at the one he had come for. It was rather thick and took a few moments of jostling to get it dislodged from its position. Once it was free, Baze stared at the manila folder. What secrets did it contain? What answers were waiting for him here?

With a deep breath, Baze turned about and left the office, knowing he was one step closer to the endgame.

Arroyo's gut felt like someone had poured a vat of lead into it, and her head was aching with the first traces of a migraine. She rubbed inattentively at her right temple, as if she could massage the pain away. But she couldn't. The hurt would slowly become overwhelming until nothing but agony dominated her thoughts. She looked from face to face, feeling self-conscious. She had failed. And she knew it.

"Carson Welsh has gone missing," she said softly.

No one said anything. Owen Anders and Marcus Austin, the two forensic techs, bowed their heads, as if they were somehow embarrassed by the situation. Detective Gary Fairfield shook his head in disgust, and his partner, Andre Giuliani, mouthed the word "fuck." Easton Lowry remained impassive, but somehow, Arroyo felt like he was secretly judging her. Like he was inwardly adjudicating her failure.

"Two hours ago, I called Welsh, but was sent straight to voicemail. I sent two uniforms into the Comfort Inn to check on him. When we knocked on his room, there was no answer. Everything was still there. His suitcase. His phone. No sign of a struggle. But Welsh is gone."

There were a few beats of nothing. Fairfield and Giuliani exchanged looks, and Anders and Austin kept their heads down like they were engaged in some sort of prayer. Lowry shifted in his seat and then waved his hand around in the air in a confused gesture.

"Are we certain that this isn't of his own volition? I mean, could he have just left?"

"Without his phone or his wallet?"

"Welsh is kind of an odd duck. I wouldn't put it past him."

"No," said Arroyo quickly. "He knows how closely we are monitoring his situation. He wouldn't just disappear without telling us."

Lowry clicked his tongue.

"So... Macabre took him?"

There was a penetrating void of quiet, and Arroyo felt like this was her own personal rapture. Like everyone in the room was inwardly scrutinizing her and deeming her unworthy of her position. How could she have let this happen? With a surge of irritation, she wondered where Baze was.

It was just like that asshole to skip an emergency meeting.

"I, uh… I don't know."

Like water through a broken dam, an angry energy crashed into the room.

"Jesus!" hissed Giuliani. "How could we have let this happen?"

"I thought you were hiding him!" added Fairfield fervidly. "I thought no one knew where he was!"

"I can't explain it," said Arroyo quietly. "I don't know how this happened. We moved him. We told no one where he was. It… it doesn't make sense."

"Seems like Bob the Butcher seems to know our next move before we even make it," said Lowry silently.

"The hell is that supposed to mean?" demanded Fairfield.

Lowry shrugged, and this seemed to provoke Fairfield even more.

"No, kid, I know exactly what you are implying, and you better just shut your mouth."

"Gary, calm down—" began Giuliani.

"No, Andre, I won't calm down! We just lost our only witness! Also, where is that scumbag Baze? He is your official consultant, right, LT? Isn't he supposed to be here *consulting*? I mean, I guess it is not surprising, considering your expert always stinks of whiskey and cigarettes. Probably passed out at the bar."

"Gary, enough!" Arroyo suddenly no longer felt like she was under the microscope. Her shame was quickly replaced by a slow burning ire toward Fairfield.

"This whole investigation wreaks of incompetence," continued Fairfield. "You would think we are trying to find the Holy Grail and not a serial killer. Shit, even if we found the Holy Grail, we would probably just lose it!"

"Gary, either cut the shit or get out!"

Arroyo's voice, at its loudest pitch, was warped and terrible. Her screaming prompted total silence from the rest of the room, and their facial expressions made it seem like she had just transformed into a dragon. None of them had ever seen her yell with such vehemence and absolute ferocity. Fairfield suddenly looked embarrassed.

After a few beats of quiet, Arroyo pressed on. They had no time to dwell on anything other than what needed to be done. "We have several roadblocks set up in the area around Welsh's hotel," she said, and her voice was a little hoarse from the scream. "We have uniforms posted up, stopping cars, taking license plates, everything. I am about to hold a press conference to release the info, so we can get all sets of eyes in the city limits looking for Welsh. If it is anything like the previous victims, we have a short window where Macabre will keep him alive. We have to act quickly. I want everybody down at the hotel, canvassing the area, and asking if anybody saw anything. If he got him directly from the room, there will be security footage to look at. I'm working on getting a subpoena for that footage as we speak. Waiting to hear back from Judge Milton."

Arroyo took a deep breath, and placed her hands on the table, leaning forward like she was about to share something intimate with all of them. When she began again, her voice was much softer.

"This meeting was not called to wallow in our sorrows, or to tell each other how big of screw-ups we all are." She eyed Fairfield, who shifted in his chair uncomfortably. "We need to get out there and stop this. Once and for all."

Nobody said anything. They all were gazing at her like they were seeing her for the first time.

"What are you waiting for, people? Move your asses!"

67

The pain in his back was now worse than it had ever been; it felt like several hot knives had been plunged into his muscles. An uncontrollable thirst squeezed at his throat, and he wondered how long it had been since he had drunk water. Disorientation touched everything. He couldn't see. He couldn't feel most of his body. The only thing tangible was the darkness. Everything was dark.

For five minutes, or it could have been five hours, he lay there, uncertain if he was even still alive. If he was, one thing was certain; he didn't have much time left. The smell of the room around him told him so. It was rank with the stench of blood and decay. Eventually, his senses became more in-tune, and he arrived at the stark realization that he was very much still alive and lying somewhere foreign. How had he gotten here? In the blackness, Welsh tried as hard as he could to recall what had led him to this. It took all the effort in his body to conjure up the memory of the Comfort Inn. Sitting there, ruminating on David Kane, when the door had opened.

That was it. That was the last memory he had. And now he was here. Alone. In pain. It didn't take much longer for the recollections to flood back into his brain. Macabre had taken him. He had finally made his move. Just as Welsh arrived at this horrible conclusion, the light turned on with a crack, and something danced in his peripheral vision. Welsh slowly turned his head to the left, to see what had moved.

It was in that moment that he realized he was about to die. Standing over him was something that could only be described as the devil incarnate. The man was massive and muscular, and Welsh could almost feel the hatred radiating off of his body. On his face was a goat mask almost identical to the one that had been on Tracy Dinwoodie's lifeless shell when they had found her hanging from a tree in Mount Tabor Park. It was dementedly poetic, and cyclical. Here at the end, Macabre was wearing the same mask he had donned the first time that Welsh had seen the killer, in that haunting video. Macabre took several slow steps toward him, and Welsh's eyes locked onto the silver butcher's knife in the man's right hand. Through the darkness, the knife began to rise.

MACABRE

With a grunt, Arroyo shifted her vehicle into park, as if the motion of pushing the gear shift had taken her last bit of energy. The tendrils of a tension headache were creeping up the back of her neck and tickling her scalp; it felt like mere moments before it would turn into ear-splitting pain. But the discomfort was nothing compared to what she felt inside. After pouring every ounce of her being into this case, everything had come crumbling down in a heap. Welsh was gone. She was certain of that. His body would turn up somewhere, mutilated and destroyed, and that would be that. Robert Macabre would finally show that this entire time, he had been in control.

The press conference had been short, but still tedious. The reporters had peppered her with questions and she had given them nondescript, stock answers. "We will not give any details about an ongoing police investigation." Or, "I can't comment on that at this time." It had all been fairly inconsequential really, except for the fact that the public was now on high alert, and the police department was now going to be flooded with anonymous tips about Macabre sightings, and reports of neighbors who would swear someone was being held hostage in the basement next door. It was up to her subordinates now to sift through the tips, and, unlikely as it was, hopefully find something that would prove to be the breakthrough they needed. As with most things in this investigation, it felt like the odds were not great.

Arroyo had been receiving regular updates from her detectives and deputies, who had been searching a ten-block radius of the Comfort Inn for hours. Canvassing the area had yielded squat. No one they had talked to had seen anything. No large men in animal masks. No Carson Welsh. As far as the footage from the hotel, someone had tripped the breaker that fed electricity to the cameras on the third floor. Their only hope was to recover footage that showed an intruder heading for the electrical panel, but somehow, Arroyo knew that this wouldn't produce anything either.

It was now two a.m., and Arroyo had been forced to call it a night. There was nothing more to be done for the time being. If there was any sort of development, whoever had discovered it would call.

But now, as difficult as it would be, it was time to try to get some sleep. She would toss and turn all night, and for every minute of rest she actually got, it would likely be matched by a minute of restlessness. But she had to try to sleep. She could not function tomorrow if she stayed awake for much longer. Therefore, with her chest tight and her gut feeling like someone had repeatedly punched her in the midsection, she clomped out of the front seat of her car, and trudged up toward her front door.

When she got to her porch, her heart suddenly pounded at a frenetic pace, and her diaphragm clenched. Something was wrong. She had no idea what it was, but the hairs on the back of her neck began to rise, and an eerie feeling swooped down upon her like some sort of wicked, otherworldly entity. Arroyo subconsciously reached for the gun that was holstered on her hip, and her fingers fumbled for her keys. Seconds later, the lock clicked and the door creaked open. She took a silent, powerful breath, and stepped over the threshold.

Someone else was inside. She was sure of it now. In the foyer that segued into the rest of her house, light crept around the corner. One of her lamps in the living room must have been turned on. She swallowed, getting ready to pull out her phone to call 911, when a voice called out to her.

"Red? Is that you?"

Arroyo nearly keeled over in shock. After a couple beats of feeling like she could jump out of her own skin, she moved forward and rounded the corner in front of her into the living room. In one of her recliners sat Baze, looking at her through squinted eyes.

"Took you long enough. If my heart wasn't racing a mile a minute, I might have dozed off."

"What the hell are you doing here?" she hissed. "How did you get in?"

The faint traces of a smile worked at the corners of Baze's lips, but he suppressed it.

"Do you know nothing about me?"

Arroyo's mouth expanded and contracted rapidly, as she struggled to find any words to express how she felt. That was, until the rage came flooding into her body.

"What the *fuck* is wrong with you? Breaking into my house? I could arrest you right now!"

"You could, but you won't."

"Wanna bet, asshole?" she shouted.

"Fine then. Put me in cuffs. I'll have to tell you the breakthrough I've made from behind bars."

Arroyo narrowed her eyes. "Breakthrough? What kind of breakthrough? *What the hell do you think you're doing?*" Her voice was a screech now, and Baze stood up and put his hands out in the air, as if telling her to calm down.

"Relax, Red. You know I ain't here to do

anything crazy."

"Breaking into my house is pretty goddamn crazy!"

"I know. I'm sorry. But I need to keep this all a secret. You are the only one I can trust. We need to move fast, before anything gets out."

Arroyo shook her head in a frenzy, and her normally pale skin was tinged with a striking redness that reflected her wrath.

"What are you going on about, Baze? How long have you been here?"

"About an hour. I figured you would be here when I arrived, and when you weren't, I figured you would show up eventually."

Arroyo threw her hands up into the air. "Why didn't you just fucking call? Why did you have to break in?"

Baze's voice got a decibel quieter when he responded to this. "Because I needed to tell you this in person. I couldn't risk someone else listening in. It is too important."

"Why didn't you just wait outside?"

"Doesn't feel safe out there. Not with what's going on."

"Jesus Christ. You almost gave me a heart attack. You... You were waiting here in my *house*." Arroyo realized that she had now repeated this sentiment several times, unable to fully grasp the lunacy of the concept. She placed her hands on her hips and bent over, breathing deeply like she had just finished the 100-meter dash.

"I'm sorry."

Baze stepped toward her and she subconsciously recoiled, moving back with her shoulders tensed. He let out a chuckle at this.

"If I wanted to attack you, do you think I would have stopped for a friendly chat before doing so?"

"There are many things this conversation is, Baze, and friendly isn't one of them. Why would you do this? This is crazy!"

"Every second I spend apologizing is one less second I have to explain what I have found."

"What you *found*," replied Arroyo in a mocking voice. "Where were you earlier, then? Normally, when someone calls you to an emergency meeting, it is customary to actually show up."

"I was preoccupied."

"Oh, you were *preoccupied*. That's interesting. Well, while you have been preoccupied, Carson Welsh has been abducted. Were you aware of that?"

"I—"

"That's right, asshole. He was taken from right under her noses. While you were *preoccupied,* our only witness to the killer was snatched from his goddamn hotel."

"Red—"

"*Stop calling me that!*"

It was Baze's turn to recoil. He stepped back,

as if her shouting could physically harm him. This somehow empowered Arroyo, and she moved forward, feeling unbridled fury at everything that had transpired over the past twenty-four hours. Baze was going to be her outlet. He was going to receive the brunt of her frustration—and it served him right. Who the hell did he think he was? He had gone too far this time—coming into her house in the middle of the night and acting like it meant nothing at all. She was going to cut him loose. Whatever insight he provided, this was the last straw.

"I am done with you! It's over! Welsh is gone, Baze! It won't be long before we find his body! We failed. We *lost*."

Arroyo was expecting him to fight back. She was expecting a shouting match to ensue and the anger that was almost certainly bubbling in his chest to boil over. There was a point where a man like Baze would reach a breaking point, no matter how aloof and blasé he always tried to act. Judging by his contorted facial expression, he was finally about to explode back at her. But shockingly Baze didn't yell. In fact, his voice somehow got even quieter.

"No, Red. I don't think you will find his body."

Blank shock washed over her. It took her several long seconds to digest what had come out of his mouth. But it wasn't just the content; it was the tone. The way he had hissed out those nine words made her certain that he had figured it out.

Whatever massive secret had shrouded this whole case in an opaque cloud, Baze had found the answer. Arroyo let a drawn-out pause take hold, suddenly feeling a sense of unbearable anticipation. And yet, she couldn't find the words to prompt him. Her tongue did not want to move, and her gut did not want to unclench to allow her enough air for the words. So she just had to wait for him to explain, and the seconds stretched out for an eternity.

"You won't find Robert Macabre," he continued. "You won't find David Kane either."

Silence. Arroyo was completely dumbfounded. She finally managed to find her voice again, but only through the strength of a whisper.

"Why?"

Baze let out a deep breath and closed his eyes.

"Because Carson Welsh, David Kane, and Robert Macabre are all the same person."

Robert eyed his various masks with intense focus, as if one would physically reach out to him, beckoning him closer. Each mask was hung on a nail on the wall; there were seventeen in total. There was the goat and the fox. The rabbit and the raven. The pig and the bull. All of the various creatures that had haunted his victims in the moments before their deaths.

In that moment, he recalled their faces. Calvin. Rachel. Tracy. Jacey. Maria. Carrie. Not to mention the others. The others that remained nameless even to him. His experiments. There were several of them. He could still envision their expressions in their final moments. They always looked... relieved. To realize that they could let go. Forget their pain, and their loss. That was the funny thing; the epiphany had always come just before the end. Before they could see what living meant with their new understanding of the world and its nihilistic tendencies.

Carson Welsh was dead. The shell of his body was still walking and sweating and breathing, but Robert was fully in charge now. And it was time to make his final move. His last mark on the world, before disappearing. He had planned it for some time. And the night had finally come.

Robert walked toward the table in the middle of the room that was tainted with the blood of all the women he had taken. If he had been caught, this would be the most damning piece of evidence that they would've found. But he had never been worried. If the police were not clever enough to realize what had been in front of them the whole time, how would they be shrewd enough to find his table?

When David would speak to him, he was angry to discover that the man actually made a good deal of sense. Robert was sick, that was all. A diseased animal, needing to be put down or locked up. But it wasn't Robert's fault. That was what David had said. It was nature that had made him this way, not nurture. That it was the chemicals and physical structure of his brain that led him to hurt people. But David had begged him to turn himself in. The man had urged Robert during every moment of weakness to concede defeat. But Robert was robust and resilient. And by the time that the bullet had gone through the deputies' skull all those years ago, the compulsions were far too strong to repress.

His eyes flitted from mask to mask, like a child in a candy store trying to decide which treat was the most tantalizing. The goat had run its course, and most of the other animals were specific to each individual victim. It would not be right to wear the face of the deer; that was meant for Jacey. The rooster was Carrie's. The pig was for Maria.

So what then? What would he wear for his final victim?

At the far end of the wall, there was a mask that was unlike the others. It was a deep shade of black, and its features were altogether more haunting than anything else that was hanging next to it. It wasn't an animal. It was the face of a demon, with sharp teeth curved upward into a taunting smile and small gashes for nostrils like that of a snake. Its bright yellow eyes contrasted vividly with the rest of the dark mask. Silhouetted above the face were two sharp, pointed horns, each six inches long.

Robert removed the demon mask from its nail and strapped it around his face. The eyeholes were a little thin, but not enough to completely obstruct his vision. The fingers of his right hand tickled the hilt of the knife that was attached to his tool belt, and his erection pulsed rhythmically against his pants.

This would be his masterstroke. The ultimate twist. Something the rest of them would never see coming. When Welsh had disappeared, surely the police department had been horrified, but not surprised. After all of the letters, and malice that Robert had shown Welsh, it would probably be fitting to them that he had finally vanished. But this one, they would not suspect.

For no one knew that Emily Arroyo had been the final target all along.

70

For a second, gravity seemed like it no longer existed. Arroyo was vaguely aware of her own body, but for a passing moment she felt more like a ghost than an actual person. And through the strange sensations she was experiencing, Arroyo became acutely aware that she would remember that moment for the rest of her life. She would never forget how Baze suddenly seemed to be standing at the end of a long hallway, or that feeling that the shock pulsating through her was an actual electrical current. Arroyo let out a long breath, and after five long seconds of searching, she found her voice.

"What?"

The word came out feeble and strange. Baze rubbed at his temple, and the skin where the scar crawled down his face was now taut as he clenched his jaw.

"Welsh *is* Robert Macabre. And David Kane.

Or, at least, Kane only exists in Welsh's head. He's crazy, Red."

"What?" Arroyo wasn't even aware that she had repeated her question. The surprise was too overwhelming to be cognizant of such things.

"Why don't you sit down, Emily? Let me explain it."

It took Arroyo a few seconds to process what Baze had just said. For whatever reason, she was focused on the fact that he had called her by her actual name for the first time.

"Sit down. I will show you." Baze gestured toward the couch that was next to him. With her legs shaking slightly, she hobbled over to the couch and perched her bottom on the edge of it, but stayed sitting forward. She was too tense to recline back. It was then that she noticed several documents cluttering her table that did not belong there.

"What are these?" She reached for one of the pieces of paper in front of her, but Baze touched her hand softly, and held it in place.

"Let me just explain it to you."

Baze stayed standing and reached for a piece of paper that was on the right side of the table. He picked it up and held it in front of her face. The document seemed to be a printed news article, and the headline took up a good portion of the page.

District Attorney Suffers Serious Injuries In Fatal

Car Accident.

"This article was written on December fourteenth of nineteen ninety-five. Welsh was coming home from work the night before when a woman named Lydia Cross ran a red light and hit Welsh's car going seventy miles an hour. She had consumed more than three times the legal limit. They think she was killed on impact, but it was difficult to tell, being that the car caught fire and she was burned to a crisp."

Arroyo took the article from Baze's grasp and began skimming. With each line she read, her heart beat faster.

Baze's voice floated down to her as she hungrily consumed the words on the page. "In that article, it just says that Welsh had serious injuries and was in the ICU. Thanks to HIPPA laws, it was almost impossible to discover the extent of Welsh's injuries, at least from the doctors who treated him in ninety-five and early ninety-six. However, in the past few months, he has been seeing a psychiatrist named Leonard Freidenberg, who kept Welsh's entire medical history dating back to the accident in ninety-five."

Baze reached down toward the table and picked up another piece of paper. Instead of handing it to Arroyo, he held it in front of his face and began to read.

"'The patient suffered significant head trauma during the accident, including damage to the orbitofrontal cortex and prefrontal cortex, which has acutely impacted his thinking and behavior. He exhibits some subtle signs of DID (Disassociate Identity Disorder) and schizophrenia, though he is able to mostly conceal his symptoms. The patient was on a regiment of long-term psychotherapy with Dr. Kellen Frank, beginning six months after the accident and ending in two thousand three. Along with the psychotherapy, Frank prescribed Fluoxetine, an SSRI, which the patient has taken intermittently since nineteen ninety-six. There was a brief period in mid two thousand and four where the patient abstained from his medication, but he has regularly taken it since July of that year. Notably, the patient seems to distance himself from the medication and it's true pharmological purposes, often referring to it as his 'back pills.' The patient experienced a small fracture to his third thoracic vertebra during the accident, as well as a ruptured disc.'"

Baze looked up from the paper at Arroyo, who was staring at him with wide eyes.

"Does that seem strange to you? The fact that Welsh stopped taking his medication for a period in mid two thousand and four and then began re-taking it in July of that year? Right after Willy Tennyson was blown to hell?"

A million frantic thoughts were jostling for the top position in Arroyo's mind, but for some reason, the one that she vocalized seemed like the most inconsequential.

"Where did you get these?"

Baze ignored this and used his index finger to skim along the paper until he came to the sentence he was looking for.

"It says here that Welsh missed his last two appointments and has not been returning calls to Dr. Freidenberg. Little odd, don't you think?"

He cast the paper back on the table and then reached for another in his stack of haphazard documents. Arroyo just there on the couch, still feeling like she was having an out-of-body experience.

"Now, if you are wondering what led me to this, I did a deep dive on all the unsolved homicides in Oregon dating back thirty years. That didn't yield much of anything. At least, not pertaining to this case. Therefore, I began probing the quote unquote 'solved' homicides. That's how I came across *this*."

Baze slid a piece of paper across the table at her. She picked it up, holding it like it was carrying some rare disease. Again, a headline took up a good portion of the page, yielding its way to another news article.

Deputy Slain By Convict.

"That article says that the officer was murdered by some tweaker named Eddie Hayes," said Baze quietly as Arroyo's eyes flitted from left to right. "Two other officers found Hayes two miles away from the scene. He had a gun on him. Ballistics of the gun matched the bullet that killed Deputy Calvin Kane."

Arroyo slowly looked up, with comprehension dawning on her face. It was like the world was suddenly upside down, and everything was getting jumbled together. Her stomach did a backflip and her chest constricted as she looked up at Baze. His expression was ominous.

"I will give you one guess what Kane's middle name was."

Arroyo looked back down at the article. "Jesus," she hissed.

Baze nodded darkly. "The case file says that when Hayes was arrested, he kept saying that the gun wasn't his. That the 'bird man,' gave it to him. Obviously, the detectives thought he was just cracked out of his mind. I mean, wouldn't you if some junkie tells you that a 'bird man' gave you a murder weapon? But now... It seems like he might have seen what he thought he saw."

"Bird man," whispered Arroyo. A horrifying image of a man's body with the head of a crow manifested in her mind's eye.

Baze exhaled deeply as he transitioned. "It took me awhile to fully flesh out the theory in my head. But once I started to really delve into it, it all made sense. Welsh is the only one who ever actually saw David Kane or Robert Macabre, see."

Baze cleared his throat and began pacing back and forth. "This is how I see it. Welsh gets bulldozed by Lydia Cross, and it addles his brain. Rearranges everything, like scrambling an egg. He starts hearing a voice. A violent voice. His consciousness creates this sociopathic alter-ego for him to live out the fantasies that are infiltrating the damaged part of his brain. Before he knows it, Robert Macabre is taking control for long stretches of time. Well, during one of these episodes, Welsh, or rather, *Macabre* is driving around one night, and he gets pulled over by Kane. Kane gets clipped, and suddenly, Welsh has visions of the first person that he ever killed. Eventually, he hears Kane's voice too…

"See, I think the persona called David Kane is his conscience. If Robert Macabre is evil personified, then Kane is the yin to Macabre's yang. His conscience manifests itself into his very first victim, begging Welsh to stop killing. Kane is the good, Macabre is the bad, and Welsh is… Welsh."

Arroyo shook her head so rapidly that it seemed more like a twitch. "How could this be possible? How could Welsh maintain his position without anyone catching on to his mental condition?"

"But people *did* catch on, I am sure of it. If you were to interview those who knew Welsh over the years, I am guessing all of 'em would have some story about him. None of it would be all that extreme. Just little tidbits here and there about a time when Welsh acted a little crazy or demonstrated strange behavior. And it's the drugs, too. They act like a shock absorbent. With the psychotherapy and the pills, he was able to suppress most signs of his mental state to the point where when he was acting strange, those around him just thought of it as him being eccentric or something."

"But how is that *possible*?"

"There are many known cases of those who suffer from DID being able to mostly hide their condition. Hell, for a long time, DID wasn't even recognized as a mental illness."

Arroyo narrowed her eyes. "So what, all of Welsh's sightings of Kane and Macabre were hallucinations?"

"I believe so, yes. Most people who have DID and schizophrenia experience auditory and visual hallucinations."

Arroyo mulled this over for a bit. She placed her head in her hands, as if her arms could somehow carry some of the weight of intense thinking.

"So in this scenario… Welsh blacks out when Macabre takes over? And then doesn't remember anything that he's done when he comes to as himself again?"

"Something like that… I don't know exactly. What I do know is, no one has ever seen these two men besides Welsh. And the letters and messages from Macabre now make a lot more sense in this context than they do, as if they were coming from someone that Welsh had sinned against in his past. It's an internal struggle between the two personas. Hence the deep-seated hatred that was conveyed in those letters. Macabre wants to be the dominant personality and kill Welsh. Metaphorically, at least."

"Jesus," hissed Arroyo again. "So what, he stabbed himself in the leg then?"

"Yeah. Imagine what that scene would have looked like if there was an actual eyewitness. Welsh struggling with an invisible foe and then jabbing a knife into his own hamstring. It would be funny if it weren't so nuts."

"He stabbed *himself* in the leg," repeated Arroyo.

"Yep. And killed his own wife. Like I said, he's crazy, Red."

"It can't be possible… It *can't*."

"It can, and it is. This is our distorted reality, Lieutenant."

Arroyo rocked back-and-forth one time, and then she began pressing her index fingers to each temple, rubbing in a circular motion. It was like the big reveal had been too much for her mind to take in, causing her headache to get exponentially worse by the second.

"So... How does Will Tennyson fit in to all of this?"

Baze gave her a shrug. "He killed the cops, but not those girls. Welsh set him up."

"How did Welsh...?"

"The theory I explained to you during our first meeting. Tennyson was Welsh's supplier. It is where he got the drugs to make the fear serum that he injected into the girls. On the night that the hand was left on Welsh's porch, Welsh had arranged to meet Tennyson somewhere nearby, hence why Tennyson's car was at the gas station. Tennyson delivered the LSD in a box, and then Welsh used the box to house said hand, so that Tennyson's prints would be on it. Bingo, bango, bongo."

"So... whose hand was it in the box?"

"No idea," Baze admitted. "An unidentified male that Welsh killed. Sort of confirms that there are more victims out there that we don't know about."

Arroyo let her gaze fall toward the ground and allowed this idea to consume her for a while. Fear and disgust boiled in her stomach, and the headache now had a vice-like grip around her scalp. How many were there? How many people were buried in shallow graves somewhere out in the Oregon wilderness? After a few more seconds of brooding, she looked back up at Baze, possessed by a new question.

"How did Welsh figure that when we went to arrest Tennyson it would end with Tennyson dead? How did he know that we wouldn't capture him and eventually figure out that Tennyson wasn't our guy?"

"I can pretty much guarantee that Welsh had been to Tennyson's cabin before. He knew that the guy was armed to the teeth. And remember how you found the remains of the infrared sensors and cameras buried inside the cabin? Welsh must have known that Tennyson had a plan should any unfriendly people find their way onto his property, you know? And even if you did catch him, when does innocence ever trump physical evidence that points toward guilt?"

Suddenly, Arroyo felt a heat rising in her chest. An anger like she had never felt before made her entire body quake. It was a dark cloud of loathing that expanded inside of her, and she felt her nostrils flare and her cheeks flush with red.

"He set us up. He knew what Tennyson was going to do. He set us up. Oh my God, *Ray*."

She slammed her clenched fist onto the table,

and Baze jumped.

"*I'm gonna kill him!*" she screeched. "That motherfucker! Ray died because of *him*!"

Baze took a couple of steps back and held his hands out in a gesture that told her to take it down a notch.

"Red, it's okay. We are going to get him. Tonight, we are going to get him."

Arroyo was shaken out of her fit of fury by this sentence. She looked up at Baze with a blank expression on her face.

"Tonight? What do you mean, tonight?"

"I know where he is, Red. It's the same place he takes his victims. You've been there before."

A platoon of goose bumps came to attention on her arms, and chills tickled her spine.

Baze continued quietly. "Where do you think he would take them? Where do you think he would keep them bound while he tortured them? Where do you think he killed them?"

The answer to Baze's prompt was quickly on the tip of her tongue, almost as if it had always been there.

"Wilsonville. The house in Wilsonville," she whispered.

Baze nodded. "I think he has a basement, or some storage shed behind the house. Robert Macabre's own personal killing shed."

"Jesus," she murmured for what felt like the

hundredth time.

"We have to go there. We have to stop him. *Tonight*."

Arroyo dipped her head twice, and then her nods slowly got more forceful with every passing second. "Tonight," she repeated, as if it were a foreign concept.

Arroyo began running her fingers through her hair, trying to concoct a cohesive strategy on the fly. Her mind was racing a mile a minute, and it was difficult to focus. She found that her palms were profusely sweating, and she wiped them absentmindedly on her jeans. Finally, the stampede of thoughts charging through the synapses in her brain streamlined into a plan.

"All right... All right. First, I will wake up Judge Milton and get a warrant. These medical records are enough probable cause. After we get the warrant, I'll get everybody in on this—SWAT, uniforms, detectives... Everybody. Me and the cops will surround the house from a distance while the SWAT go in on foot. Have a team hit the front and one come in the back. We'll come in with M84s to stun him, and hopefully we can take him alive."

Baze nodded eagerly, looking enthralled with what was going down. "Sounds like my kind of party."

Arroyo paused, looking at Baze skeptically.

"Who says you are invited?"

"I mean—"

"You are a consultant, Baze. You don't do field work. And you sure as hell aren't trained in combat."

"Not many lieutenants work the field either, Red."

Arroyo practically bared her teeth at him. "This is *my* case. I get to finish it."

Baze didn't respond to this, but the muscles of his face seemed to twitch as if he was warding off a smile.

"Don't even think about it," warned Arroyo. "Don't even go there."

Baze put his hands up in a mock-defensive gesture. "Hey, I never said I wanted to be part of this. I wouldn't know what the hell to do with myself anyway."

"Go to the station. You can listen in there. I can communicate with you if I need to."

Baze didn't say anything.

"I know you will never go back home. Not right now. And since you are the one who brought me this, it wouldn't be fair to ask you to. But *please.* Don't go out there, Baze. Go to the station."

There was a strange gleam in the man's eye when he responded.

"You got it, Red."

Once Baze had gone, Arroyo began making phone calls. She started with Judge Milton, who groggily agreed to issuing a warrant after she explained what they had discovered. Arroyo then called all the detectives on her investigative team: Lowry, Giuliani, and Fairfield. All of them were sleeping, and initially seemed fairly disgruntled to field a phone call in the middle of the night, but when she had told them that there had been a major break in the case, their tones changed. It looked like something had finally broken their way, and the eagerness was palpable. Lowry in particular seemed like he had been waiting for that phone call for his entire career.

Arroyo then moved onto the SWAT. She rang Rafe Evan's, the SWAT commander, and gave him the coordinates of the place in Wilsonville. Evans barely spoke during the conversation, and she knew that it was because he was already mentally planning the tactical portion of the operation. Next, Arroyo phoned Mike McGrath, the current chief of police, who had just been promoted to the position by the mayor three months before. Since he was new to his position and Arroyo was already familiar with Macabre, he had been almost completely hands off during the entire investigation. However, the excitement in his voice when she told him the news was obvious.

Finally, Arroyo called the phone that had once belonged to Ray McCabe. It was a land line that had been disconnected for fifteen years, but the voicemail still accepted messages. On several previous occasions, she had called the number, yearning for some connection to her old partner. Arroyo didn't normally consider herself much of a spiritual person, and logically, she knew she was doing it for her own emotional benefit, but part of her wanted to believe that she was somehow cultivating something more. She kept the voicemail short and sweet.

"We are going to get him, Ray. This is ending tonight. I am sorry it took so long."

After ending the call, Arroyo tossed her cell phone temporarily onto her bed, feeling hot tears swell in her eyes. She slid her rain jacket over her shoulders, pushing away the sentiment. There would be a time for sorrow, and even a time to celebrate, but it was not now. While smoothing out the wrinkles in her jacket, she strode over to her dresser, reaching for the lanyard that her keys were attached to, and snatching them up into her hand.

In a flash, Welsh's face flickered in her mind's eye, and she felt deeply disturbed. All this time, the answer to all of the conundrums and riddles was right in front of her. How had she missed it? It seemed obvious now. Every piece of the puzzle that Baze had assembled made complete sense, to the point that she felt idiotic for not seeing it herself.

While she was busy consuming herself in self-loathing, a jolting noise nearby almost made her jump two feet into the air.

Clunk-clunk-clunk.

Somebody was knocking on the front door. After a half a second of confusion, she let out an irritated groan.

"God damn it, Baze," she muttered aloud. Apparently, the man had decided he could not wait idly by at the station. Either that or he had forgotten something inside. Arroyo snatched the cell phone off of her mattress and opened her messages, sending Baze a quick text.

Just come back inside. It's still unlocked.

Arroyo slid her phone into her jeans, waiting for it to vibrate. She expected to hear the sound of her front door creaking open, but instead, she heard three more knocks.

Clunk-clunk-clunk.

"Jesus!" She stomped out of her living room with haste, irritated as hell. *Look at your damn phone,* she thought, and clomped through her living room, rounding the wall into the foyer. With much more force than what was necessary, she swung the front door open.

"You broke in the first time when I wasn't even here and *now* you insist on knock—"

Her words were stolen right out of her mouth. The cold muzzle of the pistol against her forehead almost made her heart stop. Standing two feet in front of her was a hulking figure wearing all black, holding a gun firmly against her flesh. His face was concealed by a demonic black mask with haunting yellow eyes, and when he spoke, his voice was dripping with a thick southern drawl.

"Evenin', pretty lady. Mind hitchin' a ride with me?"

The car chugged along at a glacial pace, ten miles below the speed limit, the tinted windows preventing any passersby from seeing the happenings inside. Arroyo's hands were on the steering wheel so tightly that her fingers had lost all of their color and most of their feeling. The only sensation she was in tune to was the sharp pain of the metal being pressed underneath her armpit, ready to explode and shatter her ribcage and internal organs. She couldn't help but see the logic in the man's action; holding the gun to her head would guarantee instant death if something went wrong, but if any bystanders looked through the windshield and saw the silhouette of a large figure in the passenger seat pressing a gun to the driver's skull, it was game over for him. This way was much subtler.

Arroyo was so focused on the gun that the feeling of the handcuffs clasping her wrists to the steering wheel almost went unnoticed. Welsh had ratcheted two pairs of cuffs tightly to the wheel and then snapped the other ends of the cuffs onto each of her forearms. She had enough slack that she was able to turn the wheel if needed, but she was still strapped firmly in place.

"You don't have to do this, Carson."

Welsh tilted his head to the side and gave her a funny glance. He had taken off the demonic mask as soon as they were in the car, apparently to avoid suspicion on the off chance that a pedestrian was to catch a glance through the windshield. Arroyo also assumed that he was no longer worried about concealing his identity to her now, for shortly, her voice would be forever silenced.

"If you are going to attempt to beseech my emotional sensibilities with that tone, at least come up with something original. They all say the same thing."

His voice reminded Arroyo of a rich southern oligarch from the 1800s. Not full-blown backwoods Alabama redneck, but still with a heavy drawl. It was doused with a sort of contrived class, but filled with menace as he over-enunciated his surprisingly eloquent response.

"Who?"

"You know who," Welsh replied calmly.

After a few seconds of dead silence, Arroyo cautiously moved the conversation forward.

"What do they say? The people you kill?"

"They say, 'You don't have to do this.' Tell me, out of all the shrewd ways you have of talkin' me out of my compulsions, why try and appeal to my empathetic side? It's the hallmark of a sociopath to be devoid of compassion. You know that."

The twang in his voice was laid on so thick and convincingly that Arroyo wondered how long he had practiced perfecting the voice.

"Carson... Please." Arroyo couldn't think of anything else to say.

"Stop callin' me that. It's off-puttin'."

"It's who you are."

"Carson Welsh is dead."

"This isn't your fault, Carson. I know what happened. I know about the accident. You wouldn't be doing this if not for that."

Welsh let out a strange, almost feminine laugh. It was high-pitched and staccato and lasted far longer than a normal chuckle.

"Is this where you try and get me to see the error of my ways, Emily? You think I am going to stop this car? Let you go, unscathed and unencumbered by this encounter? If you thought this had a happy endin', then maybe you aren't as cunning as I thought you were. And I ain't much for negotiatin'."

She had no retort for this. It was difficult to speak in general; her breathing came in short, rapid intervals, coinciding with her frenetic heartbeat.

"Carson Welsh *is* dead, Emily. I killed him."

"No," whispered Arroyo. "No, you didn't."

"I killed him. I killed *them*."

"Them?"

"I killed them all," said Welsh.

"All of those girls," said Arroyo softly, her voice filled with horror and sadness.

"All of those beautiful women."

Arroyo felt a prickle of anger beneath her chest. "Proud of yourself, huh?"

Welsh stopped and contemplated this. As he did so, Arroyo's eyes flickered onto the street lamps above them brightening the sidewalk. She prayed that nobody would be walking by. If they were to pass a bystander, she didn't think she would be able to suppress the urge to scream for help. And if she did, a bullet would tear through all of her internal organs. Thankfully, there was not a soul in sight.

"Proud? Of what? My work? Is the ocean proud of makin' waves? I'm a killer. It's what I do. Plain and simple."

"Plain and simple," repeated Arroyo, disgust thick in her voice.

"Just like you," he whispered.

Her mouth dropped open. "Like me?"

"Like you. Like your colleagues. Like the politicians, like their constituents. Hell, like the guy that counted the till at that liquor store this evenin'," said Welsh, nodding at a building that they passed that had the words Liquor Outlet emblazoned in red on top of it. "We are all killers, Emily."

The lighting from the street lamps casted patches of dark yellow haze in increments along the street. Every time they would pass underneath the lights Welsh's face would briefly illuminate before being cast back into shadow, and it seemed like each time she saw his face the menace in his expression would slightly increase.

"How do you figure?" asked Arroyo.

Welsh let out a low whistle and cocked his head to the side. "Well, take you for example. Remember that creep you arrested all those years ago? Wyatt Shaw? You were the one who got him, remember? Your first big break as detective. Probably a big reason why you eventually made lieutenant. You were the one who started the chain of events that put him on death row. Because of you, he got the needle."

Arroyo felt her stomach roll in repugnance. "He murdered a seven-year-old ki—"

"That's right. And then you and your band of merry policemen murdered him. Killin' is still killin', no matter which way you try to frame it."

"There is a big difference—"

Welsh pressed the gun harder against Arroyo's ribcage, causing her to let out a groan of pain. "No, Emily. There is *no* difference. Think of all the times you drowned a spider in the shower. Think of when you were a child, steppin' on ants on the sidewalk. Even when it's not so blunt, every choice we make gives life... And also takes it. You drive to work instead of walkin' or ridin' a bike. Some kid in the inner city inhales too many fumes and gets lung cancer. You vote for a mayor who rolls back gun laws in the city, and a couple of thugs in the ghetto get shot. You get sick and still come to work, and the virus spreads until it touches someone whose immune system is *compromised*. Every choice you make is done with your own interests in mind and elicits a butterfly effect that ends with someone else sufferin'. Even advancement in your career. You promote and climb the ladder on the backs of those poor saps who weren't preordained for your position. Your rise causes someone else to fall. Those at the top are fueled by the blood of those at the bottom. We are all just playin' one big game of king of the mountain. Some of us are just more straightforward about it than others."

Arroyo scoffed. "Well, aren't you just the fucking philosopher."

"Language, miss," said Welsh, and jabbed her again with the muzzle of the gun, causing a spurt of pain to shoot through her diaphragm. She let out a hiss.

"Don't try and spin what you do, and why you do it. You're a sadist."

"I am. But that doesn't mean I'm not right. You see, we all want to assert our dominance. I just revel in it a little more than other people." Welsh's face contorted into a leer.

"You are a sexual sadist. You get off on causing pain."

Welsh smiled. A horrible, full-mouthed grin. "We all like what we are good at. Or maybe we are just good at what we like. Take this exit."

Arroyo looked up at the green sign that had an arrow pointing south. It had the Interstate-5 symbol on it and said Salem. She slowly pulled the wheel to the right, dipping the car off of the highway and onto the exit, increasing her speed as she did so.

"We are going to the house in Wilsonville, aren't we?"

Again, Welsh let out that feminine, bizarre chuckle. "You are an astute little lady, aren't you? Not too fast now. Start speedin' and my finger may accidentally brush this trigger and paint my car with all of your insides."

Arroyo gently pressed her foot on the brake, swallowing and trying to suppress some of her fear, but it was next to impossible to do so, knowing the horrors that waited for her out at the house in Wilsonville.

"I debated tyin' you up and puttin' you in the back there, like I did with Dinwoodie. But she made one heck of a racket. Almost made me pull over the car a couple of times. Plus, if I had put you in the back, we wouldn't have been able to have such stimulatin' discourse, would we?"

Arroyo kept the vehicle at forty when she got onto the freeway, hoping beyond hope that the slow pace would give some highway patrolman pause. Apparently, Welsh had this same thought.

"You can go just a *little* faster now, Em. Don't want any deputies to notice our little foray to my, um, *lair*."

She had to think. Had to come up with something. Arroyo would be damned if she let him get her to his target destination without a fight. She couldn't see a logical way of escape. But she sure as shit would make Welsh go down with her if she was going to die anyway. And a violent death on the freeway was far superior than days of torture and rape. Perhaps she would intentionally cause a wreck, but could she do so before he caught on and pulled the trigger? She had to keep him talking while she concocted some sort of strategy.

"A deputy like Calvin Kane?" she asked slowly, while pushing the car to fifty-five.

Welsh let out another one of those effeminate, haunting giggles.

"So you've met David, eh? Real gentleman, ain't he?"

"He doesn't exist, Carson. He is in your head. Just like Robert Macabre."

Welsh punched the gun deep into her side, and she let out a grunt of pain. For a fleeting moment, her lungs had been robbed of air as her body fought the pain.

"I *am* Robert Macabre! I am everything that I am supposed to be. And you? This is your predetermined fate. Do you even *see* the futility of all of this? Do you realize it now? Everything in your life was pointing toward this moment. You. Here. In this car. With me. How does that make you feel? Would you have changed the way you lived your life if you knew the whole time that on this day in two thousand nineteen, it would end like this?"

She did not reply to this. There seemed to be no words that existed that could form an appropriate response. For several prolonged seconds, complete silence filled Arroyo's ears. She couldn't help but contemplate what he had just said. The thought was so depressing that her mind could barely handle it. He was right. It had all been in vain. Utterly futile. Her legacy would be defined by what was about to happen to her, and the evil that she had eventually conceded to.

Almost as if to ward away this brooding thought, she blurted out the next thing that came into her head.

"Why the animal masks?"

At this, Welsh let out the longest cackle yet. He

doubled over, overcome with mirth, all the while keeping the gun trained on Arroyo's midsection. For whatever reason, Welsh found this question deeply amusing, and his guffaws were almost like that of a child's. When he finally regained control, the explanation he gave was nebulous and strange.

"The disguise does not hide that which is within."

"That doesn't... I don't understand," muttered Arroyo.

"All you have to understand is that that the devil can wear many faces."

Arroyo let this proclamation hang in the air. She could think of nothing that could logically follow this statement. Welsh's ramblings were suddenly deteriorating into something strange and somewhat incoherent. Insanity was like that—It often masqueraded as intelligence for a while before devolving into complete nonsense at the drop of a hat.

When the man spoke next, his voice was a whisper. "I can't wait for you to be on my table. Can you imagine how it is going to feel to have my knives cut through your skin like hot butter? To have your tongue tickled with a switchblade? The tips of your fingers sliced off? Blood drippin' down the insides of your thighs?"

The tears leaked down Arroyo's cheeks, and her lips were suddenly quivering. It was like the reality of her situation had just hit her. She had never been afraid of this man until this very moment. And a paralyzing terror had taken hold. Her fear was a cold fist gripping her heart.

"Don't cry, miss. That ain't reason for tears. Can I tell you a story? I got a great one for you. Might make you feel better."

Welsh grinned like the Cheshire cat, and his eyes gleamed with malice. "I met a woman some time ago on the street, right? 'Bout five foot nine, long blond hair. And green eyes. Bright green eyes. Oh, those eyes. And the smell of her hair."

Welsh inhaled through his nostrils as though he could still smell the woman at that very moment. "Well, Ms. Green Eyes was hookin' on the corner downtown when I found her. Introduced myself. Got to chattin'. Well, one thing led to another and there she was tied up on my table. But this time I brought some *friends*."

Arroyo shuddered, wishing that she no longer had ears.

"Three little rats. Stuck them on her gut and put a bowl to keep them in place. It took about three hours for the rats to get hungry, but when they got to that point they were *ravenous*. I still remember her screams as they nibbled away at her flesh. The little holes all over her tummy. So when you think about it, the knives really ain't that bad."

Anger tore through Arroyo's body like a virus.

As she imagined all of the poor women who had suffered the fate of being on Welsh's table, Arroyo wanted to punch every bit of him she could reach. She wanted to destroy him, like he had destroyed all of them. For an evanescent second, she imagined *him* tied to the table, and her standing above, wielding the scalpel. She loathed him with every fiber of her being.

"You won't get away from us, Welsh. My team knows who you are."

Another wild, high-pitched chortle. "If they knew who I was, would we be having this conversation?"

"The breakthrough just happened tonight. As clever as you think you are, we still figured you out."

"Then why did you have a press conference saying that Welsh had been abducted just a few hours ago?"

"You were part of the system, Welsh. You know how this works. A few hours is an eternity in an investigation, and you know it."

"Even if you are tellin' the truth, which you aren't, my identity is superfluous. None of your people will ever see me again."

"Screw that. Suicide is too good for you," hissed Arroyo.

"Suicide? You mistake me. Only a coward takes his own life."

"Where are you going to run to then, Welsh? There is no place on this earth that my people won't find you."

"Enough talkin'," said Welsh, and his voice was suddenly much louder than it had been. "I have heard enough of your voice to last me a lifetime. For the rest of this ride, every time you speak, that will be one more hour of the scalpel, ya hear?"

"I thought you found our conversation stimulating," spat Arroyo, ignoring his threats.

"Sarcasm is a language lost on many. And that is one more hour, you filthy whore."

"Fuck you!"

Welsh jabbed her so hard with the muzzle of the gun that she was knocked off balance, and the car swerved a little. She moaned in agony, feeling like he had cracked a rib. The pain was overwhelming.

"You got spirit, I will give you that. But since you seemed fairly undeterred now by the scalpel, how about this? Every time you talk, that is one more of these."

He thrusted again, and she let out a cry as the metal crunched against her side. The tears were now flowing down her cheeks, but it was mostly from pain, not fear. It took her a while to subdue the desire to slam her foot on the brake and let Welsh pull the trigger; anything to get out of this hellhole. But she had to keep going. She had to figure out a way to end this.

After she had recovered from the blow and subdued her tears, the threat of immediate pain was enough to keep her quiet. And, while not speaking, it was easier for her brain to keep devising a plan. For ten excruciatingly long minutes she kept silent as Welsh watched her drive along Interstate-5. The road sloped downward and then went back up, and with a sense of panic, she realized they were getting close to the destination. Just as she came to this conclusion, Welsh broke the silence.

"This is our exit, little lady. We are almost there."

She had to make her move now. Had to do something. With a turn of the wheel in her hands, the car was banking sharply to the right. This particular exit was an overpass that went some twenty feet above the highway, before descending down into the small town of Wilsonville. The car curved, and then she pumped the brake as they hit the stoplight before the bridge. Frantic thoughts were skittering through her mind. When they got onto the overpass, should she try flipping the car off the bridge? Would that guarantee death for both of them? Almost as if he could read her thoughts, Welsh moved the gun away from her ribcage and then placed it firmly against the side of her neck.

"If you try anything, this bullet will sever your spinal column before you can say the word, *dead*."

Could the car even scale the side of the bridge? There would be a four-foot column of concrete on either side. Even if she floored it, the car would probably just ram into the barrier, and Welsh would fire. What could she do?

Before she could formulate another thought in her head, the light turned green.

"Easy now," whispered Welsh.

Arroyo turned the wheel slowly and edged the gas pedal down. Two seconds later, they were on the overpass. She looked to her left and all the headlights of the traffic below, passing underneath like an army of ants carrying flashlights. The barriers on either side were even bigger than she imagined. There would be no way to flip the car onto the freeway. They were almost there. What on earth should she do?

The answer to her question was provided by a sudden blur of movement in front of her. A white impala rushed onto the opposite end of the bridge, swerving wildly and then straightening toward them. Even if she didn't recognize the vehicle, the strange movement of the thing was somehow enough to communicate that it was coming to rescue her. But she *did* recognize the vehicle. She knew exactly who was behind the wheel.

"What the fu—"

For a moment, Arroyo thought the Impala was going to hit them head-on. Bewildered, she prayed that she was wrong. Why let three lives be lost, when there only needed to be two? But then, at the last second, it swerved to the right until it was horizontal across both lanes of traffic before coming to a screeching halt. If Arroyo had had time to process what had happened, she might have tried to avoid the collision. But she didn't, and a half second later, the sound of metal compacting rang through the night like an explosion, and Arroyo and Welsh were thrown forward. Her head slammed against the steering wheel and bounced back, before crumpling down to her chest. There was one more moment of consciousness before the darkness came flooding in.

Pain. So much pain.

Robert's body ached. The agony was everywhere, but concentrated in his head, after having slammed his skull against the dashboard. He stayed slumped forward for a few seconds, trying to suppress the feeling. But it was too much. It made him nauseous. He took a deep breath, wondering if he might vomit. Then, with his pulse beginning to increase, he remembered what had happened. The white sedan deliberately blocking their progress. The direness of the situation acted like a shot of morphine, and he sat up, gun still in hand. Robert shot a glance over at the Lieutenant, and she was slack against the steering wheel, her red hair coating her face. Unconscious? Or worse? Robert quickly pressed his index and middle fingers against her neck, and with relief, felt the pulse. Still alive. That was good.

With a click, he unfastened his seat belt, and began to rustle around, making sure that the crucial parts of his body were still intact. Everything seemed to be in working order, so he pressed against the handle of the door, and with an enormous effort against the pain, he lifted his leg and stepped outside.

The white Impala had taken the brunt of the damage. It was completely compacted in the middle; if there had been a passenger in the back seat, that person would be seriously injured. But as Robert walked toward the destroyed vehicle with the gun pointing forward, he saw that the only person was in the driver's seat. A gruff looking man with a mustache was collapsed against the steering wheel, unmoving and definitely unconscious. Who was it? One of Arroyo's associates? How had he known where they would be? Had he followed them from the house? Anxiety began to rise in his chest, which quickly morphed into flat dread. This was not good. Arroyo hadn't been lying after all. They had somehow been onto him. He had to get out of here.

Run. He had to run. But first, he had to clean up his mess.

Robert walked toward the side of the Impala until he was a foot away from the passenger side window. He saw the mustached man lying forward and noticed a snake-shaped scar slithering up the man's cheek. It was strange and absorbing, and Robert couldn't help but stare at it as he raised the gun and pointed it at the man's head.

A loud, blaring sound made his heart jump in his chest, and he whirled about, pointing the gun wildly at the commotion. It was the sound of a car horn. His own. But there was no movement. Arroyo's head must have slid down and pressed against the middle of the steering wheel. The noise was so amplified and jarring that in the blink of an eye, Robert realized that it was likely to wake his unconscious prisoner.

Frantically, Robert tucked the gun into the waistband of his jeans before hustling back to his own vehicle. He went around back, passing the trunk that had once held Tracy Dinwoodie, all the while fighting the temptation to cover his ears as the horn continued to shriek. Eventually, he staggered to the driver's side front door, and wrenched the door open. Arroyo was still slumped there, now farther down, her forehead pressing against the middle of the wheel. Robert shoved her roughly to the side, and the noise stopped. He exhaled in relief.

After a couple of beats of regaining control over his breath, Robert reached down and fumbled in his pocket for the keys to the handcuffs. He would have to move her back to the trunk and take her into the woods. He would shoot her there, dump the body and run. Not the way he wanted it, but this was no longer about his work. This was about survival.

While groping for the cuffs, he noticed that the woman began to stir. His heart leaped into his chest, and for a frenzied moment, he wanted to shoot her right where she was. Robert took a deep breath, trying to remain calm as he worked to remove the cuffs. Almost there. Almost off.

Just then, Robert felt the world quiver, and he was thrown forward, landing on top of Arroyo. There was an unmistakable scraping sound, like nails on a giant chalk board, and the car wiggled wildly. With his heart feeling like it was imploding, he pushed himself off of the lieutenant, staggering backward onto the street. His head snapped around, and he saw with horror that the Impala was now free of his vehicle, the front facing him. It began to quickly move in reverse, retreating ten feet before Robert could overcome his shock and react.

"No!"

He shoved the key to the cuffs into his front pocket, and then charged, pulling the gun out of his pants. The adrenaline gushing through him was temporarily masking the ache in his body. He aimed the gun at the windshield of the Impala, firing two quick shots. The vehicle stopped, and Robert thought for a second that he had hit the driver. But then it moved forward. Right toward him.

Bang. Bang-bang-bang-bang.

Robert continued to volley shots at the driver, shattering the windshield in the process. But there was no one visible in the spot behind the wheel. The mustached-man was ducking down, avoiding the bullets. Robert had to aim lower to make contact. The car was only feet away.

Bang. Bang.

The first shot hit the hood of the car with a plunk. The second made its mark. Robert saw the body of the man flop back against the seat, a red cloud spurting against the windshield. The man then came forward against the steering wheel, before sliding to the left. The Impala spun, its back end hurtling toward Robert. He backtracked, fully aware now that the driver had lost control. It was at that moment that he realized that it was too late.

The car was going to hit him.

Robert frantically leaped backward against the barrier, flailing his arms above his head. With a sickening chomp, the Impala slammed against the bottom of his legs, pinning him in place. Like a feral animal, Robert let out a bizarre, warped screech. It was a terrible, wretched noise; one that he had only ever heard from the women that had been on his table. The cold bit at the back of his throat as he yelled, his body now limp over the side of the bridge. His screams only stopped when he needed air, and after he had inhaled more oxygen, he bellowed some more. The pain would surely kill him. Both of his legs were broken.

Blood rushed to Robert's head as he dangled there. He let his head recline fully back, and he saw the highway below. Two cars darted along I-5, apparently oblivious to the serial killer flailing some twenty feet above them.

Once Robert was able to temporarily stifle his screams, he craned his neck and torso up, looking at his predicament. He had to wriggle his way free. Slide out of the crushing power of the Impala. Even if his broken legs wouldn't carry him, he could at least try to crawl. Anything to get away. Robert writhed, and as he did so, a fresh wave of agony rocked him.

"Argh!"

There would be no escape. He would be trapped here until the fire department came to dislodge him from the barrier.

Robert Macabre was stuck.

The sound of wild screaming made her stir.

Arroyo groggily wiped at her face, with sweat percolating above her eyelids. Utter confusion dominated her senses. Where was she? What the hell had happened?

With a start, everything came rushing back. The black, demonic mask with the yellow eyes. Riding in the car, the gun jammed against her ribs. Welsh's horrible threats. The scalpel glinting in her imagination.

The white Impala blocking their progress.

Arroyo jerked backward. Oxygen rushed into her lungs, and it was almost too much air for her body to process at one time. She looked to her right, just then noticing that Welsh was no longer there. She peered out the windshield, assessing the situation. The back end of Baze's Impala was crumpled against the left side of the bridge, and a man with a thick torso was pinned against the barrier by the Impala, with half of his body over the side of the overpass. The man was gyrating wildly, apparently trying to wiggle out of his predicament.

Welsh.

Arroyo looked in the driver's seat of the Impala and saw a huddled mass below the steering wheel. Even from the distance she was at, she could tell that Baze was either seriously injured, or worse. Her eyes flicked back toward Welsh, and she noticed that the gun was still in his hand. The man was going to go down shooting, that was for sure. There was no way to safely get out of the vehicle and approach him to try to make an arrest. She could leave the car and call for backup, but even when the cavalry arrived, was there any guarantee that Welsh wouldn't take one or two cops down with him? She had to remove all doubt from the equation. Arroyo was going to personally make sure that Carson Welsh was not going to hurt anyone else.

Looking to the left over the barrier, Arroyo saw several vehicles moving down the freeway. Some were slowing down, finally noticing the commotion above. Some continued full-speed ahead, including a gargantuan red semi-truck in the middle lane.

Now was the time to act.

She slammed her foot onto the gas pedal. With a lurch, the car darted forward. Arroyo's eyes were latched onto Welsh, waiting for him to react. His head turned toward her and he let out a wild cry of anguish. He did an awkward sit-up and raised the gun, aiming at her. The one shot he was able to fire flew wildly into the night sky, nowhere close to her person. She tightened her grip and braced for the impending wreck, ready to be thrown back into darkness.

Just before the cars made contact, Arroyo caught one last glimpse of Welsh's face. It was mostly pure loathing. An unadulterated, unfiltered hatred of the woman who had bested him. But also, there was an element of confusion in his expression. It was as if he couldn't understand how he had been outwitted. Like the realization that he was not invincible was utterly perplexing. Then, in the last millisecond before impact, Arroyo saw terror light up his eyes. With a tremendous *boom,* the car slammed into the Impala, pushing it forward, and Welsh was thrown like a rag doll over the barrier, tumbling toward the freeway below.

For the rest of her life, Arroyo would remember the sound of Welsh's frantic screams as he hurtled downward. She would always be able to recall the wild yells pinging around inside her ears, the last primal cries of a cornered predator. But most of all, she would never forget the sound of the red semi-truck blasting into Robert Macabre as he was still in the air, obliterating his body with a massive *crunch.*

72

The television screen continued to project rapid images, and in her state of mind, it was difficult to process what the voiceover was saying. The barbiturates and opiates in her system mixed together to create a strange, drowsy haze. It was like she was completely detached from her own body. Like she was watching herself watch the news. There was a buff man with a large forehead speaking in front of a line of yellow tape, followed by a flash of red and blue lights. Arroyo only caught a few words from the voice over; not nearly enough to string together in her head and form a coherent sentence. Among the phrases were "former district attorney," and "lieutenant," and "overpass."

Her room was small, but at the moment, everything felt large. The walls swam. She had no idea what time it was or how long she had been here, but Arroyo was vaguely aware of an unsettling feeling underneath her chest. Something was wrong.

There was movement out of the corner of her eye as a figure sauntered inside, but due to the fact that her body felt about as mobile as an overweight sloth, Arroyo let the person pass by without taking the time to try to register who it was. Two seconds later, an unnecessary amount of light flooded into the room from an overhead bulb, and Arroyo turned her head to the right like the illumination was an alien invader. She made a groggy sound and rubbed her cheek, trying to massage some feeling into her face. Suddenly, a plump face was hovering over her, looking concerned.

"You doin' all right, sweetie?"

The nurse reminded Arroyo of her grandma, with a wrinkled, sun-kissed complexion and kind blue eyes. Arroyo was vaguely aware of her situation, but her mind could not quite process the details yet. And she had to know more. Her voice was raspy and hoarse when she spoke.

"What hospital is this?"

"The Adventist Health Hospital."

"Adventish wha'?"

"Adventist Health Hospital. Correct. You have a small skull fracture and two fractured ribs. You have been here since three thirty-two a.m."

"What time is it now?"

"About seven a.m."

Arroyo looked to her left and then to her right,

as if by observing her surroundings she could verify the nurse's story.

"What is your name?"

"Carla, hunny. My name is Carla."

Arroyo nodded, like she had been expecting the woman's name to be Carla all along. The drugs were numbing her senses quite a bit, and even in that moment, she could feel herself drifting back off to sleep. But she fought it.

"What did you give me?"

"What's that, dear?"

"What drugs did you give me?"

The nurse swallowed thickly and looked uncomfortable. She straightened up, increasing the distance between herself and Arroyo before answering the question.

"Vicodin, and a small dose of lorazepam to calm your nervous system. Also, promethazine. You were... nauseous."

"Drugs combating the side-effects of drugs. That's iconic."

The nurse frowned. The mole just above her left eye came downward by a fraction, and Arroyo found herself strangely absorbed by it.

"Iconic? Did you mean ironic?"

"No... I meant ironic."

The nurse had a completely befuddled expression on her face, and Arroyo would have laughed if she had the energy.

"Why don't you get some sleep, hun?"

Arroyo wanted to stay awake and have all of her questions answered, but she couldn't fight the sensation of her head feeling like it was concrete, while her neck and shoulders were jelly. She let the back of her dome fall into the pillow, and decided that later, when she was more alert, the nurse would fill her in. Almost instantaneously, she fell asleep.

When she woke not long after, her brain was even more muddled by the different chemicals splashing around in her bloodstream. The nurse must have upped the dose. Arroyo couldn't string together a coherent thought, let alone a sentence. But that didn't seem to bother the two harsh-looking men that were now sitting in front of her, peppering her with questions. The men, in their dark blue rain coats and dress slacks, made her walk through everything that had happened, and it was halfway into this exercise that Arroyo realized that she had no idea if the details she was providing the men were actually accurate. The words, "Welsh," "Kidnapped," "Gun," and "Bridge," kept coming out in strange, staccato increments. It was like her mouth was moving of its own volition and spewing out everything that her mind had held on to. But the explanation that she gave seemed to suffice, because the men kept nodding and taking notes, and eventually, they left. It was only after she began to fall asleep again that she realized that the men had been federal agents.

Sometime later, her eyes fluttered open once more, and Arroyo found herself instantly more aware of her surroundings. She still felt confused, but this time, it was a standard confusion; not exacerbated by the drugs, and the episode with the feds felt like a dream. The Vicodin must have been wearing off. There was now a hard pain in her head and when she tried to move, hot fire stabbed at her side. She winced and noticed that it was very difficult to breathe. Her diaphragm was tense, and she knew that her muscles were hardening around her internal organs due to the crack in the outer shell that was her ribs. Like the muscles knew that they were the last line of defense now.

Arroyo noticed something dark in her peripheral vision and turned to the right to see what it was. Easton Lowry, in a black jacket and blue jeans, was looking at her with apprehensive eyes. The man was sitting in an uncomfortable-looking chair, and on the bedside table next to him, there was a bouquet of flowers in a vase. Arroyo's eyes narrowed at the sight.

"Do I look like the type of woman who likes flowers, Easton?"

Lowry shifted in his seat and gave her a broad smile.

"I figured it was customary. Besides, don't get excited, they were cheap. How you doin', LT?"

Arroyo groaned, like the question itself caused her physical pain.

"How do I look like I am doing, Lowry?"

"You look like you are alive. If I am being honest, that's all I care about."

Arroyo gave him a warm smile and then grimaced when the pain hit her again.

"I wish I could say the same."

"You will be all right with time. The human body can withstand a lot."

"I would prefer not to have to test those limits."

Lowry grinned, but did not reply. For a moment, he looked away, apparently contemplating the impending discussion. He looked like he was struggling with something he could not quite wrap his head around.

"Well… We got him, didn't we?"

Arroyo scoffed, then immediately regretted it due to the stabbing in her side that it brought.

"Yeah, no thanks to me."

Lowry's mouth opened in shock. "What the hell do you mean? You were the one who brought an end to this."

"Yeah, and if I had been a halfway-decent detective fifteen years ago, I could have saved all those lives before it got to this point. A decade and a half, and he was right in front of our eyes the whole time. How did I *miss it*?"

Lowry shook his head vigorously. "You

weren't the only one. All of us. Everybody missed it. I hate to say it, but he was one clever man. No DNA. No prints. Nobody even saw him near a crime scene. If you want to beat yourself up over the fact that we weren't able to catch him sooner, I can't stop you, but one, it is a waste of imagination to concoct all of the ways you could have solved your problems sooner than you did, and two, it won't change anything. Yeah, you could have saved all those lives if we had caught him sooner, but imagine how many you saved by catching him now."

For a while, they just looked at each other, and Arroyo felt something gnawing at her. But she wasn't sure what. It didn't pertain to the current conversation. It was the same thing that had been bugging her during the exchange with the nurse, but she didn't know what it was.

"I just don't understand how we could be so short-sighted," Arroyo finally retorted, trying to push aside the unexplained anxiety. "He was the only one who ever *saw* Macabre, or Kane. And those letters… How was suspicion never cast in his direction? How come nobody ever even asked the *question?*"

Lowry didn't respond right away. He looked up at the ceiling, as if a higher power could somehow manifest an appropriate rebuttal in the air in front of him. Then, his eyes flickered back toward her and they were suddenly cloudy, like his thoughts were far away and vague.

"Because it's ludicrous. Even now, it is hard for me to contemplate the fact that Carson Welsh... *The* Carson Welsh... Esteemed district attorney and heartbroken widow, was a vicious, violent sociopath."

"Yes. It is still hard for me to wrap my head around too," said Arroyo. "Then again, if you would have seen the way he spoke while he was... *in character.* He had this crazy southern accent. And this look of just wild, uncontrollable intent. If you had seen it, you would have known he was nuts." Arroyo exhaled, trying to push her traumatic recollections away. "Also, remember the golden rule, Lowry. The husband always did it. Always."

"I don't know much about that. I was only fourteen when his wife was killed."

Arroyo rolled her eyes. "Jesus, that makes me feel old."

"Think of it this way. You settled the score by ramming him off that bridge. You brought justice for Ray and all the others."

Arroyo felt her face harden, and her heart sink. She stared daggers at Lowry, and the man leaned back a little.

"Carson Welsh didn't kill Ray McCabe."

"Not directly, no... But he was responsible. If it weren't for him—"

"*Don't.*"

Arroyo's voice was harsh, and Lowry recoiled. She felt her eyes get hot and was acutely aware of the tears that were now swelling in them. Fifteen years had passed, and she still could not completely cope with the pain of losing her partner. Every time she dwelled on it, she pictured his head being ripped open by that bullet, and it was like a giant invisible hand was tearing the scab off of her heart so that the wound could bleed some more. They said time healed all wounds. But some wounds would never heal, no matter the hours, days, or years since the moment had passed. For some wounds, there was a before, and an after. For Arroyo, that was McCabe's death.

For a long time, there was dead-silence in the hospital room. Lowry looked extremely uncomfortable, and he shuffled around a bit in his chair.

"So… A big rig, huh?"

Arroyo didn't process the question.

"What?"

"A semi-truck took him out. Crazy shit."

"Oh. Yeah. A big red one."

"Was that your intention?"

Arroyo blinked.

"Was what my intention?"

"To knock him off of the overpass so that he could be belted by the semi?"

Arroyo narrowed her eyes. "What do you get out of the answer to that question?"

"My curiosity satiated. Don't worry, LT. No one is going to turn on you. When the investigation happens, they will see that he had a gun, and he was firing it. You did what you had to."

"Well, let's just say I was not *unaware* of said semi." Arroyo rustled about in her bed, and instantly regretted it. It felt like her side might split in two at any moment.

"What a way to go out," mused Lowry, oblivious to the lieutenant's discomfort.

"I will never forget the sound it made," said Arroyo through gritted teeth, trying to mask her pain. "Not for the rest of my life."

For an evanescent moment, she pictured Welsh's body exploding in a red cloud, his guts flying through the air like tossed meat. She hadn't actually seen the impact. She had just heard it. That *crunch*, followed by a penetrating silence. That had only lasted a moment before the screams from below, of the people who had seen the carnage. Then, with one final glance at the busted Impala in front of her, Arroyo had passed out.

The Impala...

Suddenly, the feeling of dread that had been lingering in her gut made perfect sense. Everything came rushing back in a flood of traumatic memories that burst the dam of her consciousness. That was what had been bothering her. That was what had been lingering under the surface, poking and prodding at her mind like an unfriendly visitor.

"Oh my God. Oh my God, Baze. *Baze.* I just remembered! What happened to him? Is he alive?"

The grave expression that came over Lowry's face made Arroyo's heart sink.

The room was dark. The sunlight was impeded by the dense blinds that covered the window, and inside, all was still. A cloud of quiet hung over the room, nearly impenetrable apart from the birds occasionally chirping outside. The place stunk of sweat and musk, like rotten fruit, and the smell was concentrated entirely around the man lying there on the bed.

Arroyo found herself feeling hollow, and she wondered where the feeling was coming from. She had just stopped one of the most iniquitous, depraved serial killers that had ever lived. And yet, there was no joy or triumph. Mostly, there was just a sense of loss. Like the fact that the case had finally come to a close had allowed the reality to sink in. All of the lives that had been taken flashed in her memory like someone turning through a flipbook, and with each face that appeared in her mind's eye, she felt herself becoming melancholier.

Perhaps it was also the loss of purpose that afflicted her. The end of the case also brought the end of the most important pursuit of her career. Catching Robert Macabre had defined her life. She hadn't felt this way when they had reached their initial conclusion of the investigation in 2004. Perhaps, because deep down, she had somehow known that Bob the Butcher was still out there, lingering in the periphery. But now that they had finally destroyed the perpetrator of the heinous crimes, it was like her purpose had also been destroyed with it.

Probably though, the feeling was coming from the fact that her body lacked decent sleep and solid food. Being immobile in a hospital wasn't exactly conducive to a happy lifestyle. Maybe she would feel better once the pain in her side and head abated. Or when she finally heard the voice of the man in front of her.

Arroyo watched the man with apprehension. His chest rose and fell, and she found herself inhaling and exhaling in rhythm with his expanding and contracting diaphragm. It was almost a form of meditation, and with each passing second, she found herself more relaxed. Arroyo pushed the wheels of her wheelchair forward to bring herself closer to him, and she began to subconsciously hope for him to wake. She wanted to speak with him, more than she had wanted to speak to anyone in her entire life.

Almost as if her thoughts had stirred the man, he began to rustle around in his bed, and his eyelids slowly peeled apart. It took him a minute to register her face, but when he did, Baze's face broke into a wide smile.

"Well, fancy seeing you here." His voice was raspy and sounded like it was coming from the very back of his throat.

For a moment, Arroyo again envisioned the bridge. It had only been roughly forty-eight hours since the event, and yet, it felt like it had happened a lifetime ago. The gun pushed forcefully against her side. All faith in the world extinguished, like a thousand candles being blown by a powerful gust of wind. She would never forget how it felt knowing to a certainty that your life was over. Realizing that the only thing left for you was pain and torture. And then, in the last moment when every last drop of hope had been sucked away, there had been the wild movement of the Impala onto the overpass. Her savior, riding in on a white steed. Her chest had had a fleeting moment to balloon with triumph before the impact of the accident had thrown her into darkness. But somehow, she had known as soon as she had seen the vehicle swerve onto the road that she was going to live.

"They say it is a miracle that you survived surgery," whispered Arroyo. "The bullet was inches away from your spinal cord."

"I have a habit of beating the odds, Red. You should know that by now."

Arroyo instantly felt her lips quiver and her chest clench. Before she could stop it, the tears flooded down her cheeks, and her entire body convulsed in one giant sob. Baze's smile faded.

"You never struck me as much of a crier, Red."

His voice contained no trace of the emotion that had possessed her, but his face conveyed something else.

"You... You saved my life, Anton."

For some reason, vocalizing this thought made the crying even worse, and Arroyo found herself suddenly embarrassed. This sort of sobbing was usually only done in private, or in the presence of one's mother. Baze raised his upturned palm in the air, and moved his callused fingers in a motion that said, "Come closer." Arroyo moved her wheelchair as close to the bed as it would go, and when she was only a couple of feet away from the man, he gripped her hand and squeezed.

"You saved a lot more than that. You finished it."

Arroyo envisioned Welsh's face, and she pictured the hatred it would show if the man could see this moment. The downright loathing of the two people who had beaten him. Imagining this gave her a surge of selfish pleasure. Especially now that she knew how close he had come to killing Baze.

The initial impact had knocked Baze out and given him a concussion. The man also had several deep lacerations all over his face, from being showered in glass when Welsh had fired through his windshield. But the real damage had come from Welsh's second-to-last bullet, which had traveled through Baze's chest cavity, missing the vital internal organs but finding a home inches away from his spinal column. Baze had been in the ICU for twelve hours, and Doctor Francis Silva, who had performed the surgery, had been expecting his patient to end up as a paraplegic at the very least. There was almost no way for the procedure to be performed without causing serious, life-altering changes, if not death. And yet here he was. In a few months' time, he would be somewhere close to full strength.

"Lowry told me that you were probably going to die."

Baze's face suddenly had a playful, enduring quality to it, like he was in on a joke that she wasn't. Arroyo swallowed and continued.

"You know what my first reaction was? Anger. I was pissed that you weren't going to give me the chance to say thank you."

Baze laughed. It was a deep, belly-shaking laugh, and seemed to cause him considerable pain, which Arroyo promptly felt guilty for.

"That is the Lieutenant Red that I know," he said, wincing.

"I was also mad that I wasn't going to be able to hear you explain how you found us. Or how you even knew I was in trouble."

An enigmatic, meaningful look came over Baze's face.

"I knew because you told me."

She narrowed her eyes. "I told you?"

"Your text. You said, 'Just come back inside.' And I was already two blocks away. That's how I knew you had another visitor. And pretty much anyone who makes a house call at two in the morning doesn't have good intentions."

"So you turned around…"

"So I turned around. And I got to your house right when another vehicle was pulling out of your driveway. When it drove by, I saw a flash of your red hair through the windshield."

Arroyo raised her eyebrows.

"So you followed us."

"So I followed you. I couldn't let him realize that I was behind you, so I consistently stayed a block behind. My biggest concern was that he would take a random turn and I was going to lose you. Imagine my delight when he turned onto the freeway...

"It didn't take me long to realize where he was taking you. Especially after our last conversation. My initial plan was to wait until he got you inside the house and then make my move. But then I realized that if I let that happen, it was far more likely to end with one of us dead. A tiny house with only one way in or out of it makes it difficult to pull off an ambush. Plus, if I confronted him in public with potential witnesses all around, I thought there would be a good chance that he would run and leave you behind. You being alive was more important to me than him getting away."

Arroyo felt a swelling of warmth for the man lying in front of her.

"Three exits before our overpass, I got off the freeway. One of the best things about living in the same city for thirty-plus years is you learn all the shortcuts. I was flying at that point. Eighty miles an hour in a thirty-five. Ran two red lights. I'm sure I will get a ticket or two in the mail in a few months. But I managed to head him off. The only thing I was worried about was seriously injuring you in the wreck. Which I didn't really avoid, did I?"

Arroyo rolled her eyes. "Listen, Baze, what do you think I would choose if you gave me the option of broken ribs and a fractured skull versus days of torture and rape and a violent, horrific death? Don't be silly."

"Well, that is kind of what I figured," Baze agreed. "So I pulled the trigger. Well, metaphorically at least." The man rustled about uncomfortably, apparently thinking of the trigger that had been pulled when the gun was pointing at him.

"What was your plan after? What were you hoping to do once both cars had stopped?"

Baze closed his eyes and exhaled through his nostrils, causing a slight ripple in his mustache. He flexed his jaw, making the snake-shaped scar on his cheek puff out.

"Well, I had my pistol attached to my hip. I was hoping to absorb the brunt of the impact and then hop out of the Impala with my gun pointed at Welsh's head before the man could react. What I wasn't planning was to lose consciousness. My bad on that one." Baze gave her a sheepish smile.

"I think it was actually *my* bad. I sped up at the last second. It was sort of out of surprise, really."

Baze nodded, like he was agreeing to a point made about the weather. "I can see that."

"What happened after the wreck? When I

woke up, there he was, pinned to the barrier by the Impala, screaming his head off. I'm slightly curious to know what happened in the interim."

Baze closed his eyes, as if it were difficult to summon all of the details in his hazy brain. "Well... I can tell you that I was stirred by the blare of a car horn. I came to and saw him fumbling with you in the driver seat. He was bent over you, fiddling with your seatbelt, I think. I didn't have a clean shot from my vantage point, and I couldn't get out of the car. I didn't know if he was going to shoot you right there, or what. I knew I had to act. When I got the Impala off of his car and put it in reverse, that was when he started firing. After the fourth bullet I said fuck it and decided to mow him down. He hit me just a couple seconds before I made contact."

Again, Baze moved about awkwardly in the bed with a pained look on his face. Arroyo felt a surge of guilt hit her chest, and she looked down at the ground.

"I'm sorry, Anton. I am so sorry that you got involved in all this."

Baze suddenly had a look of irritation in his eyes. He gave a minor shake of his head and then let out a massive sigh.

"Sorry? You are sorry? For what? You weren't the one who sparked my obsession. You weren't the one who made me fixate on this case for all those years. It isn't your fault that Frank Bruno namedropped me, and it isn't your fault that I was so eager to join your team. I'm sure you have lots of things to be sorry for in your life, Red, but that isn't one of them."

There was a long pause. The two of them made eye contact for a while, but it was too intense for Arroyo, so she looked down.

"By the way, I don't know if they told you… They found his little torture chamber."

Baze squinted at her, like he had to re-focus on what she had just said. "What?"

"There was a loose floorboard at the house in Wilsonville. The guys pulled it up and found a hidden entrance to the basement. Inside, there were his masks hung up on the wall. Sixteen of them. All of his animal faces. There was also a wooden table with four shackles attached to each leg of the table."

Baze groaned, and shook his head like he didn't need to know, but Arroyo continued.

"Our guys found a big red toolbox in the corner of the room. There were scalpels. Knives. Saws. Tweezers. You name it. They are all being tested for DNA. Results already came back on one of the scalpels. And we had a match. Tracy Dinwoodie."

Baze had a pained expression on his face, as if he had been punched in the gut.

"The table had DNA on it too. We are still waiting for results on that. But rest assured, there will be a match to some or all of his victims. That is where he kept them, Baze. That is where he took their lives."

Arroyo felt the tears permeate in her eyes again, and with them, a burning of agitation. Why was she getting so emotional all of the sudden? This wasn't who she was. Sentimentality didn't suit her. And yet, for some reason, the yearning to cry was so powerful in her diaphragm. She wanted to heave and sob and rid herself of this dreadful, morose feeling.

"You know, I just wish… I just wish things would have gone differently."

Baze looked at her with resolve. "Don't we all? That is the problem with being human, isn't it? We wish that things had gone differently. But that isn't up to us. We don't have any power over what happens in the world. All we have control over is our reaction. All we really can control is our thoughts."

Arroyo nodded slowly and then felt herself drifting away. A hundred different events flickered through her mind; a series of snapshots of different faces, places, and occurrences that had come to pass since she had first seen the video of Tracy Dinwoodie strapped to that table with Carson Welsh standing over her in a goat mask.

"Can you believe it? Everything that has happened to the people in this city because of him? Everything that has happened to us? It is hard to fathom. Hard to really grasp."

Baze's eyes misted over, and he turned his head toward the window, with the light falling over the snake-shaped mark on his face.

"You stopped it, Red. It's over now. Soon, it will all just be a scar."

EPILOGUE

Lieutenant Arroyo pored over the document in front of her, going over it line by line. It was filled with dense, opaque language that could only be described as legal-speak. She could feel herself getting tired just by reading it and now regretted returning to work so soon. Each word seemed to bring her one step closer to crumpling up the packet of paper and hurling it out of her office window.

She bent forward slightly, adjusting in her chair, and felt a twinge of pain in her torso. The Vicodin mostly masked the hot fire that had been raging in her ribs since the muzzle of the gun had been jammed viciously against her side, but every once in a while, it would feel like someone was forcefully kneeing her just above her right hip. Arroyo let out a hiss of annoyance. Perhaps she would sneak to the bathroom and pop another pill, even though her next dose wasn't set to take place for another six hours. This was how people became addicted to opiates. The prospect of a pain-free afternoon where she could get work done was so enticing that she was seriously considering breaking her regimen of taking a pill once every twelve hours. But the voice in her head that told her to ignore her worse impulses was still louder.

It had been nearly three weeks since Carson Welsh had been obliterated by the semi-truck that carried boxes and boxes of Greenberg's Whole Foods. For twenty days, she had been bed-ridden, watching two whole series on Netflix and reading three books. Arroyo had been so restless by the tenth day that it was a miracle she had waited another week and a half before returning to work. But now, absorbed in the doldrums of a mind-numbing legal document, she was beginning to wish that she had prolonged her leave a little bit longer.

What made the consumption of the file even more difficult was the stuffiness of her office. Outside, the searing heat beat down upon the Portlanders relentlessly, like Mother Nature was cracking the whip on their backs. It had already been the hottest summer on record, with forty days above ninety degrees. And there was still nearly a month left of summer. Arroyo wiped at the sweat that had been pooling on the back of her neck and then rubbed her tainted hand on her slacks. Her office was air-conditioned, but there was only so much that could be done when the city itself felt like it might catch fire.

Arroyo had been in contact with Baze regularly over the last month. They texted frequently and had even shared a phone call or two. The man had finally returned home from the hospital and had been sleeping for a majority of the time. He said he was still in pain, but that the drugs the doctors had given him were keeping it mostly at bay. His only complaint was that they had told him not to mix the meds with alcohol, and he had a fresh pint of Wild Turkey waiting for him in his cupboard. "Guess they don't want me to have too much fun," he had said grumpily when reporting the news to Arroyo.

Arroyo fixed her focus back on the trial summary that was sitting on the desk in front of her. It had been written by Wendell Friar, the State's prosecuting attorney for the case in question. The case was a relatively minor one; some wannabe gangster had held up a Plaid Pantry at gunpoint and stolen five hundred dollars in cash from the register. Friar had filled his summary with an annoying and unnecessary amount of verbose language, and Arroyo was beginning to wonder if he had written the report using a thesaurus.

A knocking on the door broke Arroyo's attention away from the summary, which she was incredibly grateful for. Before she could instruct the person outside to come in, the door was flung open unceremoniously, and Easton Lowry clumped in, a dark expression on his face.

"Lowry, what are you do—"

"Come with me, LT. You need to see this."

Her interest piqued, Arroyo pushed herself up from her sitting position, ignoring the grumbling that her body put forth by way of a stabbing pain in her ribs. The look on Lowry's face told her that whatever it was, it was significant.

Arroyo followed Lowry, and he led her through a row of cubicles to the elevator. Once inside, he jammed the button that would take them to the fourth floor with vigor.

"What is going on?"

"I'm not going to explain. You will just have to read it."

"Read what?"

Lowry didn't reply. They stood there in awkward silence for a few more seconds until the elevator dinged and the doors opened. Lowry then moved forward quickly, beckoning Arroyo with a demonstrative hand wave. He zigzagged to the right around a wall and then to the left down a hallway, eventually coming to a door at the end of the hallway that had been left open. He ducked in the open door to the evidence room and Arroyo followed, her heartbeat rising by the second.

Two other people stood in the room. One was a forensic tech that Arroyo did not recognize, and the other was Detective Andre Giuliani. Behind the pair was a massive expanse of shelves and boxes labeled alphabetically.

"Hello, LT," Giuliani grunted. The tech didn't say anything, but his eyes were wide. In front of him, there was an open envelope and a piece of paper sitting on a desk.

Lowry walked over to the tech and reached past him to grab something that was just out of Arroyo's line of vision. Then he turned around and handed her two blue latex gloves. Without saying anything, Arroyo pulled them onto her hands.

"We are still cataloging everything that we found at Welsh's apartment and at the house in Wilsonville. We all thought the animal masks and the various torture equipment would be the most substantial pieces of evidence that we found. We were wrong."

With that, Lowry gestured toward the table, and the forensic tech picked up the piece of paper in front of him and handed it to her. Apprehensively, Arroyo brought the paper closer to her face, and saw that it was a letter. Several paragraphs of slanted, sloppy writing covered the page.

"This was left on Welsh's kitchen table in his apartment. The envelope was sealed. Welsh apparently hadn't read it."

Arroyo looked up at Lowry, and he gave her a meaningful look.

"Go ahead."

She took a deep breath and began to read.

Hello, Carson.

My hand is shaking like crazy right now. I can barely breathe. It is difficult to put this into writing, knowing that one day you will see these words and have your world be ripped apart. I know this apology will be patronizing, but I still have to tell you how sorry I am. I have been so sorry for every waking moment of my life in the last fifteen years. I feel like the worst person who has ever lived. But my guilt pales in comparison to the pain you have suffered because of me.

It started with the affair. I don't know how it happened, or why I was drawn to infringe on something so sacred, but it happened. You see, Wendy and I shared a connection that I cannot describe. I consider myself a level-headed person, but I was attracted to your wife in a way I cannot explain. During those months, when you two would spend your days and nights arguing over every minor thing, she found comfort in my company. It was an intense, mutual attraction. But eventually, she saw the error in her ways. She broke it off. She told me you were the most important thing to her, and made me promise not to tell you what had happened. But now she is dead and I am soon to be, so I must break that promise.

You see, I thought it would be easy. I thought I would be able to move on just as easily as she did. But for some reason, I couldn't. I loved her, in a way that I had never loved anything. I made my advances, and every time she continued to turn me away, my attraction to her would grow stronger.

As you well know, Carson, I have a drinking problem. I tried to cope with my feelings for Wendy with whiskey and beer and wine, and just like my feelings for her would not stop, my compulsion to drink would not stop either. When I came to your house that night, everything was hazy. I was so drunk that I could barely form a coherent sentence. But I managed to tell her that I was still in love. That she was the only thing that mattered to me. I confessed that my feelings for her were still unshakeable. Naturally, she turned me away. She told me repeatedly to go home. But I didn't. I stepped closer. That was when she grabbed the knife.

From that point forward, it was all a blur. I became angrier than I ever had been in my life. I slammed her head against the wall and heard something crack. I grabbed the knife from her hand and turned it on her. One firm stroke and that was that.

I still have the blade, Carson. The same knife that she had used to try to defend herself against me

In the years that have followed, I almost wish that I had stayed there that night. I almost wish that I had sat next to her body until you came home. Whatever horrible way you would have killed me, it would have been far easier to deal with than the burden that I have placed on myself for the last decade and a half.

By the time that you read this, my body will be decomposing in the soil. I thought this would be a secret that I would take to my grave, but I can't. I have to apologize for my miserable existence and try, however incrementally, to make things right. And that begins with a confession.

See, I need you to hate me as much as you hate Robert Macabre. I need penance, in this life or the next. For it was I who killed your wife, Carson. I hope it soothes your conscience a little knowing that I am now rotting in hell. But I know that it won't.

I am forever sorry.

-Mo McCray.

Made in the USA
Las Vegas, NV
02 September 2021

29483493R00423